For Justin and Emily, who have known Philippe since his conception. May his growth, and mine, be meaningful to you.

And for Cheri and the Writers of Restoration, Who have suffered with me through the growing pains.

Passing Though Fire: Philippe's Smile

By L. A. Willard

Chapter 1. Therapy

"So, tell me why you're here, Philippe. What is it that you'd like to talk to me about today?" He liked the way she spoke. Her voice was deep and had a sort of sultry hum that came along with her African American, New Jersey accent.

"Well, to be completely honest with you, I'm not entirely sure where I should start. I..." He paused for a moment. He was taken by her deep relaxed chocolate gaze as she patiently waited for him to express his needs. He smiled wide and his eyes dropped down to a blue hummingbird that was woven into the fabulous carpet beneath his feet. He moved one of his shoes a little to the left so that the full beauty of the hummingbird and the pink blossom that it drank from could be seen. "Would it seem crazy," his head continued to bend towards the carpet but his bright blue eyes moved up to focus on the deep brown eyes of the woman before him, "if I had no idea why I was here? I just, wanted to see a therapist."

"No, it wouldn't seem crazy at all. Why don't you start by telling me a little about your life? Do you have a job? What is your job like? What are your friends like?"

"Well, I'm a model-"

"Oh. That explains why you look so familiar." She threw her arms up and leaned suddenly back into the supportive cushions of her chair. The satisfaction of her recognition fully set into her shoulders. "I've probably seen you on a magazine somewhere."

"Oui. Yes. Probably." He lifted his chin a bit and that sweet smile lit his cheeks. "Do you enjoy fashion? It's a bit of a passion of mine."

"Why don't you go ahead and tell me about your passion for fashion Philippe."

"I think I've probably been in love with fashion since I knew what clothes were. I can only imagine the style of baby pajama I must have worn." He chuckled pleasantly. He could indeed imagine what his mother must have dressed him in as a baby. He realized what he was doing though. He was trying to make pleasant conversation. The kind of conversation that you make with the barista at the cafe, or the cute bartender boy behind the counter. Not the sort of talk that you have with a therapist. When he looked back into her deep brown eyes, they gently told him that they knew it too. But they were patient eyes. Oh so patient.

"The truth is I've never had a lot of money. Having nice clothes always made me feel," he shrugged, "some sense of security I suppose."

"A fashion for security then. Is that why you're a model?"

"I suppose yes. I suppose I fashioned that security for myself." He smiled at the small play on words.

"And why did you fashion your life that way?" He figured he'd go ahead and cut to the chase. People were always supposed to want to talk about their parents and their childhood right? So he might as well just dive in. "Because my mother couldn't fashion a good enough life for me. So I had to fashion it myself."

"And how do you feel about that? How do you feel towards your mother?"

"I... I mean, I haven't really talked to her in a while, but I send her care packages now and then."

"But how do you feel about her?"

How did he feel about his mother? He knew exactly how he felt about his mother. He didn't want to say it though. Because it was mean. He didn't like being mean. "I'm... sure that she did the best that she could. She had.... has... a horrible addiction that really got in the way of her parenting. But I took care of myself okay." He smiled.

"A horrible addiction-"

"Oui. Heroin." Philippe finished the thought before she could finish the question.

"Okay. Philippe." She took a deep breath and crossed one knee over the other. "How do you feel about your mother's addiction?"

"Well, horrible!" he laughed at his obvious answer and then elaborated. It's horrible to see the way she treats her body. She's been hospitalized a couple of times but she keeps going back." Silence fell on the room. Philippe said nothing. It was uncomfortable. His eyes dropped back down to the hummingbird. The woman appeared just as patient and comfortable as she had been since the session started, but Philippe felt like his skin was crawling.

He was avoiding the question. He knew he was avoiding the question because he knew exactly how he felt about it. Come to think of it, when people go to therapy, it's often for the purpose of becoming aware of feelings that you didn't even know that you had. But he knew precisely how he felt about his mother. So it begged the question, if he already knew how he felt, why did he need to tell someone else about it? He'd already figured it out himself. In fact, he prided himself on being extremely aware of his own emotions. What could he discover about himself that he didn't already know? And yet, here he was.

"You don't have to talk about it if you don't want to." Said the therapist. He exhaled a sigh of relief that he hadn't even realized he was holding in.

"Oh thank god." He exclaimed and rubbed at a crease in his forehead.

"Well Philippe, what else would you like to tell me about yourself?"

"Well, I'm from Paris, you can probably tell by my accent." He smiled broadly. "I like to read books, I love sports cars. As you already know I love fashion, I have no need to tell you that. Let's see... I never knew my father, I was molested when I was nine, and my mother is an addict. But I love art, I love music, and strawberry gelato is my favorite. I try not to let my childhood get me down and I want you to know that even though I've obviously had a rather difficult time talking about it with you today, I do, in fact, know exactly how I feel, so you needn't worry." He took a deep breath.

"Well. Alright then. So, same time next week?"

"Ha!" He nodded. "Yes please."

"Alright then." She said again. She nodded with understanding and stood up to see her patient to the door. The weight lifted off of Philippe's face immediately as he rose from the sofa with a smile that would make one think that he was floating on clouds.

"I'm so glad to have met you." He said, and kissed her on both cheeks just as he had when he'd entered. Too swift and soft a peck to protest. She shook her head with a smile as he moved to exit the room.

"Oh Philippe, one moment." One hand still clinging to the door frame, he turned around with a deflective beam on his face.

"Yes?"

"I have a homework assignment for you. Write a letter to your mother. You don't have to send it to her. Just write it. In the letter, tell your mother everything that you feel about her. Just to get it out there on paper." The smile that lit his face never left, but it somehow seamlessly shifted from a jovial gleam to an apprehensive glow. Slowly he nodded. More to himself than to her.

"Alright." He said it, but his tone was less than convincing. "Merci." And with that he turned. Though his stride was graceful and his face happy, his pounding heart all but fled the building.

The unnecessarily automatic door closed behind him and he made a beeline for his Vespa. When he reached the Vespa he gripped onto her handlebars for a moment before mounting. He wished that it was his car back in Paris. He missed his car. He sat on the seat and picked up his helmet but held it in his lap a moment and took a deep breath.

There was a light breeze. It was a pretty day. A day worth having. His eyes scanned along the New York City horizon. He imagined the view for a moment, as a black and white silhouette. The skyscraper shapes that would be ever recognizable were before him as a black sea against the sky.

He decided that, at least for now, he would keep the fact that he was seeing a therapist to himself. No one really wanted to know about that anyway right? He supposed that he might tell his fiancé, but maybe he'd just see how the therapy went first.

Chapter 2. Botox

"Philippe darling!" exclaimed the slightly inebriated hostess of the evening as she opened the front door to the spacious apartment.

"Oh Elizabeth!" Philippe exclaimed in return and quickly closed the distance with her. He held his hands out to the side as he held a bag in each and pressed his cheek and the corner of his puckered lips onto both sides of her face with a verbal kissing noise on each.

With an exclamation of "Oh!" She returned the greeting. "Oh I love how you do that darling. Never stop, never stop." Her thick British accent was worth adoring. "And you can call me 'Liz' darling, none of that 'Elizabeth' business. This party is all about getting rid of those silly formalities and getting back a little of that beauty we were born with." They laughed together, as if something incredibly witty had just been said. Liz was a tall black British woman who needed no enhancing, but modeling was all about enhancements and they would let no advantage go unclaimed.

Philippe could hear the chatter of the other people in the apartment. He was eager to go in and join them all, to hear what they were talking about, and to know who they were gossiping about. Generally, these things were in the "girl's night" category, though Philippe had often proudly made himself an exception to the rule. But among the swirl of words that he could not quite make out at that distance, he heard the deeper tone of a man's voice, and discerned that he would not be this evening's only exception.

With a smile he held up his bags as they turned to join the throng. "I've brought wine and cheese. Not to keep things too original."

"Oh well now, what kind of cheese? We've had a little too much brie this evening if I may admit that. Mind you, I love brie with the best of them, but to be completely honest, I wouldn't mind something a little sharper."

"Well, does a smoked gouda count?" And for a moment he wished that he'd picked up that blue cheese he'd been looking at.

She put her hand up to her mouth as if she were hiding her words and whispered. "Well, it's not brie now is it?" And with a smile, she relieved him of his bags of wine and cheese, and turned to head into the kitchen. "Go sit down with everyone and I'll bring you a glass of the open bottle."

"Let me help you with something?"

"No no, just go sit. I won't be but a minute."

"Oh look! Speak of the devil. Philippe is here. Come over here Philippe." Philippe smiled towards the calling voices and the hand waving over the back of the fine sofa.

"Were you saying something devilish about me?" He took off his jacket and folded it over his arm. It had not been cold outside, but it had been somewhat wet, just a midsummer sprinkle. He walked over to the living room to see half a dozen women lounging around a coffee table which was cluttered with wine glasses, cheese, and makeup products. There was only one other man in the room, Aurelio, a rugged Spanish beauty of a specimen whom Philippe had met once before, during a shoot. He was new to their modeling scene, and had probably been invited as much out of curiosity, and a chance to scope the new meat, as anything else. As a man, he was no threat to any of the women's modeling careers, but Philippe felt certain that no one in the room would mind a night spent in bed with him.

"We were just saying," began Margarete, a frail, delicate cheek boned, Russian blonde with a thick accent but perfect pronunciation, "That even though you are barely in your twenties, you need this Botox. Do you know why?" Never could a room be filled with so many cultures unless it was a room filled with fashion models. They were collected, like gems, from every corner of the world. Though their childhoods may have all been wildly different, they all had one motto in common. Beauty is life, and they were all willing to pay the price for it.

"Speaking of the devil indeed!" Said Philippe and put his hand over his heart as if he'd been struck a fatal blow. "My beauty has been called into question by the goddesses of youth! If indeed my beauty is leaving me so young, then I beg thee to enlighten me as to why!" Dramatically he fell to his knees behind the sofa so that only his blond head and blue eyes could be seen by others.

Everyone laughed at his ridiculousness and Margarete couldn't help but laugh along. "But seriously Philippe. You've never had it, and I'll tell you why you need it. It isn't to replace beauty lost my dear, it's to bring out the beauty you have deep down in those muscles under those creases in your cheeks that are there because you smile too goddamn much!" With that she reached her arm over the sofa and playfully slapped the side of Philippe's smiling face. Then patting the almost invisible laugh lines made by his grin, the ones that, if left to their own devices, would become deep and pronounced in his old age, the ones that would tell the world that he'd lived a long life full of joy and laughter. But they all knew that creases of any kind didn't look good in pictures. The less work you made for the Photoshop team, the more valuable you were.

"Oh how could I, I forgot to take your coat!" Liz had come into the room holding a glass of red wine and a plate with the Gouda that Philippe had brought. "Here, why don't you just get up off of that dirty floor and I'll trade you this cheese and wine for your coat." Philippe had almost forgotten about the jacket still slung over his arm. He stood up and made the trade while the group behind him turned back to idle chat.

"Thank you so much Liz, you're a most wonderful hostess."

They traded items and Liz turned toward the coat rack by the door with a, "Well I do my best." Philippe went to sit on a chair across from Margarete. Liz called back over her shoulder. "Oh and by the way, the floor is in fact not dirty at all. I cleaned it this morning so you can all have a nice lay about on it if you really want to." Everyone giggled at that.

"So when is the Botox lady supposed to get here?" Asked Angela, one of the two women who were actually American. Her hair was a very average brown color, but it could be made into some of the best waves and ringlets. Her eyes were something of a hazel brown, but they always made them green in the photos. She had made most of her early career in makeup advertisements and hair products, but she truly became a model for the fashion and only did the makeup gig to pay the bills. She was thus, somewhat star struck to finally be sitting with a room full of La Facere Magazine's cover models. A peer group that was perhaps too good for her.

"They should be here in thirty minutes or so." Replied Liz, re-entering the room and taking a deep breath as she finally got to pick up her glass of wine and settle down back onto the sofa next to Margarete. "Just enough time for us to drink ourselves numb, don't you think?" She took a sip of her wine and smiled as she patted the side of her face to see if it felt numb enough yet.

"Cheers to that." Said Philippe, and everyone took a sip of their wine.

"Philippe," Continued Liz, "Angela here is our other Botox initiate."

"Oh is she? Everyone else here has done it before? You too?" This last part he directed with a polite nod and a flirtatious smile to Aurelio.

"Oh yes." Replied Aurelio. "Many times. In Spain I was initiated," He smirked at Liz as he borrowed her word. "In Italy too with the beauties who took me in there in Milan. In Paris once, though only once. I was only their briefly on my way to London where I did it again. For an ongoing effect it is best to do it once every few months or so, though I confess I've only been able to do it twice a year or so."

"You're really quite the veteran then?" Philippe met Aurelio's dark swarthy eyes under his black tantalizing eyelashes and something silent was communicated between them. Though anyone in the room could have noticed these unspoken words, they were left to hang in the air instead. It was just par for the course.

"Does it hurt?" Asked Angela and everyone sort of smirked at the question and the obvious newness of the asker.

"Oh you're so cute dearie." Answered Margarete. "No it doesn't really hurt. It's just some little pin pricks. You hardly even notice. And if you don't mind me saying so Liz, I went ahead and sprang for the real professionals rather than the ones you suggested."

"Oh?"

"Yes. It's really very important that you have very trained hands. People that are downright medical about it. Because it really is a medical procedure. And if they put the needle in just the wrong spot because they don't know the muscles of the face quite well enough then it could be absolutely disastrous. You wouldn't be able to put your face in front of a camera for months until it wore off."

"Oh that would be terrible!" Exclaimed Angela.

"Oh it would indeed. Especially for you since you have your very first shoot for La Facere tomorrow. You have to look your absolute best if you ever want a call back. But don't worry dear. I've made sure that you'll be in the best of hands." With this she gave a sideways glance to Liz.

"Uh oh, it's time for a roommate discussion." This came from Ellen, the other American in the room.

"You know," said Liz to Margarete, "The lady who I suggested is someone I've used many times and you've never seen me come in with a saggy face now have you? I trust her."

Margarete had a response to that. But at that moment Philippe was distracted because he felt Angela's fingers suddenly clutch the corner of his sleeve. He glanced at her. She was obviously trying to be discreet about her discomfort as she turned ever so slightly towards him and said in a low quiet voice, "Saggy face?"

Her eyes seemed to plead with him, as the only other person in the room who had never tried Botox. He could tell by the tone in her whisper and the almost invisible quirk in her lips that, though anxious to fit in, and anxious to be successful at her shoot tomorrow, she was terrified and looking for someone to share her fear with.

He smiled comfortingly at her and reached out and held her hand. He knew that this was a mixed situation and there were several social rules that he was juggling in a single moment. Angela was new blood, and unlike Aurelio, she was a threat to the other women. On top of that, she didn't exactly exude confidence. Aside from her fear of Botox, she practically worshipped the successful fashion models that she sat with and wanted to be like them, and to be liked by them. Unfortunately, this fact was more likely to make her a target. Though Philippe felt the need to shelter her from the scorn of the other models, he also had no intention of falling out of their good graces. This meant that cards had to be played carefully.

There were a couple of advantages at his exposal. Like Aurelio, he was a man, and that meant that he was no threat on a career level. But unlike Aurelio, he had also been safe zoned by the other models, which meant that no one felt the need to compete for his attention. That gave him the advantage of being able to give his attention to anyone, at just about any time, whilst avoiding jealousy.

The only possible mistake he could make, would be to give this girl too much of his attention and time. She would eventually cling to him for security, and the others would then see Philippe as her attachment. Then, the only way for them to get rid of her, would be to get rid of him also. He was not willing to put himself into that position. But at least for a moment, he could comfort her some.

He squeezed her fingers warmly and smiled. He matched her quiet voice to make the conversation a tad more intimate. They could have a private conversation even in a room full of people. "Don't worry. These girls are experts. If they've all done it a hundred times, then I'm sure we'll be fine. And who knows, with a little Botox, maybe someday Veronica herself will ask for you to be on the front cover." He winked at her flirtatiously.

"Yeah." She nodded and seemed to be mustering up the courage. "You're right. It's never good to be worried about the worst case scenario."

"Exactly. Stay loose. Just have fun." He raised up his glass, and clinked it against hers and they both drank.

Veronica was the one they all lived for. She designed the fashion, she owned La Facere magazine, and she had all of the agencies in the palm of her hand. Beyond that, she was more beautiful than anyone in the room and anyone would give anything to be hand-picked by her.

Then came the knock at the door.

"Oh! That must be him now." The argument was ended and the winner declared as Margarete leapt up from the sofa and headed towards the door. She collided for a moment into the wall, due to how much she'd had to drink, despite her ability to keep speaking without a slur.

"Hello, I'm Preston, do I have the right address?"

"Yes you do my dear Preston. Please come in."

Turning to Angela, Philippe lifted his glass. "Bottoms up." He said with a smile and lifted it to his lips and drained it.

In walked a very well dressed man in a suit and tie as opposed to medical scrubs. He was in his forties. He had a neat haircut, wore thick rimmed glasses and carried an expensive looking leather case. He was an incredibly good looking man, but his demeanor and dress said that being good looking wasn't the main focus of his life quite as much as a side benefit.

"Hello ladies," he said as he entered the room, "and gentlemen." he added when he noticed Philippe and Aurelio. "I'll be your doctor today if you'll have me." There was a collective cheer from everyone in the room as a response.

"Would you like a glass of wine doctor?" Asked Ellen in an obvious though jokingly flirtatious way.

The doctor smiled pleasantly. "I think I had probably better wait on the wine. No one wants a drunk doctor putting Botox into their face." Everyone laughed. "So who's first then?"

"Oh! Do me. Please, do me." exclaimed Margarete, coming around to stand in front of him. "I'll show them how it's done."

"Oh DO me!" Hollered a very drunk woman named Maria with a very sexual connotation, mocking Margarete's eagerness.

"I think we should let one of our initiates go first." Liz waved her wine glass in the direction of Philippe and Angela. "They weren't invited here just to watch us, Margarete. And there is only one Preston."

"Oh all right then. Angela, why don't you go first?" Preston raised his eyebrow above his professional looking glasses as if to invite Angela over to him. Philippe felt a subtle change in the temperature and perspiration of Angela's hand. So he gave her hand a little squeeze and then let go of it and stood up.

"I would gladly volunteer myself, as one who has never had Botox." He put his hand over his chest and smiled flirtatiously at Preston. "Well sir, where do you want me?"

"Oooooh" came the general consensus of the room. "Indeed. Where DO you want him?" chimed in Maria. Philippe was keenly aware of the fact that Preston had absolutely no sexual interest in him whatsoever, quite apart from the rest of the women in the room. But that hardly had anything to do with any of it.

"How about here on the sofa." And with that, Liz practically leapt up to get out of the way. "Oh no, you're alright miss, he doesn't need the entire sofa. Just sit down and get comfortable, try to relax your face and neck."

Philippe sat down, and leaned his head back into the corner of the sofa. He could see Aurelio staring intently at him, so he smiled. Liz passed in front of him, cutting off their locked eyes and returned to her seat next to him and held out his glass, newly filled.

"Here you are darling, take town some of this first." Gladly, he took the glass and drained half its contents.

Meanwhile, Preston had cleared off some of the coffee table and had opened up his leather case. Inside it were needles and bottle and some small sterilization products. He started to pull on some latex gloves. Meanwhile Ellen walked over and changed the music to something a little more danceable, Aurelio got up from his seat and moved to be closer to Margarete and the two of them whispered quietly together as they watched Philippe. All the while, with curiosity and trepidation Angela's eyes were locked on Philippe.

"Alright, now just take a deep breath. A few of these doses will be on the house for you, since it's your first time. Where would you like it?" Asked Preston in a somewhat medical tone.

"You're the expert." Replied Philippe, "Where would you suggest?"

"Maybe a little around the corners of your eyes along here." Philippe felt as the tacky gloved pinky finger ran along the side of his face by his right eye. "Perhaps some in the forehead above your eyebrows. Places that tend to crease with your facial expressions."

Philippe nodded, "That sounds fine." The doctor blinked as if he thought that Philippe didn't fully understand, but he did not venture to explain anything further. He raised the small needle above Philippe's face to get the best angle. It looked a little different than the syringes that he'd seen his mother have, but still they reminded him of her. He took a deep breath, and closed his eyes.

He could hear the giggling and chatting of the others as they danced and gossiped around him. He could smell the wine and he knew that they had plans to bring out something stronger. He could hear as flirtations on Aurelio were taken up a notch. And though Liz was sitting right next to him saying, "Now just relax darling." he knew that she had been there, and done that, and was truly more interested in whether or not the hors d'ouvres platter was well stocked. But all the while he knew that Preston's singular focus was him, and his face and the points into which his needle would pass.

A sterilizing wipe was rubbed over every point on his face before the Botox was administered, warning him of the next location that he would feel the tiny prick. But practically before it had begun, it was over, and Philippe admitted silently to himself that he had enjoyed the attention, and wouldn't have minded some more.

Then all of a sudden he was up, and another was in his place. He was being cheered as the new member of the Botox club as if it had been a rite of passage. Liz handed him his glass, again full, saying, "drink up darling, you've done it." and pressed a clean cloth against his barely bleeding face. Aurelio clapped him on the shoulder as if Botox were the manliest thing he'd ever done. Maria and Ellen pulled him into an inebriated dance, and Angela snuck into it all to ask him if it had hurt very much.

He told her that it hadn't really hurt at all. That was true, but she seemed somewhat unconvinced and went back to watch Preston work on Margarete.

"What about Veronica?" asked Angela to Ellen, a little later while they sat to watch Liz get the Botox. "Do you think she gets a lot of Botox?"

"Well I don't know how the hell else she'd be keeping her face so perfect. That woman ain't doing' anything au naturel to make her face look like that."

"Mmmmm" Groaned Liz as she tried not to twitch and respond to the talk.

"I wonder what she looked like when she was younger." Piped in Philippe.

"Do you know she's like thirty years old? Maybe even a little older," Said Margarete and she gently dabbed at the edges of her face. "And she still has skin like a baby. And I don't think its all makeup either. She obviously had a perfect complexion in school."

"I mean, makeup can do some pretty miraculous things sometimes." Said Angela.

"If you see her in person, you'll agree with Margarete, trust me." Said Liz as Preston moved away from her face.

"Have you guys actually met her?" Asked Angela anxiously.

"On rare occasions, she actually comes into the shoots." Said Philippe, "She can be very particular about what kind of shoots are being done. I don't know how it is that she has the time, but it's actually possible that you could meet her."

Angela's eyes widened.

"Not that she's likely to take the time to attend someone's first time shoot, Philippe." argued Margarete, "But maybe after she's done a few." She added for Angela's consolation. "Oh Preston! She said suddenly to the doctor as he was quietly cleaning and organizing his materials. "Are you finished? Are we allowed to offer you alcohol yet?"

"Oh, I believe I still have one more to do?" He tilted his glasses down towards the end of his nose and looked at Angela over the top of them with a smile and a raised eyebrow. "Yes?"

Philippe could see clearly the moment of truth. He could tell by her posture that Angela did not want to do it. But under the pressure of the eyes of La Facere's best, her determination for acceptance and success got the better of her. To walk away now would be an utter disgrace.

So with a deep breath and a nod and a glance at Philippe that sought the smallest shred of comfort, she said, "Let's do it."

"Then have a seat sweetheart." Liz yielded her seat to Angela, and started fussing with some of the coffee table mess. Philippe watched along with Margarete as the first prick was made, but when he glanced up to see Liz juggling an unnecessary number of dishes, he couldn't stop himself.

"Okay Liz, you have to let me help you with that."

"Oh Philippe, you needn't but I wouldn't mind." He took a number of things from her hands and headed towards the kitchen. He watched as Ellen, Maria, Aurelio and a couple others disappeared into a back room, but he just walked straight on to the kitchen, with Liz right behind him. He had a guess what that room was likely to be filled with. Chances were, that the good drugs were in there.

"I know this party was your idea," said Philippe, setting the dishes down on the counter next to the sink, "but I feel like your roommates should be more equal in their hostessing."

"Oh no," she sat a few empty wine bottles next to his dishes on the counter. "I'm just a bit of a neat freak really. More booze is what makes a party for them, not a clean room."

"Well, if that's what makes you happy." He turned and leaned his hips back against the counter and wished that he hadn't left his glass back on the coffee table. That had been the reasonable place to leave it when carrying an armful, but now he wanted it. He put his hand out in front of him and squeezed his fingers as he would if they were clutching the stem of a wine glass.

"Oh no, you poor thing." Said Liz and instantly opened up the cupboard. "Oh it appears as if we're using all of them. Damn." She added an endearing stamp to the floor on the last word.

"Whatever will I do," Philippe joked, putting his hand to his forehead as if he might faint. "Strange." He said, less jokingly as his knuckles touched his brow. "I tried to raise my eyebrows just now and it just feels tight." He tapped his brow gently, and smiled with a flirtatious look at Liz. "Am I raising my eyebrows right now?"

"No, as a matter of fact, you're not. That's the Botox dear. And it's probably a good thing that you can't raise your eyebrows very much because that'll keep the wrinkles at bay now won't it. But here, you need some wine to make you feel better. It'll feel normal in the morning. Or rather, you'll get used to it tomorrow." She started to uncork another bottle, but was too drunk to get the corkscrew on center.

"Allow me." Said Philippe, aware that he'd had a few less than her. He pulled the bottle open and handed it to her. "You are still in the wrong room for a glass though mademoiselle."

She grinned and lifted the bottle to her lips. "I'm beyond proper glassware darling." She took a swig, and handed the bottle back to him, swaying slightly. He drank, and then leaned over and kissed her. She leaned into his kiss, and reached up to grip the side of his face.

Just then, they heard a distressed screech from back in the living room and their kissing was cut short.

"I said don't move!" They heard Preston yell. Philippe grabbed Liz's hand and pulled her along with him into the living room. He found that Margarete had stepped back from the sofa a couple of paces and was standing with her hand over her mouth.

"What happened?" Asked Philippe as he came up alongside her.

"Well um, she… um…"

"She jerked!" Said Preston, as he stood up and pulled his leather case closed.

"Oh good god, you didn't" Said Liz, making a beeline for the sofa. Angela was curled up with her face buried in the throw pillow.

"It hurt." She muffled through the pillow.

"Never jerk!" hollered Preston. "Never twitch! Never move, you amateur!"

"You hit a nerve." Said Liz, coming suddenly to Angela's defense. "It hurt her because you hit a nerve. She wouldn't have jerked otherwise. You're the amateur here."

"That isn't what happened, you weren't even in here. She twitched right before the needle came down."

"Just get out of my house this instant you unprofessional, incompetent…"

"Hey! I have been doing this for twelve years and nothing like this has ever happened."

"Oh just get out!" Yelled Liz. Preston puffed up his chest and gritted his teeth. He pushed his glasses up the bridge of his nose, grabbed his case with angry force, and headed towards the door. "And we WILL deal with you later, doctor!" Added Liz as the door swung closed behind him.

There was a long cold silence, broken only by the ill placed beat of the music. Philippe stood motionless next to Margarete who still had her hand over her mouth, until she moved it aside to break the silence.

"This has never happened before." She said calmly, as if trying to convince herself that it still had not occurred.

"What is everybody doing!?" came the sudden clash of happy giggling as the door to the back room opened and out came Ellen, Maria, Aurelio and the others, wiping their noses and looking thoroughly satisfied with themselves. They laughed as if they had just been sharing some amazing joke, when they were confronted by the utterly different vibe of the living room. "Hey, what's wrong?" asked Ellen as she stumbled sideways into Aurelio's chest.

"If you had just called the woman that I had suggested, this would have never happened." Liz suddenly shot a dark glare of accusation towards Margarete.

"Huh!" grunted Margarete, and turned and stalked angrily down the hall towards the back room. Aurelio met eyes with Philippe, but then backed up away from Ellen, and quietly followed Margarete down the hall.

After another moment of standing in silence, surrounded by people who appeared not to know what to do, Philippe sighed abruptly and elected to at least do something. He walked around to the front of the sofa and sat down close to the still crumpled Angela, with her face still buried into the pillow and reached out to gently touch her hair and tuck it behind her ear.

"Angela?" He said quietly, leaning down towards her.

"This is my worst nightmare." She whispered so that only he could hear. He glanced up at Liz and Liz seemed to understand.

"Alright everyone," She said, turning to the remaining guests. "What do you say we take the party out to the patio? We can bring the music and disturb the neighbors." And with an unnecessarily noisy cluster and cheer, they made their way outside.

"Angela, where do you live?" Said Philippe quietly. "I'll take you home."

"Do you think I'll have a saggy face?" She whispered.

"Have you ever heard of Dana Delaney?" The corner of one of her eyes peaked up at him from the throw pillow. She was obviously racking her mind for the name and coming up blank. "She played in Desperate Housewives, which, yes, I did watch." He smiled at the silliness of that fact. "Well, this is what she looks like." He pulled out his phone and showed her an image from Google. "She's in her fifties, and she's gorgeous isn't she."

Angela rolled more out of the pillow so that she could better see the picture and hear what Philippe had to say. "Well, of course I did a lot of research before coming to this party. I always do, I'm a research addict. Google is amazing. But while I was researching, I found an old article about Dana Delaney and a horrible Botox mistake that she went through. A nerve was hit, and she actually lost all feeling to that part of her face and she claims that one of her eyes now droops lower than the other. Can you tell?" He turned the phone towards her again to show her the picture.

She propped herself up a little to look closer at the picture and Philippe could see a red, slightly inflamed mark next to the corner of her eyebrow. He reached out and ran his finger ever so gently along that side of her face.

"Can you see it?" She looked a little worried at Philippe's sudden interest in that side of her face.

"My point," continued Philippe, "is that I think you are young, and resilient, and you can look even better than Dana Delany, no matter what has happened here tonight. If she can still manage to be gorgeous even with permanent damage, then you can be amazing, even if it takes a little time to heal." He leaned in to her and gently kissed her face next to the red skin.

"You're sweet." Said Angela, "But tomorrow is probably my only opportunity with La Facere. Veronica probably wouldn't give little old me a second chance." Philippe leaned down and gently kissed her lips.

"You never know." He said with a smile. "And like you said, makeup can work miracles. Now will you let me take you home?"

Chapter 3. Sleeping Around

Philippe sat naked on the edge of Liz's bed, staring at the blank notepad on his phone. But it seemed that no matter how long he stared at it, his head was just as blank as the screen. What kind of letter could he possibly write to his mother? Why did he need to do it anyway? And on top of that, were therapists often in the habit of handing out homework assignments? And what was the point of writing a letter that you wouldn't send? He understood the idea of writing your feelings down just to get it out, but that would be so much easier to accomplish if it didn't need to be addressed to someone. This way, he was forced to imagine that his mother was the one reading it. Even if she never actually did, the thought of it was almost as bad.

He sighed a deep sigh and then heard as Liz shifted under the covers.

"What are you doing?" She asked sleepily, eyelids only half open.

"Just checking my phone." He said, as he closed out the notepad and locked his phone. He dropped it on top of his pants which had been wildly abandoned to the carpet and turned to smile at this night's lover.

"Couldn't sleep?" She asked as her own eyelids struggled not to sink down again. He shook his head. "I can't stop thinking about Angela." She continued. "How bad did she look?"

"It was just sort of a red mark at first. But it got worse as I was taking her home." They both knew that he had been gone too long to have just taken her home. It didn't take two to three hours to go anywhere in New York City. Philippe had returned with another bottle of wine as some excuse for his extended absence, because that was just what you did. Why they all felt the need to conceal who they slept with was anyone's guess, because everyone was sleeping around and everyone knew it.

"Do you think she'll make it to the shoot tomorrow?" He shook his head with a regretful smile.

"No. And if she's smart, she'll call and cancel. She'd be more likely to get another call back if they didn't get a chance to actually see her."

They were still for a short time as if they saw it fit to remember Angela's plight with a moment of silence. Philippe watched as Liz's eyes, black as the night sky, sank until they sealed shut. She suddenly took a breath and said, "Come back to bed Philippe. I miss your warmth."

Philippe chuckled pleasantly and then leaned over her and kissed her gently. "I'm afraid I can't. I'm going to get myself a glass of water if that's alright. And then I have to go home."

"No, silly boy, don't go home." She was obviously only half awake as she spoke.

"That's where all my clothes are dear."

"You can just wear mine." She muttered as she sank fast to sleep. Philippe smiled and shook his head.

"Sleep tight. See you tomorrow." He said, though she could no longer hear him. And he got up and put on his pants, and tucked his phone into his pocket. He pulled his shirt over his shoulders, but left it unbuttoned for now. He picked up his socks and shoes, and quietly tip toed out of the room and down the now eerily silent hallway to the living room.

He put his shoes down by the sofa where he found Maria passed out where she'd finally crashed from her cocaine high. She was still fully dressed and snoring and drooling peacefully on a throw pillow. He shook his head with a smile and covered her with a small lap blanket that he found folded neatly next to one of the chairs. She looked just a little more comfortable, and that made him content before he went into the kitchen for that glass of water that he truly did feel parched enough to need. He reached into the cupboard and pulled out a tall glass. Clean and unused due to it not being a wine glass, and filled it with tap water.

"Philippe." Said the voice of Aurelio behind him. He turned to see Aurelio's chiseled figure leaning against the archway into the room wearing only what appeared to be boxers of an extremely comfortable looking blue fabric. Philippe felt certain that he had grown a centimeter or two of stubble since he'd seen him earlier that night, or perhaps it was just the light.

Philippe smirked, not only because Aurelio was there and ruggedly handsome, but because of the way Aurelio had pronounced his name. He had chosen to pronounce the "e" at the end of his name, effectively adding a third syllable. Not just Fee Leep, but Fee Leep Aye. Philippe even amused himself by imagining that in his mind, Aurelio had spelled his name with an F. In which case, Aurelio had called him by the Spanish version of his name. Filipe. Philippe could tell that this decision was quite intentional.

"Aurelio, I didn't know you were still here." Philippe said politely. But Aurelio cocked his head slowly to one side.

"That is a lie Filipe." These words came in French, Philippe's own language, but still pronounced his name the Spanish way. Philippe had found, in this life that he was more often the one to do the wooing. But there was nothing quite like the experience of being wooed. Just a slight tweak to his name and suddenly he felt as if Aurelio had made the world to revolve around him. To feel valued, and important. These were subtle tricks that worked every time. No stranger in the world had to work very hard to woo him, but it was still nice to be wooed. The alternative was faster, but subtlety and wit were sweeter.

And Aurelio was indeed right. When Margarete had excused herself in a huff from the group, Aurelio had followed her, and at that moment, Philippe had known that Aurelio wouldn't be leaving for some time. This was especially obvious since neither he, nor Margarete were seen for the rest of the evening.

Philippe turned back away from him for a moment and drained his glass of water quickly, and set the glass down next to the sink. Keeping his back to Aurelio, he looked over his shoulder. "When is your next shoot?"

"Whenever Veronica wants me Filipe." Philippe turned his shoulders more towards Aurelio and looked at him more squarely. Did Veronica want him often? He wondered.

"I guess I'll see you there then." He turned, with a flirtatious smirk, and made to walk past Aurelio back towards his shoes and the sleeping Maria. But in the archway, Aurelio grabbed him and pinned him with his hips against the frame. They were locked with each other there, with their hands in inappropriate places for only a moment, before letting go at the sound of Maria turning in her sleep. They looked at each other, and Philippe stepped away and went to put on his shoes. There was an unspoken agreement to take things further sometime, but not now. Now, to be completely honest, Philippe just needed some sleep. After all, he did have a shoot tomorrow, and therapy after that.

Chapter 4. The Mirror's Routine

The peppy jazzy French vocals took a few minutes to seep into Philippe's groggy mind. His face was smooshed into his pillow and with one eye half open he stared at his phone, lit up and noisy on the floor, plugged in next to his bed.

Suddenly he leapt up and felt his face. He remembered reading something about how it was bad to lay on ones face after Botox, but he wasn't sure how much time had to pass before it was okay. He then realized how many hours had passed between his Botox and his sleeping and felt like it would be ridiculous for someone to need to stay awake for longer than that in order to avoid a problem. This thought comforted him, but it didn't comfort him enough to keep him from getting out of bed and setting off for the mirror to make double sure of the truth of this thought process.

He was right, there was absolutely nothing wrong with his face. He pressed at the still tight sensation in his forehead and leaned against the sink and stared at the ever so subtle ways that his face had changed. He smiled so see the way his face was effected. It caused a slightly stiff effect around the corners of his eyes. True, the crinkles that usually lit up his face were lessened. But it also seemed to him that it was harder to tell if he was smiling for real, or just posing. To be fair, posing was what he'd be doing most for the pictures, and that was what the Botox was for. So he considered the effect a practical success, and picked up his tweezers to work for a few minutes on the line of his eyebrows.

He put the tweezers down after a minute and lifted his elbows and shoved his fingers into his hair and stared at his naked chest in the mirror. He was blessed enough not to have to worry about shaving any chest hair. His hands weren't as delicate as he wished they were, but he supposed that he had to have at least one masculine feature. He was tall and thin in an almost anorexic way, but not quite. He was devoid of muscle but sleek in his figure. He could reasonably be called lanky, but he held himself with such an intentional posture that it didn't matter.

He looked at his underarm and decided that he needed to shave. So he dropped his arms to his sides and got into the shower. Shaving and showering, then lotion for his body and moisturizer for his face. He put on some tight pants and a button up shirt that had a mottled pink and gold texture. He set his light blue moka pot on the stove top to make some espresso and then went back to the bathroom to apply a little makeup.

He lived in a tiny studio basement apartment. He hated it because it didn't have windows but he could hardly complain because he was getting to stay there for free thanks to Veronica. But he had no idea how long he would live there before his engagement became public and he would move in with his fiancé. So he didn't spend all that much energy into making it a wonderful home. He preferred to spend most of his time being out with people anyway, and only came home to sleep.

He applied makeup lightly because he was on his way to a shoot. He wanted enough makeup to look good when he showed up, but not so much that it would make too much work for the makeup artists. Besides, once they got a hold of his face, they would work wonders on him that he would never be able to replicate, and then he would be able to wear it all day. There was also the fact that, if he wore too much makeup in the wrong places or of the wrong shades, it would be assumed by strangers that he was cross dressing. Not that he had anything against crossdressing, but it wasn't really what he was going for.

He tilted his head in every direction to make sure that all the angles and the light worked well together. He would be in a room full of lights though, and bright ones. So he pulled out his phone and shined the flashlight onto the side of his face and then tilted his head around again and made a few adjustments.

Then back to the stovetop he went and poured hot espresso into a tiny espresso shot cup and sipped at it while perusing the social media on his phone. Then with a look at the clock it was go time, and he set the cup in the sink and headed for the door.

Chapter 5. Flashes

The flash of the lights burned his eyes but he loved it. He was wearing a long coat, open at the chest and shoes shinier than any he'd ever owned and a fedora that was tweaked to the side as if it could fall off at any moment. And that was true, it could fall off at any moment. But luckily if he stayed as steady as he was being told to stay, then the precariousness of the hat didn't matter.

His cheek was gently pressed against Liz's and they both tilted up their chins so that they were looking down their lashes towards the camera. His own lashes were full of mascara but Liz had glittery false lashes on. They held their lips pursed but at the same time were made to hold their mouths just slightly loose and open.

Flash, another one down. Photographers avoided flash for the most part, preferring more often to control the effects of the light with huge lamps made to reflect against various screens and sheets. But on this occasion, the photographer decided to use a flash. Philippe didn't ask why, though the question swam in his head. He figured it was better to let the specialists handle such things.

He was just a prop. Of course, he and Liz were both props for the clothing and for Veronica, but more than that, Philippe was a prop for Liz. Elizabeth Dower was the focus of the photo.

"Now turn and put your back into him." She did. "Now lift up your head a little." She did. "No, the other cheek, a little towards me." She did. "There we go, now just hold that." They did.

Veronica was the master of a few male fashions, which Philippe was certainly wearing, but her real niche was women's attire, which Liz was utterly bedazzled in. Philippe could almost always expect to be the accessory to the women's clothes, but that didn't bother him in the slightest.

Liz's big kinky hair had been made to stand in a way that would have been completely impractical for just walking down the street on a day to day basis, not to mention impossible without at least three hours work each morning by a team of specialists. Philippe could smell the product and perfume that she had been drenched in. He enjoyed the smell. It seemed necessary to him, as if scent were something that could be caught on camera.

Her dress was just as unlikely to be seen hanging in a department store. Veronica didn't have time for department stores, the class of human to which she advertised would never set foot in one. But magazines would line the shelves for five dollars a pop, so that the average reader could peer into the world that they wished they lived in.

Veronica made dresses that one might see at an upper class courtly dinner, or a masquerade ball. She made some lighter summer dresses and long gowns too of course, but her real passion was in things that were fully plumed and utterly extravagant. She would have made wonderful wedding dresses if she weren't so utterly opposed to classic traditional weddings as a whole. If Veronica were ever to get married, it was anyone's guess what she would wear down the aisle. So as it was, her dresses were beautiful, but they were never white, and could never be worn by a bride.

The magazine that they were shooting for wouldn't hit the shelves until the end of August, so Liz was wearing a rusted red sort of autumn color. It hung with long lengths draped across the floor so that every time Liz moved into a different pose, someone had to run out and move the train into the best visual location. Philippe wondered if that very dress would make it to the Fall Fashion Week back in Paris. It was abstract enough. Philippe of course, was wearing burnt sienna and black with a few blazing accents to match Liz's ensemble.

The room was not quiet while the photos were taken. One of Philippe's favorite parts of the model life was the utter bustling of life and movement throughout the room. Camera men here and there, light specialists, makeup specialists, computer specialists and every other kind of specialist were moving around as if this was the most important moment on their mind. Agents with clipboards were just adjacent talking to models who hoped to someday be in the exact location that Liz and Philippe were standing in. And models who had already made the cut were standing with an air of superiority whilst at the same time patiently, or not so patiently, needing to wait their turn in the literal spotlight. There was a pulse that could be felt pumping through the room. It surged with so many people, all so full of themselves but too distracted by the hustle and bustle to see themselves clearly.

Philippe held his pose perfectly still as another series of flashes burned his retinas because he refused to let himself blink. But it became that much more difficult when he suddenly had to catch his breath as his heart skipped a beat, and into the room walked Veronica. He felt for a moment as if he were reliving the moment that he first saw her. It always felt that way whenever she walked in. And he could remember every second vividly.

Silence. In fact all the sound in the room seemed to have been sucked out through the ventilation system despite what logic would dictate. The flashes of camera lights were blinding where before Philippe had hardly been bothered by them. But now, the brightness, even though it caused her skin to glitter with a sheen of beauty not fit for this world, even though the flashes of light were like a rhythmic blinking metronome causing Philippe to fall into a trance, even though the flashes were there to capture her beauty forever, they were blocking his vision. They were getting in the way of his eyes. He wanted a clear long look but the cameras only existed to remind him that time was actually passing. That the moment he was experiencing, which seemed to be standing still, aside from the lights, would soon be gone.

There she stood for the longest second in history at the end of the catwalk. She wore a black gown that said that she clearly assumed her worth to be worshiped as a goddess. Her pluming skirts fell no lower than her knees in the front to show the splendor of the silver jeweled heels that she wore, while the back of the skirt hung an inch or two dragging along the runway because when you're a goddess, you have more than enough wealth for excessive dry cleaning.

In slow motion she turned her head, the first wave of turning to ready herself for the walk back. Her dark perfect ringlets cascaded down her shoulders like water and hung, almost floated at the middle of her bare spine. Her bare shoulder turned as the second wave of turning came. Her black fur covered sleeve started halfway down her arm and, covered in lace, it ended at her wrist. Then the twinkle of the silvery flower pieces in her hair caught his eye. He swore diamonds clung to the center of each blossom, waiting for little golden honey bees to come and drink from them. The third and final wave of the turn came and her soft fur covered breast was turned toward him. An excessive pendant rested against her sternum but on her it seemed that it wasn't nearly gaudy enough. Her lips were full and painted red like rose petals but her eyes were the green emerald thorns to all those that would touch her.

Her turn came full circle and suddenly the sound was back and time worked normally again and the flashing of cameras fell again into their proper place in the background. After the silence, the sound was booming of music and people and clicking of cameras. She walked with the sultry but commanding step of royalty. "Mademoiselle Veronica!" said the announcement. She had the spectacular audacity to be modeling her own newest design. Her other models were there only because she couldn't wear all of her outfits at once. She had a right to her audacity. She had lived a life that had earned it. She had it all. And she knew it.

Philippe knew it too. She walked with confidence towards him to exit her glory on the catwalk. He was thankful that he and the other models with him were not next in line because if that were the case, then no one would remember them. But as she left her rightful place on the throne behind her she looked at him. Her eyes bore into his with every step until she passed him. Her head turned ever so slightly, to keep him in her sights for an extended moment longer. Her expression unchanging. She would not give an inch to longing or emotion. She would not surrender to weakness or the pull of love. But she would have what she wanted. She would always have what she wanted. And Philippe knew, as she passed, as the breath returned to his chest, that he would find a way to follow her, and she would find a way to claim him. He knew that he was trapped. Love at first sight had struck him. He had never in his life believed that it was possible to love any one person more than another. All people he could love, fully, equally. But Veronica proved him wrong.

With a small clack that could barely be heard over the noise of the room, his hat hit the floor.

"Oh come on!" Said the photographer, as if this was the most aggravating thing that had happened all day. "Well, pick it up!" he said, which was arguably a silly thing to say when someone is already bending down to do so. Philippe put the hat back on his head, but how he did it was obviously not good enough because the photographer walked right up to him and adjusted it. Philippe could feel his own heart pounding. He had indeed followed Veronica to this place. "We're gonna do one more shot." he muttered, almost to himself. He grabbed Philippe's hand and set it against Liz's waist so that it was barely touching. It was interesting how, for professional photos, very unnatural poses needed to be held, in order to make it look natural at all. And Philippe and Liz said nothing, and just allowed themselves to be molded like clay.

"Okay," said the photographer as if he was talking to anyone at all. "Let's continue." Flash, flash, flash. "And we're done! Next set."

"Come on Philippe." Liz's voice snapped him out of the gaze that Veronica was holding him in. The same unmovable, inescapable look she'd caught him in that first time. But as he exited the set with Liz, he glanced back at Veronica, and saw that she was now engaged in an awkward looking conversation with the photographer. One where the photographer was stumbling over his words, and Veronica had every leverage in the world and knew it. It was as if that gaze had never happened.

In a flurry of movement, Liz and Philippe exited the shoot and their places were taken by other models, but they had no time to wait and watch. Like lightning they found themselves back in the dressing rooms changing out of and putting on the things that they were told to. Philippe found himself in a beige suit with a button up ruffle shirt the color of autumn leaves bursting from beneath his coat. Makeup was washed off and reapplied and though no one really knew where they were supposed to go next, they somehow ended up right where they were supposed to be.

The next set was supposed to be a little more light and playful, it would be Philippe and Liz, paired up with Aurelio and Margarete. Aurelio and Margarete had already done their first set. Philippe very much suspected that the magazine would feature each of them in pairs looking romantic, and then all four of them together looking playful and friendly. But he wouldn't know for sure until the issue came out.

"Bonjour Filipe." Said Aurelio to Philippe in a quiet tone as they made their way out towards the next shoot.

"Hola." replied Philippe with a sly grin. The four of them rounded the corner but one of the agency people, a woman with very neat dirty blonde hair and a not so casual business dress, put up her hand for them to stop. Philippe tilted his head around the corner to see what she was looking at.

It was Veronica. She was wearing one of her extravagant dresses, with ruffles and furls. It was likely not even a dress that she would have made for anyone. She held a delicate lace parasol that would be good for shading her from neither rain nor sun. She looked like a porcelain china doll as she gazed at the camera with complete comfort and ease. No one needed to schedule her time, she would be scheduled whenever she wanted. Every magazine featured her in one of her special creations that no one would likely see on anyone other than her.

"Is she not the most radiant beauty?" Said Aurelio to Philippe quietly.

"She is indeed."

Photos would only be finished when she decided that they were finished, no matter whose schedule it disturbed. But eventually she decided that she was done with the photographer's time, and stepped down from the photo area. Philippe and the members of his set were then waved up and Veronica glided past them without a glance.

This set involved the fans. While the wind was blowing in their hair, between the autumn leaves that they were dropping down gradually on top of them, Philippe saw, with mild horror, as Angela entered the room. She had obviously tried to work her magic with the makeup miracles with only marginal success. Not because she didn't have the skill, but because the damage was too great. The mistake made by her eyebrow had unfortunately seeped down into her top eyelid, which had thus puffed up. Philippe couldn't quite tell from between the leaves, but it seemed as though she was walking a little funny, as if she was perhaps having a little trouble seeing.

He was then told to turn his head towards the camera and smile a wide laughing smile with no noise escaping his mouth. By the time he was able to turn his eyes back towards Angela, she was gone, and instead he saw the back of Veronica's perfect curls in the place where she had been standing. She stood there, still as a statue with her arms crossed and her posture thoughtful. The leaves tickled Philippe's cheeks as they fell.

He knew that it was impossible for Veronica to let Angela be in a shoot with a puffy eyelid. But he wondered, how did that make her feel? Would she call her in a few months to see if the damage had lessened? Or would she forget about her in an hour? It was always hard to say with Veronica. No one could really ever see what she was feeling. It was a mystery, and Philippe loved mysteries.

Chapter 6. Hind Sight Twenty-Twenty

"Did you do your homework?" It had been an entire week, and Philippe felt like he had finally gotten used to the tight sensation from the Botox in his forehead. The hummingbird on the therapist's carpet was still pretty, but looking at it in the same thought as Botox caused its thin, fuzzy beak to vaguely remind him of a needle. He looked up at the therapists dark patient eyes.

"I confess, I didn't" He wondered if her psychoanalyst's eyes were all seeing enough to recognize the tightness in his brow.

"What kept you from it? I don't mean to make you feel obligated. This is your time."

"Oh, you don't make me feel obligated." He said with a smile. "And it isn't that I didn't want to. I tried actually, but I just couldn't think of what to write."

"Do you often feel as if you're unsure what to say to someone?"

"Never." He replied confidently. "But you did ask me to write things that I would never actually say to her face."

"Alright, alright." She conceded, "Fair enough. In that case, why don't we try just talking about it instead? And I won't make you pretend that you're talking to your mother." Philippe was quiet for a while, and he looked back down at the hummingbird, drinking nectar from a flower.

"I think that, my mother just never had a real chance at life. She just wasn't dealt the best hand of cards. She was never able to be better than the hand that was dealt her. She never grew." He looked up at his therapist warm brown cheeks and her heavy set shoulders. "She always stayed the same. I think that, she did her best, but there was no one around who was willing to teach her better, no one willing to invest in her. And I guess that includes me."

"How do you suppose that includes you?"

"Maybe I should call her."

"Do you think that calling her would make you willing to invest in her?"

"It would be better than nothing."

He was staring at the way her hands were laced together. There was a large diamond wedding ring on her left hand that was being pinched by her skin as she clenched.

"Last week, you said that you had fashioned a better life because your mother couldn't fashion a life good enough for you."

"Do you think that's selfish? That I came here seeking fashion?"

"No, not at all. I think that your mother wasn't able to make your life secure when you were a child, so now you're seeking fashion as a means to make up for that."

"Well," he said with a grin. "I also just love clothes."

"You are able to love clothes and feel secure Philippe, one does not need to be a means to the other." He blinked. "I'm sorry Philippe, I'm starting to preach."

"I'm not offended," he said, shaking his head with a smile, still blinking at the thought. "You have good insight. I always appreciate good insight." She smiled warmly and folded her hands gently in her lap and leaned back, more relaxed in her chair.

"I'm willing to bet that your mother did not do nothing for you. But the security, which a child seeks from its mother, seems to me to have been broken somehow. Is that true" There was a long pause and Philippe just stared at the woman. But he wasn't actually looking at her. He was sifting through his thoughts.

"As always Philippe, we don't have to talk about these things if you don't want to. Like I said, this is your time. You can choose what to focus on."

"No, no. I do want to. Last week I didn't, but I guess maybe this week I've had a little more time to emotionally prepare myself." He smiled thoughtfully. "I suppose, maybe I could talk about Armel."

"Alright." She said and shifted one foot and tucked it up under her right thigh, just getting comfortable. "Then, let's talk about Armel." Philippe, on the other hand, was sitting in the exact place that he had been since he came in. His back was straight and his knees were tight together and his hands were tucked neatly between them with his elbows close at his sides. "Can you tell me who Armel is?"

"He was one of my mother's drug dealers. They were romantically involved for a while."

"How long of a while?"

"Year and a half or so."

"And how old were you?"

"About eight or nine."

"Alright."

"I'm not really sure how to talk about this, I guess I'll just try to be blunt. Armel was the one who molested me I suppose."

"You suppose?"

"Oui. They say hindsight is twenty-twenty right?" The therapist raised an eyebrow. Philippe thought perhaps the saying seemed a little out of place. Would he now need to explain what he meant by it? Was he the only one who would need twenty-twenty hindsight in order to see clearly that he had been molested? He supposed that sort of thing was obvious to most people. He crossed one knee over the other before continuing.

"I had never thought to use the word 'molested' until my best friend Aimee, back in Paris, pointed it out to me."

"I see." She said, tilting her head slightly to one side. "Most eight or nine year olds probably don't know the word, and therefore wouldn't think to apply it to themselves."

"Oui." He said, his spirit somehow lightening a little. "I guess that's true." A smile lit his cheeks, but didn't quite make it into his brow. "I used to call him my 'boyfriend' back then. I would say I had a boyfriend but I would never say who he was. I told myself that I wouldn't say who he was, so that my mother wouldn't get jealous."

"How long did this go on Philippe?"

"For about a year. Until after my mother overdosed and had to be taken to rehab. She came home unexpectedly and caught us. Or well… caught him I guess."

"And what did she do?"

"Well, she screamed and yelled and kicked Armel out and called the police."

"And when she did that, did it return some security to you? Or did it make you feel less secure?"

"Well…" He thought about that convoluted mixture of emotions, like some horrible rancid stew, all mixed up together. "Well, I guess I felt… scared, at her yelling, sad because I had made her feel horrible, angry, because everything changed so fast and… and I just wonder why it took her so long."

"Yes. I see that. That's a lot of feelings."

"Oui. It took me a long time to see all that as something that had happened to me rather than something that I had done."

"When did you find out?"

"Late Middle school. A couple of friends had started having sex and they were whispering together about their experiences." He smiled thoughtfully with a smile of mixed discomfort and nostalgia. "You'd never believe the look they gave me when I told them that I'd had sex too. Way before any of them had" He shook his head, remembering the looks of utter confusion, pity and even disgust. "Then Aimee took me aside and we talked about it."

"It sounds like Aimee was a good friend."

"She is, she's still my good friend. Though we've fallen a little out of communication since I came to New York. She's still my best friend as far as I'm concerned."

"I'm glad to hear that you have someone like that in your life Philippe." She glanced at the silver watch on the inside of her right wrist. "Well, it looks like we're coming up to the end of our time today Philippe. How are you feeling?"

"Sort of relieved. It's nice to be able to talk about those things."

"Good, I'm glad to hear that. Will the same time next week work for you?"

"Actually, I have a shoot this time next week. Can we make it a day earlier?"

"Certainly. And if you feel up to it, you can still try your hand at writing that letter to your mother."

"Well… Alright. We'll see."

Chapter 7. Aurelio

"What is so interesting about the ceiling, Filipe?" Aurelio stepped, naked, from the bathroom and tilted his head slightly. "You look as if it speaks volumes to you. Or perhaps, it is your mind, that his speaking volumes to the ceiling." Philippe smiled. He'd been laying naked on his back with his fingers laced behind his head, staring thoughtfully into the air above him.

He felt exhausted, but at the same time refreshed and exhilarated. "I'm reliving the last hour, over and over again in my mind." He replied. It wasn't the whole truth, but it was at least part. In truth, he'd been feeling the subtle sensation of a moment of growing freedom in his heart along with the hour he'd just spent expressing it.

"I sense that there is something else going on in that mind of yours Filipe." He started walking over to his shoulder bag which had been dropped by the foot of Philippe's bed. "Your face looks more as if you've seen an angel. I do think very highly of myself, but perhaps not quite divine." He smirked mischievously and then squatted down and started rustling through his bag.

Philippe rolled onto his side and propped himself up on his elbow to watch Aurelio. Aurelio pulled out a small bag of white powder. "Perhaps you were thinking about Veronica." Philippe raised his eyebrows invisibly. Aurelio certainly did seem fond of talking about her. But it also seemed as if he were fishing for something.

"She is about as angelic as human skin can get isn't she."

"No," Said Aurelio, standing up and coming with his baggie to sit on the edge of the bed next to Philippe. "I think that an angel must have actually touched her face. That is the only possible explanation." Aurelio smiled with his stubbly cheeks and Philippe could still feel the places where that stubble had rubbed his skin like sandpaper. "Will you do a line or two with me Filipe?"

"Oh," Replied Philippe looking at the bag of powder. "No," He said shaking his head a little. "You go ahead though." He smiled to show his contented acceptance of Aurelio's habit.

"You sting me." Said Aurelio, putting his hand over his chest as if his heart hurt. "Why do you refuse?"

"Oh it's nothing. Bad experience."

"What if this experience were better? You do have me here after all. Your humble Aurelio."

Philippe chucked. "It's not you. My mum has a drug problem so I've always preferred to stay away from most of them."

"Oh yes well, my father has a drug problem and I always thought that he looked like he was having so much fun that I decided to join him." They both chuckled as if this were more funny than sad. "But you say most of them you do not do, allow me to guess what is your fancy." He reached to the floor where his jeans were laying and pulled his keys from the front pocket. Then he used his key to scratch his chin thoughtfully. "Um... I say, Ecstasy? You seem like you would like Ecstasy."

"I probably would but no." Said Philippe, smiling at the pointless guessing game.

"You have never even tried it? Ay! I cannot believe that."

"It is true."

"And not cocaine?"

"I've tried it once."

"Your bad experience?"

"Right."

"So no Cocaine, no Ecstasy, you would a probably not be smoking heroin either if you're a scared of drugs."

"No."

"Do you even smoke grass?" Philippe giggled at Aurelio's utter disbelief. But drugs were the one habit of models that he'd somehow managed to avoid.

"Marijuana puts me to sleep. I'd rather stay awake so that I can get laid."

"You don't do anything! Do you drink coffee!?"

"Haha! Oui. I do drink coffee."

"Well at least there's one upper for you, how about I snort this cocaine and you go get yourself an espresso." He shook his head jokingly and filled the rim of his key with white powder and put it up to his face. He inhaled sharply through his nose with a sound reminiscent of the ones that children make in the winter time when their noses are running and their parents tell them to get a tissue. "At least I know you drink. I've seen you do it. And you fuck, and that is the best drug of them all."

Philippe smiled and leaned back against the disheveled pillows and watched Aurelio wipe his nose. "Veronica is perfect, isn't she?" Said Philippe after a moment of waiting for Aurelio to clear his sinuses. Aurelio turned his golden brown eyed gaze onto Philippe. Now they were both fishing for something. Aurelio nodded reverently.

"In between the curls of her hair, I can see stars glitter. Her eyelashes are never fraud because she was crafted by angels by hand. When I look into her eye, I can see that which I cannot see. Like standing on one shore, and knowing that there is another, somewhere across her vast ocean."

"But would she ever let you see it?" Philippe whispered. "Or is it a land shrouded and hidden, like Atlantis, impossible to find without losing your breath?"

"My breath is lost Felipe. Can a man woo a goddess? He will never be enough. Her ocean is too great, but still I would swim until I perish utterly into her depths."

"And what if she is but a woman, and we are but men? Then her deepest secrets are treasures that only she can choose who to bestow them on. And the question is, will she? Or will she keep them hidden in her heart forever?"

"She cannot be wooed if she is not worshipped."

"But can you worship a woman Aurelio? I think you can." They stared at each other, a secret pact made, a secret rivalry born, however friendly it might be.

"What were you thinking about earlier Felipe? When you were giving your soul to the ceiling." He looked down at his keys, and then put the end of them into his mouth to suck off the last of the residual powder. He then dropped the keys and set the baggie on top of his pants, and leaned over, close to Philippe and reached over and ran his fingers through his hair.

Philippe contemplated what to tell him. Was it time to tell his secret? He knew himself well enough to know that he couldn't keep his own secrets forever. He'd wanted to tell his fiancé before anyone who cared less. But at that moment, he didn't quite see the point of that. What was the worth of keeping this secret? And he liked Aurelio, and wanted Aurelio to be someone among those whom Philippe trusted. Philippe was known to trust too easily.

"Well, don't tell anyone yet, but I've been seeing a therapist."

"Oh? And has it helped?"

"Actually, yes. It has." Philippe smiled.

"Is it about your mother?" Philippe nodded.

"Mostly."

"If it is helping, then I am glad. Therapists are good people who are good at helping others. They have a selflessness that I wish I was capable of." Philippe smirked.

"All of them?" He joked.

"You know what I mean." And with that Aurelio kissed him. Philippe's tongue became ever so slightly numbed by the tiny remnants of Cocaine in Aurelio's mouth. But not enough to worry about. So what did it matter?

Chapter 8. Repressed

"Alright Philippe, why don't we talk a little bit more about your childhood."

"Sure, no problem, where would you like me to start?"

"Well, why don't we keep it basic for the time being? How about you tell me about your earliest memory."

"Sure, just let me think, um..." Dark. Cramping muscles in his legs. Breathing slowly, quietly. Very quietly. He furrowed his brow and for a strange moment, didn't remember why his forehead felt so stiff. "Um, well it's a little blurry. It's more of a feeling really. I'm not sure if it's really a memory." He thought hard, trying to make it a little clearer. "My mother's voice..."

'Chut. Rester en bas. Soyez silencieux. Ne laissez pas les hommes que tu trouver.' Hush. Stay down. Be quiet. Don't let the men find you.

"No, no it's really blurry. It doesn't really make any sense." He furrowed his brow a little harder and rubbed it with his fingers, causing a slight crease on his forehead.

"Can you describe the feeling?" He was staring at the hummingbird again, obviously lost somewhere in that memory. "Philippe?"

Bright light. Hurt his eyes. Men.

'Allez sur l'enfant.' Come on out child.

'Non. Ne laissez pas les hommes que tu trouver. Non.' Dark suits. Kevlar. Hands. Bright light. 'mère. Non. Ne laissez pas les hommes que tu trouver.'

"I think it's probably a very important step that you process that memory in your native language Philippe. I should probably let you know though, that I don't speak a lick of French.

"What? Oh. Oh I'm so sorry. I didn't even notice that I was speaking." He rubbed his eyes with his knuckles as his mind came back to the present. His face lit up with a smile that echoed through his whole body. "So where were we? My earliest clear memory was when my mother and I moved into an apartment. It was small, but it was home. My mother was so hopeful. I think that must have been before she got into the heroin. She got a job working fast food and we scraped by." He shook his head and smiled. "But the first memory was of the door. The door to the apartment. Number 36. She opened it and said, 'Oh isn't this wonderful Philippe? You'll have your very own room. And then she proceeded to dance around the apartment as if it was the most beautiful thing in the world." He chuckled pleasantly

"Interesting." Her deep chocolate eyes considered Philippe for a moment. "And what did you think about the apartment? How did you feel about your room?"

"You know, thinking back on it, it's a little strange. It was a very small place, like I said. But when I first walked in, it all seemed very huge. Too big really. Maybe just because I was so small then."

"How old were you?"

He shrugged and rested his fingertips thoughtfully against his lips. "Five? Six maybe."

"Hmm. Interesting." She put her elbow in her hand, leaned back and rested her chin in her open palm. It was the first expression of curiosity that he'd seen in her so far. Curiosity and perhaps, he thought he also saw concern etched into her dark brow.

"What?" He chuckled slightly with a grin.

"What do you know about memory repression?" He wasn't expecting that. His clean smile faltered and he tilted his pretty blonde head to the side.

"It's the idea that if an event is more than one can handle, they'll sometimes forget that it ever happened."

"In a nutshell yes. You see, just a moment ago you were saying something in French, and I've an inkling that you weren't talking about your mother's apartment." She tapped her chin thoughtfully. "Then again, five or six is not too old for an earliest memory. But you seemed to be a little lost in thought when you were speaking. Do you know what you were saying?"

Philippe shook his head. "I was saying something?"

"Yes Indeed. Philippe, would you have any reason to believe that you might have a memory that you're blocking out?"

"Blocking out? Why?"

"If it was too traumatic for you to handle at the time."

"But I've had plenty of traumatic things happen to me that I haven't blocked out. Are you saying that there could something even more traumatic than the things that I DO remember?"

"Perhaps, but there's also the possibility that you were simply too young to be able to process whatever it was. It's possible that it's something that you would have no trouble dealing with as an adult, with the emotional resources that you've built up since that time. But you were so young. You may have the option of opening up that memory now that you're older and have more resources at your disposal."

His hands were pressed against his cheeks, smudging slightly the subtle makeup that he'd applied that morning. His elbows were hugged in close to his ribs, and his eyelids were half closed in a thoughtfulness that pursed his lips.

"You don't have to Philippe. I, as your therapist, think that it would be of potential benefit to you. But you would not be the first to decide that what was once buried is probably better off staying that way. As far as practical functioning goes, you seem to be doing just fine without unearthing those things."

"No no. I don't think that way. If there really is some memory that I'm blocking out then I'm earnestly extremely curious and will not be satisfied until I've discovered the answer." That bright sunshine smile of his lit his sky blue eyes again.

She chuckled. Philippe thoroughly enjoyed watching her white teeth smile and her overweight shoulders roll under the weight of her laugh. It just goes to show that there are all manner of ways to make people feel good. And Philippe was a connoisseur of good feelings.

"Well all right then Philippe. Where would you like to start?"

"Well, maybe Paris. Maybe I should go back home and see what I can dig up. Maybe I should talk to my mother and see what she remembers, though she's never really had much interest in talking about the past."

"Why do you suppose that is?"

"I dunno. Maybe for the same reason that I can't remember it."

"Well, I can see that you are very excited for the whole thing, which is wonderful, but I wouldn't necessarily go hopping on the first plane to Paris."

"Why not? That's what youth is for isn't it?" His goofy grin widened.

"Just don't burn yourself out too fast. I'm not even completely certain that a blocked memory is what you're dealing with. Why don't you just try thinking about it for a while? Your earliest clear memory is when you were five or six." she shrugged, "Where do you think you were at four? Where do you think you might have lived before you lived in that apartment with your mother?"

"I have no idea."

"Well, maybe just thinking about that would be a good place to start then."

"Alright. I'll do that." And with a smile, he stood up. It was time to go. She stood to show him out.

"Same time next week then?"

"Well, if I'm still here, that will be fine." He gave her a flirtatious wink, and walked out the door.

Chapter 9. Veronica

Philippe woke, warm and snug and naked on satin violet sheets. He groaned softly and pressed his face into his pillow. Then looked over to his fiancé. She lay with her back to him, softly inhaling and exhaling life into her body. Veronica. Philippe had fallen madly in love with her from the first moment he saw her. He smiled at her resting shoulders and her ribs expanding and compressing. He reached quietly to her and gently ran a fingertip down one of her long dark curls from the scalp to the tip. How she managed to keep herself perfectly primped even when asleep was beyond him.

Up and at'em! He dressed casual, but gorgeous of course, applied a light layer of makeup and brushed his teeth. In Veronica's kitchen he set out two plates and set a croissant on each with some butter and jam nearby. He smiled pleasantly at the small table setting but something was definitely missing. Coffee of course was next, and if he'd had a flower to put into the middle of it all, it would be perfect. Well, you can't have everything, so coffee it is. He started some water boiling and pulled the French press out of the cupboard. He set the press down on the counter and began the search for the coffee. Drawer after drawer, cabinet after cabinet, none in the pantry. He was at first under the opinion that it was simply impossible to find anything in Veronica's house, but he soon had to admit the truth.

They were out. Out of coffee. The coffee was gone. He looked back at his little breakfast setting which was beginning to look more and more sad. He thought perhaps, that if he left quietly enough, he could be back with coffee and a flower before Veronica woke up. He decided to try.

He sneaked quietly back into the bedroom and slipped his wallet and phone into his pockets. Then he quietly made his way to Veronica's black alligator hand bag and began searching for her keys. He found them, and slipped them into his pocket. Long lashes. Perfect lips. Either she wore bed resistant makeup while she slept, or her face was really that remarkably beautiful. All the model girls wished that they were her, and Philippe had to admit that so did he. He smiled at her sleeping face before standing up to sneak to the door. He would kiss her cheek before he left but it wasn't worth the risk. Who was he kidding, of course it was.

He turned back to steal a kiss as she slept only to find her green eyes open and her perfect lips smiling back at him. "And where are you off to sweet Philippe?"

His face lit up instantly with a grin. "We're out of coffee my love. I was planning to steal away while you slept to return with the perfect morning in my pocket for you." He crawled onto the foot of the bed and made his way to her and kissed her perfect lips and gazed into her perfect eyes, green like ancient jade. "But you dearest, have spoiled my master plan."

"I make it my job to spoil all master plans. I like the chaos.

Makes things more exciting." She kissed him back and their morning descended into giggles and pillow feathers for a time. But time was of the essence, and they had places to be. Philippe wished that they could linger there all day, but he knew Veronica better than that. He knew that she was a woman of business, she had the world at her fingertips, and she would not leave it wanting. Life was a popularity contest that she intended to win. And she certainly couldn't accomplish that by hiding her perfect face indoors. Philippe of course, had every intention of helping her succeed. But he wished that she could take at least one day off.

"Are you ready for your shoot today Philippe?" the sound of the running shower falling over her body seemed to him like the sound of thousands of diamonds being poured onto the floor of the Taj Mahal. If she could wash herself in diamonds, he was sure that she would.

"I'm always ready dearest, I'm too beautiful not to be." The sound of the shower ceased.

"Well now, look who's getting cocky. Perhaps I've been too easy on you."

"Is it time to crack the whip on me?" He watched her reflection in the mirror as she dried herself. He was mesmerized by the curve of her spine.

"Only if it forces you to become even more beautiful than you are now." Her eye caught his in the reflection. A tenuous balance of coy and dead serious. "So I never asked you. How have your secret therapy sessions been serving you?"

"Well gee, as long as they're still secret, they're going fine." He smiled as her eye turned back away from him and she hung up her towel.

"Well, my lips are sealed of course, but you should do a better job of watching what you say. You never know who you can trust." She always talked like this. It was part of her allure. It was hard to tell how much of what she said was what she meant. It made her a mystery. Philippe loved mysteries. "But since you can trust me, is there anything you would like to say about it?"

"Well, as a matter of fact, since we're on the subject, I might be taking a trip back to Paris soon."

"Who says that I can spare you? You must give me more notice than that. You're scheduled for several shoots this month. You've got work to do my love." She started working on her hair, as if it needed any work. Her eyes met his in the mirror. She stared at him as she absentmindedly combed products through her hair. "There will be Fashion Week in Paris in a couple of months. I'll need you to be there."

His smile to her was sweet as honey and soft as velvet. "So be there I shall." His memory could wait a little longer. It wasn't urgent.

"So why has secret therapy called you to return from whence you came Philippe?" Her eyes returned to her own face as she began to apply makeup. As if you could tell the difference.

"Oh, well it's quite exciting really. You see, it seems I've some dark tragic memory buried deep within my psyche. So much so that I cannot recall it unless I visit the place in which it was formed. Who knows what I may find. Perhaps I witnessed a murder, or the tragic death of my heroic father in his effort to save me from vicious vagabonds. But whatever it was I do not know. I've blocked it out. Should be interesting." He grinned.

Her face did not make light of it the way his did. She set down the makeup tools that resembled medieval torture devices and walked over to the bedside where her beloved perched. She rested a delicate hand on each of his cheeks. Her palms felt like rose petals against his skin and smelled like it too.

"When I was sixteen, I was assaulted. My father refused to allow me an abortion because he was Catholic, and he believed that to do such a thing would be to destroy the life of an innocent, even though an innocent life had already been taken. I simply could not go through with the pregnancy though, so I sought out other means. My insides are still scarred from the procedure and I'll never be able to have children again. I was hospitalized for a month while I healed and I continued to bleed for some time after. The pain in my womb has never quite gone away but I've learned to live with it.

Philippe, I've spent years trying to forget that any of it ever happened but the memory is still as vivid as it ever was. Perhaps learning what dark secret your psyche has kept from you will give you peace of mind. Or perhaps you're just lucky that you've never had to remember it. But after you find it Philippe, you'll never be able to forget it again. So I hope, because... because I love you, that you find what you're looking for. And should you choose to unearth it, that it makes you a greater man. More beautiful, inside and out. I hope that it's worth the pain that will come with it." She caressed his cheek and then slid her finger under his chin to close his jaw which he now realized had been hanging open slightly.

He stared up at her in wonderment. She had been open with him. That was a gift that she did not give to just anyone and he couldn't help but feel that he was not worthy. He wrapped his arms around her legs and pressed his ear against her wounded womb. "Thank you for sharing that with me Veronica." He kissed her just below the navel.

She knelt down in front of his face. "As long as you also heard the point of my story, you're welcome."

He smiled softly and nodded. "I think I did." He leaned forward to kiss her lips but she backed up just out of his reach.

"Ah ah. Makeup. And we've got work to do. We need to get you into the studio in under an hour, the makeup artist will be miffed if you're late."

"Well, we wouldn't want her to be miffed." He said sarcastically as he stood up.

"If she gets too miffed she's fired so I'm sure she'll keep things under control." She smiled and winked at Philippe and pulled on a dark dress that was so beautiful it had no right to be worn on just any old day. One would think that she was dressing for an occasion, but the truth was, she dressed this way every day.

"Coffee Veronica." They were headed towards the door.

"Get some for me too. Meet me at the studio in twenty. If you're late, you're dead."

"Yes ma'am." He handed her back her keys and headed out the door. The croissants sat, lonely on the table, for the rest of the day." He was a model. He couldn't actually eat them. But they were certainly pretty to look at. Though they would have been prettier with a flower.

Chapter 10. Diamonds last forever

They split ways at the door, Veronica towards the studio and Philippe towards the nearest coffee shop. Philippe put on his red helmet and got onto the back of his little red Vespa.

After buying the coffee Philippe strongly contemplated getting flowers since that had been on his to do list before, but he figured that the studio was perhaps not the best place to give Veronica flowers since their engagement was not yet public. He was thinking about flowers and about Veronica as he was walking back towards his Vespa with his hands full of coffee and contemplating how he was going to safely transport it, when he passed a jewelry store. He stopped at the window and looked inside. Engagement rings. Philippe had never been a man of commitment, so the thought of marriage had never really been something he'd thought about. Not until he'd seen Veronica. Even then, not until she'd asked him to marry her.

He stepped a little closer to the glass and peered in at the glittering stones. Diamonds. A symbol of something lasting forever. Veronica had never asked him to be faithful and he knew that she never had been either. But was there a different kind of commitment in a marriage? Was marriage about who you slept with? Or was it about being with someone forever, no matter the challenges. Could he do that? With her? Could he commit to being with her forever no matter the challenges? Since she had been the one to propose, he'd never had the chance to buy her a ring.

"Would you like to take a closer look?" The handsome well-dressed store clerk had stuck his head out the door. He was already hurting for time, he'd spent too much of it looking in this window.

"Um... Sure." Philippe smiled. "Why not?"

"Hey, why not? That's a good question. Come on in." Philippe stepped into the store. He smiled flirtatiously at the handsome clerk. "Have a special someone you're thinking of?" Said the clerk. He raised an eyebrow at Philippe's smile.

"As a matter of fact yes." He stepped closer to the glass covered displays and looked at the beautiful rings.

"Planning on popping the question?" Philippe couldn't help but grin at that.

"Actually, I believe I've done this in the wrong order. We're already engaged and yet her finger has been left naked." A ring on her finger would be a public declaration. One that he hoped they were ready to make.

"Well, let's remedy that. I have a few sugges-"

"That one." Tiny braids of tiny diamonds weaved around a silver band like ivy climbing a garden wall. They made their way around the band, swerving together and away from each other until they wrapped and swirled up into the bloom of a diamond rose. It was perfect. Just like she was.

"A good choice sir." The clerk pulled it out and put it in the little black box. "Would you like it wrapped?"

"No thank you. That would make going down on one knee far less dramatic."

"As is then." Philippe balanced the coffees in one hand while he made his purchase. He picked up the ring and tucked it into his pocket. He gave the clerk one last flirtatious glance and spotted a clock behind his left ear.

"Oh no! Crap, I'm late." He pushed his way through the door and rushed out to his Vespa. He tucked the coffee safely between his feet and got on the road. He certainly hoped that he was worth more to them as a model than he thought he was, because he had never been late for a photoshoot before.

He had a harder time than usual finding parking and by the time he was parked, he was half an hour late and the coffee was getting cold. But he picked up the coffee anyway and started walking the extra three blocks to the studio.

He didn't walk too fast. He was late as it was and if he was in for it, he was in for it. No matter how late he was. And on another note, as cold as his coffee was, coffee it was, and that was good. And on top of that, there was a diamond ring in Philippe's pocket. So despite the things going wrong in that moment, Philippe walked with an extra skip in his step and a slightly Botox impeded grin on his face.

There were sirens up ahead by the studio though. The red and blue lights danced off the windows of the buildings all around him. Philippe quickened his pace. Something felt wrong. There were six cop cars and an ambulance right out front. Officers in headsets speaking pure gibberish into the mouthpiece. Philippe began to run. Yellow tape was wrapped around an area right in the middle of the sidewalk. Officers were everywhere. There was a stretcher standing outside of the ambulance but no one was on it. There was a news crew, and cameras. The police were doing their best to keep the reporters at bay.

Philippe came around the ambulance to see that, in the middle of all the yellow tape surrounded by officers, was Veronica. She was lying face down on the ground. Her delicate fingers were covered in blood. Her beautiful curls were thrown haphazardly over her face. And she was laying there, on the ground. Cheek against the pavement. Dead. Very dead.

He dropped the cold coffee with a splash as it fell against a gutter. "No." He whispered. He couldn't believe what he was seeing. Before he knew what he was doing he'd crossed most of the distance and was swerving past the officers and ducking under the yellow tape. His foot slipped in the blood that had drained away from Veronica's body and as his knee hit hard against the red pavement he reached his hand out to try and touch her curls.

His hand didn't get far before it was grabbed by one of the officers and he felt himself being pulled away from his beloved. As her pale face grew more distant he saw her eye peeking out at him. Her green eye. No longer green like jade. The light was gone. Mascara ran into the blood around her heart shaped face. Her perfect lips were partly opened and her lipstick was smeared. It was smeared all across her blush-less cheek. "No... Veronica!" he tried to struggle against the officer but he was no body builder, and the officer surely was. "No, please, that's... that's Veronica. Please, let me go!" Another pair of hands grabbed on to him.

"Sir, you can't be here, it's disrupting evidence." Philippe turned to face his aggressors. Dark suits, Kevlar, hands. All the sound went away from Philippe's ears. He could see the man's lips moving but no sound came out. He felt all his muscles give out as his body went limp. Darkness, cramping in his legs. Dark suits, Kevlar, hands. Bright light. Can't see. Too bright. He felt a thumb and forefinger pulling his eyelids apart. Bright light.

When he came to, he was wrapped in a thermal blanket, laying on the floor of the ambulance. His face was wet with moisture from his eyes. He supposed he must have been crying. No, he was still crying. His body was shaking and his face felt scrunched. His chest was hurting and a noise was warbling through his throat that sounded an awful lot like sobs. Lights were still flashing on the buildings from the sirens which had since been silenced. He rolled onto his side and curled up as small as he could be. He let himself cry for as long as his body wanted to. He cried until he was numb. He let himself just be numb for a while. He couldn't feel the grief on his face. Why should he feel it in his heart?

"They're tracing her with chalk Filipe." Philippe looked down towards the big doors of the ambulance. The ambulance was open. Aurelio was sitting on the edge watching the bustle of the cops doing their work. "There's only so many of them here because she's famous. If she weren't famous they would have left her in the gutter like everyone else."

Philippe sat up and scooted over, with his thermal blanket, to sit next to the Spanish hunk of a man. He stared at the ground at first, but slowly he allowed his eyes to lift. There she was, on the ground still. And sure enough, a cop was outlining her body. He looked away again. But ultimately decided to force himself to watch.

"What do you think this will do to the magazine?" Aurelio asked. "This is certainly going to give us some interesting publicity." Aurelio scanned his eyes around at all the cameramen and heaved a great sigh. "It is a very, very sad thing, to lose such a beauty."

"She was the love of my life Aurelio."

Aurelio snorted. "How many loves of your life can you have at once Philippe? Can you have all of them?"

"This was different!" His grief flared for a moment into tears of anger. "I was going to marry her Aurelio. I would have been with her forever. And forever had only just begun. You wouldn't understand. She's the first person I've ever wanted that much."

Aurelio heaved a great sigh. "As did I Philippe, as did I."

Philippe looked away from the scene in front of him, to the face of his Spanish companion, as mournful as his own face. Had they all loved her so much? He didn't doubt it. And who was Philippe to say that his love for her was of any greater worth than someone else'. Tears of empathy covered his anger. "She was well loved."

Aurelio nodded solemnly. "That she was." Philippe rested his head against Aurelio, and offered a bit of his thermal blanket. Aurelio wrapped an arm around Philippe's shoulder, and took him up on the offer. So that even if their hearts were left a little colder without her. At least their beds would be warm.

Chapter 11. Tabloids

Rumor has it, world renowned fashion designer and editor of the fashion magazine 'La Facere', Veronica Diarmada has died in a tragic accident.

Rumor has it, she was murdered by a colleague.

Rumor has it, she was murdered by a business rival.

Rumor has it, it was a random assault by one of New York's many small time criminals.

Rumor has it Veronica Diarmada was sleeping with her models. Scandalous! But surprising?

Rumor has it that one of these was an up and coming model named Philippe De' Leon. But were they more than that?

Rumor has it they were engaged to be married.

Rumor has it that Philippe cheated on her.

Rumor has it that she cheated on him first.

Rumor has it that Veronica's fiancé, Mr. De' Leon, slept with a MAN on the very night she was murdered. Betrayal!

Rumor has it, they have no idea what they're talking about.

Has Mr. De 'Leon always known that he was gay?

Would she feel betrayed if she were alive to know?

Did her fiancé truly love her? Or was he just pretending to be straight for her money?

"People with disabilities and parents with young children may now board." A woman in a neat uniform spoke into an intercom phone that rang from the speakers above his head. For the moment, Philippe ignored her.

He couldn't help but read the slander in the tabloids. They always did such a good job of making a big deal out of things that no one would have cared about or batted an eyelash at otherwise. Everything was chaos. But through all the aftermath he could hear her voice inside his head 'but you should do a better job of watching what you say. You never know who you can trust.' Perhaps not Aurelio.

"Oh, Philippe, I wasn't expecting a call from you. You know, you missed your appointment last week." Her deep voice displayed the appropriate tone of concern.

"I know." He replied to his therapist.

"I saw the news. Are you doing all right?"

"I'm sad. But I'm okay." His voice was full of emotional exhaustion.

"Would you like to come in for an appointment? I have an opening tomorrow."

"No, I just wanted to let you know that I'm on my way to Paris." He turned the diamond ring over and over again in his hand. He couldn't really put his finger on exactly why he felt the need to inform his therapist that he was leaving. Maybe it was just to help him process that fact. Maybe he was just being polite.

"Are you sure you're ready for that Philippe?" He couldn't help but smile at that.

"No, I'm never sure that I'm ready for anything."

"Will you be able to call me while you're there if you need to talk?"

"I'm not really sure. I don't think I have the money for the international calls right now. This is a one way trip and the last of my savings really." He held the ring a little closer to his eyes. So much money for such a tiny piece of rock. He wiped a tear from his eye and put the ring back in his pocket.

"Business class may now board." Said that female voice. Cold. Immune to his emotions. Unthinking of the true weight of her words.

"I have to go." He couldn't keep the quiver out of his voice, not that he'd really tried all that hard.

"When you find what you're looking for Philippe, call me if you can." He nodded, to her invisibly, and smiled as he wiped another tear from his eyes.

"Okay. I will. Thank you for everything."

"Good luck Philippe." The warm deep velvety chocolate sound of love in her voice resounded in his ear, as did the cold hard click of the line breaking. He slipped his phone into his pocket where it clinked uncomfortably with the tiny black box that held the ring. Two lifelines in one pocket.

"Flight from New York to Paris, final boarding call." He stood and collected his luggage. Time to go home.

Chapter 12. First Love

Philippe came out of the airport and made his way toward the parking lot. He was a smidgen disappointed that his mother and Aimee hadn't been there when he showed up but he shrugged it off. He wasn't particularly surprised, and he knew his way around like the back of his hand.

Then he saw his car. The moon seemed to pick it out from among all the others. 1971 Mercedes-Benz 280SE 3.5 Cabriolet convertible. She seemed to glow with a red and radiant beauty that Philippe knew only to be rivaled by the beauty of Veronica. Oh if he could only have seen them together. His car, together with the beauty of his sweetest love. The splendor of Rome would have been rebuilt in the instant the two were seen together. If she hadn't died, if they had been able to come to Fashion Week in Paris as planned, perhaps he would have seen such a magnificence. But as his fantasy died so too did Rome collapse.

But Philippe smiled, because out of his beautiful little red convertible came Aimee from behind the wheel. The only person who he would trust to steer her true. He turned his trajectory towards her and picked up his pace.

"Aimee!" He called her name and when he reached her, he dropped his luggage and threw his arms around her and kissed her on both cheeks. "Il est très agréable de tu voir." It's lovely to see you. His own language rolling from his tongue felt wonderful. No matter how fluent he was in English, there had always still been an aspect of needing to check his language before he spoke it. But French. It felt warm, and comforting. Yes, French felt like home. Taken for granted before, the words felt like a novelty now. Like a decadent truffle, melting on his tongue

"Philippe, it's been too long already. It's good to have you back." Yes. Hearing French was even better. "You must tell me everything Philippe, we're going to stay up late tonight!"

"I wouldn't have it any other way." He held her out at arm's length and looked at her. She was pretty, she had always been pretty. Ever since primary school she had been pretty but she had never been the prettiest girl in school. Her nose was just a little too long and bony, her cheekbones just a little too pronounced, and her chin just a little too thin. She had nothing on Veronica, but who did?

Her hair though, had always been the perfect auburn color. Her bangs were cut just over her pencil thin eyebrows that were too often furrowed and her ponytail was a little longer than it had been before, which accentuated the fact that things had changed since he had left. If she put on her glasses and stood behind a counter, he would think that she looked a little like an irritable librarian.

But her loving smile was as sincere as it had always been, which had always made up for the fact that her lips were a little too wide and thin. Though, due to childhood braces, her teeth were perfect. Some things would never change. No, wait, there was something else in her eye, barely concealed by the contacts resting on her irises. Philippe could see it, he had a knack for such things. There was a weight on her smile that hadn't been there when he'd left. But maybe he was just projecting his own troubles.

It wasn't that he hadn't noticed his mother, he just hadn't looked at her yet. But now that she was opening the passenger side door, he turned his eyes to look at her. She was thin, as always, but who was Philippe to judge that? He wasn't much thicker. Though their thinness came from different external forces. Hers was drugs, and his was enforced beauty for the camera. Were they so different though? Philippe didn't like to ask such questions.

"Hello, mum." He let his hands drop from his best friend and he walked over to his mother.

"Philippe my son! I'm so sorry that we're late." She grinned past her chapped lips and her sunken and unfocused eyes and she hugged her son as close to her as she could. Their features were remarkably similar. He had taken a lot of his mother's genes. But his yellow hair had a life that hers, mousy and pale, had long ago lost. His eyes were blue like the sky and hers had lost their luster. He knew that she was somewhere in her mid-thirties, though life had never allowed her to be young. Philippe found himself making up for that. He wanted to live his twenties to a fullness that she never could.

He hugged his mother, and pressed the corners of this lips politely against her cheeks. His fears had never stopped him from loving her. But they had made them somewhat distant. The truth was that he had come home to attempt to learn from her, something that she had never been willing to share. He knew that as scary as it would be, he was coming home to face the fears that he had about being close to his mother.

Chapter 13. Aimee

Aimee flipped on the light switch of her petite apartment, and turned to hug Philippe before the door had even fully closed. With one arm wrapped around her, he pushed the door shut with his other hand.

"Are you okay?" asked Aimee. He took a deep breath and smiled against her ear.

"I'll be alright."

"Asshole. I know you better than that. Let's try this again. Are you okay?" His smile was glued to his face. But despite that, he felt the tears coming up from his chest and he could do no more in response but shake his head slowly. Then he just hugged her back and allowed himself to be comforted.

After a time he reached into his pocket and pulled out the little black box.

"No… Oh Philippe. Oh honey." Her eyebrows were etched with every sadness that he felt. She took the little box from his hand and opened it then led Philippe by the hand and brought him in to sit down on a small white loveseat. Her eyes didn't leave the beautiful diamond ring. Nor did her face stop portraying the tragedy of it.

Philippe slipped the Allen Edmonds shoes off of his feet and pulled his knees up to his chest and leaned back against the cushion.

He picked up a midnight blue throw pillow, hugged it into his chest and ran his finger over the threading. His finger found the end of a loose thread and twirled it back and forth. Careful to not exacerbate the damage.

He finally turned his moist eyes toward Aimee as she pulled the ring out of the box and turned it over in her hand.

"It's beautiful." She put it in her palm and set the box down on the end table. "You should have gotten it engraved."

"I should have. 'Perfect love', it could have said. I didn't really have time to think about engraving it though."

"You should have called me." She lifted her eyes to look at Philippe.

"Now that, is definitely true. I'm sorry. I just… I didn't want to talk about it over the phone."

"Did they ever figure out who did it?" He shook his head slowly in response.

"They assured La Facere magazine that they would do all they could to find out, but chances are as high as ever in New York that they'll never catch the culprit. Even if they do, I'll probably never know unless I see it in a news article."

"I'm sorry Philippe." She put her hand on his arm tenderly. She had a pink and white manicure, though the left thumb nail had a small chip in it. She probably hadn't noticed it yet. "How about wine, and chocolate mousse?"

"Mmm sounds delish." He smiled at her. Her eyes were green with one brown fleck in the left. Though sometimes they turned more hazel when she was really fired up about something. He sat hugging the pillow while, after setting the diamond back in its case, she got up and walked not far to the small kitchen.

Philippe had always jokingly called the little apartment her bachelorette pad. It was perfect for her. From the bar stools at the tall counter instead of a dining table, to the tastefully painted nudes hanging on printed canvas over the sofa. One bedroom, and as much room to express herself as she needed. What more could a bachelorette want?

He watched as she pulled two long stemmed glasses from the rack above the counter and a Burgundy wine from the beautifully polished wooden rack below that. She opened the drawer below that and pulled out her favorite blue corkscrew.

"And how are you Aimee?" He watched as her hands moved with precise mathematical twists to turn the corkscrew. He could tell that he wasn't the only wounded puppy here.

"What?" She glanced over her shoulder at him. "Oh, I'm fine. What makes you ask?"

"Because it's been a while. And I know you. What's going on?" With both glasses poured, she reached up and pulled down two lovely dishes with cherry blossoms painted on the sides and began dolloping generous amounts of chocolate mousse into them.

"I'm… I'm not ready to talk about it yet." Philippe's stomach lurched. Had it really been that long? Had distance really done something to them? He looked down at his pillow, the loose thread was coming from the last letter of Aimee's embroidered name. He set the pillow aside and slapped a wide smile onto his face and stood up.

"That's alright! I know that what you need then is a good time with yours truly." He made his way over to the small kitchen. He opened one of the drawers and withdrew two dessert spoons. He scooped a small bite of mousse from one of the dishes and lifted it to Aimee's lips. "Am I right?" He beamed at her and she couldn't help but smirk at his exuberance. He was always the perfect medicine to lighten one's spirits.

She accepted the bite offered to her and then took the other spoon from his hand and offered him a bite in return. "See, that's what friends are for." He said, as the sweet chocolate settled onto his tongue.

"Yeah?" She smiled and took a deeper drink than necessary of her wine, and then set the glass down carefully. "I thought friends were for…" She paused as she dipped her pinky finger into the mousse, "This!" Philippe leaped back from her as swift as he could but the small dollop of chocolate had already made it to the tip of his nose.

"Ha! Oh I see how this is. The tables have turned. From friends to enemies! We'll see where this goes, we'll see." Leaving the mousse on his nose and watching her carefully from the corner of his eye he took a more tempered drink from his own glass than she had from hers. But despite being eyed carefully, she decided to take the risk of smearing chocolate on his cheek. But he was too quick this time! Bouncing nimbly on his toes he escaped the attack. But his quick defense came at the price of sloshing pinot noir into his own face, dripping down to his lapels.

He held the glass out at arm's length as he dripped and by this time Aimee was in a fit of giggling. "This is a new shirt!" he gasped.

"First spill." Aimee said through laughs, pointing at him.

"Oh you're going to pay for that!" And with grins and giggles the fight was on. He set down his glass and the chocolate mousse took on a purpose not so intended for it. Before they knew it they had descended into laughing fits that took them to the floor of the kitchen, covered in mouse, each holding their respective wine glasses, and on to their third bottle.

The giggling finally subsided and they both sat on the floor with a glow of silly contentment. They had taken a break from life. A break much needed.

"So what really brought you back to Paris Philippe? Is it that tragedy simply gave you a yearning for home?" She lulled her head against the lower cabinet of the counter so that she could see him better and then pulled the scrunchy from her now thoroughly disheveled hair. She wound it around and around her knuckles as she listened to him.

"Well, for one thing my agency is 'taking some time off from me'." He made air quotes with his fingers and then took a drink from his glass. "So I figured I really didn't have much reason to stay there."

"Why did they fire you? That's terrible."

"Whoa now, you don't need to use words like fired." He winked at Aimee with a smile. "I don't mind I guess. It's sort of insulting. I think they let me go because," He paused for a moment. "Because of

Veronica." He took another drink.

"Well that's stupid, we should boycott." She set the scrunchy aside and lifted her glass to her lips. "So you came home because you missed me huh?" She winked and then set the glass back down next to her.

"Oh of course!" He smiled. "In all honesty, aside from just being homesick, I've been seeing a therapist."

"Really!? Did someone besides me realize that you're crazy?"

"Haha. But sort of. She said that she thinks I have a repressed memory. Isn't that fascinating?" Philippe smiled and reached over to pick up the abandoned scrunchy and re-commenced its winding habit around his own fingers.

"A blocked memory. Like what?" She picked up her glass and looked at the swirling red, and then put it back down without drinking any.

"I don't know. I'm thinking of trying to pick my mum's brain about it."

"Oh. Ooh. That sounds like fun." She said sarcastically.

"Yeah. I'm nervous." Aimee just stared at his face. A little smile and a mildly unfocused look was in her eye.

"That's cool Philippe. I'm happy for you."

He chuckled. "You're happy for me?" He turned to look at her with an extra dose of surprise in his tone to make up for the disbelieving expression that the Botox wouldn't allow.

"Yeah. I think it'll be good for you and your mum."

"Huh. I see. I think you've had too much wine." He grinned and then leaned over and licked a glob of chocolate off of her cheek.

She chuckled, and then she turned and kissed his lips. They lingered there in that kiss for several moments with their eyes closed. At the end of it he would have kissed her again but instead she spoke the words that she'd been too scared to say until now that she'd had enough to drink. "Philippe, I'm pregnant."

His eyes opened suddenly and he couldn't stop blinking in surprise. He glanced at Aimee's empty wine glass. "What?" But before she could respond, she got up and made a quick lunge for the bathroom toilet. He watched her throw her guts into the porcelain and he was sure that she wasn't there for any kind of morning sickness. He was so startled that he almost forgot his best friendly duties of holding her hair back. But though delayed, he managed to remember.

She sat up and wiped her mouth on her sleeve looking disgusted and exhausted. Philippe, still holding her hair, couldn't seem to take his eyes off the side of her belly. She wasn't showing at all. Or, had she gained a little weight that he hadn't noticed? But wait. "It's not mine." He said, still processing it all.

"Well duh Sherlock. If it were yours it would be born and screaming and pooping by now. You've been gone that long." Of course he knew that… that's why he'd said it. But after another long flabbergasted pause he said timidly,

"Wait, you knew you were pregnant and we've been drinking all night?" She shot him the dirtiest glare he was sure he'd ever received from her. "I'm sorry… I just… It's okay." He wrapped his arms around her and pulled her against him. She stayed there in his arms for a while. Tables had turned and now she just allowed herself to be comforted for a moment. Until round two of porcelain love making came and Philippe managed to hold her hair without delay this time.

"Uhg." She choked, "Gross." He tucked her hair behind her ear and shifted into a more comfortable cross legged position on the floor next to her. They could be here a while. He let the silence linger as she wiped a tear of strained heaving out of her eye.

"So, whose is it? Do I know him?"

"No. And you'll never meet him either cause he's long gone."

"I'm sorry. You should have called me." She chuckled at that and turned to look at him.

"Yeah, I guess we should both remember that next time we're apart for so long."

Philippe shrugged. "Or we could write lengthy letters with perfect handwriting, tied with ribbons. I for one would have put perfume in mine. It could have lightened things up a little for you. I'll remember that next time." he smiled kindly and re tucked the hair behind her ear.

"Yeah alright it's a deal. Long handwritten letters are better than zero calls and fun frivolous snaps and Facebook posts just don't cut the distance. Besides, when you open your mailbox it's like Christmas."

"See, that's the idea." They paused and Aimee gazed at his comforting smile for a long moment.

"But what am I going to do Philippe? I'm going to turn into a single mother with no future." A flash of his own mother burst into his eyes and he gave a mild shudder that he hoped wasn't too visible. A one bedroom bachelorette pad was perfect for just Aimee. But to add a baby into the mix was to make the whole set up look just a little too much like the one bedroom apartment that he himself had grown up in.

"Who says?" He said sounding almost gleeful. The smile on his face grew, for no smile was out of place to Philippe. "You have every future possible Aimee."

"How?" A tear came from her eye that was not from exhausted heaving. "I dropped out of school. My father found out about me going to school for journalism, said I have no future, and disowned me. They don't even know that I'm pregnant. I'm working at the cafe right now to pay the rent, but how am I supposed to keep that up with a baby?"

"Because I'm going to help you and you're going to go back to school and you're going to make all of your dreams come true or else." He winked optimistically and found a clean hand towel to wipe the mixture of tears, chocolate and vomit from her face. She was quiet while he did, but the feeling of guilt welled up too high and before she could stop it she yelled at him. She didn't mean to but she did.

"No!" He was startled and taken aback by her sudden hostility. She had that hazel splash in her eye. "No." She repeated a little tamer. "I refuse to let you take care of me!"

"Um. That's what friends are for?"

"No. Because you have dreams of your own, and you might need to go back to New York for your modeling career and you have a blocked memory and shit with your mom that you need to work out. I refuse to let you put all that aside to take care of me."

That feeling came up in his stomach again accentuated by the sloshing wine of Burgundy. Had time done that much damage? One year? Was it too much? So much that they couldn't rely on each other anymore?

"Did you really feel so abandoned when I left?"

"No Philippe, you had dreams you had to follow. And just because I don't get to have mine doesn't mean that you shouldn't have yours." Philippe was nothing if not empathetic. She had said the polite answer that her parents had taught her, but he knew the real one.

"So who was this guy?" He asked.

"Just… A guy. I just, ran out of luck I guess. It's what I get for liking the bad boys you know? Bad boys have more important shit to do than become mister daddy. One ear full of the news and he was long gone. He didn't even say goodbye." There was a long silence while Aimee contemplated whether or not the toilet bowl was calling her name again. She decided that it was going to let her off easy this time and decided to take the risk of brushing her teeth. She stood up wobbly and leaned against the sink wondering whether or not her stomach was going to change its mind.

"I don't think that you should give up on your dreams Aimee."

"No. I know. I've been thinking about an abortion too. I probably should have figured out a way to stay in school, but my dad pulled my funding and I guess I was a little too freaked out to think about it." Philippe looked up at her from the floor and said nothing. Finally Aimee decided to take the next step and pick up her toothbrush and unscrew the tooth paste. He watched as she, with a drunken sense of depth missed the toothbrush on the first pass and dropped some toothpaste down the drain. She got it the second time.

She finished brushing her teeth and then zoned out on the water running down the drain. Philippe finally stood up. He put his hands on her shoulders and said,

"Come on. Let's get some sleep."

She nodded into the sink as if it had been the one to give the suggestion and then turned to allow her childhood friend to lead her to the bed.

He pulled back the violet and white flower covers and guided her into the sheets. He took the uncomfortable layer of clothing off of them both and then climbed in next to her. They were both asleep within moments. His last thought was that Aimee had forgotten to take her contacts out of her eyes. But that was no longer tonight's problem. Let tomorrow bring what it will.

Chapter 14. Armel

He parked his car in front of his mother's apartment and for a time just sat in his car looking at the home he'd grown up in. Everything he'd ever owned as a child was still in that building. Or at least, he assumed it was if she still used his five-year-old t-shirts as dish rags. He had long ago learned to never keep anything of real value there. No. This was the place he'd grown up in. But it was never his home.

He reached to open the driver side door to get out when the door to the apartment opened. It wasn't his mother who came out. It was a man. Some ten to twelve years ago the man had been rather good looking. That is, he was good looking if you took all his ill-fitting clothes off and then gave him a thorough bath and a shave. Now he appeared as if that ten to twelve years had been working double time.

Philippe's fingers froze on the door latch and the man froze when he saw him. It had been about ten to twelve years since they had last spoken. Philippe hadn't ever expected to see him again. And in all truth, he hadn't even expected the man to still be alive. Yet there he was. Frozen on his mother's doorstep.

"Is that . . . is that you, Philippe?" He had a deep, raspy, smoke-inflicted sound to his voice. It hadn't sounded quite that bad all those years ago, but Philippe knew it was him. Even with the raspy voice, the sunken eyes, the gray hairs and the very unfortunate change to the quality of his skin, caused by years of neglect. He'd had rather nice skin back then.

Philippe pressed his spine firmly against his seat as if he hoped that glue would miraculously keep him stuck there in his car. Ten and two, his hands gripped the steering wheel with deadly force. He hoped that his muscles would soon respond to his commands well enough for him to be able to turn on the ignition, just in case he suddenly felt the need to remove himself from this scene. But just in case they didn't, he threw up what he knew was his best defense. His only defense. The defense that had gotten him out of just about everything so far since he'd learned how to do it.

He smiled.

"Hello, Armel."

"Oh wow. It is you. Hey uh . . . I thought you were in America."

"I guess I'm back." If he could have felt anything in his stomach at that moment, he would have felt sick that this man knew anything at all about his whereabouts. But in truth, Philippe couldn't feel much of anything. It was as if he were somewhere far away from anything that his body could have felt. "What are you doing here, Armel?"

"Oh . . . You know. I was just visiting your mum."

"Where have you been? It's been a long time." His words felt monotone even though he could clearly hear them being perfectly and appropriately cheerful. He was sure he could guess at least one place that Armel had been for at least a few of those years. He supposed prison hadn't treated him well. When he had been taken away,

Philippe had, over time, grown to hope, even to believe, that he would never see Armel again. But that bitter tone was left quite cleanly out of his words.

"Ah." The man chuckled and smiled an awkward mustache bristle smile. Ten to twelve years ago . . . he'd had all his teeth. "Well . . ." He put his hands in his pockets and rocked back and forth on the balls of his feet a couple of times. "Yeah well, it has been a long time hasn't it . . . Hey uh . . . So I was just on my way out so, maybe I'll catch you later." He turned to walk away down the street back to wherever he'd been surviving. Philippe nearly let out a breath of relief when the man turned back around. "Hey," he said, one hand in his pocket, the other hand with his palm facing up as if to show that he was about to bring his heart and soul out into the open. Philippe swallowed hard past his smiling face. "I never hurt you. I think, that if you think back, you'll remember that." He paused for a moment and Philippe couldn't take his eyes off the man. "So, have a good night." He turned on his heel and disappeared into the shadows.

Philippe's hands instantly dropped from the steering wheel into his lap. For reasons that he wouldn't have likely been able to explain to anyone, he pulled down the visor mirror and checked over his face carefully. Eyes blue. Lashes, perfect. Lips, lightly glossed. Skin, soft, supple, and completely free of blemishes or breakouts. He was beautiful. He knew it. He could see it right there in the mirror. That was why he was a model. He was beautiful, he was made for it. He breathed a huge sigh of relief as if his beauty had been in question.

He flipped the mirror back up and opened the door. He braced himself to discover that which he did not wish to see. Whatever that man had done to his mother. Had he sold her drugs? Had he traded her drugs for other . . . 'merchandise'? Nothing would surprise him. All the same, he hoped that there was no evidence of anything when he walked in. He knew better. But it was time to decide whether to confront her about it.

He closed the door to his car and tucked the keys safely in his pocket.

Chapter 15. Mother Dearest

"How was America, Philippe? I loved the scarf that you sent me." The warm water from the sink was running over his hands, and suds were forming an excessively thick lather as he listened to his mother's question. He'd sent her the occasional package while he'd been gone. Once a month or so. Just something small. A scarf, a postcard, a keychain of the Statue of Liberty. Always sent with a note no longer than two words. "Avec Amour." With love. Never a phone call. Never a longer explanation of what his life was like. No. His mother was lucky that she even knew that he was going to New York to be a model. The packages made him feel a little better about the whole thing. He wanted her to know that he still cared.

"It was . . . great. I thought the lilac was a good color for you." There was a clink as he set the now glittering plate onto the drying rack. It was the same apartment. The very same one that they had moved into when he was little. It was worse for wear but it probably hadn't been much better when they first moved in. He never quite felt like he was in his own skin here. Or perhaps, he felt like he was a little too much in his own skin here. He could easily belong here if he wanted to, and he desperately did not want to.

"How was model life? Did you blow them all away?" The tea kettle began to whistle. He picked up a dirty rag and used it as a potholder to take the hot kettle off the element. He poured the boiling water into a chipped mug and dunked the loose-leaf tea strainer twice before setting it aside to steep for a few minutes.

"Of course I did." He smiled and tilted his head to glance flirtatiously over his shoulder at his mum. She was sitting at the small table. It was actually quite a lovely table that was meant to be out in a garden or on a patio. The kitchen wasn't really the place for it, but function was its purpose. Besides, she would have put it on a patio if she'd had one.

"Are you here to stay, Philippe?" He said nothing as he contemplated his response. How should he bring up to his mother his reason for being here? How much of his reason should he share? "Can't you just be a model here Philippe? Please tell me that you'll stay for a little while. I know you. How can New York be better than Paris? You love Paris."

"Of course I love Paris mum, it's in my blood." He turned off the water and elected to let his hands air dry rather than use the dirty rag. He gingerly picked up the steaming mug of tea and turned to face his mother with a beaming smile on his face. "We're Parisian, it would be a heinous crime to think of any place in the world as better than Paris." He set the mug delicately in front of his mother. "And I tell you the truth. There is no place better than Paris." He shook his head with a grin and sat down next to his mother.

"So that's why you've come back then?" She smiled weakly, hoping that her son had truly returned only to be closer to her again. "You're not going back? Did they move you here?" She leaned back as if to brace herself. "Or did you just have some vacation time?"

He didn't particularly want to tell her about Veronica or her death. Nor did he wish to tell her that he had in fact been "put on temporary hiatus" from that modeling agency for nothing more than bad publicity. "Just until all this murder stuff blows over," they'd said. He had no idea where he was going next. But he knew that he was young and there was plenty of time to figure it out. Until then, he needed answers. "Mum, where did we live before this apartment?"

"What?" She looked startled. Her sunken eyes seemed to sink a little deeper. "Well that question was a little out of the blue don't you think?"

"Well," He fixated on a small brown stain that had been on the cream-colored table top for years. He rubbed his thumb over it again and again as if he would somehow now be able to remove it. "I randomly decided to talk to a therapist while I was in New York."

"Why?" His mother scrunched her brow and seemed suddenly on the defensive.

"I don't know, it was just sort of a random decision, like sometimes you're just curious if someone else can tell you about how many problems you have that you didn't know that you had. Does that make any sense?"

Her expression seemed chiseled onto her sallow face. He noticed that she was holding her breath. Waiting to see whether this would be fight or flight. Waiting to see if the moment would just blow over. He took a deep breath and decided to push forward.

"Well, the therapist, she asked what my earliest memory was, and I told her that it was when I first saw our front door. Number thirty-six. But she thinks that I'm repressing a memory. From before that." He managed to lift his eyes up to look at his mother. She was quite a bit smaller than him, but he couldn't help feeling tiny in that moment.

She started to shake her head in an almost shivery way. "We're not talking about that. We're talking about your life as a model. I know they loved you. They all loved you."

"Mum. I came home to Paris to try to learn this. I want to know where we lived before we lived here. We must have lived somewhere, didn't we?" His mother stared at him as if she couldn't believe that he would continue this conversation. This was the subject that she'd always adamantly avoided. She wasn't about to stop now.

"No . . . no, we've always lived here."

"Mum, if my first memory is of the day we moved in when I was five or six, then we haven't always lived here. Mum were we homeless?" It wouldn't have surprised him in the slightest. But his mother shook her head just slightly and reached out her hand to rest her tiny fingers on Philippe's forearm.

"Stop, Philippe." She whispered.

"Mum." His voice became soft. He could hear the strain in her whisper. He could see the pain on her face that she was always running away from. Running to men, running to drugs, running away. Always away. But he needed her to make an about face now. Because maybe, just maybe, if he could get her to face her pain, then he could start to understand his own. He didn't feel selfish or guilty for that because he'd spent his whole life watching her run. Whatever she was running from couldn't possibly be more painful than watching her run. It couldn't possibly be worse than nursing her back to health from nearly dying. It couldn't possibly be worse than calling an ambulance when he was nine because he thought his mother was dead. It couldn't be worse than watching her detox and shake and shiver only to watch her run away again. "Mum. I know that if it's a memory so bad that I've blocked it out," He put her hand between his own and gently kissed her knuckles. "Then it must have been something so bad that you've been trying to block it out all these years. But mum, we can't block it out forever."

She shook her head and smiled at him with cracked lips. She put the palm of her other hand against her little boy's cheek. "You're the only good thing I've ever had in my life Philippe. Please. Don't ruin that. We can just be right here. Right now. Good times." She slid her hands away from Philippe and clutched the tea between them to feel the warmth. She still had not taken a sip. "Besides, you just got back."

His eyes dropped down to look at a crease in his pants that had been poorly ironed. He rubbed it with his palm as if he could iron it with his hand and then sat up straighter, resolving not to look at it. "Alright. Well, let me take you out for some brunch then." He smiled at her. "Or let me cook something for you."

"No, I. . . I think it's alright Philippe."

"Why not?"

"Well, I suppose I had a rather large breakfast." Of course, there was nearly nothing in the house. Philippe took a deep breath. He hadn't attempted any kind of quality time with his mother since he'd graduated school. Even if she wasn't hungry, she could at least go out with him. But maybe he was wrong about that.

"Mum, why was Armel here?" The smile fell from his mother's face. "I bumped into him in the parking lot." He felt a hot tear fall on his cheek and could feel his face begin to flush. "Did you buy drugs from him? Is he your boyfriend again?"

Warm tea was splashed across the table into Philippe's lap as he felt his mother's weak slap against his face. It was immediately followed by her squeal of sudden guilt. She bit down on the ends of her fingers then threw herself on her knees before Philippe and wrapped her arms around his legs.

"I'm sorry! I told you to stop talking about such horrible things. Oh Philippe, I'm sorry. I'm so sorry." She hadn't hit him often as a child. Almost never in fact. The only times that she ever had were if he became accusatory for any reason. Whether his accusation was true or not.

She'd slapped him when he confronted her about stealing his money. She'd slapped him when he'd accused her of making her living in the red-light district, though that had been an empty accusation. He'd hit her exactly once as a child. He supposed he'd been trying to emulate the men in her life. The only father figures he'd ever had. But unlike with them, she'd slapped him back. That was the only time he could remember getting an honest scolding.

The message, whether she'd intended it or not, was quite clear. Other men could hit, but Philippe was not really a man, so he could not. In fact, he'd become quite the pacifist and had turning the other cheek down as an art form. The only person that he knew he could confront was himself. And that fact was probably his favorite quality about himself. He could always figure himself out.

His face had been slapped to the side, he'd submitted to the abuse, resigned himself to turn his face and weather through the emotional outburst. But now he turned back to his mother and smiled past his tears. "It's okay, mum."

"I didn't mean it." She sobbed into his knees.

"I know, mum."

"I'll never talk to Armel again!"

"Mother. It's okay." She looked up again. Her sunken eyes were red and puffy and bloodshot.

"It's not okay. I haven't seen him in forever and I knew better. For your sake, I knew better." Philippe shook his head.

"You shouldn't do everything just for my sake. You should do some things for your sake also. I'm not mad at you, mother. Just worried." He smiled warmly down at his mother's tear-streaked face. Her eyes were gray like clouds, but he felt sure that they had been as blue as his own once. "Now, would you please get up off the floor?"

The truth was that her reaction was completely predictable. He knew that she wouldn't tell him about her past, about his past. But he had to try, didn't he?

Chapter 16. Marcello

The other line was ringing as he walked somewhat aimlessly down the street. He'd needed a little fresh air and a break from his mother before he went back in for round two. He held the phone against his ear as he glanced down the direction that he was sure he'd seen Armel walk, and elected not to go in that direction.

"Philippe." Said an Italian man's voice on the other line. "I should have called you first. Are you still in New York?"

"No, I'm not. I'm back in Paris. How are you Marcello?"

"I'm well, but I admit I've been a little worried about you."

"Well, I'm alive."

"That is true my boy. You know, it just seems like bad business that they let you go. If I'm ever in the same room with any of those agents, they'll get an earful from me."

"Oh that's alright Marcello, you know they're just trying to protect themselves."

"They'd better watch how they go about that then, because so far it just looks as if they're trying to cover it up as much as possible. That's the agency but the magazine's gone a step further. You know I just got the August issue of La Facere and they didn't put in Veronica's usual self feature. She's not in the book at all and I know for a fact she got some pictures taken."

"I know, I was there when she took them. They cut them out?"

"They did, and they cut you out also. Your face doesn't show up once." Philippe stopped abruptly. He hadn't been paying much attention to where he was going, and found himself standing at a busy crosswalk waiting for the light to change and the cars to stop.

"I'm not in it?" This was just adding insult to injury. But the pictures were owned by the magazine. It was their prerogative.

"I was just as upset about it." No he wasn't... Philippe sighed and decided not wait for the crosswalk or the drivers who didn't care, and he turned around to head back towards his mother's apartment. "But Philippe, I want to give you my assurance that here in Paris, we'll take you back. You have my word."

"Alright."

"You're still my model as far as I'm concerned Philippe. And that means I'll take care of you. Veronica treated you like gold and that agency should have taken that into consideration. I thought you would be with her for the rest of your career, but know that you still have a home here. Give it about a month and then call us alright? Or I'll call you."

"Thank you Marcello, I appreciate that a lot. That isn't really why I called though."

"What's on your mind son?" Philippe had reached his car again, sitting buffed and beautiful outside his mother's apartment. He ran the back of his knuckles against the red paint on the side mirror as if he were caressing a lover.

"I guess I was just calling a friend."

"Well Philippe, I'm happy to be your friend in high places. How's that car of mine? I hope she was well treated while you were in New York."

"She was safe and sound Marcello." He smiled. Now this was the kind of shallow conversation he was looking for. But how often did someone call a friend and ask them for some well-placed small talk?

"You know if you ever go leaving the country again, I'm always happy to hold onto her for you." Philippe chuckled.

"I think if I did that, I might never see her again."

"Oh now Philippe, I promise I'd give her back. But you owe it to me. Give me the wheel and let me take you out for a spin one of these days."

"It's a date."

The call ended abruptly. Philippe looked at the screen to see that the battery had died and the phone was powering down. He cursed quietly to himself that he'd not charged it at Aimee's house. He'd been too drunk to remember to plug it in. So with a sigh, he tucked it into his pocket and resolved to properly have a conversation with Marcello later. For now, it was time to face his mother again.

Chapter 17. Overdose

All he'd done was go out for a walk. He'd needed a bit of a breather after his confrontation with his mother. He'd needed a change of clothes from out of his car too. The pants he'd been wearing before smelled of Earl Gray. With a clean pair slung over his arm, he unlocked the door to his old home.

Somehow he could feel it as he turned the lock to. It's was a strange familiar foreboding sensation. He pushed the door open to apartment number thirty-six and the familiar sensation continued. The place was dead quiet and he could see the lamplight at the end of the hallway that was blocking his view of his mother.

"Mum?" But there was no answer. He'd started the endless walk down the hallway but before he came to the corner a subtle and sickening smell accosted his nostrils. It smelled like death and fear to him. It smelled a little like vinegar and sweat. It was a smell that rose chills on his skin and threw him into a panic.

With a crumpled thump his clean jeans were dropped to the floor and he rushed into the room to find his mother lying on her bed with the needle still in her arm. He pulled his phone out of his pocket only to find that it was still quite dead. So he leapt over to his mother and pulled the needle out of her arm and cast it onto the bedside table. He put his elbow over his mouth and bent over as if he might vomit. But he didn't have time for that.

He didn't check her pulse. Instead he was nearly tripped by his jeans on his way back down the hall. He flung open the front door and ran out to the car. His duffel bag was still in the passenger seat. He yanked it open and began throwing designer clothing haphazardly across dashboard. Shoes, shirts, buttons, cuff links, one fedora. Slacks, sweaters, silky pajamas. Socks, boxer briefs, a pair of blue sweats that said the word PINK in all capital letters up one leg. Down near his excessive stash of condoms he finally found his phone charger. The one he should have been using ages ago.

He ran back into the apartment and shoved the charger into the nearest outlet and hooked it up to his phone. "Come on, come on, come on!" As if it could hear him. "Turn on… faster." He gritted his teeth. He was sweating. Partly from the running and the anxiety but it was also like his body was trying to push the heroin away from itself. Like it was afraid that it was in the air. Like maybe his own body would be flooded to death with the stuff next so he'd better just start the detox early.

As he waited he bit the inside of his lip and tasted a small drop of blood on his tongue. Slowly and painfully he turned his head to see his mother's limp fingers dangling off the side of the bed. He felt a horrible pressure in his heart. Like it could stop beating at any moment.

How could he forget such an obvious thing? He was so used to living off of only his cell phone that his brain had utterly blacked out the existence of his mother`s landline. How much time had he wasted looking for his phone charger? His ears began to ring. One long high squeal as his vision continued to pan, past his mother's overdosed figure to the phone hanging silently against the kitchen wall.

He picked himself up off the floor and flew past the tunnel vision and practically fell against the hanging phone. He dialed the numbers one and five. "Hello, five, zero, one, six, Avenue Rue Morand room number thirty-six, my mother has overdosed on heroin." He paused and strained to listen past the incessant ringing in his ear. "I haven't checked her pulse or anything yet no." He didn't want to. This wasn't the first time this had happened and there were few things that he hated more than getting close enough to her to see whether or not she'd actually managed to do herself in this time.

He looked again over to his mother's still body and then at the phone cord connecting the phone to the wall base. Would it reach that far? With the phone still to his ear, he took a few steps towards his mother. "Okay." He said to the woman on the line. He knelt down on the floor to try to inch just a little closer to his mother's limp fingers.

"Just a minute." He said into the phone and then held the phone away from his ear so that he could inch across the floor close enough to touch her. With his arms stretched out wide, one hand holding the phone and the other holding his mother's chill fingers, he put his fingertips against her wrist and stared at the scars on her arm next to the new puncture wound. At least he knew that an ambulance was on its way. He didn't need to hurry anymore. He closed his eyes and tried to focus on whether or not blood was pulsing through his mother's body. "I don't know." He dropped his mother's hand like a hot iron and pressed the phone back up against his cheek. "My hands are shaking too much."

He dropped the phone and the wire wound back up until the phone dangled just above the floor and clacked against the wall a few times. He made it to the kitchen sink just in time to lose the sick that he'd been holding in. At least there weren't any dishes in there anymore. He'd managed to clean those before this. Thank goodness because who liked cleaning vomit off of things?

The woman on the phone listened to him throw up and waited patiently for a moment for him to pick up the phone. But she soon realized that he was not going to pick it back up and there were other emergencies that needed to be attended to, so she broke the rules and hung up on him. She was strongly reprimanded later that day.

Philippe sat slumped against the kitchen counter and stared across the room at the dangling phone. He had no intentions of picking it back up or putting it back on the wall. He hugged his knees to his chest. He had no intentions of trying to check his mother's pulse again either. He heard the sirens in the background. Soon he would be able to give this whole thing over to those more qualified than himself. He tried not to think about the time that he'd wasted. He tried not to think about the fact that he may not have truly had any time to waste.

Chapter 18. Luis

Sitting in the waiting room. Now this was the easy part. Strangely enough, this was only the third time that he'd been able to sit in the waiting room to wait for his mother since adults tended to get a little uncomfortable when there were kids in the waiting room by themselves. The first time was ten or twelve years ago only because Armel had been there with him. So Philippe wasn't a child by himself. The second was some time after Philippe had gotten his car.

He sat next to an outlet finishing the charge on his phone. He hadn't sent a text to Aimee yet to tell her what had happened. He wasn't really sure whether or not Aimee would want to know. It wasn't the first time. Then again, Aimee probably loved his mother more than he did. Or she at least had a more loving tolerance for her. It's a different relationship as the son's best friend rather than the son himself.

"Monsieur De 'Leon." Philippe looked up as the husky doctor stepped out of a door into the waiting room. Like a shadow, he thought he saw someone slip into the door behind the doctor. But he didn't see that as any of his business. He stood up to be greeted.

He found himself sitting in an office, watching the doctor's mouth move. He knew what he'd just heard. He just didn't believe it. This had happened before. There was no reason why the next phase of this act shouldn't be played out. Counselors would talk to his mother. Agonizing controlled chemical detox would ensue. There would be a hospital stay. Sooner or later they would send her home and he would have to nurse her up the rest of the way with chicken noodle soup. That was how it went. It was a good thing they were in France, because in New York they would have acquired quite the medical bill.

He back to his senses just in time to hear the doctor say, "We haven't had a chance to contact her family in Sweden yet, but we thought that perhaps you would prefer to be the bearer of that news."

"What? Sweden?" This was just too many things to wrap his head around all at once. They had family in Sweden? He had family? Of course, just about everyone had grandparents and aunts and uncles, but family had been on the list of undiscussable topics with his mother. But why Sweden? Was Sweden where they had lived before they came here? Was he actually born in Sweden? No! Was he not French!? Why was this the first he was hearing about it? Finally he said, "Why... why is there family in Sweden?"

The doctor looked at him somewhat mournfully for a moment and wondered if Philippe had heard anything else that he'd said. "Here." he pushed a piece of paper towards Philippe. "I don't know if that is still their contact information. Maybe it is. Or maybe they've moved, but it's worth a shot."

Philippe stared at the paper. Nordin was the surname, not De 'Leon. So he must be at least a little bit French. Maybe they were very distant family. Or his mother had once been married? Anything was possible. He just wished that she would have told him.

"If you wish, we'll give you a moment in the room alone with her before we move her." Philippe looked up from the paper to the doctor's round face.

He nodded. "Okay."

He stepped into the room with the tubes and the machines that had been turned off. No beeping. No sound of a flat line. Just silence. He closed the door behind him and looked at the shape lying on the hospital bed. A white sheet was pulled up all the way over her head. Anyone could be under there. Perhaps a mannequin used to educate medical students. The sheet down by the legs of the bed swayed slightly as if there were a breeze, though the air was still.

He pulled a chair up next to this horizontal human figure but he didn't sit in it. Not yet. It was a little bit chilly and the room smelled so sterile. So cold. So clean. So quiet. He reached up to uncover her face.

Even though he'd known that his mother would be beneath the sheet he couldn't stop the sensation of surprise that knotted suddenly in his chest cavity when he saw her sunken, pale, empty expression.

"Mum." Some part of him was trying to tell himself that she wasn't worth grieving. But he knew, that somehow, if she wasn't worth grieving, then he wasn't worth grieving either. "Mum." He felt a choke in his throat and he suddenly felt himself gasp for air. "Mommy!" The tears came. He grabbed onto her punctured arm and shook her. "Mommy. Mum! I'm sorry!" He collapsed down into the chair and buried his forehead against her needle wound. He reached his arm over her tiny belly and just held onto her like a small child clinging to his mother's skirts.

"I'm sorry I wasn't there mum. I'm sorry I left. I didn't stay. I'm sorry I went to New York. I'm sorry I left you to deal with Armel again. Mum I'm sorry I pushed you away. I'm sorry. I'm so sorry. Please. Please give me another chance." He didn't take the moment to notice the way that he sounded so much like her. He hated ever to think that he was like his mother but he felt like her now. She said sorry when he was nine after a whole year spent with Armel. She said sorry after she'd already used the drugs that she'd spent his money on. She said sorry always too late. After the damage was irreversible. And now Philippe said sorry, because he should have tried to fix things a long time ago.

"Why is everyone dying?" he said softly, then he just sobbed against her no longer rising and falling rib cage. "I'm sorry." He whispered repeatedly between sobs. "I'm so sorry."

It was in a quiet moment when the sobbing had lulled that Philippe heard the sound of breathing. Quiet slow breathing. Like the breath of someone who was trying not to breathe too loudly. At first he put his palm over his mother's nose and waited. But of course, he felt no breath. He choked on the lump in his throat and put his forehead back down on her arm and forced himself to take a deep slow breath. "Who are you?" His voice cracked slightly. But there was no answer from the breathing.

He tipped his head down to look under the bed. Lying on his back was a young man dressed all in black. Philippe guessed that this was the shadow that he'd seen slip in behind the doctor in the waiting room earlier. But he hadn't expected that shadow to come here to this cold room. The boy was maybe in his late teens or early twenties. He was wearing converse shoes, black skinny jeans with a hole in one knee, a black beanie over his long brown hair and his hands were tucked firmly in the pocket of a black hoodie that said 'Seattle' in big letters on the front. Sort of far from home.

"Who are you?" Philippe quietly repeated, this time in English. He felt a tear tickle on his cheek and drip down onto the linoleum.

"Um..." The boy's eyebrows were raised obviously wondering if he was in for it. But Philippe was too laissez faire to mind him being there. He was just wondering why. The guy could be a necrophiliac for all he knew. "Luis... uh...sorry. I uh..." He glanced towards the empty space on the other side of the bed. "I didn't... mean to interrupt."

"It's okay." Philippe smiled weakly down at him. He turned his eyes back to his mother and took a deep breath. He knew that he should wonder who the boy was and what he was doing, but instead he opened his mouth and said, "I hated her you know." He put his hand over his mouth as tears started descending again.

This definitely wasn't why Luis was here but hey, sometimes you get called to unintended jobs and you just gotta buckle down and do them. So if he was gonna play counselor then he'd go ahead and play counselor. "Why did you hate her?" Luis took his hands out of his hoodie pouch and laced his fingers behind his head. He thought of his own mother, and how he would feel if she died. He hoped that he didn't live long enough to see that day. That wasn't a ghost that he wanted to ever have to deal with.

"She was..." Philippe opened his mouth and tried to get the words out. He hated saying mean things. It was mean, the way he had always felt about her and he'd tried to push that feeling away his whole life. She was his mother after all. Sure she wasn't the best mother in the world but that didn't change the fact that she'd given birth to him. She'd always tried to do her best. Her best just wasn't very good. "She..." his voice lowered to a tiny whisper. "She was a selfish bitch." He latched onto his mother's hand and sobbed.

Luis had no idea how lucky he was. That was the first time Philippe had said that to anyone. Not even Aimee had heard Philippe utter those words about his mother. They were the truest words that Philippe had ever spoken about her.

"She knew," Philippe went on, "She knew what was happening with Armel way before she kicked him out. She just turned a blind eye until she walked in on it and couldn't pretend anymore. She knew, but she didn't want to risk losing the boyfriend and the drugs. She hated being alone so she'd hook up with losers and I had to be along for the ride. Now her body is so worn and used and covered in track marks that no one wanted her and she crawled back to Armel while I was gone. I guess maybe she thought that if I wasn't there then it wouldn't matter. It wasn't until I left the country that she finally noticed that I'd been gone for years. I took as many extracurricular activities as I could in school just so that I wouldn't have to go home. The library was the best home I ever had. Or my car. My car was the best home I ever had. She never noticed that I'd been practically living in my car. Coming home for showers. Or staying with Aimee or Marcello all the time. Anything just so that I wouldn't have to be home. So that I wouldn't have to be with her. So that I wouldn't have to watch her kill herself every day. I refuse to let her take me down with her. I refuse to be like her. I refuse to live in squalor and filth. She can't keep me down." He descended into loud sobs and wrapped his arms as tight around himself as he could digging his fingers into his ribs and gritting his teeth past the pain of his loss.

Luis bit his lip and looked over at the empty space on the other side of the bed. He opened his mouth to say something but before he could get a word out, Philippe continued. "And when I was finally old enough to get a job... She was clean then. For a little while. She was clean and working at McDonald's trying to pay the rent. She was having a hard time with it so I thought..." He started laughing with mild hysterics. "I thought, I know, instead of buying myself new clothes, why don't I be a good son and help my mother pay the rent. That's what good sons do. And she was trying so hard and I just wanted her to succeed and..." He gasped a little as the sobbing tried to take over his vocal cords. "I knew something was messed up when I was paying half the rent and she still wasn't able to pay her half. She'd started using again and since I was picking up the rent responsibilities she decided to use her cash as play money. Drug money. Without knowing it I enabled her. She failed because I enabled her." He let the tears flow for a moment. "Stupid... Selfish… Bitch." He just couldn't bring the last word above a whisper.

Luis thought a moment about how lucky he was. He listened to Philippe cry and decided that he should give his mom a call at his next available opportunity. Just to tell her how awesome she was and how much he loved her. He looked over to the empty space on the other side of the bed and opened his mouth, waited a moment to see whether or not he was actually going to be able to talk, decided that he was, and then spoke his message. "2320 Rue Veron."

"What?" Philippe sniffed and pulled a silk handkerchief out of his pocket to wipe his nose.

"2320 Rue Veron.... it's where you guys lived before..." Luis paused for a moment staring into that empty space. "Before... thirty-six?"

Philippe leaned his head back down to look at Luis. "Rue Veron?"

"Yeah um 2320... you might wanna write that down unless you've got a good memory. I'm sure as hell not gonna remember it. Or, unless you know where that is." Philippe just stared at him.

"Who are you?" Philippe repeated his question from earlier. He could now no longer ignore the fact that this kid needed a little more explanation for his existence in the room.

"Uh… Yeah well..." Luis rolled over and decided it was time to come out from under the hospital bed. It's not like he was hiding anymore. "I'm Luis. Um. I know, you probably want to know more than that but I'm really nobody so I don't think I'd be able to give you a very satisfactory answer." He pulled up a chair next to Philippe and sat down so that they were both facing the body.

"But how did you know where we once lived? And why are you here?" Luis only shrugged in response. Philippe stared at him silently until it became clear that the boy had no intention of answering that question. "Why do you keep your hair long?" Philippe decided to ask instead. Luis shrugged again.

"Cuz I'm like one eighty-fourth Native American and also long hair is supposed to hold spiritual power." He smirked to himself. "Also, the real reason is actually cuz my dad always had long hair so I decided to do it too. I think it looks kinda cool. Also I just miss my dad and it kinda keeps him close you know?" Luis turned his eyes to look at the body. A vacant shell.

"I never knew my father." replied Philippe, "I don't think she knew who he was. And I certainly didn't want to keep *her* close."

"Naw… I don't think that's true. That you didn't want her close, that is. She was probably just never really close in the first place. Not for real." Luis noticed Philippe's expression. Staring. As though he expected Luis to spit out an answer to all his personal mysteries. "I mean, I'm just guessing." He shrugged. "I mean, I didn't know her. And I really doubt that I'm the right person to be talking to you about forgiveness and shit."

Philippe smiled at him, intentionally ignoring the lie of not knowing her. "You should braid your hair." He reached over and pushed Luis's hair back from his shoulders, his fingertips brushed gently against his neck.

'Alright…' thought Luis, 'time to bail…' "Yeah…" he said awkwardly, "uh… hey I gotta go… uh... What's in your pocket?"

"My pocket?" Philippe cocked his head, a little perplexed at the sudden irrelevant question. "Um... well, I have my phone, my wallet, my keys and my..." He pulled the little black box out of his pocket. "And my dreams that are gone." He opened the box and looked at the beautiful diamond rose. Luis looked over Philippe's shoulder into the box and then reached out and took the ring out of the box. Philippe was startled. He didn't expect this guy to just reach over and grab it.

"Oh, sorry uh… may I?" Philippe nodded reluctantly. Luis looked at the ring dubiously. He held it up to the light and squinted his eyes at it. Then he looked again over to the blank area on the other side of the hospital bed. Philippe followed his line of sight to see if he was looking at anything in particular. But all he could see was blank screened medical equipment and a painting of the coast of France. "Huh." He handed the ring back to Philippe.

Philippe raised an eyebrow at him. "Alright?"

Luis shrugged. "What are you gonna do with it now?"

"I don't know. Probably sell it to pay for the cremation."

"Yeah, that makes sense. Um… I think she would have loved it."

"Yeah. I think so too." he gently put the ring back into its box. "It seems like everyone is dying. I feel like I'm too young for everyone in my life to be dying already."

Luis nodded. "What did you know about her? I mean, the girl the ring was for." He glanced across the room again. "I mean, about her family and stuff."

"Um," Philippe squinted, a little perplexed by all the strange questions. "I know that she didn't get along very well with her father. He was over controlling and Catholic. That's about all I know about him. I know her mother died when she was young from jumping from a building. Veronica had a hard life. I admired every inch of her. The way that she faced her life. She took hold of it and refused to let it run her. Exact opposite of my mother. Why do you ask?"

Luis just shrugged and continued. "Did you ever meet her parents?" Philippe blinked at Luis. He had brown eyes and one freckle on his right cheek.

"No, I didn't."

"Pretty bold move huh? Popping the question before even meeting her parents. Don't think Catholic dad woulda liked that."

Philippe smiled. "I guess I didn't care about his opinion enough to think to ask his permission. That's so archaic." They sat in silence for a moment. It felt like it was getting towards time to go.

"Well..." Luis lifted his hand and then after a moment of deliberation brought his hand down awkwardly onto Philippe's shoulder. "It'll be alright man. And if you can find a way to forgive your mom, your life will be transformed. Those are my only wise words for the night so I hope you take that to heart cuz I mean it." He stood up. Philippe stood with him and pulled him into a very close hug. 'Hugging...' Thought Luis, 'hugging strangers... cool... what ev's...'

"Thank you." Said Philippe into his hair. Luis patted Philippe on the back with a nervous sort of deliberation.

"No problem man." Philippe giggled lightly and kissed Luis once on each cheek and then held his face between his hands and beamed down at him.

"I still don't know who you are, or why you're here or how you know so much, but it was lovely to meet you."

"Uh… You too man." Philippe winked.

"And do put your hair into a braid for me at least once someday."

"Yeah okay..." Philippe smiled and tucked Luis's hair behind his ear.

"Good. Go now." He let his hands fall to his sides away from Luis's face. Luis nodded and glanced at the body and at the empty space across the room.

"Good luck man. Have a good life."

"You too."

He smiled bemused, as Luis backed away awkwardly before he left the room. The door clicked shut and he turned to face his mother. He took a long deep breath and then let it out. He walked over to his mother's side and felt the tears well up and drip over his still smiling cheeks. He reached out and touched his mother's hair. He squeezed his eyes closed and just let the tears fall. Then put his hands on the edge of the sheet.

"Goodbye mum." His lips quivered as he spoke. And his hands shook as he lifted the sheet up over her face and let it settle down. "Goodbye mum. I'm sorry."

Chapter 19. Who was Luis?

"I'm Aimee, I'm Five. How old are you?"

"Um… I don't know."

"You don't know how old you are? That's pretty weird."

"Yeah..."

"Well, when's your birthday?"

"Um… I don't know."

"You don't even know when your birthday is? No wonder you don't know how old you are."

"I guess..."

10 years later.

"So I was reading this book and I found out that I'm a Libra. Check it out! I got it from the library. See, there's my birthday. That means that I'm a persuasive, sociable, self-confident and an independent natural leader. Doesn't that describe me perfectly Philippe?"

"Yeah! It really does. Hey that's a cool book."

"Yeah. It's called astrology. I wonder what your sign is. Let's see, June first. It says that you're a Taurus. Wow. You really don't seem like a Taurus to me..."

"What are you talking about? I'm totally a steady, reliable, slow to excite but holds a bull like grudge kind of guy... No I'm not. You're right. Haha. That's funny. I wonder why it got you so right but me so wrong. I guess you can't put all your eggs in the astrology basket."

"Yeah I guess not. You seem more like a Gemini to me. On the one hand you're fluffy and fun to be around and seem really shallow and emotional... no offense. And on the other hand you're actually a deep intellectual. Or maybe you're a Pisces. You are kinda weird sometimes.... Or maybe you're more like a caring Cancer. Or a wild, no attachments Aries. Huh. I don't know, but you definitely don't seem like a Taurus. That's for sure."

10 hours later.

"Hey mum. I was wondering, do I seem like a Taurus to you?"
"What?"
"Yeah, you know, like Astrology."
"I don't know Philippe. I never really thought much about Astrology."
"Oh, okay. Well hey, Aimee and I were thinking of trying to do a full astrology map just for fun. But I need my birth time and place. I was born here in Paris right? What time was I born?"
"Uh... I don't know Philippe, I don't remember."
"Oh, okay. Do you remember the general time of day?"
"Um... I don't know... morning maybe?"
"Hey I know! Can I look at my birth certificate? I bet that would say."

10 minutes later.

"There's no location on here. Was I not born in a hospital?"

Silence.

"There's my birthday. June first. No father listed… Time unknown? So… I guess that explains the hospital question. The doctors would have known that."

Silence.

"Wait… This birth certificate was made 10 years ago… it says so right here. I was like 5 years old then."

Silence.

"Mum… when was I born? was it really June first?"

10 seconds later.

"Philippe I can't understand you when you're crying so much. Talk a little slower, what's going on?"

"My birthday is a fake! My mum was so drugged out of her brain that she doesn't even know what month I was born in. She just made something up when she finally got around to getting a birth certificate for me because she needed one to enroll me in school. I was probably born in her bathtub or something."

"Well… I guess that means you're probably not a Taurus… It's okay Philippe. Astrology doesn't mean anything anyway."

Philippe opened his eyes. He was laying on Marcello's king sized bed with the dark sheets and the ostentatious headboard.

Marcello was gone. He'd always been an early riser. It was dark, and quiet. The sun wasn't up yet and the heavy curtains covering the window wouldn't have allowed for light anyway.

Philippe wrapped his arms around his stomach. It was too quiet. Too quiet to avoid his thoughts. Yesterday his mother had died and suddenly, despite the warm bed, left cold by Marcelo's absence, and despite Aimee, his best friend who still had no idea that his mother had died, he felt lonely. Really, as he laid there, he imagined that he was a little child, who just wanted his mommy to hold him. No substitute would do.

He scrunched up his face and cried into the pillow for a while before getting up. Yesterday was beyond horrible. But he somehow felt sure that today would be worse. Because today was the day that he had to suck it up and keep his composure. Today he had to be able to hear sentences and words. He had to be able to make decisions. Choices. He had to find out how to pay for a funeral with no money. No, his mother didn't need a funeral. She wasn't religious and there was no place to bury her. So instead, he needed to pay for the cremation. That tended to be cheaper, but he was still broke.

He looked around at the expensive room. He knew that he could probably ask Marcelo for help. But he had somehow gone the whole night without telling Marcello that the only reason he was there was to distract his tired heart. He didn't feel like making Marcello a part of his life quite that personally. He thought that maybe Marcello would help with no questions asked, but that would hardly change the facts, and he was no beggar.

He stood up and pulled on his pants. He felt the bulge in his pocket and reached in to pull out that engagement ring. He opened the tiny black box and looked at it. It was no use just hanging on to it. It wasn't as if he could give it to someone else. He supposed that perhaps the best use for something made to make people hold onto each other, was for him to use it to let go instead.

He sighed and slipped the box black into his pocket and finished buckling his belt. He walked through the dark quiet room and went over to the huge heavy curtains and drew them back to look outside. He was suddenly blinded for a moment by the sun that he was sure hadn't risen yet, but either the darkness of the room had thrown off his sense of time, or his grief and upset stomach had.

He rubbed his eyes and waited for the black splotch to leave his vision. Then he took a proper look out the window to look at the countryside of France. Marcello did not live in the middle of Paris and Philippe had needed to drive quite a ways to get there. But with the stresses of that day, he hadn't minded the escape of a long drive.

He cracked open one of the double doors that led out to the balcony and took a deep breath of the crisp morning air. He had never thought that he'd feel the need to ask himself this question, but now he caught himself asking it. What was he going to do without his mother? It wasn't as if he'd ever actually needed her. He could do anything and everything without her. He should be filled with a sense of relief and freedom.

2320 Rue Veron, that boy had said. Rue Veron. Who was that kid? Rue Veron was a tiny little street a little ways from Boulevard de

Clichy, just a hop skip and a jump from the Moulin Rouge. Why would a complete stranger, only a few years younger than himself be able to tell him that he and his mother had once lived a few blocks from the red light boulevard? Unless his mother had started taking young lovers. But even that would have been out of character for her, and no young lover would have been benefited by the experience. But he could be wrong.

2320 Rue Veron. But there was a bigger strangeness than the fact that he'd had an answer to Philippe's question. The bigger puzzle was the fact that Luis had known that Philippe had asked his mother such a question in the first place. It had been barely an hour between his asking her, and her overdose. It just didn't add up.

He took in another deep breath of the morning air. At least he knew what he would do without his mother. He would keep searching for answers. He would go to 2320 Rue Veron and see if the whole thing was just a silly dead end. But before that, his mother needed to be cremated. So he put on his shirt and grabbed his keys, and like he had always done, he left Marcello's house without saying goodbye.

Chapter 20. 2320 Rue Veron

He held onto the urn that contained his mother's ashes. It was lilac and it had tulips carved into the sides of it. It was cute. Philippe thought perhaps he was a little odd to want his mother's ashes in such a bright container but lilac really had been her best color. He'd always felt that lilac would have been the color of her soul if her soul had been more healthy.

There had been no memorial service, but Aimee had sat with him while they waited for her body to burn. Philippe had hocked Veronica's engagement ring in order to afford the casket that his mother was burned in. How poetic. One ring. Two deaths. It was like he'd purchased two lives for the price of one but he had acquired neither. Even though it was just burned along with her, he somehow just couldn't bring himself to stuff her into any old box. It had to be a beautiful one.

He sat in his car with the ignition turned off staring down at the flowery jar. The casket had had angels on it. Brown burgundy angels with cream satin lining on the inside. The ashes of that box, he knew, were among the ashes of his mother in the urn. Maybe those angels, bought with a ring for a lost love, would carry his mother away to a better place. One that was sweeter than the life that he'd seen her live. He looked out the convertible window through the pouring of the

Paris rain at the boarded up old building he was parked in front of. He hoped those angels would carry his mother to a better place than she'd ever lived.

2320 Rue Veron. This was the place that the boy Luis had told him was the residence of him and his mother before his earliest memory. How Luis had known this was beyond Philippe's understanding but from the looks of the place, he hoped that the boy had been wrong. He supposed he would soon find out.

He set his mother's urn safely at the foot of the passenger seat and got ready to open the car door. He stepped out into the rain without an umbrella. He had a feeling that he was going to require the use of both of his hands in order to get into the old boarded up building.

He didn't care about the fact that the baby blue blazer that he wore had a tag that said "dry clean only." Why he'd chosen to wear the blazer today in a situation where it was likely to get ruined was anyone's guess. Why he'd chosen to take no precautions against ruining it was another question one could ask him. He likely would have no answer. Or he would have an answer that meant nothing like 'oh my goodness you're right, what was I thinking?' or 'It's okay, I have ten of these at home.' or even more likely, 'I couldn't help it, I love baby blue in any weather.' In any case, he stepped out into the rain with no regard to the wealth of his clothing at all.

It was an old Paris street and it was deserted. The old buildings were built with no space between them. No alleys for lurkers. No cracks for rats. As Philippe crossed the street from his car to the place of his lost memories he wondered when it was that the cobbles had been laid there. How much history was in the very ground that he walked over? How many others had lost or gained memories here?

He finally reached the other side of the soaked old city street, only one lane wide. He looked up at the two story building. It was covered in rotting boards and graffiti. The number 2320 was missing the number three so it read, 2_20. He stood looking at it in the rain. His hair was quickly becoming plastered to his forehead and he could feel the makeup beginning to run.

The door was locked in the same manner as most Parisian buildings. He would need a key to get into the entry way or courtyard, and another key to actually enter the building. He had neither. So he was going to have to find another way. It didn't take him long. The windows were long and narrow and the ones at street level were covered with thick black iron bars. But one set of bars looked as if they had been forcibly wrenched off their bolts and then subsequently boarded up with plywood.

He walked over to the building and began feeling around the edges of the spray painted slabs. He found a weaker spot and began to pull. Anyone could look at him and know that he was no body builder. He had nearly no upper body strength. No woman could ever hope to feel protected with him around. He wouldn't last a minute in a fight.

He squealed a pathetic whine as he pulled his hand away from the board to find a splinter lodged into his finger. "Ow.' He whimpered to himself as he pulled the sliver out of his finger and watched the blood run down in the rain. He winced and put his finger in his mouth and looked back up at the building that challenged him.

He searched through his mind but he could find no memory of the place. Maybe it was just because of the boards and the graffiti but the building didn't look familiar at all. Maybe that kid had been wrong and this place had nothing to do with him. He didn't want to give up yet though. He put his hands back against the scraggy board, holding his hurt finger up away from the wood and into the rain.   He spread his feet for traction on the slippery cobble ground. His shoes would need a serious shine after this. The leather wasn't made to be worn in the rain or used as leverage. His feet were getting wet and a strange frothy lather was beginning to form on the tops of his shoes. He stood as firmly as he could, and pulled.

There was a small crack sound and the wood gave just a little. He stopped to take a breath for a moment and then pulled again. There was a louder crack and his hands slipped from the board and he landed sitting in a small puddle of water. He was happy that no one was here to see this. He was happy that this was a solitary experience.

He looked up to see that the board had mostly cracked in half and the crags of a broken window were visible. He stood up and looked at his hands. His fingers were sore and the one was still bleeding. He walked over and considered pointy shards of glass sticking up from the old window sill. He pushed the board away with his shoulder to get a little closer to the window. It didn't look safe. But it was the best way in that he could see.

Past the foggy broken glass was nothing but pitch black. Before finding a way in through he decided to pull out his phone and turn on the flashlight app. He put his hand in through the opening to try to get a better angle. As far as he could tell, the place was ransacked, and deserted. He slipped his phone back into his pocket and using the arm of his blazer, began breaking away at the sharp glass points to make himself a way in. He'd had about enough of the rain anyway, he was soaked to the bone and shivering.

Once the glass had been cleared away enough that he thought he could probably make it inside without slicing a major artery, he decided to hoist himself inside. This part wasn't difficult for him. He was plenty nimble despite the shivering. He was tall enough that he was able to simply put his leg through first and then follow it with the rest of him. He felt a shard of glass snag against his pant leg, but it missed his skin.

Once he was inside he pulled his phone back out of his pocket and turned the light back on and shined it around. He wiped the rain water and hair out of his eyes and turned around one hundred and eighty degrees. It looked like a living room. The walls were lined with old squashy moth eaten couches and a very old square television. There was a half fallen poster of a naked woman but other than that there were no wall hangings. The place smelled of old dust and mold but any other smells had long ago fled the place.

As his turn made full circle, before his light touched it, he noticed the smell of body odor extremely unwashed and sickly. His light came to an archway in the corner of the room and landed on the form of a man standing on the threshold with one arm shielding his eyes from the light. Philippe gasped a little startled by the unexpected human presence and quickly lowered the light from the man's face.

"Oh I'm sorry." Philippe said quietly, but his voice seemed to ring like a bell in this silent, drafty place.

"Who izzat?" The man slurred. Philippe felt his stomach lurch and sink down to his loins. The voice of this homeless bum was familiar to him, but he didn't recognize who it was. He lifted the light back up towards the man's face but the man again covered himself from the brightness.

"Shine that at yourself!" His voice was annoyed but also demanding. He meant it. Philippe knew the bum wanted to see his face. He lifted the phone up to his own cheek so that the man could see him. He stared out into the pitch black of the room wondering what the man was seeing in him really. He could hear his own breathing being kind of shaky. There was no other sound for a long moment. The bum said nothing.

The moment seemed to drag on silently for far too long and Philippe began to wonder if the man was still there. He hurriedly turned the light around and nearly jumped out of his skin when he found that the man was standing directly in front of him. He let out a startled yelp and took a step back.

"What's your name?" Said the bum. His face was covered in a patchy disheveled beard speckled with dandruff and body grease, and he was missing most of his head hair. His smell was hard to stomach.

He smelled of body odor, booze, urine and what was likely his own cum. His thin brow was furrowed, wrinkling his obviously once broken nose. His eyes squinted and focused on Philippe's face, trying to make out his features in the dim light.

"Uh um..." Philippe wasn't prone to stuttering but he couldn't seem to get his own name to come clearly out of his mouth but much to his astonishment this shade in front of him said it for him.

"Ph... Philip... Philippe?" The man blinked and raised his eyebrows as he remembered the name. "Philippe!" Philippe just stood gaping in horror at this pathetic walking corpse of a man. "You're so tall. I didn't think you'd get so tall." He leaned back a little and chuckled. "Oh damn you got so beautiful. Damn it!" He shook his head from side to side as he marveled up at him. "Damn it. You would have been so good." He reached up and moved a stray wet strand of hair from Philippe's forehead to the side. Philippe shuddered at the man's greasy touch and bony pale musky smelling fingers. The slight scratch of the man's chipped fingernails were grating like running them down a chalkboard.

Philippe continued to stare at the man. He didn't want to ask. He didn't want to know. The memory was best left buried. What was he doing here?

"You have no idea who I am do you kiddo." Philippe shook his head slowly. The man chuckled. "Did you come here to see your old ghetto? Hmm? Nice place huh." Philippe couldn't bring himself to speak but he felt as tears began to run down his cheeks. The kid had been right. This was the place. But the memory was still buried. "Oh now don't start cryin' on me now kiddo, I thought you would be over that by now. God you look just like her. How's your mama doin'?" Philippe just shook his head. His breath was only coming out in short spurts as dictated by the tears. "That good huh?"

The man started to slowly walk around Philippe never taking his hand off of him. Philippe let his phone lower down to his side. No need to keep using it right now. He stared off into the black of the room and waited for his eyes to become slowly accustomed. He wasn't sure why it had taken so long, but he suddenly felt very unsafe. Like there was a chance that he wouldn't leave this building alive or unmolested.

"You're skinny." The man felt at Philippe's waist and hips from behind him. "There's a market for that." Philippe swallowed hard and forced words to move past his vocal chords.

"A… are you my f… father?" the man laughed in response. A high pitched somewhat maniacal laugh.

"You kidding? You sure didn't get your tall gene from your mother. And as you can see, you didn't get it from me." His hands ran down the back of Philippe's thighs. Philippe suddenly turned around to face the man and took a step away from him and shined the light into his face. The man dropped his hands to his sides. "I'd love to take credit for your creation kiddo. But it seems damned unlikely. No. Some other angelic stud made you."

Philippe gasped past his tears. "What is this place? Who are you? What… what did you do to my mother?" The man tilted his head to the side and looked at Philippe.

"You that dense kiddo? You really don't remember anything? Want a tour?" Philippe shook his head. No. In fact he wanted to leave. But his feet were glued to the spot. He began wondering if this guy was armed. He could have a knife on him. "Sure you do, come on, I'll show you your old bedroom." He walked up to Philippe and reached out to his baby blue blazer. He ran his thumb down the collar and then buttoned one of the big buttons on the front. "Come on, follow me."

The bum walked through the archway and down a hall. Philippe just stood there. He stared at the dim light coming in through the broken window. He could do it. He could run right now. He could make it out that window before this creep even turned around to see if he was following. But then he'd never know. He'd never get that memory back. He knew he didn't want it, but it wasn't about whether or not he wanted it. It was about knowing everything about his own life. It was about knowing the whole story. He needed to reclaim the part of his mind that he'd cut off from himself.

He turned his head and looked towards the dark threshold. He knew already that whatever the memory was, it was a bad one. Veronica's warning came firmly to mind. She'd wished that she could block out her past. She'd envied the fact that Philippe had forgotten his. But what would he do if he didn't go down that hallway? He'd return to his shallow life. He'd get another modeling job selling his body to the highest bidder and he'd never know what would have happened if he'd just walked down that hallway.

He took a deep breath to steady himself and walked under the arch holding his light out in front of him. As soon as he walked through the archway, strange things started happening. He started hearing things. Voices. Memories. There was the scream of a woman. There were muffled conversations. There was the loud repetitive squeaking of springs and the thud thud thudding against the wall. He suddenly wanted nothing more than to be back in his mother's tiny apartment. He wanted to be six years old, huddled in the closet because it was safer in there.

The paint was peeling off the walls in the hallway and the floor was lined with trash and abandoned clothing. He could see the form of the bum in front of him but for a moment another reality was transposed on top of this one. One where the lights that hung from the ceiling turned on and weren't covered in webs. The room was bright and Landers was younger. That was his name. Landers. He was dressed like a man of sophistication. He was taller than Philippe because Philippe was small. 'You're the prettiest baby I've ever seen kiddo. Never believe otherwise. Maybe in a couple of years you'll be pretty enough to get a job huh? What do you say kiddo? Sound like fun?'

Philippe rubbed his eyes to try to get them to see things right again. But when he opened his eyes Lander's was kneeling down in front of him with a perfectly trimmed mustache and a friendly smile. 'Hey kiddo, I was thinking maybe in a few hours you and me could go out father and son style. What do you say? Maybe get your ear pierced?' He reached out to Philippe's tiny body and buttoned the front of his little blue sweater. 'That way you can have one that matches mine.' He lifted one finger to the gold ring on his left ear and with his other hand reached out and pinched Philippe's left ear. It hurt.

Philippe reached his hand up to his ear. It was never pierced. He'd never had an ear ring. He'd wanted to go with Landers to get his ear pierced. But it never happened.

The hallway was suddenly dark again and Landers looked like death. He was standing in front of a door that was half way off its hinges. Philippe looked behind him at all the rooms they had passed. He realized that he didn't remember the way back and they had climbed a flight of stairs.

He watched as Landers tried to heave the door into the room. Since it was only on one hinge it was dragging across the floor, leaving a long horrible scar on the hardwood that made Philippe cringe until it ran into a room sized floral rug. "This was your room..." He heaved at the door, pushing with his shoulder. "Where you and your mama lived."

Suddenly the phone in Philippe's hand began to ring and vibrate. It startled him so bad that he dropped it and it lay on the old dusty wood, ringing loudly face up. 'Aimee calling' it said on the caller ID. When Philippe looked down at it. He didn't move. Landers stopped heaving and looked at Philippe. He had a stern and somewhat threatening look on his face. Philippe looked between the two, not wanting to make any sudden moves. They just stared at each other in a sort of stalemate until the phone stopped ringing. Philippe swallowed hard.

Landers turned back to the door and shoved it open with one last big heave that caused the rug to wad up under the door. Light filtered in from a window. Landers looked into the room and then stood to the side and gestured for Philippe to enter.

Philippe bent down and picked up his phone from the floor and tucked it into his pocket. He looked at Landers to see if for some reason he was going to have an issue with that but Landers said nothing. Philippe swallowed and walked into the bedroom.

Chapter 21. The Blocked Memory

"Hush Philippe." She put her finger up to her red lips thick with lipstick. She smelled of lavender perfume and beauty products that covered up the bags that she had under her eyes. "Shh. Stay down, be quiet, don't let the men find you okay." She smiled and picked up a stuffed bear with one button eye. "Here's your bear okay? So just stay in the armoire and be really quiet okay."

"But mommy it's broked. Look at its eye."

"I know about its eye Philippe!" She took a deep breath and tried to lower her exasperated voice. "Just hold onto it for now okay, and after I'm done working I'll fix it for you and I'll sew a new button eye on it."

She sat up straighter and turned her head towards the door. Little Philippe could hear muffled men's voices coming down the hall towards the bedroom. She hurriedly fluffed the flat pillow next to Philippe and had him sit down on the old wooden floor of the armoire on top of a thin blanket. His little body was tucked just under the dresses hanging above him. "Okay now hush Philippe. Don't make any noise at all. Just stay down, be quiet, and don't let the men find you."

"Okay mommy."

"Hush hush hush." She kissed his pale forehead leaving red lip marks on his skin. "I love you Philippe. Sleep tight. Stay down, be quiet. Don't let the men find you." Quietly, the door of the armoire creaked shut and the darkness enveloped him.

This was a night like all the nights. Philippe laid down on the flat pillow and pulled one of his mother's sweaters over his legs for warmth. He hugged the one button eyed bear to his chest and proceeded to not sleep a wink. He fiddled at the one button remaining instead. He felt the way that the eye with a button felt different than the eye with no button. He felt the way that he could still tell where the other button should be because there were still the ends of little threads there. He felt that the eye locations weren't perfectly symmetrical. The eye with the button was a little closer to the nose than the eye without. It didn't occur to him of course, that maybe he shouldn't fiddle with his bear like this, as this was in fact, how it had lost the first eye.

He heard the bedroom door open and the sound of his mother's excessively cheerful, overactive voice. He knew it was fake because he knew what his mother really sounded like. She sounded tired and annoyed. Not cheerful.

'Hush. Stay down. Be quiet. Don't let the men find you.' He said it silently in his head like a mantra. 'Hush. Stay down. Be quiet. Don't let the men find you.' He knew that if he didn't think it to himself over and over again that he might forget it and make a noise. He might say something, or sing something. And that would be bad. It would be bad because then he would be heard. If he was heard, the men would find him. He knew that was bad. He had no idea why that was bad, but he knew it was bad.

He heard Landers's voice and he looked up towards the tiny crack between the hinges of the armoire door. "No bruises or I cut you. Have a good night!" He heard the door shut. He wished that he could get up and go out into the hallway with Landers. It would be better than laying here. He looked longingly towards the small crack but then reminded himself, 'Stay down. Be quiet. Don't let the men find you."

He heard the sound of the man's voice in the bedroom talking to his mother and clapped his hands over his ears, letting go of the comforting bear. It wasn't long before he could hear the sound of the bed springs squeaking rhythmically and the bed frame banging against the wall. His hands were never enough to block out the noise. He tried wrapping his head in the pillow and that worked a little bit better. 'Stay down. Be quiet. Don't let the men find you.' Never cry. Never yell. Never sing. Never breathe too loudly.
'Keep him quiet.' he'd heard Landers say once in a while, just as a reminder. 'The minute someone notices he's in there, I'm putting him to work.' So, 'Stay down. Be quiet. Don't let the men find you.'

Eventually his arms got tired and he had to let go of the pillow in order to give his muscles a break. The noises persisted. He took a deep breath and let it seep out very slowly and quietly. He rolled over and reached for his bear, hugging it again to his chest and returning to his fiddling with the eye button that his mother had told him to stop fiddling with.

He looked up through the dark at all the fabric hanging above his head. He'd seen all those dresses. He reached up and touched one of the long tassels that was dangling down near his face. He tried to guess which dress it was just by the feel of the fabric. It was a little game he often played with himself. He loved all the fabrics. Some were silky, some were fuzzy and soft, and some were thick and hard to move. His favorite was the satin lilac colored dress that he felt sure he was touching. His mother looked pretties in this one.

'Hush. Stay down. Be quiet. Don't let the men find you.' his little fingers grabbed a little tighter to the soft dress. The tighter he held it the more he felt like his mother was close to him. The loud voice he heard from her now was not her own voice. His favorite voice was when she said things like, 'I'll sew your bear's other eye back on after work.'

His mother wasn't very good at sewing. That eye had fallen off five times already. Landers said it was because her own mum never had a chance to teach her. Maybe she'd teach him to sew and then he could fix the bear's eye. And he could fix her lilac dress too because it had a tear in the side so she hadn't worn it in a while.

The noises and the banging and the yelling started getting louder so Philippe clapped his hands to his ears again. But he forgot to let go of the dress and it and several other dresses dropped down on top of him all of a sudden. He heard the wire hangers clank loudly against the wooden walls of the armoire and despite his mantra he let out a small yelp of surprise as the fabric fell over his face.

All the noises stopped.

He scrambled to push the heavy smothering dresses off of his face and he sat up with his back to the wall and held one hand firmly over his mouth, trying to get his breathing to slow down and perhaps suck the sound of his voice back into his throat. The other hand wrestled madly with the last button eye of the bear.

'Stay down. Be quiet. Don't let the men find you.'

"What the hell was that?" The man's voice was so accusatory. How dare a noise break his concentration.

"Nothing! That was nothing. My clothes must have just fallen off of the hangers."

Pop! Off flew the button from Philippe's bear and clacked really quite quietly against the door of the armoire, but amidst the hush of the moment, it sounded to him like a gong.

There was a creaking sound of the springs and then quick footsteps which were suddenly followed by the very loud scream of his mother's protest.

The armoire door was flung open and there stood the man naked with his mother clinging to his arm, trying to pull him back, screaming, "No!"

"What the hell is with the brat!?" Yelled the man. Philippe started yelling too. He clapped his hands over his ears, scrunched up as small as he could, squeezed his eyes tightly shut and started yelling his mantra as if somehow that would turn back time.

"Stay down! Be quiet! Don't let the men find you! Don't let the men find you! Don't let the men find you!"

He'd been only a moment away from dealing with the anger of many people when the bedroom door burst open and everything started happening at once. His mother got a hand free to slam the armoire shut and Philippe shoved the blind bear into his mouth and bit down. There were many men's voices now. Everyone was yelling. Something thudded against the door of the armoire but Philippe kept his eyes shut, and kept his jaw clamped.

The noises eventually subsided and he could hear his mother talking swiftly and frantically with someone whose voice he didn't recognize who was speaking very firmly. The muscles in his legs and arms and jaw were starting to cramp and hurt but he couldn't get them to let go. He didn't want them to let go.

But then he saw the first person in his home who did not live there, work there, or get his entertainment there. The first person who was neither selling anything, nor buying anything. The only other people he'd talked to were the clerks at the grocery store but this was someone who was none of these. When the armoire door creaked opened there were two people in black with thick Kevlar vests and utility belts with guns at their hips.

"Come on out child." The one in front of him said. Philippe's jaw unlocked and his legs started kicking trying to scramble against the tangled pile of dresses beneath him, wishing that there was a hidden door in the wall behind him but not finding one. So he started yelling again.

"No! Don't let the men find you! No!" He could see his mother wrapped in a robe in the background sitting disheveled and defeated on the floor. "Mommy I'm sorry I pulled down the dresses I'm sorry I was too loud."

"Hey hey. It's alright. We're not going to hurt you." The man in black put his hands up to show that they were empty and he meant no harm. But if Philippe knew anything, he knew that an open hand was just as dangerous as a closed one. There was only one truth, one rule that had been violated and now he would be put to work.

"No! Don't let the men find you. No." He shook his head and hugged his little blind bear as tight as he could.

Another person all dressed in black walked into the room straight to his mother and pulled her up onto her feet. "Come on, you gotta come out with the others."

"But my kid's here, he's scared, let me take care of my kid."

"We'll take care of him. You need to come out with the others." His mother looked at him and the sorrowful look in her eyes made him wonder if he would ever see her again. She was led from the room and Philippe started screaming louder.

Fifteen years later, Philippe opened his eyes to find himself in a silent room lying on the floor of an armoire that he now barely fit into. He couldn't stretch out his legs anymore. He was too tall. The knees of his half folded legs leaned heavily against the old wooden wall of the armoire.

He could remember what happened next. He'd screamed and cried the mantra again and again until the officer finally just had to hoist him out and more or less toss him over his shoulder with as much care as he could. Philippe didn't see his mother again for two sleepless nights until he was finally released back into her custody.

That explained it all then. He was literally the bastard son of a whore. She'd done the best that she could to protect him under the circumstances and at least in the brothel, she'd succeeded.

Chapter 22. Drugged

His dreams while lying on the floor of his mother's old armoire were plagued by images and noises that his mind hadn't been old enough to correctly categorize. The result was that it was trying to categorize them now but it was left with only mushy half understood visuals to sift through. Disjointed people and fragments of fabric strewn about the disorganized muddle of his brain space.

His eyes opened briefly and he saw the lilac urn filled with his mother's ashes sitting on the worn floral rug below the open armoire door. Or was it floating? He couldn't tell. Back into the ebb and flow of a time that no longer existed, he let his sleepy mind wander through the hallways of this old brothel building.

He remembered that it was always crowded with people who loved him sometimes, and found him an unfortunate nuisance other times. He remembered that there was no one his age there to play with, and also that he never really knew that someone around who was his own age was something that he should want. But also now, from his older perspective, he could remember that many of those faces were young enough that they could have been his older siblings. Though they would have been much older siblings, ten years older perhaps, it didn't change the fact that they weren't much older than children themselves. They were adolescents who had never had a chance to go to middle school.

His mother was one of them. Now that he thought about it, he couldn't remember a time when they had ever celebrated her birthday. Then again, he couldn't remember them ever celebrating his birthday either.

He was laying on top of a pile of musty old clothing. He knew that they hadn't been moved at all since the night that he'd pulled them down on top of his head. They'd been abandoned there, along with the memories and the lacy underwear that he knew were in the armoire drawers beneath him. If he'd had the energy, he could have pulled out that old lilac dress that he'd loved so much when he was small. He gazed at the urn of his mother's ashes, and realized how much of a tragedy it was that he'd put her in that color. Bottled her up in it. Like lilac was her color, and she'd never escape it. He regretted that he'd never actually asked what her favorite color was. It disturbed him now that he didn't know.

It occurred to him that he probably shouldn't be laying there on those clothes though. For all he knew, there could be spiders or mice that had made a home in them. He didn't care about that now though. No, he just wanted sleep.

He closed his eyes again and returned to the swirling images. It occurred to him that he'd probably slept with as many men as his mum had. Only no pimp had ever told him to do it and he'd never gotten paid. Was his mother ever really paid? Or had Landers taken it all? He had no idea. What was the difference? Maybe that was what he should do whenever he finally got out of this place. Head to the bar to find a hookup.

He'd looked up to Landers he realized. Children find a way to admire whatever you put in front of them. He was probably lucky that he'd turned out nothing like the man. But his life wasn't over yet, and he wondered if it were possible for him to go in that psychological direction.

His lips parted and he was startled to hear himself let out a small moan of discomfort. He felt a painful prick and opened his eyes just enough to see Landers kneeling beside him, slowly pulling a syringe away from the crook of his arm. Philippe thought that he should be angry about this, but he wasn't.

"Sorry kiddo. Habit. Just try to relax." He heard Landers voice as if it were some soft bird singing in the tree just outside the window.

He lulled his head against the dresses and found himself rocking off into what he was surprised to find was a comfortingly familiar sensation. He'd never done drugs. That wasn't true. He'd snorted cocaine exactly once and had managed to resolve to never try that again. If he was an exuberant person on a normal day, he was ten times that when amped up on cocaine. It would have been too easy for him to decide that people liked him better that way, because chances are it would have been true.

Other than that, he'd never done drugs. He'd seen what they'd done to his mother and he'd had no intentions of following in her footsteps. But he was sure following in her footsteps now, in more ways than one. Landers too had been her introduction to such things.

The familiarity of the warmth came out of nowhere. Where had he felt this before? It was like being rocked back and forth like a baby in his mother's arms. It was like the love that he'd always wished that his mother had for him. It was like a love all the way around him, enveloping him in its womb. A mother who loves her baby as it grows inside her feels like this, he thought.

He felt an unexpected pang of anger towards Aimee for even thinking of aborting her child. How could she not love it? That was a cruelty that Philippe empathized with and he resolved for a split second to give Aimee a piece of his mind about it. But then the moment was gone, and he was back in his mother's womb, being swayed gently from side to side.

His hand reached over to close the armoire door and thereby seal himself fully in the womb sensation but his knuckles simply clacked against the wood and then fell back to the cushioned dresses by his side. He stared at the urn sitting next to Landers as he sat cross legged just watching.

With every breath Philippe felt like his mother's love was being pumped into his belly through an umbilical cord, nourishing him. For a moment the feeling turned sour though. His mind flashed to his mother dead on the bed with a needle in her arm. No, maybe she hadn't been dead yet. Dying. How many times had this feeling tried to kill her? How many times had Philippe's body tried to sweat out the memory of the feeling he was having right now?

He suddenly rolled over towards Landers and found that Landers was holding a large saucepan in his hands. He tucked the saucepan under Philippe's chin because he'd already known that

Philippe would need it. Philippe heaved and a little bile and mucous escaped his lips, but the truth was, he hadn't eaten anything in at least twenty four hours. He let his head lay down on his mother's old scratchy work outfits.

"You used to cry a lot when you were a baby you know." Landers voice sounded like story time. Philippe felt no urge to respond to him. So he just listened. "Always hungry for mama's milk." Landers reached out his hand and ran his fingers through Philippe's hair. Philippe thought that this should bother him. But it didn't. Instead he heard himself sigh at the sensation of every follicle on his head.

"You remind me right now of when you were a baby and your mum finally gave in to your screaming and gave you some. Tastes pretty good huh?" Philippe felt as a soft cloth was rubbed gently against his lips to wipe them clean of any sick. "You were the one I was saddest for losing when they busted the place. Men don't get as much for their efforts as women you know. But boys. Ah. Pretty boys like you would have gotten me somewhere. I had a feeling that you were gold. I shouldn't have waited so long. That was my mistake. There was a market for you. I was just being too nice. Too nice to you and your mom, letting her keep you all safe in this armoire like that. And they wouldn't let me do it. I shouldn'ta been so nice. And I shouldn'ta listened to them." Philippe felt as Landers picked up his hand and felt at the skin between his fingers. He turned his hand over and scrutinized his well-manicured nails. "I think maybe it was the innocence too you know. I kinda liked ya. Kinda wished you were my own. Made it hard to spoil you. But I guess I missed my chance didn't

I?"

He put the tip of Philippe's pointer finger into his mouth and bit down on one of his fingernails. Philippe felt the vibrations of the snap of his nail ripple down to his toes. It felt like the vibration of being wrapped in his mother's womb feeling the base of loud club music reverberating through the amniotic fluid all around him. Philippe thought that he should feel uncomfortable with that, but he didn't.

The hair stroking continued. Philippe looked up at Landers's scruffy emaciated face and his left ear that was now empty of any gold ring. He felt his eyelids begin to close of their own accord. "You were born wanting the stuff. Now you finally get what you wanted. How's it feel?" Philippe's voice only let out a creaking moan in response. "Yeah? Feels like mama's milk. Your mum fed you mostly formula, until your crying got too loud. Kept you quiet and happy."

That explained why he couldn't remember where he'd felt this before. He'd known this feeling since before memories were formed. His eyelids sealed shut. He felt the cracked bristling sensation of Landers lips against his own. He thought he should feel disgusted by this good night kiss. But instead he dropped off to sleep.

He had no idea how long he slept passed out in the old cramped closet space in which he'd spent most of the first five years of his life. He opened his eyes again to see that the sun had gone down outside his baby bedroom's window. The lilac urn was still sitting on the floor next to the bright blue image of a swallow landing on a twig, but Landers was gone. The swallow sort of reminded him of the humming bird back on the rug in his therapists soothing office.

He elected to try to sit up, only to find that at the sensation of moving, he was filled with vertigo and a euphoria that put him back down onto his back. Hatred for the sensation flushed over him. Hatred for the control that it had over his body. Hatred for what he'd seen it do to his mother. Hatred for what he knew it could do to him. And hatred that it seemed to be winning him over. How could he fight it without hatred?

The hate dribbled away like rain down a drain pipe and was replaced by a worry that he might throw up again. He turned over and reached out to where he thought the sauce pan must be, but instead his hand bumped into his mother's urn and knocked it over. It was sealed shut, but as his hand clacked against the pottery, and as he watched it roll heavily onto its side, it finally occurred to him, that it was really there and not some mental apparition.

His stomach lurched and he lay dry heaving into his mother's dresses for a minute. It wasn't so much that he was worried, simply that he was following his own mind's foggy train of thought. If the urn was really in this room and wasn't a dream then…

He reached his hand into his pocket only to find that he had no pocket to reach into. He looked down to see that he was dressed only in his boxers and socks. His blazer was gone, as were his pants and his shoes and his shirt.

He closed his eyes and much to his own surprise, he started giggling. Laughing. Something about this seemed tremendously funny. Like how embarrassed one feels in their dreams when they look down to see that they're giving their school report naked. You could run screaming from the room, or you could take the opportunity to find some humor in it. It didn't make any sense really, because Philippe's situation was not anything like that.

He gazed silently at his mother's urn once the laughing had subsided. Maybe if he looked into her lilac colored soul long enough it would give him the answers. He could see his reflection along one of the glossy tulip petals. He looked purple. Purple eyes, purple hair, purple pupils. His face was dressed in his mother's color. Then of course, in his reflection of his mother, the answer finally came to him. He opened his mouth and spoke to himself, to his reflection, the first words he'd spoken in hours.

"I have to get out of here."

Chapter 23. Sweet Resignation

Somewhere in the background of his groggy drugged out state he thought he could hear Landers's voice. It wasn't speaking to him though. It was talking to someone else but he couldn't hear the someone else it was speaking to, nor could he make out the words that were being spoken. He had to get up. He had to stand up and get out of this armoire and out of this building.

He was wrestling for the urge to do so but the only thing he could cling to was his knowledge. He didn't want to leave. All he wanted to do was keep laying on the armoire floor and fuck whatever happened to him as long as he could keep this feeling that he was having. That was everything that his body told him but at least his mind knew better.

His mind knew just how much danger he was really in. His mind could extrapolate that if his pants were gone and his mother's urn was sitting there in the room then chances were that he wasn't going to have any hope of driving his car away from this place or using his phone to call for help. His mind was keenly aware of the fact that he'd been robbed, he'd been drugged, and only worse was likely to happen after that.

But his body didn't care about any of that. No, he had to use the knowledge of his situation for the sake of knowledge only. He couldn't use the power of fear. He wasn't scared of what would happen to him, he only knew that technically… it would be bad. He knew that if he were sober, he'd be terrified.

So he rolled over onto his belly and slowly started trying to make his body do what his mind told it to do. He rose himself up onto his hands and knees and promptly collapsed, tumbling out onto the floor of bedroom next to the urn. He lay breathing for a moment, staring up at the ceiling, his feet still propped up into the armoire. He turned his head and saw the blind face of that old musty stuffed bear, having fallen out next to him. Blind and button-less. He turned away from it and tried to get his hands to grasp onto the container that held his mother's ashes. He didn't want to leave that here if he could help it. The blind bear could stay. He managed to get his hands around it and wrapped it up in his arms against his chest.

His eyes reached across the room towards the darkened window. That was going to be his first destination if he could go that way. But between him and the window, he saw one of his pant legs dangling off the edge of the bed. So he decided to aim for that first.

Slowly he crawled to the edge of the bed and propped his back up against it. He had a momentary lapse into the throws of sensation but he felt sure that it was starting to wear off. He reached his hand over his shoulder and pulled his pants down on top of him. First things first, he checked the pockets. Predictably, the pockets were empty. No phone, no keys, no wallet. He wondered what Landers had done with his shoes and blazer… and his car.

He tipped his head back to look over the edge of the bed to

see if there was anything on top of it. It smelled like cobwebs and mildew. There was his wallet lying open on top of the musty disorganized sheets. He had no reason to believe that there was any cash still in it, but it was a nice wallet, so he reached his arm over the bed and grabbed it. Free of cash as expected. Landers had been kind enough to leave Philippe's photo ID, though it had obviously been studied. His bank card was gone also, but that was the least of his worries. He slipped the wallet into his pants but decided not to take the time to try to put them on, he was sure he heard footsteps coming down the hall.

He tossed the pants over his shoulder and grabbed hold of his mother's ashes and pushing himself up on the bed, he made it to his feet. He took the four steps to the window and braced himself against the sill. He felt around the bottom of the glass looking for a latch to open it but soon realized that these windows were painted shut. Besides which, the tree outside wasn't anywhere near to the window, and it was a two story drop to the ground with no ledge. "Shit." He whimpered loudly. It was definitely wearing off. The fear was starting to creep in.

Just then the footsteps closed in and the bedroom door was pushed open.

"Philippe," Landers voice sounded quizzical. "What are you doing?"

"Landers." Philippe leaned his forehead against the window shaped blockade.

"Hey. You remembered my name. Wow. That's really cool."

Philippe had moved maybe ten feet from the armoire to the window, but he was breathing as if he'd been running a mile.

"Landers." Philippe smiled and chuckled over his shoulder at his childhood role model. "Landers I gotta… I gotta go." Out of the corner of his eye he could see Landers shake his head and smile. The bum was wearing his baby blue blazer.

"I don't think so kiddo." The urn slipped from Philippe's loose wavering grip and fell with a dull thud to the ugly carpeted floor. His eyes looked down at it and he tried to keep his weak knees from buckling lest he follow the urn's example. "You don't really look like you're in any condition to go anywhere. You should rest and sleep it off."

"My friends will know I'm gone Landers." He rested his cheek against the window and turned his body enough to look at the man more fully. To his distress, Landers was holding up Philippe's rose gold colored cell phone.

"Your friend Aimee thinks you're doing just fine." Landers slipped the phone into his grungy pocket, and cocked his head to one side. Philippe had nothing to say to that. He took a deep breath and looked longingly down to the filthy Parisian sidewalk below. He resigned himself to his situation here. This was how things were going to be until he found a chance to get out of here. Fighting that fact would only make things worse. Waiting for the right moment was what brought hope, and hope was something Philippe often had in abundance.

Landers walked over and took Philippe gently, but with

conviction by the arm. Philippe turned to look at him and smiled.
Sweet resignation. Sometimes giving up on having any control
brought a sense of peace. He'd had so very little of it. Why expect any
now?

"That a boy."

Chapter 24. Dirty Little Thief

Philippe's eyelashes fluttered open. His body had had just about enough of sleeping but he couldn't seem to stop dozing off. His arm was sore but for now the pain felt more like a caress or a massage. A dull aching pressure. Sooner or later his body wouldn't be able to function without the stuff, and then he would have a reason to stay rather than a reason to go. The two would be one in the same.

He was laying on the bed and was almost certain that he'd felt something creeping through the covers earlier but at the moment, that thought wasn't bothering him. He had the time, and yet time was utterly of the essence. So he closed his eyes and tried to think of a way out of this place. He found that his mind took him back some ten years ago to a time when all he wanted was to fit in at school. Not that much had changed since then aside from his methods.

"Nice Jacket Philippe. Where did you get it?" Aimee had said, eleven years old with a highly freckled nose. Freckles that no amount of foundation and powder could cover.

"Abercrombie. I'm glad you like it." He'd answered as if it were the truth. He hadn't been a half bad liar back then. It was a skill he'd since tried to unlearn with marginal success.

"Did you get an extra-extra small to try to find one that fit? It looks a little baggy in the arms." He remembered how she giggled and reached over and poked the edge of his sleeve that was a little too long for him. But Philippe had played it off as funny rather than suspicious. He'd just smiled with a pleasant chuckle and then returned his gaze back down to his salad. Not that he'd eaten much of it so much as picked at it.

"But who gave it to you?" He'd looked back up at his friend. She had always seemed to be able to see right through him. That's what would make her a good journalist. The ability to see the truth.

"Um… no one."

"But then… How did you get it?"

At least now he knew where the skill had come from. Years spent hiding in an armoire in a brothel full of threatening situations had taught him things. Not least of which was how to stay hidden. He knew how to hide. He knew how to be quiet. He knew how to sneak. And he knew how to steal what he needed. Or more often, what he wanted.

He opened his eyes again and gazed up at the dark cracked ceiling. It wasn't just the one jacket that he'd stolen. He'd stolen shoes, hats, pants and wallets right out of people's pockets. He hated that part of himself. The dirty little lying thief in the night. He could imagine where that would have led him if he'd followed that road to its end. But now he needed to call to that inner thief. He needed that thief to steal him away from here. But it had been a long time, and he wasn't sure that he would remember how.

Chapter 25. Escape

Thud.

He landed hard on the floor next to the bed. His head hit the corner on his way down and knocked the lamp off the bedside table with a crash. Not the best start. But as if something else were for a moment taking over his dazed and bruised body, he heard two sets of voices and footsteps coming down the hall, and felt himself roll under the bed.

He heard the door swing open. They didn't turn the handle when they came in. That meant that it hadn't been shut all the way when they'd left. That meant, if they remembered that it hadn't been shut that is, that they could potentially assume that he had escaped the bedroom without making the sound of an opening door, and therefore they might not think to check beneath the bed, and would instead make haste to the nearest exit.

"Where is-s he l-Landers?"

"Shit. Where'd he go?" He vaguely saw one set of feet kick for a moment at the broken lamp. It wasn't Landers. This was the one with the stutter. He heard Landers then, as he flung open the armoire door, perhaps assuming that Philippe would be there like he had been as a child.

"Oh little Philippe my boy!" He called loud enough that it could have been heard quite a ways down the hall. That must have meant that Lander's didn't necessarily assume that Philippe was in this room, now that he'd found the armoire empty.

As one set of feet began to hurriedly follow the other pair, Philippe felt a third set of feet scuttle over his arm. But there were probably at least four feet on this thing. Each tiny foot covered in tiny claws that felt like tiny needles on his skin. Philippe bit his lip and tried to hold as still as he could. He felt a little whiskered nose sniffing at his hand. He heard the men take a few quick steps towards the door. He could barely see from beneath the sheets hanging down from the mattress, as the pairs of shoes stepped over the threshold. But Landers's feet wore shoes that were polished. In fact, Landers was wearing Philippe's shoes.

He felt a harsh pinch as the four legged one sank it bubonic teeth into Philippe's finger just to see what it tasted like. Air hissed through Philippe's nose and he yanked his hand away from the creature and held his bloody finger tightly over his face to keep his breathing quiet. Luckily, by the time he'd done this, the feet were already halfway down the hall. He hoped that his finger wasn't infected or plagued but he shoved that worry aside to replace it with a more imminent one.

He pulled himself out from under the bed. His breath was held. He didn't trust his own vocal chords. The rat scurried from under the mattress over to the armoire and disappeared beneath it. Philippe's childhood home had become the home of rats instead. Not that it had been much better when he'd lived there. It had still been the home of rats. Those rats just had less fur.

On hands and knees he crawled, not towards the door, but towards the window. Though he felt keenly that time was of the essence, he also saw clearly that the vision in his right eye was blurry and red and he felt that his balance had much to be desired. Probably from his fall against the bedside table.

His hand wrapped around his mother's urn. She was going with him. He refused to let her be left in this place again. His pants were lying on the floor next to the urn and he took a moment to deliberate whether or not to put them on. It was a moment that he regretted wasting. Especially on top of the moment that he decided to take struggling with gravity and vertigo to get the jeans onto his legs. But eventually he found himself, pants on, shirt gone, holding his mother's incinerated corpse, and leaning against the door frame to the room, listening hard for those that he must evade.

He could hear his name being called with Lander's voice somewhere below him. He remembered that the stairs he had come up were to his right. So that was the way to go if he wanted to go out the way he came in. He looked down the hall to his left and saw a boarded up window at the end of the hallway and another room across the hall.

Suddenly he heard quick steps trotting up the stairs and thought 'sometimes you have to go backwards in order to go forwards.' He quickly hid himself in his childhood armoire. Wondering where the rat was, he huddled down, and waited to hear what the feet would do.

As he'd expected, someone had thought that perhaps they should have checked that last room down the hall. He heard the feet run past his mother's old bedroom door and he waited. He waited to hear the feet again. He smelled the must and mold of the moth ridden clothing and felt his stomach lurch a little. He remembered the other times that he'd waited for the sound of footsteps.

Waited for his mother to return and for the sound of men leaving. Waited for someone to come and find him. Waited. He'd waited for security guards to walk by. Waited for flight attendant's tapping heels. Waited for Veronica's sure and authoritative step. So many feet had he waited for. So many strides could he recognize just by their sound.

The feet walked hurriedly back through the hallway. They were Lander's steps. Philippe would recognize the sound of his own shoes anywhere. But there was one truth about all this walking, and that was the fact that the back room, was now a safe one. Safe enough anyway. It was the wrong direction, but sometimes you have to go back, in order to go forward. Perhaps the window in there would be better than the window in here.

He lifted himself up, hugging the wall with his left shoulder to keep himself from keeling over. He hoped that their hearing wasn't as good as his was, but he was walking in his socks, so that gave him an edge. He made his way to the back room and left the door ajar. It was a room not too different from his mother's, but this one looked a little more lived in. Or rather, stashed in. The bed didn't look like a place to sleep so much as a place to store one's stuff. Philippe hadn't expected Landers to have stuff to store, but when he thought about it, it made some sense.

On the bed was a broken and dismantled television, VCR, DVD player and a few other assorted old electronics. There was a stack of worn looking leather coats, and shoes that all had a hole or two in them. There was one large backpack that appeared to be currently empty and a bunch of wrappers from various nonperishable grocery items.

All these things were on the bed which had been shoved all the way to one side of the room. On the other side of the room was a desk with a scale, a cutting board, and a razor that had all been set up just so.

Philippe made a beeline for the window and pushed back the heavy curtains. The window was boarded up, but a bit of the wood had been cut away. Probably so that Landers could see the street. Philippe let his head thud against the splintery wood. He recognized that street. It was the one he'd parked his car on. His car wasn't there. He'd expected that. But seeing her absence put a sudden gap in his heart. He looked above the buildings and saw that the sun was setting. How long had he been here?

He was wasting time. He would mourn his loss after he gained his freedom. He walked over to the desk and opened the top drawer. Inside, there was a small stack of cash, and the drug stash. He stared at the bag of powder in the drawer and the small pile of needles resting next to it. He was startled out of his thoughts by the sound of his name being yelled more frantically than before. He grabbed the cash, the bag and a couple needles, and shoved them all into his pocket. He pushed the drawer closed, and picked up the razor blade from atop of cutting board.

He'd never had to cut anyone before. He'd managed to avoid violence. Any violence that had ever been inflicted on him were things that he knew were passing. They would end. All he had to do was put up with it for a bit, then get in his car and drive away. But that wasn't the case now. He had no car and he had no intentions of being stuck here forever.

The dizziness was starting to fade and his head was starting to clear. He made his way back out into the hallway and towards the stairs. He could hear doors being slammed and things being rummaged through. One of them would surely check outside in the nearby streets, and if he knew addicts at all, Landers would likely be heading up the stairs soon to check on his stash again. Because you never know what could happen when you have a thief loose in the night.

Just as Philippe was cringing at the squeak that the first stair made when he stepped down, he heard Landers running towards the stairs as expected. Philippe turned against the wall into the nearest room. This one also looked much like his mother's but it was empty of everything but the bare mattress, and it had no windows. He heard Landers run up the stairs and fly past the door that Philippe had cracked open. He could see the old bum wearing his nice blue blazer and already scuffed shoes as he passed. But Philippe let go of that when he heard the door of the room at the end of the hall bang open and he knew that hell was about to get a lot hotter.

Back to the stairs, he skipped the first step so as not to cause any squeaking. But that meant very little very soon when he heard "Philippe!! You little CUNT!!" and decided to pick up the speed rather than the quiet. Unfortunately, the combination of the transition from quiet to quick while skipping a step, wearing socks, and over estimating his recovery from the vertigo, was not the best mixture.

In mid slide he had options, given that there were two rails to cling to. He could drop his mother's urn and hope it survived the fall, while grabbing the rail and keeping his weapon. Or he could drop the razor blade, cling to the other rail, and keep his mother's urn intact. The third option of course was to brace himself and hope things simply fell well. The possibility of unconsciousness, bruising, internal bleeding and likely cutting himself to ribbons on the way down didn't seem very appealing. So with a click click click and a rattle on the broken tile, the razor blade landed at the bottom of the steps.

He heard a snap in his ankle as he clung to the rail, knocking his head against the wall and thudding a few steps down the stairs. He nearly lost his mother's urn anyway but was barely able to keep a hold of it. He instantly heard pounding coming down the hallway and before he knew it, he remembered another side of the Landers that he'd known as a child. The angry side.

Moving a little too quickly, Landers dropped down a few steps towards Philippe and reached out to grab a handful of his hair in rage. Philippe dropped his head towards the stairs, effectively dodging the bum's hand and taking advantage of the small moment of less that optimal balance Landers had, he reached out his foot and pushed him in the side of the torso. As Landers fell towards the hard wooden stairs, he reached out and grabbed Philippe's foot. He heard another loud pop as the force of Lander's weight pulling on his foot exacerbated whatever other damage had already been done to it. But with his elbow he managed to keep his hold on the rail and he watched as with a crash and a crunch, Lander's landed on the floor below, still holding Philippe's dirty sock.

He felt like he was hyperventilating as he gazed down with horror at the unmoving form of his first father. He swallowed hard. Was he dead? Had Philippe killed him? No. That wasn't possible. Philippe wasn't a killer. Sweet innocent little Philippe. It was simply an impossibility of the universe. He shook his head and hung there against the handrail. But then he heard a door somewhere else rattle gently, open and shut, and he remembered that this wasn't over yet. He would have to contemplate his guilt later.

"He-he's not out there Landers." Said the other voice. Philippe held his exasperated breath.

From around the corner came the stuttering man. As soon as he saw Landers he rushed over and knelt down to feel if there was a pulse in his neck. He had a short, bleach blonde, un-styled Mohawk that had begun to grow out around the edges. He wore a black tank top and a denim vest. He had washed out jeans and the sneakers that Philippe had seen from beneath the bed. There were tattoos climbing just past the collar of his shirt, and others wrapping down the side of his arm.

Without taking his hand away from Lander's neck, his head turned somewhat abruptly and he looked up at the stairs and then at Philippe. He had a large overemphasized silver crucifix dangling from his neck that thudded gently against his chest when he turned.

He didn't say anything, he didn't move. Philippe could hear the proverbial time bomb ticking in the background. Who would make the first move? Was Philippe going to have to lunge for it? Would the man notice the razor blade between his feet? It seemed that the stranger might have been thinking the same thing he was. Was this going to be a fight?

Philippe scooted his still socked good foot underneath himself so that he could stop hanging on the rail. Slowly and tentatively he raised himself to standing but winced when he tried to put weight on his other foot. He was pretty sure it was broken. Or at least something in it was dislocated, but the adrenaline was enough to walk a little.

Leaning heavily on the handrail, Philippe hugged his mother's urn to his chest, and slowly but surely took a painful step down the stairs. He didn't take his eyes off of the stranger as he inched his way towards him and Landers's still, unmoving body.

Just past the man's head the edge of a kitchen counter began to make its way into Philippe's range of vision. He glanced up at the counter for just a second and saw that his cell phone was resting there on its edge. He wanted that. When his eyes had flashed back down to the stranger, the man hadn't moved except that his fingertips were no longer resting on Landers's neck. Though he looked like maybe his back was a little straighter. He looked a little more ready to pounce on Philippe once he got close enough.

Philippe halted his descent and eyed the man suspiciously. Then again, Philippe was rather crippled here. If that man wanted to attack him, it wouldn't be that hard. He hardly needed to wait for Philippe to get close enough.

"Let me go." Philippe whispered and felt his breath seep slowly from his lungs. The man just nodded slowly and kept his eyes fixed on him. Philippe took another step and winced as he put as little weight as possible just on the tips of his toes.

Landers's feet, still wearing Philippe's shoes were propped up on the bottom step where they'd landed when he fell. Philippe carefully skirted past his feet. Landers could keep those shoes. As soon as he'd cleared the bottom step, he hurriedly hobbled and half collapsed against the counter. He quickly snatched up his phone and shoved it into his pocket. His lifeline. As long as he had that, he was okay.

He turned his head towards the stranger. He was really going to let him just walk out? The man was still watching him with a steady gaze. Philippe felt like the tension was so tight that it could easily snap at the smallest misstep. He didn't move. His eyes dropped from the stranger's face down to the face of Landers. He wanted to ask if he was still alive. But at the same time, he was too afraid to hear the answer 'no'.

"F-f-forgiveness." Philippe's eyes shot back up to the man's face. He'd broken the silence. "f-forgive him. Go. D-don't call the c-cops." His stuttering didn't seem to be out of fear. It was probably a constant speech impediment. His gaze was steady and stern. This was the second time that a stranger had asked him to forgive someone.

Philippe had a lot of questions that he felt this man could answer. But he found that he was too afraid to take the time to ask them. Not in this place. Philippe nodded. With his bad foot hobbling on the tips of his toes, he slowly made his way around the counter to move past the man. He was two feet from him, then one, then his knee was only an inch from the man's face as he made his way by. His eyes still keeping a close watch on Philippe.

Philippe looked down at him as he passed and he saw that the man was clutching the razor blade tight between his fingers. Just in case. That man obviously had no problem with getting into a scrape if things went that way. But Philippe was a lover, not a fighter. He wanted to get out of here, so that he could go back to being that way.

He rounded the corner, the man's face finally passed out of sight. There was the door, at the end of the hallway. He teetered and tottered slowly closer to it. He passed the living room with the window that he'd come in by. Despite the pain and the problems that it was causing for his foot, he picked up his pace as he got closer to the door. He practically fell into it and as his hand wrapped around the door handle, he felt a sort of sob, or a relieved exasperated whimper escape his lips. He turned the handle, and walked out into the cold twilight.

Chapter 26. Worthless

He shoved the heroin bag into the soil of the nearest potted plant when he heard the sirens outside. Maybe the man had called an ambulance, and Landers was still alive. Or maybe the sirens were for someone else and would drive right by. Philippe wasn't sure but in any case, he didn't feel like having drugs on him if they arrived before he could hobble away.

He winced his way around the block and saw the lights flashing across the building walls just as he rounded the corner. He pulled his phone out of his pocket, closed out of the text conversations with Aimee that he completely intended to read later, and dialed the number for a taxi service.

He gave them a cross street to meet him at nearby and then proceeded to that location to wait. As he stood on that corner, he looked down at himself. He couldn't think of a time when he'd looked worse. He smelled terrible, had only one sock on and his other foot was swollen like a bowling ball. Not to mention the throbbing on his head where he'd hit the bedside table. How bad did that look?

He wondered if taxi's ever turned people away. He wondered if they'd had worse in their back seats before. He told himself that they probably had and that he was just feeling insecure. True and understandable, but that realization didn't really make him feel any better.

He shivered a little in the cool air and wrapped his free hand over his bare chest. He thought his perspective was bad now, just wait until he saw a mirror. He felt that someone was watching him and he looked up to see what was obviously a street worker leaning against a lamp post staring at him. She was probably deliberating about whether or not he was going to leave or if she was going to have to find a new corner.

He smiled weakly at her.

"You look like shit." She said conversationally. He felt like shit.

"I'm on my way to a shower." He wondered what his mother's life had been like.

"Mmm hmm." He got the impression that she didn't believe him.

The taxi pulled up to the street corner and stopped along the sidewalk. The driver turned around and was obviously looking for someone else. Someone with more clothes on perhaps. Philippe hobbled over and struggled to open the door. He felt the awkward eyes of the prostitute and the taxi driver as he sat down in the back seat and wrestled his injured foot into the vehicle.

"Have a nice shower." Said the prostitute as he closed the door. He felt he should say something to her but he wasn't sure what to say. The door clicked shut and the driver looked back at him disbelievingly.

"You are the one who called?" Philippe nodded.

"Yes."

"Do you want me to take you to a hospital?" Philippe shook his head.

"No."

"You have cash?" Philippe nodded.

"Yes." He reached into his pocket and pulled out some of the cash that he'd stolen from Landers's stash.

"Then where shall I take you?"

He gave the driver Aimee's address. The taxi pulled out and began to drive. He watched as the streetlights went by his window rhythmically, hypnotically. But as he stared out the window, in a moment of horror, he realized that without New York, without his car, and without his mother, he was now homeless. He was slowly becoming his own worst nightmare. Worthless.

Chapter 27. Text Messages

Leaning heavily against the wall, Philippe limped to Aimee's apartment building. He buzzed her room, but there was no response. He buzzed again but the lack of response was the same. He checked the door handle, but it was predictably locked. She wasn't home. There were a few possible explanations. Maybe she was at someone else's house? Maybe she was out dancing? Maybe she was just working extra late. Though he wasn't sure why the café would be open so late. It was about closing time. This meant that it was also possible that she was just en route.

Once upon a time he'd had a key, but he had given that back to her before he'd left for New York over a year ago. He took a deep calming breath. The only thing to be done was to wait. So he turned his back to the pale stone wall and allowed himself to slide carefully down to the sidewalk, crossing an arm over his chest to shield himself from the evening air.

He looked at his bad foot. It was looking swollen, bruised, and purple. It occurred to him that he probably should have told the taxi driver to take him to the hospital. But more than a cast on his foot, he wanted a shower, he wanted a safe bed, and he wanted a friend. He would worry about his foot tomorrow. It hurt like hell, but some ice would probably help with that at least a little.

He spent some time sitting, and contemplating the kind of explanation that he would have to come up with if another tenant walked by and wanted to know why this bum was loitering outside the front door. He wouldn't blame them. He would tend to have the same reaction. But even if he told them the truth about why he was there, chances were that they wouldn't believe him. They would ask him to leave, or threaten to have him removed.

After several minutes of these humiliating thoughts, he recalled the cell phone in his pocket. He could just call her. He should have done that forever ago. He pulled the phone out of his pocket and swiped the simple password. It was just a square across his screen. He had never before been concerned about the privacy of his cell phone being invaded. He'd always assumed, if anyone was fishing through it, they were welcome to look at his 'secrets' because he didn't have any. He made a mental note to make his password more complicated.

He saw that he'd had seven missed calls from Aimee. At least one of those missed calls he remembered. But the other six must have happened while Landers had his phone. He opened up his text messages and saw that quite a few texts had been passed between her and Landers. He read.

3 missed calls.

"Aimee, what's up?"

"Hey Philippe, I've been trying to call you. Where you at?"

"Sorry, phone was silent."

"Oh ok. Np. Hey, so I did some research on that place that you said your mum is from."

"Oh?"

"Yeah. Turns out that place was shut down for human trafficking and busted for drugs as well."

"That's interesting."

"By the power of Google."

5 hours later.

1 missed call.

"Hey Philippe, would you give me a call when you get the chance?"

2 hours later

1 missed call.

"Philippe, if your mum was there, chances are that she was one of the people who were trafficked. That explains a lot of things, like why you didn't have a birth certificate until you started school. Your mum probably didn't even have citizenship."

"That makes sense."

"Yeah it does."

"You're the greatest."

1 missed call.

8 hours later.

"Philippe, did you decide to visit that address?"

"No."

"Are you thinking about it?"

4 hours later.

"Philippe what are you up to? You never responded to my

question. Would you want to talk about it over dinner? Where are you staying tonight?"

"I'm busy."

"Busy doing what? Are you looking for a job? ;)"

3 hours later.

"Yah."

"Oh… okay. Would you want to meet up sometime?"

"I'll send you a time and place when I have a free minute."

"Place? My place is fine. Hey, will you just call me? You went to that address didn't you? Don't lie."

2 hours later.

1 missed call.

If his phone was correct, then he'd only been there for about 24 hours, give or take a few. It felt like it had been days, but it had only been one.

Chapter 28. The Cleansing Process

"Philippe. Sweetheart." He felt gentle fingers run through his lank hair, deeply in need of a wash from the chemical contents of his night spent sweating. He slowly opened one eye. The other was squashed closed against the pavement outside Aimee's apartment building. He swallowed hard against the mucousy cotton in his mouth.

He turned his eye up to see Aimee bent over him with a very grave and concerned expression on her face.

"Hey, let's get you inside." She gently tried to help him into a sitting position.

"Aimee." He mumbled and wiped the drool away from his cheek that was numb from sleeping on the sidewalk. He realized that his eye still felt squashed and he wondered if he'd developed a black eye from knocking his head against that bedside table in the brothel.

"Shh. Philippe. First let's go inside and clean you up." With her pulling to help, Philippe tried to stand, but the adrenaline was long gone and he let out a horrified gasp of pain when he tried to put weight on his broken foot. He swore that he could feel the pieces grating together just under his skin.

"Oh ok. Ok. Arm over my shoulder, leaning on me. Good. Use the wall too Philippe, I'm not quite that strong." With clumsy awkward difficulty, Aimee bent down and picked up the lilac urn and then helped him through the apartment door and up a clunky old elevator. When they finally made it up to her apartment, she took him over to the edge of the loveseat and sat him down.

He watched as Aimee dumped her shoulder bag next to the love seat and set the urn gently down on the end table. She ran into the kitchen, and opened the freezer, pulling out a bag of frozen fruit and rushing it over to him. Then she knelt down on the floor in front of his swollen foot.

She tried to gently settle the clunky bag of strawberries against his ankle but frozen strawberries are anything but gentle. "Sorry." She said at his wince, not that he thought she had anything to apologize for. She got up to retrieve a hand towel. She wrapped the bag of fruit in the towel, and tried again but there was nothing that she could do to make it not painful.

Philippe took the bag from her and carefully lifted his leg up onto the cushion so that he could better get at it. It wasn't comfortable, but it was better. He settled the fruit onto his foot and looked up at his best childhood friend. "Thanks Aimee."

"Yeah. Of course hon." She paused and just looked at the sorry state of her friend for a moment. "I don't know how much it'll really help, but let me get you a pain killer."

She stood up and went into the restroom medicine cabinet. "I don't have anything really strong I'm afraid." He watched her from across the little apartment as she turned over bottles and read labels to see what all she had in there and then rushed to the kitchen for a glass. She filled a glass with cold water and tipped a couple of pills into her hand, then she decided to grab a wet washcloth as well. With the glass and the pills in one hand and the moist washcloth in the other, she walked slowly over to him and knelt down on her knees in front of him again.

He could smell the comforting smell of her shampoo and cheap perfume. The same as she'd always worn. It was inexpensive but a very nice scent. He could finally relax. He felt all of his muscles just release and cramps ease that he hadn't even known he was holding.

He smiled at his dear friend, "I'm disgusting." And he was. He knew it. He was filthy.

"Oh, just take this." She shook her head kindly at him and handed him the pills and the water. Dehydration, he supposed, was what made the water so sweet. He swallowed the pills and then sipped at the water slowly as Aimee moved to sit on the cushion next to him and started gently dabbing his bloodied face with the moist cloth.

"How bad is it?" He asked.

"I don't know Philippe. Do you think you have a concussion?" He just turned slightly to look at her with a smile. She looked focused and serious. Concern etched between her eyes as she cleaned his wound.

"I suppose," He began after a moment of quietly allowing his friend to nurse him, "That you'll want to know what happened." He smiled, tired but willing. "Like any good friend."

Aimee sighed. "I think I've managed to put a few things together myself. I'll see how right I am in the morning maybe. I don't think you should tell me anything until after you've rested up a bit and perhaps gotten your foot looked at. Unless you just want to talk that is. Then I'm all ears. Like any good friend." She glanced away from the blood on his head and smiled back at him, un-wrinkling the freckles on her nose just a little.

Philippe breathed a sigh of relief, "Maybe tomorrow then." He nodded gratefully. "Seriously though, I'm disgusting." he looked down at himself and theatrically scrunched his face in disgust.

"Well, I think you're going to have some trouble standing in the shower, or even walking over to it." She refolded the blood soiled cloth to find a cleaner side and then returned to cleaning his eyebrow.

"Well... that's true..." He'd been looking forward so much to a shower. He was sure there was a way to pull it off. He began working out a fantasy plan that involved Aimee needing to help him, which while somewhat humiliating, would mean that she would need to take her clothes off and get into the shower with him.

Aimee sighed, set the cloth aside and stood up, tucking her fingers into her back pockets. She walked to the middle of the room where she could get a pretty good view of the shower. She tapped her toe thoughtfully for a moment. "I guess you'll have to sit."

"Yeah, that's what I was thinking." It really was the most logical conclusion.

"Well alright. But tomorrow you have to go to the hospital Philippe."

He smiled comfortingly up at her. "I promise I will."

She nodded and walked in to turn on the shower and warm up

the water a bit. Then she came back to help Philippe out of his pants, which was painful, to help him from the loveseat, all the way across the apartment, which was slow and difficult, and into the shower, which was heavenly warm and cleansing.

After Aimee had left him, the door clicked shut and Philippe sat on the floor of the shower with his foot propped in an uncomfortable position. The world was out there and he was locked in a tiny room by himself with a hot shower. He'd set the bar of soap and bottles down on the floor where he could reach them. As he felt the comfort of the small warm space, too many things began to make sense in perspective. As he poured shampoo into his hand, he understood why he used to sleep in the closet in his mother's little apartment number 36. He understood why his favorite place to be had been squished in with too many blankets and stuffed animals, some of which he had stolen.

He washed himself more than once, and watched as the soap bubbles collected on the edge of the drain and slowly rinsed down with the hot water. His eyes stung as the flower smelling shampoo ran down his face and off the end of his nose but he didn't look up to rinse it away. He looked down at the bubbles draining and thought that the burning sensation mixed well with his tears. The edge on his eyelids took the edge out of his pain.

He had never minded crying in front of Aimee. But for some reason this time he found himself opening his mouth a little wider as he cried as he tried to let the air out a little more gradually, to make the sound a little more subtle. He tried to hide his tears in the stinging bubbles, and the burning in his sockets was a welcome distraction.

Finally he could find no excuse to wash himself another time. All the bubbles washed down the drain completely, and it seemed to him that the tears had washed down with them He found that a numbing calm seemed to come along with the forever hot water pounding down on his upper back and shoulders, so he sat there a little longer in the small warm space away from the world.

An involuntary deep breath filled his lungs and he felt that the rest of the cleaning process couldn't happen here. So he reached up and twisted the knob of the shower. He felt the leftover bits of water dripping from his nose, and the slow and gentle but ever growing chill of the real world as it seeped into the bathroom from the crack beneath the door.

He took another deep breath, and wiped what was either a last minute tear or a stray drop of water from his cheek. It instantly mixed with the rest of the wetness of his face as if they had always been one and the same. He pulled a towel up to his face, and dried it. His eyes were red from crying, or from soap exposure, but the stinging at least had finally washed away.

Using his good foot, he pushed himself up against the wall of the shower, and braced himself to turn towards the door. He could hear Aimee in the other room. It sounded like the clinking of earthenware plates. The one's she'd bought for herself when she first moved into the place. Her own house warming, a hurrah for autonomy.

He put his hand against the wall of the shower and balanced on his good foot while he clumsily dried those hard to reach places with his free hand.

"Aimee." He called, ashamed when he'd reached the limits of what he could do unassisted. The sound of her bustling in the other room had subsided and he decided that she must have stepped out of the kitchen. If he strained his ear a little he could hear her as she pushed a drawer closed over on the other side of the one bedroom apartment.

"Aimee." He called again. He'd never really had a lot of pride. He supposed that he'd never really had a life good enough to develop any, but it wasn't a hurt sense of pride that he felt, it was guilt. He didn't much like being in a position where he needed to be a burden to Aimee. She had her own drama to worry about without needing to spend her energy helping him get around. He thought to himself, that he really should have asked that taxi to take him to the doctor. Then at least he'd have crutches.

"Hi Philippe." Aimee's face popped around the edge of the door. "I know your legs are too long, but you can wear some of my sweats if you want." She procured a pair of pink sweats and tucked them over the towel bar. "And here's the biggest hoodie I had. Sorry for the lack of fashion sense." She tucked an old beige hoodie over the top of the sweats. Philippe recognized it as probably being something that belonged to an old boyfriend. Something that Aimee would never wear in public.

"Oh believe me dear, this is the best fashion I've worn all day."

Chapter 29. Roll Over

Aimee helped him out of the bathroom onto one of the tall chairs that sat in front of the marble topped kitchen bar counter which she used as a dining room table. On it, she'd set out two small plates and one larger platter which was covered in mostly baguette slices, olives and brie. In the center was a blue bowl which had been filled with a sorbet which she had probably made using the bag of frozen strawberries, perhaps mixed with a bit of yogurt. Aside each small plate was, not wine, but a champagne glass of cold sparkling water with a lemon wedge clinging to the brim.

Philippe looked at the food and remembered just how long it had been since he'd last eaten. He felt as though his stomach had been empty for so long that it had forgotten how to feel appropriately hungry for the morsels that were before him. He knew that he would not be able to eat much, but he knew that he should eat some.

Before he touched anything he turned to Aimee with a smile as she sat in the seat next to him. "This is lovely Aimee."

She smiled and picked up a slice of bread and a wedge of brie and set it on her plate. Instead of reaching for the food, Philippe reached towards his glass. His fingers seemed to waver as he reached and squeezed the lemon into the sparkling water. His grip was almost too loose to manage it. He lifted the glass to his lips took a small sip and felt the sour carbonation tickle his tongue. With great concentration, he managed to set the glass back down before his head collapsed onto his elbow like a pillow on top of the counter, his fingers still clutching the stem.

"Philippe?" He felt Aimee's hand touch his shoulder. "Hey." She shook his shoulder gently. He turned his head to show her that he was still conscious and smiled comfortingly.

"It's okay. I'm alright."

"Hey, maybe we should get you to the hospital tonight." He shook his head and pushed himself to sit up.

"No, I'd rather go in the morning if that's alright. I'm just light headed from low blood sugar." He smiled and kissed her fingers still resting on his shoulder. "It's because I need to eat something. Go figure." He winked at her and shakily spooned a small bite of sorbet into his mouth.

Aimee let out her breath and let her hand fall from his shoulder. She quietly watched him as he slowly nibbled. It felt a little awkward to have her just watching him eat but he supposed he couldn't blame her for worrying. Eventually she returned to her own food and they dined without much conversation.

Philippe ate two small slices of bread with cheese, one olive and about five spoonfuls of sorbet when all was said and done. He just couldn't seem to eat much more than that. His stomach didn't seem to have the space anymore. He supposed that his appetite would come back after a day or two of nibbling. That's just what happens when you don't eat for two days. But he drank all of the sparkling water, and felt that was an accomplishment.

After a short protest from Aimee about him being finished, he managed to talk her into just taking him to bed. Things would be better in the morning when he got a cast and crutches. He promised to have breakfast when he woke up, and rest was really what he thought he needed.

But when he was lying in bed, his eyes seemed to be glued open. He lay, wide awake on his back, imagining pictures in the texture of the popcorn ceiling above him. He listened to Aimee putting leftover brie and sorbet away and washing the dishes. He wondered if she was nervous to be around him. She'd said that she'd managed to put a bit of the story together herself and he wondered what conclusions she could have come up with. Her conversation with Landers had not been that detailed, but he knew that Aimee was the sort who could put a puzzle together with or without all the pieces.

He wanted to roll over onto his side to stop looking at the imaginary images on the ceiling but he didn't want to disturb his foot. Perhaps he couldn't sleep because he'd spent so much time in and out of consciousness at the brothel.

He furrowed his brow and turned his head to look at the ornate redwood chest of drawers that Aimee had had all her life. He didn't want to think about how it felt when he'd been drifting through different mental and physical states of being in the brothel. He didn't want to think about how he wouldn't mind feeling it again. Wouldn't mind feeling the sensation that had killed his mother. Her urn, he knew, was still sitting on the end table by the loveseat in the other room.

He decided, while looking at the beautiful, although dusty mirror that rested atop the chest of drawers, that along with going to the doctors, he should also call his car insurance and report his car stolen. Perhaps there was the off chance that it could be found. But he wondered if that would cause him to need to tell the police about what happened to him.

And why shouldn't he? He considered his hesitation. The stuttering man had asked him not to with a plea for forgiveness. Why had that man let him go? Why had Landers been trying to keep him in the first place? He'd already stolen his valuables. He wondered if Landers had intended on killing him. There likely wouldn't have been a huge investigation on Philippe's behalf. But Philippe felt somehow grateful to the man for his life. If Landers had intended on killing him, then he was lucky that the other man let him go. Then again, he felt somehow sure that those sirens had already been on there way to his rescue. He wondered if the stuttering man thought that Philippe had called them. It wasn't as if Philippe had promised him that he wouldn't. Why did he let him go?

Philippe heard the door creak open and saw Aimee coming into the room. The lights were off in the room behind her.

"Hey, you're still awake." She said quietly.

"Yeah." He smiled. "It's good just to rest though." She crawled into the bed next to him, careful not to disturb his foot. She settled in, and rested her cheek against his shoulder. He gently kissed the top of her head and let his chin rest against her hair. "Thanks for letting me stay here Aimee. I feel a little like a mooch right now and I know you have your own life to deal with without also needing to deal with mine."

"You're in a vulnerable spot right now Philippe. When everything you've had and have worked for just disappears to be replaced by some other life plan, it's good to have friends."

"Yes..." Philippe blinked at her bluntness. Was everything he worked for also gone? Or was her statement as much about herself as him. "That's true..." He agreed. She scooted her head back to look at his eyes.

"Sorry, I don't mean to be morbid."

"No no, it's not morbid, it's true." He shifted his shoulders to turn towards her just a little. He wanted to roll over so that his shoulders were square to hers but on account of his foot, he held back the urge. He found her hand next to his and held onto it. "I suppose both our lives are going to be changing quite a bit aren't they?" He hadn't actually given himself the chance to think about where his life would be headed after this. He'd found his lost memory, and at the same time, he'd lost everything else. That memory was hardly the climax of his existence. Right?

"I think I'm going to keep the baby." His mind emerged back from his own thoughts.

"What made you decide that?"

"I don't know. I guess maybe I just can't bring myself to do it."

"Well, if that's what you decide, then I'd like to be here to help you." He smiled at her. "So that you can go back to school and finish your degree." She didn't miss a beat.

"But what if you have to go back to New York?" His heart was saddened. A year really had been too long. "You have your own life to live Philippe." She was right. She had a point. He couldn't promise that his modeling career wouldn't pick up again. He couldn't promise that he would always be there. He couldn't promise that his life wouldn't take him far away again. She had no right to expect that of him, and she had no intentions of expecting that of him.

"I didn't go to New York for fashion you know." He swallowed hard past the lump in his throat. "I didn't go because I love the city either. I went for Veronica. I followed her there. Not for her fashion but for her." He took a deep shaky breath.

"I know Philippe." Aimee rested her palm against his cheek. "I know."

"I mean, I can't promise that there would never be someone I'd want to follow across the world again. But for fashion, Paris is the place to be." He thought about the possibility that he didn't have a drop of French blood in his veins. But he pushed that thought aside with a smile. "Besides, women like Veronica are only born once a millennia." Aimee used her thumb to wipe a tear from the brim of his eye.

"Then I guess we can be aimless together for a little while." He smiled and nodded at her,

"Yeah, alright. Deal." He put his forehead against hers and they just lay together in silence. It took him a minute to work up the courage, but eventually he decided to unlace his fingers from hers and gently touch his hand to her belly.

He looked at her and she didn't object. It was a bit awkward, but it was a boundary that needed to be breached if he was ever to come to terms with it. There was going to be a new person in the middle of it all, and her entire life was going to change. His entire friend was going to change.

He put his fingers under the edge of her shirt and ran his hand gently against her skin.

"How far along are you?" he gazed down at her belly, enthralled by the idea of there being another life there.

"I'm almost out of the first trimester." Still running his fingers against her belly he looked up to see her face. Her expression seemed tired, or perhaps melancholy.

"I'll stop drinking if you will." He smiled, half joking for if she laughed at him, half serious for if she took him up on it.

"Really?" She smiled but her smile became a sort of crack in her face and her voice choked against the tears coming up in her eyes all of a sudden.

"Yeah." He lifted his other hand up to her face. He hadn't expected such an emotional reaction to his little bargain. "Yes really Aimee."

"Okay." She said, and her agreeing to his little bargain seemed to open the flood gates and her strained smile turned into open mouthed sobbing. He took his hand away from her face and instead wrapped his arm around her. Again he wished that he could just roll over.

"Are you okay?" He asked as her crying settled a bit.

"Yeah." She said, running her sleeve over her eyes. "I'm sorry. I'm fine."

"Don't be sorry. I never am." He winked with a chuckle.

"That's true." She laughed. They were quiet again and their breathing returned to normal.

Aimee firmly pressed her hand on top of his, against her belly. "You know, part of me kind of wishes it was yours."

He caught his breath a little and looked down at her face. "Really? Why? Would you feel differently about it if it was?"

"I don't know. Maybe. At least I wouldn't have had to worry about you ditching it as soon as you heard it existed."

"Well, let's remember that I was all the way in New York at the time."

"Yeah, but you weren't ditching a baby when you did that." She sighed. "At least you would have loved it. At least you would have tried." He was thoughtful as he ran his fingers, laced with hers over the top of her womb.

He opened his mouth and closed his eyes and waited for the words to come out. He had to force them out, hoping that he wouldn't regret them after he said them. He hoped that no circumstance would later arise that would make these words the worst words he could possibly say. "You know," he began and took a deep breath to steady himself. "It could be mine." He opened his eyes to see her face.

Aimee lifted her head off his chest and looked at him with a raised eyebrow. "It's definitely not yours Philippe, we've already been over this."

"No no no, that's not what I mean." He took another deep breath. "I mean, I could sign the papers. I could say it's mine. Who would argue? The father?" He looked at her to see what her reaction was. She propped herself up on her elbow and stared at him for a long moment. He couldn't tell from her expression whether or not she favored the idea. After all, there was no guarantee that another Veronica wouldn't whisk him away someday. But even a temporary father was better than no father at all. Wasn't it?

Then she leaned over him, and started kissing him. She kissed him passionately. He wasn't sure if that was a yes, he wasn't sure that he wanted it to be a yes. But he kissed her back anyway. Several times he wished he could just roll over. Damn that broken foot. But he slept a peaceful dreamless sleep that night, free of haunting memories.

Chapter 30. Idle Hands

"Fighting crime, trying to save the world. Here they come just in time, The Powerpuff Girls!"

Philippe Sang loudly as he watched the French dubbed Powerpuff Girls fly into action upside down to take out the nefarious Mojo Jojo. His hair hung from his head just barely brushing against the faded out floral rug. One hand rested on his bare, underfed ribs, which were bowed backwards over the edge of the cushion. The other hand was reaching above his head, to the floor where a bowl of popcorn rested waiting. His broken foot, now wrapped in a clunky hot pink cast, thudded gently, though thoughtlessly against the wall just above the loveseat, and just below a large abstract painting of the lower half a woman's face.

He'd found a collection of old silly cartoons that he and Aimee used to watch together when they were younger. Littering the floor below the television screen were open cases that read things like, "My Little Pony", "Adventure Time", "SpongeBob Square pants", and "Invader Zim." Right now it was "The Powerpuff Girls." This was actually the third time he'd watched this episode. He'd watched it once in French for fun, once in English for authenticity, and then again in French to compare and giggle at the dubbing differences.

He chuckled to himself and tried to toss a piece of popcorn into his upside down mouth. It bounced off of the underside of his nostril and landed on the floor. He'd been working on this for quite a while with some success, but he groaned as he failed this time and reached to pick the piece of popcorn up off of the floor. As he arched his back to reach, the top of his head bumped against the rug and he settled his other hand on the floor for some stability. But just as he caught popcorn between his outstretched fingers, the weight became too lopsided, and he tumbled onto the floor.

After straightening himself out again, he sat with his back against the loveseat and his pink foot stretched out in front of him. He held the piece of popcorn up to his eye and glared at it as though it had betrayed him. Then squinted and aimed it in the general direction of the trash can. With little to no weight in a piece of popcorn, it fell short. It just wasn't very aerodynamic.

He looked up at the colorful tiny people on the screen. They're heads and eyes were abnormally large and he'd long ago noticed that Blossom, Bubbles, and Buttercup, were the only characters in the show who didn't have any fingers. Bubbles was his favorite. He felt that she most represented his sentiments towards life.

He picked up the pin striped fedora that had been lying on the floor and tipped his head back so that when he put the hat on, it nearly covered his eyes and his head would have to be tipped that far back in order to continue watching the screen. He smiled to himself and put another piece of popcorn into his mouth, without tossing it this time.

He sat there for a few minutes as the episode finished up and was mildly dismayed when he saw that it was the last episode. He stared at the silent title screen for a while, and then pushed the fedora back on his head so that he could see properly. He reached over to the arm of the loveseat to grab the remote that he had left there. Time for music. Jazz. Zaz, Je Veux.

He straightened out his electric blue tiger striped boxer briefs and then turned over to stand on his knees. He moved his head up and down to the tempo, and tipped his hat at no one. He reached for his crutches which were resting against the end table that his mother's urn still sat upon. He pushed himself up to standing and tucked the crutches under his arms. He tipped his hat again at his mother's urn, and then began to sing along with the music.

He looked pretty silly, but as there was no one there to watch, he didn't much care. He sang, and practiced some dance moves that involved lifting himself up with his crutches and balancing on them like stilts for his hands. He smiled at the urn and said,

"Now if I just learn how to juggle I'll be all set for the circus mum." He winked and picked up a few pieces of popcorn and tried to juggle them. When they turned out not to work so well for juggling either, he just tossed them into his mouth instead and caught them this time. One, two, three down the shoot, one after the other. "Ta da!" He said to the urn. "Fruit would work better for juggling. An apple, an orange and a plum. Or perhaps a pomegranate? Naw, that would probably be too heavy."

He turned away from the unresponsive urn and went back to dancing. He was actually a rather good dancer, he just needed to work out the best way to utilize the props. He popped his hips from side to side and generally did a good job of keeping his cast foot off the ground. Then he had a thought, and using one crutch for stability, he used the other crutch as a sort of movable stripper pole. He twisted his cast leg around it and generally started being a little more acrobatic than was probably advisable for someone with broken foot.

The song ended and he rested his elbow on the top of one of his crutches and patiently waited for the next song. He found himself staring at the door during what seemed to be an impossibly long moment before the next song came. The door was white but old. The whiteness was a little bit gray and there was a brownish area around the handle and along the edges where some of the old paint had worn away. Not to mention a scratch where the door often hit the coat hanger on the wall when it was opened.

When the next song finally started he smiled, and felt an instant sense of relief. He started dancing again but it took a little more effort to get into the rhythm so he gave up. He crutched his way over to the counter and picked up a raspberry from a bowl that he'd put out a couple of hours ago. His head was still bobbed up and down to the song.

As he sucked the juice from the small fruit he gazed nonchalantly at his mother's urn, and then gazed back at the door. By the time the juice was gone from his mouth, his finger was tapping rapidly against the countertop. He abruptly stopped tapping and looked back at his mother's urn, and then started biting his thumbnail. His head still moved to the tempo.

He stopped biting his nail and reached over towards the urn and picked up his cell phone which was laying on the corner next to it. He lifted it a little above him, tilted his hat to the side and smiled. With the artificial camera click of his phone, he took a selfie. Then started flipping through all of the many other ridiculous past selfies that he'd taken.

He smiled at a few of them, then happened upon a few that he'd taken of Veronica. He was amazed that she had allowed anyone other than a professional photographer to take pictures of her. He looked up away from his phone when he heard the click click sounds of his fingernails being clipped away by his teeth again. He lowered his phone and looked at his mother's urn. Then he looked again at the door, and decided to get dressed.

Chapter 31. Scavenger Hunt

2320 Rue Veron. Philippe hated the fact that he found himself standing in front of that building again. But at least this time, he had no intentions of entering. No matter how curious he was about whether or not Landers was still in that building, alive or dead, he would not enter. It was enough of as risk just being here.

He plunged his hand into the potting soil of the plant just outside the door that he'd fled from, but he felt suddenly terrified and at the same time relieved when he found that the stash of powder that he'd left there was gone. But just as he was about to give up and return to wallowing in Aimee's apartment, his finger grasped around something that felt like stiff paper.

Slowly he pulled what looked like a small scroll out of the soil. It was made of brown thick parchment and rolled up with a red ribbon wrapped around the outside. He quickly used his crutches to take several steps back from the potted plant and the door that it stood outside of. He glared at the door as if someone might emerge from it and nab him.

He quickly glanced up the cold cobblestone street and then down it. Then, more paranoid than ever, he squinted to look up at the boarded up window that he was sure went to Landers's room. He wondered if anyone was watching him. He wondered if this scroll was actually intended for him or if he had just had the misfortune of shoving his stash into a place that someone else was already using as a stash point.

He looked down at the scroll. The edges of the parchment were artistically and intentionally frayed and he wondered if it had been home dyed that tea color, or purchased that way. Whoever had made it had done so with care. Along with the ribbon, they had even gone through the trouble of sealing it with a red wax seal that had the letters SP stamped into it. He looked up at the accursed building that he'd been born in. He wanted to open the scroll. The curiosity was killing him, but he wasn't comfortable opening it here.

A cold autumn wind blew down through the old street and he reached up to tighten his scarf around his neck. He resolved to keep the scroll, and tucked it into his coat pocket. He then gripped his crutches, and swiftly left the sight of that building to a place more populated.

A busy shopping street was safer than an empty alley, as far as he was concerned. So he found a place to stand where people were constantly moving past him. After that, he withdrew the scroll, and broke the seal. Inside, he was somewhat surprised to find, was a poem.

I saw your face, so big and so bright.
I saw your face, so full of life.
Everything glows and tingles with fun.
Everything's better, when you're chasing the dragon.

I thought I saw you, and then you were gone.

High in the sky, so far you'd flown.

At first he held you, tight in his claws.

Then down you fell, from the dragon's jaws.

The ground may be hard, when at first you fall.

But it becomes softer, when you're under it all.

The dragon may lift you up to higher places.

But whenever he drops you, you must climb higher to chase him.

Because you go deeper, through the soil you went.

Climb up through the earth until you break through the pavement.

But then climb still higher, for the dragon he flies.

His wings stretch out wide, his breath fills the skies.

For him you must climb, for him you must soar.

For him not the highest, but higher than before.

You'd need a blimp, or maybe a jet.

You'd need a rocket ship to the moon, and yet,

A height made by man, for man is his limit,

A high sturdy building, the dragon may be in it.

So follow him up a tower, chase him with a helicopter,

Or maybe, all you need to reach him, is a very long elevator.

He read the poem once, and then he read it again. At first the poem seemed simply to be philosophical. It seemed to talk about how the body builds up a tolerance to drugs. You need more than you did the first time. "In the soil" suggested that it takes more effort each time just to get above ground, so to speak, or back to normal. But if you're "chasing the dragon" then you have to go even farther than normal to reach it. But each time you come down from the high, you go even deeper into "the soil." Yet, at the same time, soil is softer than a sidewalk. Just a compounding problem. The fact that it "becomes softer when you're under it all" perhaps suggested that you just get used to it after a while.

That all made sense to him. What didn't make sense was that, if the poem were purely a philosophical thought process, then the elevator bit would be a poor ending. He tried the idea that the elevator suggested that you didn't actually have to go that far to get the high you were looking for, but that just didn't seem to sit right. Not of course, unless the writer was trying to sell the drug. What if the last four lines, were more like directions. Or a riddle.

"A high sturdy building, the dragon may be in it." Not very clear directions if the writer was trying to suggest specifics. "All you need to reach him, is a very long elevator." There were countless tall buildings with elevators in Paris. That fact alone suggested that they were simply doing a poor job making some sort of philosophical point.

Philippe shook his head and sighed. He rolled up the scroll and tied the ribbon around it. He looked up as he moved to tuck the scroll in his pocket and call it a day when the answer to it all shone right in front of him. It was a poster on a wall advertising a local theater play. On the poster was an artistic sketch of the only building that would need no direction more specific than 'long elevator,' the most iconic building in the city if not the world. The Eiffel Tower.

A wiser man, he knew, would go home now. He'd accomplished so much in the last couple of days. He'd gone to the doctor and gotten a cast. His black eye was almost gone. He'd gotten his clothes out of his mother's apartment and gone through the steps to close out her lease. He'd moved everything to Aimee's place for now. He'd even managed to report his car stolen in hopes that it would be found, and he'd somehow done that without disclosing anything about the twenty-four hours that he'd spent being drugged by an ex-pimp. Surely getting his life back in order was worth more than this.

The need to physically, with his feet, "chase the dragon" seemed a little bit on the nose in its symbolism, but Philippe knew that he was curious like a cat, and he prayed that satisfaction would indeed bring him back because if it didn't, then he knew he was about to make an idiotic mistake. But in all truth, it wasn't the drugs at the end of the scavenger hunt that pulled him, it was the poetry.

Chapter 32. Accordions and Cellos

Philippe stood at the foot of the Eiffel Tower looking up at its brilliance as the sun set and the first of the hourly lights played up and down the stretch of it. He'd been up it before. More than once naturally. It was a beauty that he both romanticized, in its architecture and history, as well as took for granted. It was a thing for him to snobbishly brag about to foreigners but he didn't feel nearly enough love for it as he felt he ought to. He chalked that entirely up to the fact that he'd grown up looking at it. A masterpiece that was hardly worth noticing.

He contemplated the idea that his goal could be hidden somewhere around the foot of it, but he set that idea aside rather quickly. What was the use of mentioning an elevator in the poem if he wasn't intended to use it? And he would certainly need to use it. The stairs were cheaper to walk up but he didn't want to try to walk up all those steps with crutches.

As he pondered this, he glanced over at a street singing duet. A man and a woman, both wearing intentionally somewhat ruddy looking, wide brimmed hats. The woman was playing an accordion and the man held the neck of a beautifully polished cello against his chest. The open cello case lay at their feet. The woman was singing the majority of the vocals and tapping her foot in as much of a dance as she could swing while playing her instrument.

They were playing their own modified version of La Vie En Rose with a little more beat to it. Perfect for a touristy evening, with foreigners crowding to the foot of the Eiffel tower, hoping to climb to the top to see all of Paris's, night lights twinkling down below.

The duet noticed that they had an admirer and smiled at him. As much to be friendly as to encourage him to leave a donation. He smiled back. The truth was that he would much rather give his few pennies to them rather than to use it to board the overpriced elevator ride. Or spend it on whatever he hoped to find at the top.

The woman nodded her head as if to ask him to come over to them. She didn't cease her lovely singing though. Philippe sighed at his own weak will and glided on his crutches over to them.

"You're lovely." he said, and smiled. He tilted his head to the side and reached his hand into his back pocket to pull out a Euro.

"Thank you." Said the woman, breaking out of her lyrics into instrumentals. "You've been looking up." She gestured her eyes towards the tower.

"Yes." Philippe smiled at her astuteness. "I have to go up."

She shook her head and closed her eyes. He couldn't tell whether she was shaking her head at him or just swaying to the tune. "Only the staff has to go up. You have a choice." She chuckled lightly.

Philippe chuckled along with her at the polite working humor. "Actually, I'm on a sort of scavenger hunt. So I suppose I choose it."

He shrugged and smiled as if people often went on scavenger hunts by themselves to the top of the Eiffel Tower.

She nodded and smiled, then nudged the leg of her companion with her boot. He had fallen into a deep romantic, brow furrowed passion, with the thrum of the strings of his cello. Broken from his reverie, he looked up to his companion.

Her foot returned to its tapping and she nodded her head towards Philippe. He glanced at Philippe and the woman just slowly nodded her head. She closed her eyes, and continued to nod and smile and sway to her music. The man regretfully ceased the movement of his fingers against the cello strings and reached into his pocket. He looked from side to side and then reached something out towards Philippe.

Philippe, rather surprised by this, reached out and took into his hand what he was even more surprised to see, was a ticket to the top of the Eiffel Tower. Philippe looked up disbelievingly at the man and raised his eyebrows. The cello player scratched his stubbly handsome chin and smiled affirmingly. "Say hello to the prophet for us."

"The prophet?" They both just nodded and smiled and returned, quite pointedly to their music and entered into a duet that required both of their vocals. Philippe stood there a little longer, in part because he was too confused to move and in part because he was being utterly blown away by the man's baritone.

When he'd come to his senses again, he decided to do what he'd wanted to do when he first saw them. He opened his wallet, and emptied it into the cello case.

Chapter 33. Clair Eiffel

When he first set foot off the elevator, he had a moment where he felt strangely self-conscious about his crutches. Something about them seemed to supremely exude an extreme lack of class. He'd only been here with foreign friends as a way to give them the grand tour as if he himself personally owned all of Paris.

He walked over to the edge and gazed down past the grating over all of the chilly city. It was a cold night for sightseeing, but the twinkling lights, like stars below him, didn't seem to mind. The last time he'd been here, he'd been with Veronica.

There was nothing classier than spending an evening at the overly priced restaurant just a floor below his present position. And nothing more glamorous than spending it with Veronica. He'd hardly had a right to boast of his beautiful city when speaking to her. He looked down at himself and his foot, and the stark contrast when compared to that wonderful evening.

He turned mournfully away from the view and decided to focus himself on his task. If he was going to be here, then he was going to get what he came for. Whether that be drugs, poetry, or just satisfaction for his curiosity. He looked around at several people that were wandering here and there around the place. Arm in arm they were, foggy breath blowing from their lips. But then it struck him. The poem had brought him to the Eiffel tower, but it hadn't told him where to look beyond that. He had no idea where to go, or what he was looking for.

He took to wandering like the people. The cello player had given him at least one clue. He seemed to have an idea of what was going on when he handed Philippe the ticket and there would be no point of sending him to the top of the tower if that wasn't where he was meant to find something. So he was at least in the right vicinity.

He wondered how those street musicians had known that he was the person that they should send up here. He wondered if he wasn't actually the person they were looking for and they had made some mistake. Maybe this "prophet" wasn't the same person that he was seeking and they had simply gotten things mixed up. But then again, maybe everyone was on the right track and on the same page and it was simply his statement about a 'scavenger hunt' that had given him away. Or was it the crutches? Did this 'prophet' know that Philippe had a broken foot?

And what was it that he was looking for anyway? Drugs? Was this the end of the search, or was this an unnecessarily elaborate trap? Or would it be something else entirely? The exasperation of this thought process as he gazed aimlessly around the walkways below his crutches and the iron bars above his head, caused him to stop his walking. What if this was all a dead end and he was making himself crazy for no reason.

Just then, and he began for a moment to wonder if this was going to be a pattern, he heard someone call out to him. He looked up and found that he was standing in front of the Eiffel Tower's little champagne booth. 'Champagne' was written in giant letters above the man who was standing behind the small counter, ready to serve.

"You, man with the crutches." The server said.

"No thank you." Philippe replied to him with a wave, almost relieved to see that it was just someone trying to sell him something. He didn't have anything in his wallet left for champagne, and he really didn't need the drink anyway.

But the man waved him over again with a, "Just come here."

At first, Philippe assumed that the man hadn't heard him so he took a step closer and repeated, "No thank you."

"Are you looking for something?" He was nicely, if uniformly, dressed but his whiskers and his hair could have handled a trim and he had an uncomfortable looking scar on the right side of his lower lip. He appeared as someone who was doing his best to look professional, but simply lacked the practice.

Philippe smiled politely and shook his head, "It's nothing, I'm fine." Philippe turned to leave, intending to ignore anything further that the man had to say.

"Are you looking for the Prophet?" The man asked, and Philippe's eyes shot back over to him. He squinted and gave the man a more thorough gaze up and down. He was thin, but his skin hung in a way that suggested that he'd recently lost a lot of weight and had not been so thin to begin with. "Just come here." He said again, and waved his fingers for Philippe to step up to the counter.

Philippe finally went over to him. "Who is the Prophet?" The man just grinned and set out a cone shaped, plastic champagne glass and filled it in front of Philippe. He put the bottle aside and then set the glass where Philippe could take it. "I can't buy this."

The man sighed and shook his head. "On the house. But listen." He paused and scrunched his eyebrows as if he were trying to remember something. "Ah." he said to himself and smiled at Philippe. "Here it is. Ahem.

Where Eiffel sometimes liked to live,

So there did the Prophet have words to give."

He smiled at Philippe, obviously proud of himself. His little rhyme was short sweet and to the point.

"Where Eiffel liked to live?"

"Take the champagne." Philippe took the glass and looked at the man.

"Who is the Prophet?" He repeated. But the man just smiled and reached up and closed the metal door over the counter window. This was getting strange. Philippe lifted his champagne thoughtfully to his lips before suddenly remembering his promise to Aimee that he would quit drinking with her while she was pregnant. He frowned at the waste and tossed the full plastic cup into a trash receptacle, and gripped his crutches. The place where Eiffel sometimes liked to live. He took a deep breath. There, he knew he would find whatever it was that he was looking for.

Just a few steps from where he now stood, he knew there was a small apartment on display behind glass. As the little rhyme had simply stated, it was a place where the tower's creator sometimes lived. If one looked through the glass they would see a couple of creepily realistic mannequins sitting on chairs as if they were talking to one another. One was the figure of Alexandre Gustave Eiffel, the other was his good friend Thomas Edison. They sat in old chairs, hands outstretched as if making some intelligent conversational point. They were surrounded by what Philippe thought was warm, though tacky floral patterned wallpaper, next to historically out of fashion decorum. All they needed was to each be holding a fat cigar or a tobacco pipe in one hand, and a short glass of brandy in the other. Still, the image seemed cozy. Philippe wondered how and where a clue could be hidden in that tiny museum. He supposed he would soon find out.

He nodded to a silent security guard who was leaning against a rail looking bored, and walked the few steps around the corner to the window of the apartment. He took a moment to forget about the next clue and simply gaze at the figures sitting behind the glass. History preserved. He wondered how Eiffel would feel if he knew that his private living space had become a tourist attraction. The man had never allowed anyone in there while he'd been alive. Except of course for Edison. Only famous scientists allowed. It was Eiffel's own little hiding place in the middle of everything. All the city below him. Even after his death, whoever held the decision making power had elected to honor Eiffel's silent wishes to keep his apartment private. It was only within the last few years that it had been opened up as a public display.

Philippe wondered if he really was a quiet, modest man, hiding away, or if he simply enjoyed being on top of it all. Perhaps he was really just a quiet megalomaniac. For a moment, Philippe wished that he could have met the man. But that was a level of fame that Philippe never hoped to be able to reach, let alone the time travel.

Philippe smiled to himself as he imagined sitting in Thomas Edison's seat. What if he'd chosen to chase after glories of the mind rather than the body? He knew that he was capable. He could become a great philosopher and scientist if he wanted to. But was the end result really so different? Either way he would end up a mindless body, out on display for all to see. As a model, that simply happened sooner. Famous scientists could only put off the inevitable.

Philippe sighed and glanced around the small room from his own side of the glass. If he were to hide a clue, where would he hide it? Let's see, if he were to follow some of the previous patterns... he blinked and then glanced over to the quiet, bored looking security guard. He smiled flirtatiously at him and asked,

"Do you, happen to know the prophet?" The question sounded silly coming out. He felt even sillier when the guard raised his eyebrow and just responded,

"Monsieur?" looking thoroughly confused.

"Oh um... never mind." replied Philippe shaking his head and trying to shrug off his mild embarrassment. The guard just rolled his eyes, obviously looking forward to the end of his shift. Philippe felt his own thumbnail as it scratched at a small tear in the padding of the handle on his right crutch. But there had to be a clue in here somewhere. He'd finally let go of the idea that this was just his imagination.

Behind Thomas Edison was a large metal beam that ran diagonally through the little ancient apartment. Behind that, Philippe could see the top of a feathered hat. He tilted his head to see another expertly crafted, uncomfortably lifelike mannequin of a woman in a dark red turn of the century dress. Clair Eiffel. Alexandre Gustave's daughter. She stood staring at nothing in particular. Or gazing morosely at the space between the two gentlemen.

What would it have been like to have been her? The fashion was certainly different, though somehow finer. But if Philippe had to pick a time period for which he felt he would have been most suited, he would have picked the 1920's. Those were the days to live.

He shook his mental wanderings from his mind but decided to Google Clair Eiffel's life later. But for now, another curious thought had struck him. He looked at Claire's sullen gaze and then followed the direction of her face. Through the glass casing that separated her world from the real one, towards the metal grating past which was only a long drop off the tower. Much to his surprise, he caught his breath as he saw there, the edge of a ribbon fluttering in the chilly autumn wind.

He looked back at the mannequin's face. Whoever this prophet was, his mind worked just a little too much like Philippe's. Either that, or this whole process was causing Philippe to know him better and better though they had not yet met.

He crutched his way over to the grating and carefully reached his finger through the grating. He felt a heat in his face that one feels when they know that they are doing something that they oughtn't. It was another scroll, tied with the ribbon to the outside of the grating. He carefully untied it so as not to let the ribbon fly away, and turned it over to see that it had been stamped with the same seal. S.P. He took a deep breath, broke the seal, and read the poem inside.

On top of the world you are, and you can see great distances
Like the glory of a sunset though, awe lasts only brief instances.
You'll wonder where to find the next beauty in the world,
In art, words or nature, or in the dragon's arms you'll curl.

People travel across the planet to find the awe of the sun,
But of unmeasured glory, I know of only one.
Art may try to see it, words ache to describe it, nature whispers that it knows it,
But with fire, the dragon overrides it.

If you did not chase the dragon, awe may lead you to the Louvre,
But who's to say that the dragon, does not the Louvre approve?
Many an artist knew him, and was led by him to his fate,
And the only warning left by them, was awe inspiring paint.

So what, pray tell, is the difference between one who chases art,

Or one who cases sunsets or towers, or wishes to consume the dragon's heart?

What is it that makes those better, who do not with the dragon play?

Or are they simply unaware that with the dragon they play another way?

Perhaps we'll find the answer if we go where the dragon cannot,

But to find such a place whilst not inviting him in, is in all truth, a longshot.

There is a way around him, but I'll not tell you yet,

For now I'll simply let you know that he's jealous of that sun set.

Though his fire is hot he duly notes, that Sol is hotter still,

From your lofty view you'll see him, from the Eiffel's window sill.

As I've already said, he flies only as high as man can build,

But while over the horizon, the sun moves on, the horizon that it touches stands still.

At that moment, Philippe realized that he had truly stepped into a scavenger hunt. Someone had taken the drug stash from the potted plant, and in its place, had left a symbolic journey.

Philippe lifted his head and looked west. But it was early autumn, and that meant turning his head a little to the north. The sun had already set, but he could still see the last glimpses of sunlight through the clouds at the edge of the sky. He squinted his eyes at the horizon but couldn't see from that distance what he was looking at. He glanced around to see that he was standing right next to an old brass colored, coin operated telescope. He had no coins in his pockets, but the telescope was clearly pointed in that direction. Whoever the Prophet was, he had been uncomfortably thorough.

Philippe sighed, and placed his face against the eye piece. He gave the scope a jostle to be sure that it was truly locked into that position. He found himself looking at the broad green expanse of the Bois de Boulogne. A huge park covered in woods and ponds and horse racing tracks. Though it was the second largest park in Paris, it was still a good two and a half times larger than Central Park back in New York. He got the feeling that the scavenger hunt wasn't over yet.

Philippe took a deep breath and rolled the paper up and tucked it into his pocket next to the first one. Like Central Park, Bois de Boulogne wasn't always the best area to walk in at night, though during the day, it was a great picnic location among other things.

He wondered, as he headed back towards the elevator, if he shouldn't just go back to Aimee's and wait to continue this search until morning. But the search had been going along as if it had all been set up just so. The musicians at the foot of the tower, the man at the champagne stand. If he waited until tomorrow, would the opportunity still be there?

It was time to take the metro.

Chapter 34. Speechless

Philippe stared out the window of the bus watching the dim lights of the Paris underground tunnels run past him. He'd propped his crutches against the seat next to him and the most recent poem lay open on his lap between his hands.

In the first poem, Philippe had been first taken by the philosophy of it all and only realized the instruction clue on further contemplation. With the second poem he'd found himself so drawn by his instant recognition of the instruction that he'd lost sight of the philosophy. He was making up for that now that he had nothing to do but wait.

He looked back down to his lap and uncurled the edge of the paper to see the handwritten words. Whoever the "Prophet" was, they really cared about their writing. Someone who cared about the art itself had written it. The handwriting was more like calligraphy than like scrawling. Every letter intentional.

The irony struck him that one who seemed to be suggesting that a life without drugs was better than a life with them, also stated in this poem that art and words were no better. Yet here they were paying ever close attention to the artistry of every individual word and letter. Philippe didn't like to be judgmental, but either the writer was a hypocrite or they really did have a way "around the dragon". He hoped the latter, not because he wished to know the way around, but because he found himself hoping for some legitimacy on the part of the writer. For now, he'd just give them the benefit of the doubt.

"The Prophet." he said to himself under his breath as he turned back to face the window. If indeed that was a reference to the author of these unsigned poems. He wondered how he had received such a street name. If indeed it was a 'he'. Had he been known to make predictions of the future? Had the name been given to him, or was it a name that he chose for himself?

He rolled the poem back up as he saw his stop coming. He grabbed his crutches and stood up to disembark. Again he had no idea what he was looking for. But at least he now had the comfort of a resolution to keep looking.

After ascending the stairs from the tunnel Philippe stood on the sidewalk looking out into the looming darkness of the park. A very peculiar feeling came over him. It was not un-akin to the feeling he'd had when he had been standing in the black empty brothel with the squatter that was Landers. It was a feeling of foreboding. A warning in his gut that told him that if he did not leave now, he could find himself very worse for wear.

Anyone standing on the edge of the Bois at night might feel the same though. It wasn't a safe place to be. When the sun set, the park tended to turn into a forested den of robbers and prostitution. This was a somewhat different sensation though. It was as if his mind was trying to recall something. Like a memory just on the edge of his thoughts or a word just on the tip of his tongue. But he wanted to keep his mind keen enough to hide if he needed to.

He realized just how much of a disadvantage his crutches and broken foot were. He couldn't run, and even if he could somehow hide, his crutches would prove difficult to shove into a shrub and they could stick out and give him away. He decided to give himself a time limit. If he didn't find anything in the next twenty minutes, he would go home and wait 'til morning and hope that the darkness wasn't a prerequisite for this clue.

Just as he was making up his mind about this, a woman stepped out from behind a street lamp and began walking towards him. He dearly hoped that she was one of the "Prophet's" accomplices. She was somewhat petite and had thick beautiful dark hair which rested against her shoulders. She wasn't dressed like a prostitute though. She wore plain jeans, sneakers and a warm jacket and scarf. But he couldn't imagine that she would be out here unless there was someone… somewhere… watching out for her, in some way or another.

She closed the distance between the two of them and when she got close enough to hold a conversation, she stopped and eyeballed his crutches. Then she nodded to herself and gestured for him to follow her as she turned around.

"Uh, no, no thank you." Said Philippe, a friendly smile suddenly jumping up to his cheeks. She stopped and looked over her shoulder at him. He realized that if she wasn't a prostitute, then chances were that he had just said something terribly offensive. And if she was, then he was a snob who'd just denied her, her livelihood.

But her expression didn't portray any offense taken. She didn't say anything, and she didn't move on. She just stared at him as if waiting for him to follow. Philippe squinted his eyes and tilted his head, unsure as to how to either proceed or discontinue this awkward social interaction. He decided that no matter what her profession was, she was a person. And Philippe would be hard pressed to find a person that he didn't like. So perhaps the best way to proceed was to just be his usual friendly self.

"What's your name?" he endeavored to ask. He raised his eyebrows brightly and allowed his smile to rest more naturally on his face. Her response, however, caused that smile to falter unintentionally, because he wasn't expecting it at all. She turned back towards him and moved so that he could see her better. Then, to his mostly well contained horror, she opened her mouth to show him why she had not said a peep to him. She had no tongue. Or rather, she had only the stub of a tongue in the back of her mouth.

"Oh!" he said, startled and for a moment stood, trying to blink the surprise out of his eyes like a speck of dirt. "Oh, I'm sorry." She waved her hand at him and closed her mouth as if she had now sufficiently made her point, and then again turned, and gestured for him to follow her.

Philippe forced his jaw into a more socially appropriate position and hurried so that he and his crutches could walk alongside her.

"But where are we going?" he asked. She looked at him as if she couldn't believe that he was asking questions. The truth was, though he would have certainly liked to know the answer to that question, it was mostly rhetorical. He just didn't enjoy being silent and needed to fill the air.

She shook her head along with half an eye roll, and suddenly turned off of the sidewalk, and led the way into the wood.

"You know," he continued in a quieter voice as they crossed the threshold into the Bois itself. "People have been known to get mugged out here at night. Not that anyone should really be wandering around here at night. The only people that do, seem to be either looking to get laid, or looking to rob the people who are looking to get laid." She glanced back at him and then climbed over a fallen log. "I can't say as I'm particularly looking forward to the idea of getting mugged, and I don't have any cash on me anyway."

The woman stopped and turned towards him with her hand over her mouth and an expression of feigned surprise. She then put the fingers of her right hand in front of her and rubbed her fingers and thumb together. Then she put both hands, palms up, by her shoulders. Philippe read the little game of charades as, "What!? Money! You don't have any!?"

"No." He shook his head in response. "I don't have any money." He wondered for a moment if he'd read her all wrong and she really was a street worker who had been looking to sell herself in the bushes, and had just found out that her john didn't have any cash with which to pay her. But as though she'd been reading his thoughts, she suddenly grinned and turned back around, gesturing again for him to follow.

Philippe squinted thoughtfully for a moment before following. He then came to the conclusion that she had just made some sort of sarcastic joke. He then chuckled a little and became much more confident in the idea that she really was leading him in the right direction. No one ever said that being mute would rob someone of a sense of humor. So, smile happily back on his face, he proceeded to wrestle his way over that fallen log.

"All that being said," he continued with his one sided conversation. "Do you think we're safe out here right now? I feel like you and I would look an awful lot like easy pickings if anyone were to decide to pick on us. We're not the most threatening couple of people. No offense, I'm sure that you're tougher than I am. Very sure actually." He paused for a moment and tugged one of his crutches out of a bush. His companion glanced at him, but predictably, gave him no response.

"So, today has been a bit of a scavenger hunt." He managed to disentangle his crutch. "And thus far, everyone I've run into has dropped the name of "The Prophet." Do you know who The Prophet is?" She nodded to him, and kept walking. 'Great,' he thought to himself. 'The first person I find who I could ask about him, and she can't tell me.' Not, that is, unless she wished to stop and write or text it. But it didn't look like she had any mind for stopping.

They climbed through the rough undergrowth for some time with Philippe barely managing, with his broken foot, to keep up. He felt sure that the twenty minute limit had elapsed, and a quick glance at his phone confirmed this suspicions. It had, in fact, been about thirty since he'd met her. But he couldn't deny that he had found something. Someone. But he had no idea where they were going, and he was anxious to get the next clue, and get out of there.

"Just a minute." he panted. He leaned up against a tree to breath and get ready for more trudging. She stopped reluctantly with a sigh and sat down on a stump and watched him. "I wonder," he said as he rested, "Do you suppose we would find what we were looking for if we came in the morning instead of at night? Or does it actually need to be pitch black in order for this clue to be findable?" The woman only responded with a shrug. Either she didn't know, or she didn't care.

Philippe just sort of nodded at her and sighed, resigning himself to the uncertainty. "Well, alright then, I guess we'd better keep at it." She nodded and stood up and continued to lead him through the brush. But the brush didn't last much longer, and before he knew it, Philippe found himself out in the open grass under the big harvest moon, nearly full, but not quite.

"Well," he found his voice was speaking a little quieter, almost whispering. "The Bois is certainly a pretty place, even if it's not safe." He watched the woman walking in front of him as they quietly started making their way across the grass. They were going up a slight incline and she certainly seemed to know her way, daylight unnecessary.

"I wish you could tell me your name. It's something of a shame walking with someone for this long and not knowing their name. I have a hundred questions I would ask you if I could. How do you know the prophet? Have you met him in person or just poem? How do you know your way through this park so well? Where are you from?

What's your favorite color?" She looked over her shoulder at him and smiled, almost sadly but bittersweet. Philippe savored it, and smiled in return.

"Perhaps, after this scavenger hunt is over you'd let me take you out to lunch. I'd bring a pen and paper and maybe you'd let me ask all those questions, and maybe a few others." He smiled at the back of her head as they walked. But predictably, she said nothing.

As the pair crested the incline, the woman suddenly ducked low. Philippe followed suit before he'd gotten quite as far as her. He wasn't sure what was over that hill, but he was already regretting being here. She stayed there against the cold grass for a moment, thoughtfully, before she seemed to decide on their course change. Slowly she started inching along the side of the incline rather than going over it.

This was exactly the sort of thing that Philippe had hoped he wouldn't need to be doing with a broken foot. Crawling while trying to pull along his crutches. He tucked himself a little closer to the woman, and tried to work out how to effectively keep himself and his crutches unseen. But before he decided to execute his plan, he glanced over the hill.

Relatively close by him on the other side of the hill was the bank of one of the park's smaller ponds. A ripple dabbed at the edge of the water as a fish touched the surface for a moment, but that wasn't why they were ducking. Across the reflection of the shadowy trees along the water's surface, on the far side was a large grey van.

At first, Philippe considered the idea that it could be the park's caretakers. But whether or not that was true, Philippe lowered himself down to his knees and set the crutches down beside him. The woman came back over to him to pull him along, but he was elsewhere in the waters of his own mind.

Those nagging memories were resurfacing. It was like his time in that brothel was just the first stone having been removed from the dam. It had been like the gateway leading into a whole library of unopened memories. But he was so little then. So it must be a small library. Right?

He remembered he loved this place, and hated it. He would come with his mum and a few other girls and Landers. When they got there, they would park by some water. Probably a different pond. Probably a lake. With trees hanging high over the water and the moon shining on the grass.

He loved coming because he and Landers would go on long walks, just the two of them. Around the lakes, through the long winding paths through the woods. Landers would talk, but Philippe couldn't think of what he'd ever been talking about. Just that he enjoyed the attention.

But Philippe hated coming because his mum never went walking with him. She always stayed with the other girls at the van. And when Landers would bring him back to her, she would always be too tired to talk to him. Too tired to hear about all the trails he'd walked and all the watery ripples he'd seen.

He wished that he could hold those memories just as far out of context now as he had then. He wished that he couldn't put two and two together now, and see what really happened. They were never just, nice moonlit trips to the park. They were business transactions. The Bois de Boulogne was just as much a den of robbers and prostitutes then as it was now. Perhaps if he'd understood, he wouldn't have been so angry at his mother's sad silence.

He wiped a tear on his sleeve and felt the woman tugging the shoulder of his coat to get his attention. "Sorry." he whispered but she put her finger up to her lips to silence him further and then gestured, with a somewhat urgent look in her eye, for him to follow.

As quickly as he could, he somewhat crawled, using his good foot to propel him further whilst holding both crutches in one hand. It was awkward going. The woman seemed to be trying to strike an uncomfortable balance between swiftness and quietness.

A few times, his crutches clanked together loudly but they managed to hide themselves in the bushes on the other side of the clearing just as someone came up to investigate the noise. It appeared to be a young man in a uniform waving a flashlight around. It really was the park enforcement. Once the light of his flashlight disappeared over the hill back down towards the van, the two of them disappeared deeper into the thicket.

With those resurfaced memories now much on his mind, Philippe found himself being very nearly silent as they continued climbing their way through the woods. Landers and he had never climbed through the woods when he was little, they'd always stuck to the paths. He supposed that Landers hadn't felt as though he needed to be afraid, or hide from anything. Perhaps his reputation was all he'd needed at that time to keep himself safe.

Philippe was so lost in his thoughts that he didn't notice where the woman was leading him until his crutches landed on pavement instead of earth. He looked up to see that they were now leaving the Bois de Boulogne. He looked back at the shadows and wondered why the prophet had led him through there. Had he known that Philippe would find memories there? As he turned back to see that the woman was leading him towards the nearest metro tunnel, he couldn't help but feel as if, someone, somewhere, had known. Why else would they have gone through that park at night? Then again, maybe he was just being too full of himself.

The woman stopped before entering the tunnel and turned to look at him. Then she sighed and unzipped her warm coat. Philippe blinked with some surprise when he saw that she wasn't wearing anything at all underneath it. She wasn't paying any attention to that though. She reached into an inside pocket next to her bare breast and withdrew another scroll of paper, bound with a red ribbon, sealed with SP.

She zipped her coat back up to her neck and handed the scroll out to him. Philippe reached out and took the scroll but didn't take his eyes off of his puzzling companion. He wanted so much to know her story, but he couldn't help but feel certain that he would never get to find out.

"Thank you." he said quietly, still gazing at her instead of the next clue. She smiled and waved her hand and started to depart from him, to head back to the Bois. "Wait." He said before she could leave. He reached out and kissed her cheek gently and touched her hair. "Thank you." He said again. Then smiled, and backed up to let her leave.

She nodded, as if she understood that he had gained more from that walk through the Bois de Boulogne, than just a destination, or a stroll through the park. And with that, she left, and disappeared into the woods, and Philippe never saw her again.

Philippe stared at the dark woods across the street for longer than he thought was safe. This whole journey had thus far been so much more meaningful than he'd thought it would be. In the end, he wondered what the full message was that the Prophet was trying to get across. And he also wondered, why he had gone through this much trouble to say it.

He looked at the entrance down into the metro tunnel. He was certain that if the woman had led him here, then chances were he would need to get on that metro to go to the next place. So with a somewhat tired sigh, he lifted the scroll, and broke the seal.

In the whispers of the air,
In the trees and the breeze,
In the greenness of the grass,
And the ruffles of the leaves
With a midnight stroll with the moon overhead
With some warmth in your arms and a sigh on your breath
With the stars shining down but you can barely even see,
Where worshipers of the dragon can come to be free.

They come here with wallets,
Though their souls try to flee,
An offering of cash
And a bow on bended knee,
And they give away their souls to all those that would beg
They lay down all their clothes and choose bushes over beds
And though there may be moans and rustles you can see,
Deep down inside there's a muffled kind of scream.

Another place the dragon hides,
Other worshipers to eat,
Under pews, in the rafters,
In hearts called there to preach.
They bring their wallets in their pockets, bring their prayers and
their pride
From the rest of the world, they go there to hide,
An offering of cash and a bow on bended knee,
With a thousand ah father's they hope to be free.

But sitting right beside them,
Other worshipers will breath
In whose hearts are different prayers
And another kind of peace.
The dragon though, he hates them and would consume them
with fire
He'd tear off their heads and tie them to a pyre,

But another one told them that for them he'd bleed,
And because of his blood they've been untouchably freed.

You'll never know them
Sitting in those seats,
Are they these ones or those ones,
Or the ones next to me?
Perhaps go to their house and along with them sit
Where the stained glass glows when all the candles are lit.
See if you can tell which one's the dragon feeds
And which ones are strangers to the dragonish greed.

Perhaps now you know
Perhaps now you've seen
I've been leading you through Paris
Old, tall and green.
And now to another old monument you'll go
For I'm full of cliché places that I like to show
So now go to a place that thousands come to see
With the story of a hunchback and a dark history.

Notre Dame. He rolled up the scroll and tucked it into his pocket next to the other two, and descended the stairs down to the metro carefully and slowly with his crutches. He stood at the foot of the stairs and glanced at a homeless man who was sleeping against the wall under an old ratty blanket with holes. Philippe knew that if it weren't for Aimee, he might have found himself someplace similar. Hopefully at least a few acquaintances would have let him couch hop.

He sighed and turned his eyes away to look at the tracks as he waited for the metro to arrive. This clue had taken on a distinctly religious tone. He wondered if the Prophet was a religious man. That would make enough sense, given the name. Though there were certainly others in the world who would throw around the word 'prophecy' with no care at all to religious attachments. Or prediction, or divination, or augury or oracle or a hundred other words that had a different spiritual connotation to them depending on which ones one used. Though thus far Philippe wasn't sure that the Prophet had done anything particularly fortune telling.

Perhaps it had only taken on that nature due to the destination. What would he find at Notre Dame? That had never been a tourist attraction that he'd much attended or shown off to foreign friends. If he was interested in anything concerning it, he supposed it was the history. It certainly harkened to a different era of France. And not often a pretty one.

The metro arrived and he stepped on and sat down next to the window. He watched as homeless man began to move past him. There was so much pain in this world. He wondered if that was what the Prophet had intended when he wrote that Notre Dame was somewhere that people went to hide. Perhaps they were hiding from the pains that were so easy to see if one just looked.

He also noticed that over the course of the three poems, the dragon, as a metaphor, had been subtly transforming. It wasn't just about the drugs anymore. It was about something else.

Chapter 35. Lies

Predictably, the great cathedral was locked. As were the fences that cut the public off from the doors. Philippe let his fingers slip from the heavy grating and looked up to gaze at the tall building. At the arches that crested over the top of each door. He was stumped. What more could he do? He looked back at the wide open walkway of the little Seine island that he'd just gone through to get there, and decided to sit for a bit on a curb next to a hedge facing the monumental church.

He set his crutches beside him and proceeded to re-wrap his scarf around his neck a little more snuggly. It was so late that it was getting more than just chilly. It was getting downright cold.

Again he wondered at the timing of it all. He'd noticed that there had been people involved in every step of the process. Had they been watching him? Had they been communicating with each other, sending text such as, 'He just left my post and he's headed in your direction.' Or had they been individually waiting, ready to pounce no matter what hour he arrived? Should he wait here until someone just showed up? Or was it an unreasonable expectation to think that anyone would show up? Did this clue actually require him to enter the building? Because the door was really quite locked and he didn't fancy breaking and entering into Notre Dame.

He was startled from his thoughts by the sudden buzzing against his leg as his phone began to vibrate. He pulled it out of his pocket to see that Aimee was calling him. He supposed that she probably was having a little anxiety over him not being there when she got home. Considering what he'd been doing with his evening, her worries were perhaps well founded.

Hastily he answered it and pressed the flat screen against his ear. "Aimee." He said, aware that he felt as though he were trying to hide something. Like he quickly needed to come up with some excuse for why he wasn't home. He'd never been one to try to obfuscate his actions or intentions from his best friend. He knew something was terribly wrong if he did.

"Hey Philippe. Um, am I interrupting anything?"

"No, of course not!"

"Okay. I mean, I'm not really one for trying to keep tabs on your location but you know… after the other night…" She paused, "Anyway, I'm glad to hear that you're doing fine. I waited a couple hours before getting paranoid. And I didn't want to interrupt if you were doing anything romantic." She chuckled. "I'm sure there's someone out there with a hot pink cast fetish."

Philippe chuckled along with her. He wished he was doing something romantic, it would be better than his real goal. "Nope. Alas, nothing romantic yet. But the night is young. I'm just out and about. I didn't mean to worry you. I should have told you that I would be out late."

"Oh no, don't worry about it." she replied, "I was just checking in on you. I'll go put my paranoid self to bed now. What are you up to anyway?"

"Oh um… I'll tell you all about it when I get home." But even as the words tumbled from his lips, he knew that they were lies. He had no desire to tell Aimee that he was out in the dead of night chasing after drugs. No matter how poetically he chased them. His heart clenched inside his chest as he lied to her. To the only person who he knew would accept him, dirt and all. But if she knew, he was sure that she would be able to dissuade him from his goal. But though she could forgive him for drugs, could she forgive him for lying?

"Okay." he heard her voice say with a sound of relief. "I'll probably be asleep when you get home. You can wake me up if you want. Or just climb in bed and tell me in the morning."

"Alright, sounds good. Sleep tight darling."

He slipped the phone back into his pocket and peered up at the looming church building. The figures of carved saints and gargoyles seemed to stare down at him. He wasn't sure that he'd sinned against God. He wasn't sure that there was even a God out there to sin against. But two things he felt utterly certain about, he was sinning against Aimee, and he was sinning against himself too.

All at once, he seemed to care nothing for the next clue. He'd spent hours and hours chasing this wild goose but now his heart and mind were overwhelmed by the tiny internal implications of his actions. What did this say about him?

It was true that it had been a small lie. Hardly a lie at all, it was actually a simple diversion from information rather than blatant misinformation. But that didn't matter. A lie, no matter how white, could stein his heart forever. Or worse, his friendship. He had worked so hard to become an honest and authentic person. He could express every emotion on his heart at a moment's notice. This felt more like backsliding than any drug relapse.

"Tell me how you're feeling Philippe." It was as simple a question as that and then he could give every answer. And if he could not find the words to express them then at least he could show someone the truth. By the tears in his eyes or the smile on his face. By the fact that, in Philippe, those two expressions could live together in unity.

"I guess, guilty. When I was young, I hid everything. I hid what was going on with Armel. I hid my mother's drug addiction so no one would find out. I lied about where I'd stolen my clothes from. I lied to myself about everything that I was thinking and feeling." He felt his phone, warm and bright against his cheek. What time was it in New York? "But then I learned, that authenticity is better. If I can analyze everything that I feel, then I can understand myself. If I can understand myself, then I can empathize with everyone else. If I can empathize with everyone else, than I can have true intimacy. If everyone shares how they feel and if everyone knows how they feel, then there's no barriers. We can all just love each other." He smiled against his phone. "Does that make any sense?"

"Yes it does." Replied the warm deep voice of his therapist. "I'm hearing that this is really all about intimacy, and about feeling loved. How can you be sure that someone really loves you if you're lying to them?"

"Yes! Yes that's exactly it. Because then they can only love me for the fake me."

"Yet at the same time, I wonder if you've been trying to be something that *everyone* will love. That's quite the paradox."

"What do you mean? How so?" He asked and at the same time, pulled his phone away from his ear to look at it. He'd called his therapist in New York? He should have known better. He didn't have the money either for the call or for her bill.

"Well," she was about to explain as he put his phone back up against his face, but Philippe had to interrupt.

"I apologize. Something just came up and I have to go. Maybe I'll call you later, or just email you."

"Hmm. I see." She said. "Interesting."

"Au revoir." Said Philippe, and hung up the phone. What a strange monetary mistake he had just made. He must really have wanted to confess his guilty feelings.

Chapter 36. Notre Dame

Yet again, just in his moment of doubt, something in the world pulled him forward. He almost wished it wouldn't. If it stopped, he could just go home. The door to the Notre Dame creaked open. Startled, Philippe waited to see who would cross the threshold.

It was an old man that came through the door wearing a white robe that was so long, it nearly brushed the stones beneath his feet. He opened the door a little wider and seemed to shuffle with something behind it for a moment. Philippe wondered if the man had even noticed that he was there. But then, with a candlestick of four candles in one hand, he turned and gestured obviously to Philippe. "Come on in son." he said. He walked to the gate to unlock it also. Then stepped to the side of the big cathedral door, to wait for Philippe to pass through.

Philippe blinked for a moment disbelievingly, but then remembered that he was still looking for the next clue. But a priest of the church, was the last contact he had expected the Prophet to have. None of the people he'd met thus far seemed like they had any business being in a church.

He reached out and picked up his crutches and hoisted himself up with them, tucking one under each arm. He ventured toward the archway. He couldn't help but look up at the stone faces looking down on him as he passed beneath them.

"What's your name son?" Philippe jumped a little when the man asked as he came in alongside him and shut the door.

"Philippe." he said. Candlelight was the only light that lit the place. They'd been set aglow all along the walls and the pillars and the aisles. He felt sure that it was more dramatic than necessary. Likely, there was electricity to be had. But he couldn't deny the beauty.

"Philippe." The man repeated the name, nodding to himself. He was tall. Philippe imagined that the man had likely been at least as tall as himself before age had taken its toll and he'd stopped being able to stand quite as straight.

The man drew the candles a little closer to their faces to get a better look at him. He had deep lines in his cheeks and his forehead. His gray thin hairs were combed over the top of his obvious bald spot. But he had the most brilliantly blue eyes and Philippe was transfixed for a moment by them.

"Well then," the man said, "I'm glad I let the right fellow in. Sorry I left you sitting out there so long. I was doing some spiritual reading and tidying up and lighting all the candles and I'm afraid it took me a little while to remember to open the door."

"Sir, if you don't mind my asking. Why am I here?"

"Because the Prophet led you here. But you must have been in here before."

Philippe shook his head. "Only once. A friend wanted to see it. And he wanted me to come in with him. We just went up to look at the bells. We didn't stay for mass." Philippe scanned around the hugeness of the cathedral. Candles were lit near the huge stained glass windows. But the light couldn't pierce through the darkness outside.

Philippe scanned over the man from head to foot and back up to his brilliantly blue eyed face. "How do you..." But he paused for a moment to find the right words. Finding few he continued. "You don't really seem like someone that the Prophet would send me to. Am I wrong?"

"Quite." Chuckled the old man. "He wouldn't have if I weren't." He patted Philippe's shoulder and began walking along the inside of the church. Philippe was happy to be walking with someone who seemed that he too could only move at a rather slow pace. He felt surprised that the old man wasn't walking with a cane.

"But you... you're a...a priest." The old man stopped his walk and turned to look at Philippe's confused face.

"What is it that you're looking for son?"

"Well..." Philippe scrunched his eyebrows. "Don't you know?" The old man shook his head.

"No. That boy doesn't tell me everything. He even sometimes jokingly calls it 'patient confidentiality.' ha!" He turned and continued walking. "I'm just supposed to take you to the next poem."

"Sir... who is 'The Prophet'? How do you know him?" At least now Philippe could, with confidence refer to the Prophet as a 'him.'

And now he finally had someone who might be able to answer a few of his questions.

"Oh I suppose I've known him for about a decade or so. I knew him before he took that title. He was involved in a few street gangs and was looking for a way out. I suppose God put me in the right place at the right time to offer the poor boy some shelter. He'd been on the streets for too long. And I say a single day is longer than any young person should be on the street. He was fifteen, maybe fourteen. Maybe sixteen, my memory loses specifics. But now he's turned the tables on his old life. The streets have become his ministry. Speaking of confidentiality, I'm a priest you know, I only divulge this information with his permission."

"He... oh... but... but I'm not involved in any gangs." Philippe bit his tongue. He needed to try to allow himself to just speak straight to this old man. If nothing else, he would likely never see him again. No need to stutter over his expressiveness now.

"You don't need to tell me what you've done. But if you do want to confess you can. I am a priest you know. Ha! In any case, I'm just walking you to his next poem. I do find it interesting that he sent you my way. He said that he was sure that you and I have some common history. I find that odd though. I wasn't expecting such a young man to be here when he told me that. My history looks like it's a lot longer than yours. Ha!" He reached out a tapped Philippe's shoulder again. "But I wonder, do you have any idea what he could have meant?"

Philippe smiled at the jovial old priest. The man's humor was beginning to warm Philippe's heart towards him. But as he smiled, he shook his head. "I have no idea. I can't say as I understand how he could have any knowledge of my history at all, since I've never met him before. No offense, but I feel sure that I've never met you before either. Not even on the one occasion that I came into this building."

"Ah well, would you perhaps be willing to tell me a little about your life and perhaps you and I can guess? I could tell you mine but I suppose I could only tell you about the past oh, how many years… how old are you son?"

"Nearly twenty-one."

"Nearly twenty-one. Twenty-one years of history eh? Well now, let's see." The old man seemed to sink down into his thoughts for a minute. "Well, if you haven't met me and I haven't met you or at least neither of us can remember it, then perhaps is was a family relation? I suppose your grandfather might be old enough to share a history with me. What's your grandfather's name?"

"Ah, well. I've never met him. I suppose, if he's still alive then he probably lives in Sweden." Philippe took a deep breath as the jovial smile began to melt a little from his face. "Actually, the only family member of mine that I've ever met was my mother. But she passed away very recently."

"Oh I see. I'm sorry." They meandered slowly through the length of the cathedral, the light glowed against the glass. The silence seemed to carry weight. It was a full silence, not an empty one.

"It's alright." Philippe said, breaking the silence and feeling as if his quiet voice carried more than he wanted it to through the echo. "Besides, unless you frequented brothels twenty years ago, you probably wouldn't have met her. She never went to churches either."

They suddenly stopped walking. He blinked and wondered if this was where the man intended to turn him loose. He glanced around at the historically preserved museum displays for any hint of a slip of paper but found none.

"Oh I see." Whispered the old man next to him. Philippe looked to see that his stoop seemed to be a little lower. The jovial lines on his face seemed to become wrinkles sagged with sorrow and age. His bright blue eyes seemed suddenly very tired. The old man reached out and steadied himself against a pillar and stared at the flickering of his candles. "I wonder, when the prophet sent you here, was he meaning to find healing for you? Or for me?"

He looked up from the flickering flames and his blue eyes seemed for a moment to reflect Philippe's own, as their gazes met. They were eyes that were deeper than the surface.

"Or perhaps for both of us." The man said. But as the pieces of this story began to fall together in Philippe's mind, his stomach tied itself into knots and he felt sure that he must escape. The man tilted his head and furrowed his brow slightly as if his mind was considering unexpected conclusions, but Philippe had no interest in whatever thoughts he was thinking.

He gripped onto his crutches, and vaulted himself. He turned his face away and turned his back to the old man and headed for the door.

"Philippe wait!" the man called, but it was too late. Back past the pillars and the paintings, the stained glass and the candles flickering in their reflections as they lit the quiet corners set aside for time spent knelt in prayer. Philippe had pushed his way through the great front doors out into the dark Paris night. His mind was blinded by emotions and adrenaline and escape and he didn't much realize where he was going until he was stopped by the edge of the drop off to the canal below.

He looked left and right and caught sight of the steps that led down to the water, and he went to them as fast as he could go, and descended to the safety of the water side. He put his back against the wall, and lowered himself to the ground. Heart still pounding, he clutched at his chest and wrapped his arms around himself and tucked his forehead against the knee of his good leg.

The price for these stupid drugs was becoming too steep. Drugs were supposed to help one escape from reality. But these ones were leading him straight into it. Veronica had been right all along. Those doors would have been better left shut.

Chapter 37. Rue Du Chat Que Peche

Philippe was left for a while sitting in something of a daze. He watched the water slowly undulating under the cover of night with only the vague lights of the city left to reflect on its surface. But the walls of the canal made something of a barrier from the light. Philippe was invisible, sitting in the utter dark. The light of the city did not touch him.

That priest had been one of Landers's patrons. He would have been one of the many many men that came in to take advantage of the girls that had been coerced into being there. Possibly even his mother.

But that priest had seemed clean as a whistle. Not only that, but he hadn't seemed at all like those religious people who act like they're perfect but you can just see the lies under their fake smiles. He hadn't seemed fake at all. His happiness had seemed genuine. Had genuine happiness come at his mother's expense? Or others like her?

Philippe could barely breathe. Had that old man gone and kneeled in a confessional box and told his companions that he'd sinned again today? Had they just crossed their fingers over their heads and chests and told him to say a few words and be forgiven? Or had he hidden it deep in himself. His own dirty little secret from the church. Too afraid to tell them what he'd been doing lest they excommunicate him.

Philippe took a deep breath and felt as his heart rate began to slow down. He himself was the sort that would forgive a person for their past transgressions. Live and learn and let bygones be bygones. That was twenty years ago after all. Had Philippe any right not to forgive him? But this was too close to home, and it was something that had been heavy on his heart ever since his mother had passed. To some extent, he felt as though he'd already forgiven Landers. Couldn't he forgive this stranger too?

Philippe was not the sort to hold grudges, but he'd been blindsided. He, the victim, had just come face to face with the perpetrator. But that old man did not look as though his heart was feeling free of guilt. In fact, as soon as Philippe had brought it to his memory, he had looked nearly crippled by it.

Philippe reached into his pocket and pulled out his silk handkerchief. He used it to wipe the teary snot from his cold nose. When Philippe had entered that boarded up brothel, he had gone in looking for truth and thus far it had not ceased to be shown to him.

He thought about the old man and his blue eyes. The resemblance to his own eyes was not lost on him. But lots of people had blue eyes. His mother for one. That alone didn't prove anything. Nothing in their interaction could have proven paternity and Philippe had no intentions of asking for a DNA sample.

On the night that his mother had died, Philippe had asked her to stop running from her pain so that maybe she could try to heal it and maybe he could heal himself too. But she had denied him, and instead she ran towards drugs to try to take away the sting. He wondered if that felt anything like how he was feeling now, as he hid by the shadows of the canal.

He wondered if, by fleeing that cathedral, he was following in her footsteps. It would likely lead him, to the same place that it led her. To his death. So with that last thought he picked up the crutches that he had cast down to the ground and used them to lift himself up. He struggled his way up the stairs and fought his way back to the door that he'd fled from. His mother had not been willing to heal her pain, but he had to be willing to heal his own.

But when he reached the door, there on the ground just inside the relocked grating was the candlestick with all four candles still lit and flickering quietly as they held down the edge of yet another scroll of paper. The next, and what he frankly hoped was the last clue.

He lowered himself to sit against the fence, and reached through the bars to pick up the scroll. SP. There was the seal. He unrolled the paper and tilted it towards the candlelight to read.

Perhaps the road has been too long,
The mountains far too steep.
The dragon may fly too high for you,
Only the dust of his wings can you keep.

I'm sure your feet are worn and tired,
This journey seems never to end,

But that's how the dragon gets hold of you,
He gives you a taste and then ascends.

If I were to truly keep the analogy,
I would lead you on still more.
Poem after poem you would follow along,
Until you collapsed on the shore.

Because one truth you should know about the dragon,
Though his scales glitter and shine.
You may have caught the first taste of his lips,
But that will be the very last time.

Many are content to chase him so,
Until their lives fall to the dust.
But though they shall never catch him again,
Chase him forever they must.

But I know your literal feet need a rest,
And for the dragon your blood is crying.
I know my poems are pretty and true,
But they aren't nearly as satisfying.

So allow me one last final word,
Before you reach the end.
In the smallest of all alleyways, just across the Seine,

Life has been found there time and time again.

Rue Du Chat Que Peche. The street of the fishing cat. That was the only place that Philippe could think of that fit the description, and thankfully, it wasn't far at all. It was just down the street and across the river. He truly hoped that it would be the end of this scavenger hunt. His heart and his feet, not to mention the burning pits of his arms, had been taxed nearly to breaking.

Philippe rolled up the scroll and tucked it into his pocket with the others. Then he lifted his eyes over head to look up at the looming ancient church full of history. The poem was enough. He didn't need to go inside and confront the old man. At least, not tonight.

He put his hand against the bars and pushed himself up and tucked his crutches back into the pain of his underarms and set out towards the nearest bridge to cross the Seine. The street of the fishing cat was a different sort of tourist attraction than the Eiffel tower or the Notre Dame. But it was a tourist attraction just the same. It was known as the narrowest street in Paris, the smallest of alleyways. Though there were a couple of others that argued that title of fame. Without already knowing that it was there, one would never see it tucked neatly between street side nick knack and souvenir shops. But if one knew to look for it, they could walk through it to the shops on the other side whilst reaching out to touch both walls of the alley

Philippe crossed the bridge slowly. He looked down at the reflection of the lamp light on the water and felt as if he were getting just a little slower with every assisted step. Part of him wanted this whole thing to be over. But there was a heavy fear in his heart that weighed him down and made him slow. He was afraid to encounter whatever and whoever was at the end of his journey. And he was afraid of the test that he knew the drugs would put him through.

He came to the end of the bridge nonetheless. The street was dark aside from the lamplight along the river. There were no cars driving at that time of night so ever so slowly, Philippe crossed the street at the crosswalk. The shops were closed up tight and the air was cold and quiet. In the distance he could see a dark figure walking briskly with his hood pulled up and his hands tucked securely into his coat pockets.

Philippe found himself feeling a little vulnerable with his crutches. This was indeed the city's witching hour. Not that he could have put up a fight without the crutches, but he was known to be fast when he needed to be.

With these thoughts going through his mind, Philippe noticed that at his pace, the dark figure would walk past the tiny alley before he himself did, and now he wished that he'd walked a little faster before. Philippe moved to step aside as the figure came close but the man veered right into him and shoved him hard with his shoulder, nearly knocking Philippe down and causing him to drop one of his crutches.

"Hey, get out of the way!" The man grunted, and just as if the whole thing hadn't been on purpose, the man kept walking on. Philippe stood startled and watched as the man crossed the street before he suddenly remembered to check his pockets to make sure his wallet hadn't been stolen. Not that there was much in it.

He was somewhat confused to find that his wallet hadn't been touched and he began to wonder if he had misperceived the collision. Perhaps the man had not meant to bump him and had simply been on his way home from a bar and wasn't sober enough to walk straight. But then, as he was curiously checking all his pockets, he found that nothing at all had been taken, but instead, something had been placed.

He pulled out a small slip of paper. It had been folded over once and rather than a seal, it had SP written on the front of it in what seemed to only be pencil. Philippe lifted his gaze to look into the direction that the man had retreated but he was already gone. What a strange person this "Prophet" was. He sighed and turned his eyes down and flipped open the slip of paper.

Around the next corner, the last poem you'll find.
But in it you'll see, no more riddles, no more rhymes.
In it you'll find only the truth most sublime.
I promise, when you read it, you'll understand it this time.
And after you've read it, instructions you'll find.

If you can find me, I'll treat you to tea.
And along with me the dragon you'll see.
But before you can meet him, you must first speak to me.
And then on my honor, your choice only it will be.

Will you chase after the dragon, or from the dragon be free?

He folded the innocuous slip of paper and pinched it between two fingers to grab hold of his fallen crutch. His armpits felt inflamed from having them bearing his weight all day and all night and he wondered if he was chafing. He looked up at the edge of the corner that he was about to turn. At least this clue was simple. 'Go around the corner.' easy enough.

Chapter 38. Street Prophet

When he came around the corner he saw the place on the wall where there had once been a painting of the fabled fishing cat and the old man who was his companion. As the story goes, the old man and the cat were often seen wandering around the area during the wee hours of the night. The cat would often be seen by the edge of the river with a fishing pole, fishing for his dinner with the old man nearby.

Their constant presence and the oddness of the cat always fishing in the river caused those superstitious members of old Paris to consider the thought that this old man was some sort of sorcerer and the cat, his demonic familiar. To be fair, Philippe certainly knew of no other cat with the ability to wield a fishing pole. But the fear of the people one day caused a few to decide that something needed to be done about this demonic duo. So one night, they came and they grabbed the cat and threw it into the Seine, drowning it among the fish. Much to their horror, in that same moment, the old man, vanished into thin air. But the very next night, the pair of them could be seen once again, fishing by the river. And the townsfolk of Paris elected to just let them be.

An ode to the story had once been painted on the wall in the smallest of alleyways right around the corner from the little store that bore the name of the street on a sign hanging above its doorway. The painting had been a simple one but evocative. A silhouette of the old man in a hat and coat standing with intrigue and mystery next to his shadow of a cat with its fishing pole lowered into the canal. But the painting had since been removed. Philippe wished that they had left it there.

He had at first assumed that the prophet's poem would be directly in its place but it was not. It wasn't on the edge of the wall within the view of any passerby who passed the alley. No, Philippe had to walk a little ways into the alley, towards the middle, tucked into the shadows. There where one could be hidden, if only for a moment, he found the last poem.

It was like a muralized street tag on the wall over the bricks. The prophet had an artistic hand and had obviously put much effort into being able to tag a wall with the length of an entire poem. If Philippe squinted, he could make out the words, but he decided to pull out his phone and turn on the flashlight. The colors, which were easy enough to make out in the dark, became utterly brilliant in the light. To hide such artistry in an alleyway, instead of in a place where it could be seen by everyone, seemed strange to him. But, he thought, perhaps after he read it, he would understand.

The letters were written in a deep midnight blue, but not black. All around it was a swirling vortex of gold and orange and red that tapered off into the color of the wall it was painted on. Like a glowing sunset that was setting all around the poem, receding into the brick.

What does God taste like?

Have you ever tried to taste him?

Like a child wanting only rock candy pops,

Is it the taste of the sweets that she loves?

Or is it the father who bought it for her on an outing?

Do they blend?

The taste of sugar, and the taste of love.

Does God taste like a paycheck?

Honestly or fraudulently earned?

Would he let you lick him to find out?

Or would that be too much an expression of greed?

Of lust?

Can we taste of wealth and still know the taste of that which is

Holy?

Are they the same?

Where are the taste buds that taste God?

Are they in our bodies?

Are they in our mouths?

Is it a feeling in our hearts?

Or on our skin, engorged and overwhelmed,

Or coursing through our blood with the drugs that must,

I say, must, taste like God.

Is that not the only explanation?

Surely that is why it is so wonderful.

Surely that's why you're here,

Whoever you are.

Surely that is why you're sitting there,

Shooting up on the stones,

Reading this poem.

They'll wash this poem away like the fishing cat,

But not before you've read it.

Not before you find yourself here seeking the taste of God.

Like I have.

Like you have tasted before.

But before they wash this away let me impart to you some truth.

It may be a crippling, incapacitating comfort for you to know

that…

You will not find him here.

But he might find you.

-Street Prophet-

Street Prophet. S.P. That was the seal that he'd put on the clues. His title. But like the innocuous piece of paper had said, this was no clue. It was a statement. "Only the truth most sublime" it had said. Philippe read the poem over again. He wondered how long this poem had been here. He wondered how long it would stay before it was painted over or power washed off. It occurred to Philippe that it had not been put there for his own sole benefit. It had likely been put there for anyone. But it did state bluntly the point that Philippe believed the Prophet had been trying to make all along. People do drugs because they are really looking for God. But drugs won't help to find him.

Why had the Prophet led him here? Why did the prophet care so much what he did? Why him? This poem was here for anyone to read. Why had the Prophet gone through so much trouble to show it to Philippe specifically? Philippe sighed. "But he might find you." The very last line. Philippe considered the effect that the Prophet might have been going for. He tried to imagine himself as a homeless addict, hiding out in this alleyway trying to shoot up, only to look up to see this poem on the wall right in front of him. Would these words be able to turn someone like that from their present course? Is that what the Prophet hoped it would do to him?

"But he might find you." Philippe did have to admit, part of him wished that his mother could have found herself in this alleyway looking at this poem. Maybe it would at least have suggested to her, that someone would find her. Perhaps that was reason enough for Philippe to consider its message.

Consider them Philippe did. He took the poem as it was. He wasn't sure that he was looking for God, but he could at least appreciate the sentiment. And some comfort and truth could be found in the words weather or not there was a God to look for. The sentiment that there is something deeper. A deeper hunger, which drugs cannot sate. Philippe had already known these things. But it was somewhat comforting to see it in language and color. Just in case anyone had forgotten.

But now, with a sigh, he turned his purpose back to his quest. Having all but lost his appetite for the end goal, he would follow this to its conclusion. But the poem on the wall did not tell him where the Street Prophet was hiding with the supposed tea and heroin. So he shined his light about the tiny alley, looking for the clue. The final instruction. It wasn't a scroll wrapped up and sealed with a ribbon. It was more like the innocuous poem he had in his pocket. He bent down and pulled a crumpled wrinkled slip of paper out from its place wedged in a crack between two bricks. He opened it up and smoothed the wrinkles to see if it was just trash, but the instructions therein were simpler than the last.

"I am but one small alley away from you." were the words scribbled across the creases. Philippe looked up and turned off his flashlight. He was quiet. Listening for any sound or sign of the Street Prophet. It was possible that he heard something, but it was also possible that he was only perceiving the all but unperceivable vibrations of the metro somewhere in the underground below him.

Chapter 39. Stutters of Freedom

He scuffled around the corner with his crutches. It felt strange, as if his stomach were somehow holding its breath. He was about to witness that which he had been chasing after. That which he did not know. Half of him believed with complete surety that there would be nothing in the alley around that corner. That somehow, all of it had been a dead end chase. A fun and fruitless imagining. But as he saw the candlelight play against the brick, he knew that he would not be so lucky.

He caught his breath when he saw the little dark ornate iron table and chairs. It was small and round and a petite white candle was sitting under the teapot to a completely mismatched tea set. But that wasn't what caught his breath. His heart had stopped when he saw who it was that was waiting for him. He had somehow expected a completely unfamiliar face. But the face that he saw, the author of all those poems, the alleged Street Prophet, was none other than the crucifix wearing, tattoo armed, bleach blonde, stuttering man who had let him walk free from the brothel.

He wasn't looking at Philippe. He was clutching onto the worn cover of what appeared to be a well-loved leather journal and with his other hand he was feverishly scribbling on its pages with a dull pencil.

"S-sit." He said without looking up, but Philippe was already looking all around himself to make sure that there was no one else that was going to leap out of the dark. The man looked up from his book to see why Philippe had not yet sat down. "D-don't be afraid. There's no one else here."

But Philippe was having trouble getting his heart rate to slow down. He hardly had a reason to trust this man. "Who are you?" he was slightly disturbed to hear his own voice crack. He frustratedly shook his head at himself and wound up his face and threw on a very forced smile. He tried to lower his shoulders to relax or at least to appear more relaxed.

"I'm S-Sasha." He was still slouched over his book as he looked at Philippe. Good posture wasn't his highest priority. Philippe glanced around himself one more time and then inched over towards the other chair. As he came closer, he saw that right out in the open, sitting, ignored on the ground next to Sacha's chair, was the bag of heroin, and a needle. Suddenly, Philippe's body remembered why it was there. His skin felt a crawl of anxiety while his gut simultaneously felt an unprecedented sense of relief. 'Just be cool and you'll get some.' said his body to his mind.

Philippe moved his crutches into the same hand and settled them against the wall as he sat himself down on the uncomfortable iron lawn chair. He tried to get himself to say something. Something like, 'what do you want?' or 'what do I need to do?' but something about the fact that he had just gotten done reading so much of the man's spiritual and poetic, revelative genius, made such mundane questions impossible. He realized, as his mouth hung open, trying to find words, that the ball was truly in Sacha's court. Sacha needed to be the first one to speak. To stutter an explanation.

Sacha looked at Philippe for a moment, and then shoved his stub of a pencil into the pocket of his jeans. He closed his ruddy journal, and half slipped it into his back pocket. Philippe watched the excessively large crucifix as it thudded against Sacha's chest while he moved. Not only was the cross gaudy and oversized, but he could also see the tiny figure of the crucified Christ hanging from it.

"Tea?" Sasha asked, and leaned forward to pour out.

"Would it offend you if I declined?" Sacha's hands stopped in midair as he reached towards the stout little teapot.

"No." Sacha rested his hands on the edge of the table. "When you've been d-drugged against your will, I don't b-blame distrust. You have a r-right to be cautious." He picked up the teapot and tipped it into his own cup. The handle of the cup had been cracked off. He picked it up and sipped it, then slowly drank the whole thing, scrunching his eyebrows slightly against the heat. "I, however, do not mean to drug you. N-not against your will at any rate." He set the cup down lightly and poured himself another. Then held the pot up towards Philippe and looked at him questioningly.

Philippe hesitated a moment before picking up his own cup and allowing Sacha to pour the tea into it. Sacha did, and then set the teapot back in its place over the candle.

"Did you l-like my scavenger hunt?" Sacha leaned back in his seat and folded his hands between his knees.

"What was the purpose of it?" Philippe picked up the cup and held it under his nose. Jasmine.

"Was I s-so unclear?"

Philippe set the tea down and opted to perhaps give it another minute before he tasted it. He looked up at the man sitting across from him. It just didn't seem to fit. Sacha was sitting in such an un-intimidating way. He looked downright welcoming. Everything in his poetry suggested a distaste for drugs but the bag and needle sitting poised and ready suggested otherwise. Not to mention the fact that the first time Philippe had seen him had not left him thinking of Sacha as any kind of friendly saint.

Sacha looked at Philippe's still perplexed expression and sighed. He leaned forward and laced his fingers together atop the table. "From what he said, I'm guessing that you didn't go to Landers looking for d-drugs."

Philippe swallowed hard and just shook his head.

"Then I'm giving you the ch-chance to walk away from what Landers did to you."

Philippe was startled by the tears that suddenly welled up to his own eyelids. "Um..." he mumbled and pressed his knuckles against his cheek to try and barricade the tears from falling. Crying in an empty alley next to a street smart thug just didn't seem wise to him.

Sacha continued. "He told me a little of your story. I can't make you for-g-give him. He's done some h-horrible, inexcusable things. You're entitled to y-your hatred. But, I can at least try to explain where h-he was coming from." Philippe felt his face beginning to flush red hot and he felt grateful for the shadows.

Then suddenly Philippe remembered, "Is he alive?" He lowered his hands from his face and looked directly at Sacha. He didn't want to have to think of himself as a possible murderer anymore. Even if it was self-defense. Sacha nodded his head and Philippe leaned back with an incredible sense of relief.

"Oh thank god." He sighed and rubbed the anxiety from his forehead.

"Yes. Thank God." Said Sacha in a tone much different from his own and picked up his teacup and took another sip. Philippe stared at Sacha as he drank.

"So, the sirens when I left, they were from an ambulance you called for Landers?"

"No. They were the p-police. But I said nothing, and th-they found no sign of you. Another case not closed. Did you not c-call them?"

"No." Philippe answered simply with a small shake of the head.

"Hmm." Sacha's eyes looked to the side and he furrowed his brow thoughtfully. Philippe could tell that this was one puzzle that Sacha didn't have the answer to. His expression told Philippe that he had assumed that Philippe had called the cops, though he'd had no intention of calling him out on it.

"Sacha, err… Prophet. Do you know why Landers drugged me? Did you help him? Do you know what he did with my car?"

Sacha set his cup back on the table. "S-Sacha is fine. And one q-question at a time I think. No, I did not h-help him. He called me after he d-drugged you." He tilted back in his chair so that the chair was only on two of its legs. "He said, 'Prophet, I need help, I did something b-bad.' So I c-came to help him th-through whatever it was that he'd done. I didn't ex-p-pect to find you." He looked down thoughtfully for a moment and then looked back up to Philippe, almost pleadingly. "He's a sick man Philippe. There's a lot of s-sick people in Paris. Esp-specially on the street."

Philippe had been spending all of this time so far trying to figure out who Sacha was and who he was trying to pretend to be. But this was the moment that Philippe realized that he hadn't spent even a moment pretending. Sacha was being nothing but honest and even compassionate. Philippe picked up his tea, and took a sip.

"W-why did you go there Philippe?" Sacha picked up his cup and began to slowly nurse it. "I-I don't think that Landers knew the answer to that."

"Well, because I didn't remember it. I couldn't remember anything about the brothel, or Landers." He smirked and shook his head. "I think that curiosity is my worst foible." He smiled flirtatiously at Sacha. "That's what brought me to this alley anyway. And it's what brought me to that place also. I couldn't stand having something about myself that I didn't know."

"What d-did you discover?"

Philippe took a sip of his tea. He liked Jasmine. "Everything I think. My mother must have been kidnapped. Shipped here to Paris and made to be a prostitute. The only French blood that I have is from some unknown man who must have abused and taken advantage of her. Just one of many."

They were silent for a moment and Philippe drained his teacup before continuing. Sacha was patient to hear his story. "The memory that was most vivid…" he swallowed and put his hand back up to his cheek.

"I'm n-not afraid of tears Philippe."

Philippe chuckled and forced his hand back down to his lap. He smiled gratefully and affectionately towards Sacha. "Okay." He said and took a deep breath. "I was in an old armoire listening to my mother and a man and I was trying to be quiet. Trying to block out the noise. I knew that if I got noticed then Landers would 'put me to work'," he made air quotes with his fingers. ", the same as the women. He'd pimp me out as a little boy." Philippe shook his head and looked down at his lap.

"I made a noise. I got noticed. That was the night the brothel got busted I guess." He wrapped his arms around himself. "The man that was with my mum looked like he was about to beat me when a bunch of officers stormed the place wearing bulletproof vests. Some strange part of me thought that they were somehow the consequence of the noise I'd made. Like they were my punishment. My mum had told me to never let the men find me and well… they found me. I know that's not the men who she was talking about. But it was still terrifying.

I feel like I should have listened to Veronica and just let it stay buried. I'd probably be better off now. I'm not sure that any of this has been worth it." He sniffed and put the cup down on top of the table. He pulled his new handkerchief out of his pocket and wiped his nose, then leaned over to pour the last bit of tea from the pot into his cup.

"So the m-memory that you lost, was one of being rescued."

Philippe looked up at Sacha and blinked past his tears. He set the empty teapot carefully back above the flame and furrowed his brow thoughtfully. "I suppose that's true."

"Then maybe it was a b-blessing, to see the life that you didn't have to live. I'm willing to bet that it would have been w-worse if you'd lived it."

Philippe looked down at the iridescent warmth swirling in his cup as he contemplated this. His life had not been a good one, all things considered. Now he was being asked to be thankful that it had not been worse. It was true that he could appreciate the fact that he had not become a child prostitute on the streets of Paris, but that certainly hadn't saved him from molestation. How much better was it really? Had he simply traded one bad life for another? Or was there really something there to be thankful for?

He considered his mother. The trauma of human trafficking had never left her. She had never been able to heal from it, or even to cope with it. The fact that she'd somehow managed to keep it a secret for all those years was beyond him. He could hardly compare his trauma with hers. Armel had been only one man. His mother had had to deal with many. Philippe had been sexualized by one person over the course of a year, but his mother had seen new faces daily since, who knows how old she'd been.

He supposed he could think of it that way. It could have been worse. He could have been much more privy to the pain that she went through. But he had trouble with that. It was true that it could have been worse. But he couldn't see how it not being worse could be construed as a 'blessing'. It was only not as bad as it could have been.

But there were two things to bear in mind. One, was that Sacha didn't know what the rest of Philippe's childhood had been like, so he was hardly one to judge if it had been better or worse. The other, was that Sacha had said nothing about the rescue being a blessing. He'd been referring to the memory itself.

He looked up from the tea and squinted through the salt stinging in his eyes at the candlelight glowing against the old brick wall. It was like another riddle that needed to be worked out.

"Look." Said Sacha, interrupting Philippe's puzzling thoughts. He reached down and picked up the bag of heroin and the needle and set them gently atop the table. Philippe swallowed against a sudden lump in his throat and he noticed, with some stroke of empathy, that Sacha was feeling much the same way about the temptation. Sacha continued to stutter though his explanation. Now they finally came to the meat of it.

"L-Lander's d-drugged you bec-c-bec-" Sacha put his hand over his mouth and scrunched his eyebrows together in frustration as he struggled to make his mouth do what his mind wanted it to do. But Philippe interrupted his struggle.

"Was he hoping to pimp me out? Start his brothel over again? Because he must have known that it wouldn't work." Philippe shrugged, "I don't think that I would have made him much business. I'm sure someone would have taken him up on the offer, but statistically adult men make an awful lot less as whores than do woman." Philippe set his tea down un-sipped. He'd lost his palate for it.

Sacha shook his head. Then he cleared his throat. Then he took a deep breath but still he waited an extra minute before attempting to speak again.

"Y-you were a symbol to him. Of a b-bygone era." He took another deep breath and closed his eyes. "L-like a bird he hoped to cage you. To capture the spirit of what he, in an unfocused and drugged out haze, imagines was a better time. Grasping for what he fantasizes of as the glory days, he grasped you. You are from that bygone era. The last glimpse of his old foundationless magnificence and the only reminder of his fall and failure. His goals and glory crumbled when salvation sprang you from his cage. Though that era has passed he wanted to recapture you. But the only way that he remembers how to make people love him, is to make them c-chemically d-dep-pendent on him." Sacha opened his eyes and looked to Philippe. "You s-see? You have to ch-choose to let it g-go." He lifted up the bag of heroin. "I c-couldn't have stolen that from you."

Philippe sat up straighter in his chair. That's what the scavenger hunt was for. If Sacha had been intending to do him a favor, then he couldn't have simply taken the drugs. But then Philippe may have sought to buy more elsewhere. Even if he managed to fend off that hurtle, what would happen if ever someone offered him the stuff? Through that poetic search, and the test that he was facing now, he could perhaps find a deeper seed within himself to build a better barrier against such temptations. If he could say no now, then he could say no later. But if Sacha hadn't taken the drugs, then Philippe wouldn't have had the chance to say no at all. Philippe was in awe. With words like that floating around in his head, it was no wonder that Sacha struggled to get them out.

"You're not too far g-gone for this. I w-wouldn't be able to do this with Landers."

"Why are you doing this?" The amount of trouble that this stranger had gone through just for this moment was staggering to Philippe.

Sacha smirked at Philippe. "I'm the Street Prophet. Everyone you m-met along the way has a history. Most of them, you'd r-rather not hear. My m-ministry, includes prevention. I'm doing this for you. But I'm als-so doing this for Landers. For his c-conscience. Lots of p-people help the victims. Who helps the perpetrators? M-many free the captives. But what about the p-prisoners? They are victims of s-something else and I'm here m-mostly for them."

Street Prophet. That was what they called him. "You…" Philippe furrowed his brow against the thoughts now invading his mind and crossed his arms over his chest. "Prevention… You think that I could have become like Landers? You think that I have that kind of sick potential?"

"We all do b-brother." Sacha stood up and took three steps away from the table to what Philippe saw was a drain in the ground. He held the bag out in front of him in one hand, and the needle in the other. "Th-the drain is deep. But the c-candle is still hot."

Philippe felt a chill run up his spine and a clammy shudder ran through his muscles from the top of his scalp to his cast bound toes. He nodded at Sacha, "Drain." and then bit his lip and watched.

Sacha smiled. He tucked the needle into his back pocket, likely for proper disposal, then he opened the bag and knelt down to the drain. "B-believe it or not. This is h-harder for me than it is for you." Philippe did believe it. He watched with a strange mixture of grief and relief as Sacha turned the bag upside down and emptied it down the drain.

Those emotions, while uncomfortable and strange, were not unexpected. What was unexpected was that Philippe suddenly realized that he was now free to properly mourn his mother.

Chapter 40. To Start Life Over

He turned the key in the lock to Aimee's apartment. He was happy that she'd gotten around to giving him a copy of the key. This way he could sneak into the apartment without waking her up. The door slid open quietly but a sharp pang of guilt hit him when he saw her curled up on the loveseat, fast asleep on her embroidered throw pillow. She had obviously been waiting up for him despite her intention to just sleep off the anxiety. Her feet were tucked up under her and she looked a little cold though she was too busy sleeping to notice.

Philippe gently let the door click shut behind him before he unbuttoned his coat to hang it on the hooks by the door. He settled his crutches in the corner and then settled his coat on the hook. He heard Aimee inhale deeply and then groan a little.

"Philippe?" She mumbled sleepily and he looked over to see that she was shifting into an upright position somewhat abruptly as if she hadn't at all meant to be sleeping. She glanced over at the stove clock and then stood up and Philippe could tell that she was convincing herself not to mention something about the time of night. "I didn't mean to worry but…"

"Aimee," He finished hanging his coat and then swiveled on his good foot to face her. "You had every right and instinct to be worried, and I'm sorry."

"Sorry? You don't need to be sorry Philippe. It's not as if it's the first time you've ever stayed out late I just..." She put her hand over her mouth and then waved the other hand wildly for no apparent reason as she scrunched up her eyes fighting tears. "Any day, absolutely any day at all, anyone's loved one could leave the house and never come home again. But nobody realizes that unless it happens. Or almost happens."

Philippe hastily grabbed one of his crutches and used it to help him take the few steps to close the distance to his friend where he promptly let it fall and wrapped his arms tightly around her. "I'm sorry Aimee."

"No, you have no reason to be sorry. I'm just being paranoid and my hormones are out of whack." He had every reason to be sorry. There were several layers of sorry that he could legitimately be at that moment.

"Aimee," He gazed at the dimly lit lilac flowers etched into the side of his mother's urn. "I think I'm ready to start my life over now." Aimee leaned her head back from his chest and looked up at his face.

"What do you mean?"

"I mean, I think it's time to stop chasing the past. It's time to move on. Nothing in the past will ever change. The life my mother had and didn't have. The life that I did or didn't have. It's time to move on. It's time for me to admit that, no matter what happened back then, I... I miss my mum." He wept and that was what it really boiled down to all along wasn't it? From the very beginning, from the day that the lilac dress fell on his face in the armoire to the day they opened the door to apartment number 36. From the thefts to Armel to Marcello's car. From clothes to makeup to starving for food and attention and flashing lights. From New York to Paris, from Veronica to Aurelio. From love and lust and Botox to affection and caresses and heroin. He`d always just missed his mum. Only now, he could finally admit it.

So they cried, and they held each other and they slept. They woke with the sun and Aimee called in sick to work and they cried and slept some more. The urn sat on the bedside table and they talked and took the time to remember all of the good memories that they shared with his mother. All the things that they missed and would always miss when they thought of her. Aimee confessed all the times, even when Philippe was in New York that she'd gone to her house and helped with her dishes, talked to her about anything at all but mostly Philippe and how proud of him she was.

They got out of bed and brought the urn with them and ate crepes and reminisced about the times when they were young and his mother would smile at them or tell them to be careful when they played. Little endearing moments like telling them not to climb too high. And Philippe remembered the times when it was just the two of them, when his mother always seemed sick but she would still hold him and sing him a sad sort of lullaby. Or hum a tune with no words because, Philippe now new, all of the words were in Swedish.

The moments were small and few, but in them Philippe was able to see a little of who she was meant to be and who she truly was underneath the pain, and the trauma and the addiction. Those things began to peel away in his mind because he realized that they weren't her, they were things that had been covering her up. But underneath, she had still been there, and that was how Philippe would choose to remember her.

He forgave her that day in his heart, and in their own special way, they spent the time giving her their own personal memorial service. Until the sun set again and tomorrow, life would resume coarse. The future would continue. The pain in his heart had lessened a little, but the healing was only beginning. He was ready to start life over, but what that would truly mean, he didn't yet know.

Chapter 41. Freeloader

Philippe clutched the crook of his cane as he hobbled his way slowly from the bedroom towards the kitchen. Finally without a cast, his ankle was free to breathe the air and his skin felt better for it after copious amounts of lotion. But his muscles were slow to regain their strength. Being a person with so little muscle in general, he learned that he'd always taken for granted how much work his muscles had offhandedly been doing all his life. Who knew that his ankle had always been strong enough to hold him up until now? But he was still healing quickly. The doctors had suggested that he continue using the crutches for a while but he was tired of them, so instead he was working that much harder with a cane.

"Guess what." Said Aimee who, in her pajamas in the kitchen was setting a cup of espresso on the bar for Philippe to sip at. She had to turn sideways in an awkward direction to keep her now obvious belly from getting in the way of the counter.

"Don't hold me in suspense." Philippe scrunched his face for a moment as he struggled his way onto the tall bar chair and hooked his cane onto the back of it. "And thank you." He said, and lifted the espresso to sip at it.

"I'll be able to start classes again in the spring."

"Oh that's wonderful! I'm so happy to hear that."

"Yup. And I figure, when this little guy comes out, I'll just take as many online classes as I can for a while."

"That's how you're going to reap the benefits of your maternity leave?"

"I figure that three months of not needing to split my school time with work will give me the chance to take a couple extra credits."

"And some time to get to know your baby."

"I don't think I'll have much choice but to get to know him." They chuckled.

"Just don't forget to rest is all."

"Well that's what I have you for now isn't it."

"Oh I'm sure he and I will be seeing a lot of each other. Have you thought of a name yet? Or are you planning on waiting until you see his face."

"I'm not sure that the squished new baby expression would tell me a lot about him Philippe. But no, I haven't settled on a name yet. I think maybe, Lucas, or Hugo. What do you think?"

"I've always kind of liked the name Jerome." Aimee Laughed and nearly choked on her sip of espresso.

"Jerome?"

"Yes, Jerome. I think it's a nice name."

"Alright." she shook her head and chuckled, "I'll put it on the list then."

"Well, it's your baby Aimee, you should choose the name you like best."

"Hey now, if it's your name that's going onto the paperwork as the baby daddy, then you can't go thinking like that or no one will be convinced." Philippe smiled.

"Well then. I guess Jerome is on the list." Aimee shook her head at the name and drained her little cup of espresso.

"Alright. I have to take a shower and get ready for work. What's on your agenda for the day?"

"Um... Well..." Philippe pulled a culinary magazine towards himself and opened up one of the pages. "I was thinking I might make us dinner tonight."

"Who knew that Philippe would become a culinary artist? You've been doing this a lot lately. What are we having?"

"I was thinking scallops." He turned the magazine around and showed Aimee an amazing picture of scallops drizzled in something, resting daintily on a shell.

"That looks absolutely delicious Philippe. But I can't eat seafood while I'm pregnant."

"Ah!" He exclaimed and face palmed his forehead. "Right. Of course. Well, not that then. I'll think of something else."

"As long as it's a masterpiece." She winked and retreated to the restroom for her shower.

Philippe turned the page of his magazine and racked his mind for other ideas. He looked up at his mother's urn while he thought. The urn had taken a somewhat permanent central location as an ornament on the edge of the bar next to a potted plant which had started looking much better since Philippe had moved in and was watering it regularly.

There was always salad but he was feeling a little burnt out on salad. Though the dressings could be so interesting to put together, salads really took no skill to prepare. Just a few ingredients to bulk it up. Nuts, fruit, meat, what have you and various dressings tossed together with various greens. There were only so many combinations that could be tried before one just needed to taste something other than salad.

Meat then. Pasta perhaps? Not seafood, perhaps fowl. Chicken? He looked away from the urn and turned the page again looking for inspiration. But while one part of his mind was trying to put together an ingredients list, another part of his mind was considering his own motivations for cooking so much. Aimee was right, he was the last person one would expect to do so much cooking since he was the last person that one would expect to do any great quantity of eating. But it was not the stomach that he meant to satisfy, it was the tongue. With the right amount of richness, no one could eat a lot and everyone would feel satisfied after a bite or two of something so perfect.

His mind digressed into a fantasy of tastes and textures until he returned to his quandary of motivation. What if he was just spending his time cooking because he was still otherwise useless? He picked up his cane and looked at it. It wasn't a bad cane, but it wasn't the best cane. Quality being judged purely on its appearance. He found himself wondering just how photogenic a cane might be. Once upon a time, Marcello had told him that when he was ready, he could come back to modeling. While his foot was broken, he had avoided Marcello like the plague but perhaps now, he could pull it off. Perhaps there was more he could contribute to his little household than just good flavors. Maybe he could stop being a freeloader and help with the rent.

He got down from the chair and used his cane to hobble back into the bedroom where his phone was charging on the bedside table. He picked it up and stared at the blank screen for a moment before typing in Marcello's number. Just a text.

"The modeling offer still open?" It read, and after so many months, Philippe would not have been surprised if Marcello never responded. But after he hit send his stomach lurched and he suddenly regretted sending it. How would he go about telling Marcello about the car? Gone forever. And now he hoped beyond all hope that Marcello wouldn't respond at all. But barely twenty seconds later, he was still standing in the bedroom staring disbelievingly at his phone when it vibrated in his hand.

"Of course!" Was Marcello's response. Oh crap… Philippe thought. Why hadn't he considered the car before texting Marcello? But Marcello didn't give him time to think.

"When are you available?" No, Philippe wasn't ready for this. Marcello would never forgive him for the loss of that Mercedes no matter what trauma had happened to him. A freak accident could have totaled the car leaving Philippe a vegetable in the hospital and Marcello would not have forgiven him.

"I have an opening available this afternoon if it's not too short a notice." Marcello just kept texting and Philippe just couldn't bring himself to respond.

"It's actually an outdoor shoot and I think you'd be perfect in it." Philippe looked around the room as if something in it could aid him in his dilemma.

"Let me know if you can make it. Or just meet us at Notre Dame." Notre Dame? That made him think of Sacha, and he kicked himself for not having thought of this before. Sacha had been there with Landers. He had known something about what Landers had done, with whom, and why. Was it too farfetched for Sacha to have the smallest idea about what had happened to the car? The police had of course never found it, and the insurance company had already given Philippe some monetary consolation. It had been months since then, so the likelihood was small, but there was hardly any harm in asking.

"If you do come Philippe, make sure to bundle up. These are chilly winter shots but we don't need the models all covered in goosebumps." It didn't take any cold to cover Philippe in goosebumps right now. He didn't respond to Marcello at all, which he knew would irritate the man in just a few minutes. But in the meantime he could think a little. He closed the conversation window with Marcello, and opened up a text to Sacha.

"I know this is probably a long shot, it's been a few months, but Landers stole my car. Would you have even the slightest idea about what he could have done with it?" He hit send, then he waited. Sacha didn't seem to be nearly as attached to his phone as Marcello because he didn't respond right away.

Philippe gripped onto his cane and started making his way back out towards the bar counter. Philippe knew that the "just show up" suggestion that Marcello had made was complete bogus. He'd only said it because it was a nice thing to say. He knew that instead, Marcello was waiting for a response and were Philippe to "just show up" he would find himself with an earful when he got there.

He wrestled his way back onto the bar chair and then swiped back into Marcello's text. Should he? Aimee came out of the shower room with one towel barely wrapping around her belly and another twisted into her hair. He smiled at her as she walked by and went into the bedroom to find a change of clothes. Then he bit his lip and looked back down at the text screen.

"I'll be there!" He hit send. The text seemed too cheery, but he had typed it with intense hesitation.

"Great!" Responded Marcello. "We'll all meet you there in three hours. I've missed you my boy." Philippe winced and ran his fingers through his hair. Ew… now he was the one that needed a shower.

"Why is it such a pain to find a clean shirt that fits?" groaned the voice of Aimee from the bedroom.

"Hey Aimee, when you come out, I want to give you some news." His voice was so much more jovial than his nerves. Of course, just then, as fate would have it, Philippe's phone vibrated and he looked down to see a text from Sacha.

"I'll look into it." Sacha said. Philippe wished that he'd said that sooner. He wondered what hope there was that Sacha could actually find the car. There was even less hope of it being in any worthy condition. But Philippe had fixed it up once, and in his youth no less, so maybe he could do it again. Of course, it had been previously well cared for and he'd had a lot of help from Marcello. Philippe assumed that whoever had ended up with it, had likely not treated it so well.

"You look so thoughtful." Said Aimee, coming out of the room having apparently found the shirt that would fit over her belly. "What's on your mind?"

"I was actually just texting Sacha, and he told me that he'd look into the whereabouts of my car."

"Oh." She looked mostly concerned. "I know how much you loved your car Philippe, but are you sure it's a good idea to open that door back up again?"

"Well, I'd had this thought. Landers had stolen my keys and done something with my car. No idea what. Sacha had been in contact with Landers, but I don't know that he would have seen where the car went, but perhaps he could find out. It would have been better if I'd managed to think to ask him about it months ago but I didn't. We were too busy talking about WHY Landers did what he did as opposed to talking about WHAT he actually did." The truth, if Philippe had remembered was not that he had forgotten to ask, but that Sacha had forgotten to answer.

Philippe furrowed his brow thoughtfully. "You know, one part of that conversation never quite came clear to me. The most curious thing. When I escaped Landers, it was because Sacha let me go. But he asked me not to call the police. I didn't really question it much at the time. But when I left the building, I heard sirens. I assumed that Sacha had called an ambulance for Landers. But when I talked to him, he had thought that I'd called the police. I didn't call the police, and neither did he, so who did?"

"I did." Philippe blinked. He hadn't expected that curiosity to be so swiftly settled. "Yeah. You didn't know that?"

"Well, no. I was gone by the time they got there."

"Yeah, the police called me back to tell me that you weren't there but that an old man had fallen down a flight of stairs and had been taken to the hospital. I was worried that you were somewhere that they couldn't find you, and I almost went to look for you myself. I came home to change into better search and rescue clothes. Thank God I did, because that's when I found you passed out on my doorstep."

"But why did you think to call the police? I saw the text conversation that Landers had with you." She smiled kindly at him.

"You might want to read that conversation again if you haven't deleted it. You would never have a conversation so vague with me. It took me a little while to stop second guessing myself and finally call the cops. But I could tell it wasn't you. I didn't have any idea who it was, but it definitely wasn't you. But after a little research into that address and its history, I figured that was where you had gone, so that's where I sent the cops." His jaw was slightly dropped.

"You're amazing."

"Well thanks," She giggled, "but I'm just glad that you're alive." She pecked him on the cheek and then went over to the coat hanger. "Well, I've got to get to work. Please be careful with that Sacha guy. I know you trust him, but I also know how you are with trusting people, and I think it's weird that he counsels freaks like Landers." She lowered her head as she looked down to slip on her shoes. She muttered mostly to herself, but Philippe heard her clear as day. "Cause some people are just beyond forgiving." She mumbled, and then looked up and smiled at Philippe. "Alright I'm off. Don't tell me what you're making for dinner alright. I want to be surprised." And she was out the door.

That hadn't been all his news. But that was alright, he supposed he could fill her in about his opportunity with Marcello while they ate dinner. Now... what was he making for dinner?

Chapter 42. Model Reunion

There was a camera team in front of the Notre Dame as Philippe came up out of the Metro tunnel and started heading towards it. He hobbled slowly, cane in hand. He was wearing a discrete brace wrapped tightly around his ankle for the added stability. It was invisible under his pant leg, but he could feel it. And as long as he kept the laces loose, he was able to fit a shoe over it. He could see Marcello's broad back as he seemed to be having a stern conversation with one of the photographers. He half hoped that Marcello would take one look at his cane and tell him to go home. But he knew better. In all truth, either Philippe would just stand lightly on that foot, or it would be decided that the cane was a nice touch. But the small gaggle of models standing around like a pack of high schoolers was another matter. Come to think of it, at least a few of them probably were high schoolers.

"Philippe!" Exclaimed Marcello as Philippe got closer. "What on earth happened to your leg that you are needing to carry a cane?" Marcello had a thick Italian accent when he spoke French, but still commanded the language beautifully. He was a sturdy, somewhat stocky man with broad shoulders. He was strong and worked out often but his metabolism was beginning to show his age. He was however, extremely well dressed in a suit and a thick black coat. His hair was slicked back perfectly and his beard was very well groomed and neatly trimmed. He quirked a half smile and raised an eyebrow as he looked down at Philippe's cane and limp.

"It's a long story." Philippe smiled, "but it's good to see you."

"It's good to see you too." He clapped his hand hard on Philippe's back and then roughly put his arm around his shoulder like some over confident bear and kissed him on both cheeks. "Hey all you kids." He called to the models as if they were children. "This is Philippe, I think a couple of you girls know him yes?"

"Oh Philippe!" Liz, of all people, came bounding out of the crowd. If you could call it bounding that is, her skirt was too tight and her heels were too high, but she did come over with excitement. Liz was nearly as tall as Philippe as it was, but those heels put her right over the top and she leaned down ever so slightly to kiss him on either cheek. "I've been getting into the customs around here. I think I might have to stay for a while darling."

"How long have you been here?" Philippe grinned. He wondered what Liz's experience with that agency had been like since Veronica's death and how she had managed to find her way into Marcello's gentle care.

"About a month. And I'm absolutely adoring it. You grew up in this marvelous city?"

"I don't mean to interrupt," Said Marcello, obviously meaning to interrupt. "But we have a shoot to get on with. And Philippe, I think that your cane is the perfect classy touch. And you know what, for the next shoot, I'll even get you a new one. Shinier. New and improved. I have just the thing in mind. I know you'll like it. Alright!" He suddenly took his arm off of Philippe and clapped his hands loudly. "Everyone into your places!" Liz hopped away from Philippe back over to the group. "Well Philippe, maybe I was meant to be a film director instead, what do you think?"

"Um…" Philippe started, but Marcello continued.

"Well, I know this was short notice for you, so I brought along a few things for you to wear and I had just hoped that you would fit into the same things that you fit into before. Your makeup is fine for this sort of shoot, we will have some more prep next time. But for now, these amateurs," He said with a wink, "are going to start things off with the photographer and I'll give you an outfit that I want you to go change into. He gave Philippe another hard slap on the back and then disengaged from him and went over to the photographer to watch his work.

Philippe found himself holding a bag full of designer clothes for the winter fashion. He started hobbling slowly towards the Notre Dame. He wondered what sort of advertisement they were shooting for. Travel? Was someone out there trying to get more tourists to Paris in the winter months? He looked up at the ancient building that he had no need to enter. But he couldn't help but linger for a long moment next to the stairs that led down to the public restroom just a short ways off from the cathedral. It loomed above him, but with a sigh, he descended the stairs.

After he was changed he made his way back over to the photoshoot. He was wearing mostly cool colors but there was a bit of warmth to counter balance it. A thick pea coat that came down to the backs of his knees was the only black thing he was wearing aside from his shiny black shoes. His pants were gray and he wore a quite comfortable auburn sweater with the collar of an off ice blue button up shirt sticking out from underneath. He had on a long scarf wound round and round his neck and a pair of fluffy ear muffs over his ears that no one would ever actually wear. But that didn't matter, this was photography. This was art.

But as Philippe sidled up along his companions and was guided into position, he felt a little out of place. Though the poses were like second nature to him and even with his cane he was perfect, something just didn't feel quite like it used to. He felt that he honestly wished he were someplace else. Truly, he wished that he were back at home, cooking.

Chapter 43. Flashback Martini

He found himself sitting at a party with a martini in his hand. But somehow getting there had seemed surreal to him. The pictures had been taken, smiles had been made, Liz had made a comment about how she could tell that he hadn't used Botox again, but he still couldn't seem to shake the sensation that he somehow wasn't where he was supposed to be.

"Philippe," Said Liz as she sat down next to him. Her drink was mostly empty, but he couldn't seem to drink his own. "It's been too long darling and you've hardly said a word to me. Tell me, what brought you back to Paris? Not that I blame you mind." He smiled and turned his eyes to look at her more clearly.

"Oh, I grew up here. This is home. But I'm more curious about what brought you to Paris Liz. And Margarete over there, who hasn't said a thing to me all day. You'd think we were strangers."

"We came together. Isn't that nice? Roommates for life." There was a mild tone of sarcasm in her voice.

"And Aurelio?"

"I believe he took an opportunity in Milan. Though it's been awhile since we were in touch. You know, everything just sort of fell apart after... well, you know. After Veronica was murdered. It was murder you know. Premeditated and everything. From what I understand, it was a rival designer with the magazine. He was found guilty of the crime, although you know, I don't think he did it himself. I think he used a hit man. Huge scandal. And we the models just sort of got lost in the whole thing and ended up taking jobs elsewhere. I think La Facare is still tied up with lawyers."

"She was murdered by another designer?" Philippe felt so small. This was the first he was hearing about this. If the whole thing had happened just a little later, it would have been different. They would have been married, their relationship would have been public, and he would have been the first person to hear about it. But as it was, to the rest of the world, his relationship with her had meant next to nothing, and only he knew better.

"I guess there was some discussion about taking the magazine into a different direction. You know, less gaudy. Not that Veronica's styles weren't amazing, but it was a little like playing dress up princess. These women aren't children anymore. Still, that hardly gives anyone grounds for murder."

"That was the whole point of her designs." He felt suddenly defensive. Like he needed to defend Veronica's honor. "It was to remind women of their worth. To take out all the stops and dress like a queen."

"I'm not saying that they weren't lovely, I'm saying that no one would ever be able to find an occasion to wear them."

"That didn't stop her from wearing them. She was trying to show women what they could be." Liz turned to look at him more full on having taken full notice of the fact that he was suddenly arguing with her about something that she seemed to feel was only harmless gossip.

"You certainly do seem to care an awful lot."

"Well, she was murdered in cold blood over nothing but petty jealousy."

"People have been murdered for less Philippe. It was a horrible scandal and a pity for the loss but there is plenty of amazing fashion out there, for feminists or otherwise."

"I just think we should hold her memory with a little more reverence." He finally lifted his martini to his lips and took a drink.

"I get it." Said Liz leaning back and looking a little bit smug. "Aurelio knew what he was talking about. You were in love with her weren't you?"

"Would her name be worth less if I weren't?"

"I do think it probably has something to do with why you're being so touchy about it. And I doubt you were the only one in the love with the woman. Hard not to be."

"It was different."

"How?"

"We were engaged to be married."

"Oh." She looked like this was new information to her, and it was questionable whether or not she believed him. "Well… why don't we talk about something else?" He sighed and shook his head.

"No thanks Liz." He got up and drained his glass and set it gently on a counter before hobbling his way to the door. When he opened the door to leave, he looked back and saw that Liz was smiling and talking to Margarete their conversation had never happened. He closed the door behind him and left the building and stood on the sidewalk for some minutes, wondering where to go, and what to do.

He couldn't figure out why he didn't know where to go. He could go back into the party, he knew how to do it, but he didn't want to. None of them wanted to talk about things as they really were. Had he been like that? He certainly hadn't felt like that. He could only assume that they didn't either. So he could hardly blame them.

Another part of him just wanted to go back home to Aimee's apartment. But he was getting so stir crazy. The cabin fever was one thing certainly, but also if he went home, he would need to go to the grocery store first. The grocery store just seemed so mundane an activity, and he still had some time before dinner needed to be cooked. What was he going to make for dinner anyway?

He could just walk aimlessly until something came to him. His ankle didn't quite have the stamina for that though, but perhaps it could work for a little while. He decided to start with that. He gripped his cane and started walking.

Part of him was also still waiting for Sacha to get a hold of him, but he had no idea when he would do that. The idea that Sacha may have actually found his car seemed unlikely. So he mentally prepared himself for Sacha to say 'oops, never mind, wrong car.' There was also the possibility that his car was found, but totaled. For such a thing to happen to such a vintage masterpiece would be tragic, but still, he took the moment to mentally prepare himself just in case Sacha said, "This is the car… I'm so sorry for your loss."

After a time of wandering and thinking of morbid car related scenarios, he found himself walking along the river and again moving towards Notre Dame. He stopped. He had always thought of The Church universal as a symbol of purity. It was thus ironic since it was often full of hidden scandals and atrocious sins. This church was no different. In fact, it was even worse. Aside from all of the history, it was a church on display. Like a play act, everyone had his lines down. Everyone knew how to play the part. And that meant that all the dirt had to be buried deeper. No church was pure, no matter how much it tried. Churches were built on people, and people were never better than their roots.

It wasn't that Philippe held it against them. He expected people to be that way. But it just felt so dishonest. Then again, he'd just left a room full of dishonest people. Then again, at least they weren't hiding their two faced nature. They knew that they had problems. It had seemed to him that so many of Sacha's poems had blatantly stated that everyone had the same problem. Philippe felt that it was a simplistic concept, but true enough. Models weren't all that different from church goers in a way. Whatever it took to make them feel better about themselves.

In that church Philippe knew that there was a man who was a priest, who was supposed to be pure, but instead he had been a brothel patron. Honestly, for Philippe, it wouldn't have bugged him so much if the man had been one or the other. It was the fact that he was both that bothered him. But it wasn't as if he hadn't known that sort of thing to happen, and the thought had never bugged him before because he knew that priests were just men. Whatever they might think. No, Philippe discovered in himself that it was really only because of his mother. He was the only person who Philippe knew who had been one of his Landers's clients. Perhaps even one of his mother's regulars.

He wanted to leave this behind. He didn't want to chase her ghosts anymore. But he took a deep breath and took a limping step forward. Everyone had a story. Everyone had a reason for the things that they did. Philippe wanted to know his motives. He wanted to know his story. And besides that, he needed a place to sit down.

Chapter 44. Father Samuel

He walked to the archway of the door and looked up at the faces engraved around it. He remembered a few months ago when they had seemed to be looking down on him both literally, and figuratively. But they were just stone. So he crossed their threshold and passed their leering eyes.

Inside he heard chanting. Or singing. He wasn't sure which. The chairs had people in them who were all standing, or sitting, or kneeling on the hard ground. There were robed men and women standing at the front with books held open that they were reading out of. He couldn't understand a word they said, and he supposed they were probably chanting in Latin or Greek or something like that. There was also a small gaggle of tourists following a guide with ooh's an aah's as the guide led them and their snapping smartphones up a flight of stairs to go look at the bells and the home of Quasimodo.

Then the chant, or song, came to a close and those in the chairs all sat down. A man then stood up at the ever so tall podium at the front and began reading something that he did understand.

"I will hear what God proclaims; the LORD—for he proclaims peace to his people. Near indeed is his salvation to those who fear him, glory dwelling in our land." Then all of a sudden, everyone in the pews said in unison,

"Lord, let us see your kindness, and grant us your salvation." Then he priest continued his part.

"Kindness and truth shall meet; justice and peace shall kiss. Truth shall spring out of the earth, and justice shall look down from heaven." From all the way across that great room the priest's eyes met Philippe's while the congregation chanted their response.

"Lord, let us see your kindness, and grant us your salvation." The priest continued to say his part but Philippe had stopped hearing the words because he had known that face. The priest who had admitted that he had been one of Landers's patrons all those years ago.

He found a chair to sit in and waited. Twenty minutes later the service finally ended, and Philippe did not move from his seat. The giant congregation filed out of the building slowly until aside from one or two people, the chairs were empty. The chanting was over. And the acoustics caused the talking of the tourists to echo all too much. He didn't see the priest. But he waited.

One thing he did admire was the skill of Notre Dame's creators. The art, the architecture. The history of the various parts being built, or burnt down by ancient riots and then re-imagined, and rebuilt. It was worth looking at. It was worth studying. Whether you were religious or not. He sighed and if nothing else, enjoyed the rest for his foot.

"I had wondered if you would come back." Philippe looked up to see that Landers's patron priest was standing next to him. The old man wore a small smile. "May I sit?" as if that chair belonged to

Philippe. It didn't so Philippe smiled and nodded and scooted over to give the old a seat. The priest settled in beside him and was just quiet for a moment. "Well, I see that your foot is doing some better. No crutches. And that looks like a fine cane. I suppose by the time you've healed enough to be done with it, I might be needing it if you'd be willing to lend it to me. Heh heh."

"Well, then when I'm done with it it's yours." Philippe smiled though his eyes looked at his cane rather than at the man's face.

"Well thank you. I can't say as I'm looking forward to needing it, but I can tell that I'm headed in that direction." Small talk. This wasn't the time or the place for it. But it made a nice initial barrier.

"Father Samuel--" Philippe began.

"Sam. Please just call me Sam." He was smiling, but his blue eyes looked a little sad. "Though I'm happy to hear that Sacha told you my name, because I'm quite certain that I forgot to introduce myself when last we met. I'm told that I've been doing that a lot lately. I must be going senile. Ha!"

Philippe sighed. "Sacha didn't tell me your name. I looked it up. Then I looked up your career history. All the public stuff. Your education, your credentials, the time you've spent traveling around the world as a missionary. I even found out that you legally adopted Sacha when he was a teenager. You've led an interesting life." Philippe looked up from his cane at the tired, old but thoughtful face of the priest. "Will you please tell me your story Sam?"

"You know it's been quite a few years since I've had to face some of my old sins. I have had to face them now and again. It seems that this is one of those now and again times doesn't it?" Philippe couldn't quite tell if this question was rhetorical. He decided to cut to the chase.

"You used to go to brothels, but how do you know that you went to the one my mother was in?"

"It's just a guess really. I was a gross creature of habit. I only ever went to one place. Sacha would have known that."

"Why would Sacha have known that?"

"Oh, he and I have had quite the many long heartfelt talks."

"About brothels?"

"About a lot of things. You see, heh, he's always trying to help people through things, and so am I. We ended up helping each other quite a bit I think."

"Are you lovers?"

"No." Sam cocked his head and furrowed his brow curiously and looked skeptically at Philippe. "I find it interesting that that would be your first thought. Sacha came to me when he was running from a pretty terrible lifestyle living on the street. He can tell you his own story if he cares to. He had no parents and no home, and I wanted to keep him from falling through the cracks back into his old life. It's not the sort of thing priests normally do, but I felt called to do it. I mean I felt called to adopt him rather than send him through any of the other resources that could have helped him." Sam shrugged. "But I don't think that's the part of my story that you are looking for. And I'd rather leave Sacha to tell you the details about that if he cares to."

"Sorry. I didn't mean to assume. I was just trying to understand why and mostly how Sacha had sent me to someone who was one of Landers's patrons."

"Well, Landers for one. If you're wanting the how. You just told me how. You, Sacha and I, must all know the man's name. True?"

"True."

"So that's the how. Perhaps you want to know the why?"

"Who." Philippe said. "I want to know for sure if you knew my mother."

"Well…" The man took a deep breath as if this were delving a little closer to the memories themselves than he really liked. But for Philippe he was willing, so he asked, "What was her name?"

"Emilia. Her name was Emilia. Did they use their real names?" Sam's hands were crossed over his arms holding his elbows as he thought back uncomfortably on those thoughts.

"Petite thing." His voice got quiet. "Blonde straight hair. Fourteen or fifteen years old probably. Only passable at speaking French." He looked over at Philippe. "Yeah." Said Sam quietly, sadly. "I knew her."

"I only learned right after she died that she wasn't from France. Her French must have gotten a lot better. I had never managed to guess it."

"Do you know where she was from?"

"I found out that she was from Sweden. So I'm only half French at most."

"I'm sorry for your loss Philippe. And I'm sorry that I had anything to do with it. Back then I wasn't too good at thinking about consequences. I've since had to face many of them. I guess I'm looking at one right now aren't I?" Sam was looking at Philippe.

"There's no proof that you're in any way related to me." When Philippe said it, it came out a little more defensive than he meant it to.

"I'm not saying that you are my offspring. I am saying that you could be. And whether or not you are, you are still the product of an industry that I bought into. Without patrons, there would be no prostitution. In that way, I am just as responsible for your birth as anyone else, and just as responsible for your loss." Philippe didn't know what to do with that. He felt the tears welling up under his eyelids. He could find a way to take offense. He could think of plenty of people who would. He could just imagine Aimee saying, 'no, sorry old man, you can't make up for your crimes.' But he wasn't the sort to hold a grudge. And everyone had a reason, everyone had a story.

"Why did you do it? How long did you do it for? When did you stop?"

"Now I see we're getting to the why. And a little of the when, but if you don't mind, I'll just answer one question at a time."

"Sorry."

"Don't be, at least these are the kinds of questions that have straight answers. Ha! I'm used to questions like, what was God's purpose in all of this tragedy? Or, why didn't God heal my dying child when I prayed? Much less straightforward. I guess I'll start with the when. Sadly, I started seeking that sort of recreation right around the time that I was ordained. I lived a double life for too many years. I stopped around… oh… two decades ago or so. How old did you say you were?"

"Twenty… ish."

"Ah well then… Yes, around then ish."

"Why did you stop?"

"Would you believe me if I told you that I didn't think that I was hurting anyone?"

"Well I…" He suddenly thought of Armel. He remembered bumping into him outside of his mother's apartment only a few months ago. Even after all those years he had turned to Philippe and said, 'I never hurt you.' and Philippe could tell that he'd meant it. Armel truly believed that he hadn't hurt Philippe as a child, and for years, Philippe had believed that he hadn't been hurt. "Yes." He said nodding to Sam. "I guess I do believe you."

Sam smiled sadly. "I'm sorry to hear that. That tells me that you've seen too much. I stopped because I realized that I was hurting people. As we say in the church, I was convicted of my sin. The pain that I was causing was put heavily on my heart."

"How did you realize that?"

"People go way out of their way to try not to realize those kinds of things you know. I always did my best not to ask too many questions, so that I wouldn't have to try to justify the answers. Most of Landers's girls were local and they had all sorts of sad reasons for being there. But every time, I saw it as their choice, and thus not my problem. Then he started collecting foreign girls, such as Emilia. It wasn't as if I was personally responsible for his decision so I mostly ignored it. After all, it wasn't me who was running the business.

Emilia became my favorite. I say that with a very bitter taste in my mouth. But at some point I had an epiphany that even if I asked her why she had chosen that life, she would not have had enough control over the language to be able to properly answer me. But I was able to ignore that because it wasn't as if we talked all that much anyway." He stopped talking for a moment and took a deep steadying breath. Then he turned and said, his face almost pleading, "I'm so sorry Philippe."

Philippe bit his lip, nodded and said in a low whisper, "Please continue." The old man looked at him strangely, as if he had a hard time understanding why or how Philippe could possibly wish to listen to this. But he pushed on.

"When Emilia became pregnant is when I fled. I told myself that it was at least a hundred to one that you were mine but my mind couldn't seem to shake the fact that that hardly mattered. What mattered was that a girl, only halfway through her teens had gotten pregnant by a stranger. Any stranger. One out of a hundred strangers. And it was at that moment that I was convicted. I realized that weather or not she chose it, she did not deserve it. Nor did any of them. No sad circumstance could ever give anyone, not even me, the right to exploit their choices.

So I left, and I went into prayerful seclusion for several years. When I returned, the brothel was gone and I was happy for it. Then I found Sacha and when I adopted him I felt as though there was penance to be found in being able to help someone find a way out of a sorrowful loop made by bad choices. Instead of exploiting, I had an opportunity to liberate. But now it seems, it has come full circle hasn't it? You were the thing that helped me to leave that old life, and now here you are. I can't say that I quite know what to make of it."

"Me neither." Philippe said quietly. "Thank you for telling me."

"I don't know if it helped you to hear it, but that is the truth."

"The truth is best."

"Philippe, I wonder, have you ever met your relatives in Sweden."

"No. I never met them. She never mentioned them. I didn't even know they existed until she died. I don't know why she didn't tell me."

"Perhaps she was ashamed. Perhaps she didn't want to face her parents."

"Why? Wouldn't they have understood?"

"They very probably would have. But that isn't how shame works. Perhaps you should go to them."

"And tell them that she's dead?"

"Philippe, they probably thought that she was dead decades ago." Philippe looked up at the man's brilliantly blue eyes and the ever etched laugh lines around his cheeks. Not unlike the lines that Philippe would eventually have if he stayed away from Botox. "You wouldn't be going to deliver them the bad news Philippe, you'd be delivering them a grandson, and you'd be inheriting a family."

"I hadn't thought of that. But I had wanted to just move on from all of this." Sam furrowed his brow thoughtfully.

"That's what healing is. It's the same reason that I'm having this conversation with you, instead of hiding from you or telling you to go away. I could have refused to speak to you, and said to myself, "I'm moving on from that old life." I'll thank you very much, I have moved on. And that's exactly why I'm able to talk with you about it. You see?"

"I suppose I'll have to think about that."

"Indeed you will. Philippe, there's at least one more thing I'd like to ask you today if you'll hear me."

"Alright."

"You see, I believe that God has set up this world with His own kind of justice. I have done horrible things, and for that, I deserve punishment. I deserve to die you see. And Philippe, horrible things were done to you, and to your mother and in God's legal system that gives you certain power."

"Power." Philippe furrowed his brow.

"Power, yes. When someone sins against another, they must beg forgiveness from what they deserve. Forgiveness cannot be earned. And when one is sinned against, they become the holder of that right to forgive or not forgive."

"Isn't forgiveness something that you pray for?"

"I have sinned against God, and I believe that God has forgiven me. I also sinned against you. Understand this Philippe. I cannot make you or anyone else forgive me. That power, that right, belongs to the one who was sinned against." Philippe blinked. "As I am a priest, this is probably going to sound to you like a strange request for me to make but... Philippe, will you forgive me?"

There was silence as they stared at each other. Their eyes were blue on blue and Philippe could hardly fathom the choice that had just been handed to him. Forgiveness. He'd always seen himself as a person who never needed to forgive. Why forgive when you could accept instead? He had been asked to consider forgiveness now so many times that he was starting to lose count. Why would he need to forgive? He wasn't angry. He didn't feel wronged.

"You don't have to decide now Philippe." Sam's eyes seemed to reverberate with the sudden sound of his voice breaking through Philippe's thoughts.

"Oh." Philippe said simply. Sam smiled and his winkles crinkled at the corners of his eyes.

"Will you join us for mass this evening Philippe."

"Um... no I have to... wait, what time is it?" He pulled out his phone. It was nearly six o'clock in the evening and Aimee would be getting off work in an hour and he had still not decided what to make for dinner. "Crap. I have to go. What's your favorite food?"

"My favorite food? I'd say duck with cranberries and oranges sounds about right at the moment. But that might just be the season talking."

"Duck?"

"Yes indeed. Delicious bird."

"Oh... well." He raised an eyebrow. "Alright then. I guess I'm off to the store. Thank you again for your time Sam."

"No Philippe, thank you for coming back.

Chapter 45. Cooking Libido

He had made Duck a l'Orange. The smells had been wafting through the apartment when Aimee got home. The meal was a success for certain. Philippe found his mind whirring about the things that had been perfect, the moistness of the meat, the crispness of the skin. And he considered the things he could do differently. Add a little spice to the sauce perhaps. He imagined how that might taste different. He found that it was difficult to get his mind to stop considering the options, even while he slept. There was quite a lot of mathematics involved in the whole process of cooking, Philippe discovered, and his mind was going over the measurements over and over and over. One could justify the expense of cooking extravagantly if it lasted more than one night. For the two of them, that was easy.

He woke up. It was the middle of the night. The city lights glowed dimly through the curtains on Aimee's bedroom window. He had been dreaming about dinner. Had his dreaming woken him up? He rolled onto his side towards the window and looked at the curved silhouette of Aimee's sleeping form. She had taken mostly to sleeping on her left side to ease the discomfort of her sciatic nerve, so her back was to him, and she was facing the window.

He felt angst, as the perfection or not of the duck continued to whirr through his mind. It was delicious and there was much to be improved, but he needed it to stop. He reached out and gently stroked the nape of Aimee's neck while she slept. And then it hit him. This was the longest stretch in years that he had gone without sex. He rolled onto his back and looked up at the ceiling.

He'd now been in that apartment for several months and he and Aimee had made love once, maybe twice. That wasn't the abnormal part. The abnormal part was that he hadn't slept with anyone else. On account of his foot of course. The thought of the opportunity that he'd probably missed when he'd walked out on Liz at that party fluttered through his mind with a mild sense of regret.

He and Aimee had unspoken rules. They were different than other friends with benefits. With other friends, it was fine for the benefits to be an important focus of the relationship. But with Aimee, the friendship always came first. He'd never slept with Aimee when he wasn't already in some capacity sexually satisfied, and Aimee had always made the first move.

He looked over at Aimee's sleeping form. From behind, he could hardly tell that she was pregnant. Her frame was such that she seemed to carry the baby more or less right in front of her. Her pregnancy was in no way a turn off though, on the contrary, he found it fascinating how the experience had gradually changed her shape into something that it wasn't before. Looking at her from behind was like a flashback to an earlier time.

In the dead of night was hardly the time to be feeling this way. He put his arm frustratedly over his eyes and took a deep breath. If he woke her, he had no idea how she would react to his advances. Very likely she would find it odd at worst. If she had no interest then he knew she wouldn't have a problem telling him 'no'. At which point he would just go take a cold shower.

So he turned towards her again and slowly sidled up closer to her and propped himself up on his elbow. He reached out and gently stroked her hair away from her face. He could clearly see her pregnant belly from this angle, and he ran his hand along her side and felt the baby move. He smiled at that. He vaguely remembered reading something about how it always seemed that fetuses were awake at night. Much to the annoyance of their not nocturnal mothers.

He leaned down and gently kissed Aimee's shoulder and heard her moan softly in her sleep. So he kissed her neck, and caressed her thigh.

"Heh." She smiled a sleepy smile and chuckled awkwardly in her sleepy voice, eyes still shut tight. "What are you doing?"

"I'm trying to seduce you." He whispered, gently tickling her ear with his breath. He kissed her ear lobe. "Is it working?" She half rolled towards him and opened one eye.

"Mmmm, what time is it?"

"I don't see how that's important." He leaned down and gently kissed her lips.

"Why are you trying to seduce me?" She smiled lazily.

"Because I want to." He pressed himself a little closer to her and kissed her neck."

"I see. When was the last time Philippe got laid?"

"I hardly see how that's related."

"Oh, I think it's related." She chuckled

"Nonsense." He said and kissed her, this time a little more passionately.

"You really gotta get out more Philippe. I can't be responsible for this. I'm not your girlfriend, or your lover. I don't want you getting too attached." At this they both laughed. It was an ironic statement given that they were living together at least semi permanently.

"Alright, I'll start getting out more first thing in the morning." He said, and started unbuttoning her night shirt.

"Deal." Said Aimee and allowed herself to be seduced, but the message was quite clear. 'This time was fine Philippe, but not again.'

Chapter 46. Old Gossip

The flash of lights was familiar but still strange. Philippe wore a black formal jacket and slacks. With a forget-me-not blue ruffled shirt underneath, a bowtie, and a flower pinned to his coat pocket, he looked like he was ready to go to the prom. Something to get the high school girls excited.

Margarete was standing next to him in a gown with a matching blue sash and a tiara in her hair. She had a wide toothy smile on her polished and well Botoxed face as they posed for the camera. She still wasn't talking to him. He had no idea why, but somehow felt that it didn't really matter.

They took better prom pictures than any of the teenagers would actually receive at their own proms but that was rather the point. Make them see what they think they'll get, and then later, make them think that they got it. It was an old tradition. Why stop now?

"All right, that's it for the set, have a good night everyone." Said, goodness knows who and with a sudden bustle. Equipment started getting pulled down and put away and the models, at least the ones that didn't vacate immediately started collecting in little cliques to decide what to do with their evening.

Philippe changed out of his little tux and started heading in the general direction of out. He passed the clique that Margarete had joined, which was now distinctly separate from Liz across the room. He wondered if they'd had a falling out. Liz was standing by herself staring over at the giggling Margarete.

When he reached the door he remembered that he was holding the wrong cane and still needed to make sure that it got back to Marcello. He didn't want to be responsible for the loss of a family heirloom along with the car. No matter how much Marcello seemed not to care about it. He knew better. So he turned around and sighed when he saw Liz still standing there and walked over to stand discretely next to her.

"Are all of them on your bad side?" He asked quietly, gesturing to the group she was watching. She turned to notice him there.

"Oh. No. But I don't really want to make them all choose who to be friends with." That was code for, Margarete had won. Whatever war they'd been fighting, Liz had lost.

"Hey, I wanted to apologize for walking out on you the other day."

"Oh it's alright. I was insensitive."

"So what happened with you and Margarete?"

"Well you probably should hear it from her side if you want to be on the in crowd."

"Actually, I don't think she likes me much. Not really sure why."

"Oh you don't know?"

"Not a clue."

"Oh I see." She shifted her weight and looked like she was considering something.

"Are you going to tell me?" He asked with a smile. He really didn't care, but there was nothing like some good gossip to drive a conversation.

"Well… well alright. It isn't as if she and I are best friends anymore now is it? But I have to ask you. Just so that I have all my facts straight... do pardon that, that's not how I meant it… But do be honest with me, did you sleep with Aurelio?"

"You know, I thought there was something between them."

"So you did sleep with him? Well I suppose that's another point against her isn't it. Well she dumped him because she found out that he'd been sleeping with men. It's a bit bigoted of her isn't it? I had no idea that she was that sort of person."

"I didn't know that they were an item."

"Oh they definitely were. And then there was the whole thing with you and Veronica… And him and Veronica… I dunno, the whole thing sort of got her panties all up in a bunch."

"Gotcha. So, she's not talking to me, for the same reason that she's not talking to Aurelio."

"Basically yes." Somehow Philippe didn't find it odd to think that she had been angry about the homosexuality rather than the infidelity. That wasn't an uncommon preference of priorities. Then again, fidelity depended on the rules you played by didn't it.

"So what happened between you and her?"

"Well, you remember the Botox incident at our place in New York right?"

"I'd have trouble forgetting it."

"Oh if you're anything like me, then you've tried. Well, not unexpectedly, she was sleeping with that man too. But he dumped her over the whole thing and she blamed it on me yelling at him over ruining that poor girl's face for months. So you know what she did?" At this Liz wiped a tear from her eye and tried to get it to do minimal damage to her makeup. "She went and had a nice long conversation with Roger about it over dinner and then seduced him. Just to get at me. I only found out about it the other night. Roger and I were trying to do the whole long distance think you know, and Margarete thought she was being a good friend by confessing that she'd slept with him back in New York."

Philippe looked sideways and furrowed his brow at the floor. Nope… He had no idea who Roger was.

"Did I meet Roger?"

"He was my boyfriend, don't you remember him?" Philippe didn't, but he didn't say so. Instead he just pulled his silk handkerchief out of his pocket and handed it to her. She took it gratefully and started gently dabbing her eyes. "So anyways. I dumped him, for cheating on me with Margarete, and I dumped Margarete for the whole horrible lot of it, and now we aren't talking. You know I'd probably forgive her for the whole thing if she would just get that stick out of her ass."

Philippe was thoughtful. "You dumped Roger for cheating on you?"

"Oh definitely. I'm sure it wasn't the first time too."

"And you were with him before I left New York?"

"Yes," She looked at him. "You really don't remember him do you?" In fact, after this whole conversation, Philippe was completely certain that he had never met the man even once.

"Didn't… you and I sleep together?" He asked.

"Oh. Yes. We did once didn't we? You know, you're very gentle in bed, makes one feel a little like a princess. Or like some precious jewel." Philippe blushed slightly at the compliment and smiled. That sweet bit of information really honed in the sting of regret for his next comment which hadn't sounded nearly as bad in his head as it did once it had left his lips.

"It's just that, if you and Roger were so committed, maybe we wouldn't have done it." He winced and put his hand gently over his mouth.

"Oh I see. That's a very fine way to call someone a whore isn't it. Is that what you're saying? You're accusing me of being as bad as Roger was because I cheated on him first. Is that it? Well you were a part of that equation too I think, and you don't even remember Roger. So don't start thinking that you're any better." He took the verbal beating with his eyes closed and then slowly removed his hand from his mouth and replied in a voice much quieter and more sheepish than the one he'd previously been using.

"I'm sorry, I didn't mean to accuse you of anything." Or had he? He honestly felt unsure. It wasn't that he'd meant to point out the cheating, so much as the hypocrisy. And he hadn't even meant to point out her hypocrisy personally so much as the hypocritical irony of the situation. "Yes, I was there. And I wasn't trying to suggest that I'm better than you in any way. I'd sleep with just about anyone probably. But… I'm pretty sure I never met Roger, or even heard his name."

"Oh, well I wonder if that was when we were taking some time off." Liz responded looking less angry for a moment. Philippe blinked. It was only a moment. "Well that doesn't change the fact that you were trying to call me a cheater. Which I'm not… mostly... but that also doesn't change the fact that Margarete stabbed me in the back, and I was just looking for a little comfort from you." Philippe was having trouble believing that he had just failed miserably in comforting someone. Very miserably. "Here's your handkerchief back Philippe. I've got things to do." And she tossed the silk cloth in his general direction and stalked off. Philippe watched as the silk fluttered to the floor, and wondered what the heck had just happened.

Chapter 47. Jazz

Philippe had gone to another photo shoot and managed to avoid any offhanded Mercedes comments with Marcello yet again. But now he felt that he needed to track down Sacha. He sent him a text with no response so it was time to search for the source and he found himself back in Notre Dame looking for him. The church was as full as ever and a quick glance over the tops of people's heads yielded no results. Sam was not the priest up front, and that took some pressure off. Then again, he'd half wanted to see him.

The service was somber and methodical. The words that he didn't understand were lovely and comfortingly monotonous. The words that he did understand were pretty but heavy and he only half understood what they meant in context. He eventually managed to realize that the service had something to do with Christmas. He didn't know that Christmas was something that they chanted, preached and sang about before a Christmas Eve service but he supposed mid-December was close enough.

He thought about how the history of the church in France had been especially bloody and horrible, and he wondered how it was, that after all that, they still had anything to offer anyone. But the service was slow and meditative, and mesmerizing. The songs were melancholy and beautiful, and he enjoyed the fact that everyone was encouraged to sing together. Even if they did so with glum faces and solemn expressions. He found himself sitting out the entire service, enjoying it as someone might enjoy an opera or a ballet.

After the service had ended, and everyone starting filing out, Sacha was still nowhere to be found. So Philippe got up quietly with everyone else, and left the old building, empty of everyone except some priests, some tourists, and a select few still bowed in prayer.

Outside, the winter air was cold and he stood for a while watching the plumes of his own breath puffing from his mouth. He sighed a deep sigh and the oral fog faded out into the night. He pulled his coat a little tighter around his shoulders and gripped onto the crook of his cane that he felt sure he was starting to need less and less, and then he walked to one of his favorite bars.

He wasn't quite up for dancing yet, so no dance clubs but a bar would be fine. Or better yet, a bar with a dance floor. Someplace where both movement and intimate conversation could happen. Somewhere he could find someone to go home with for the evening. He remembered his promise to Aimee, but he needed at least one drink to lubricate his chances.

As he walked, the somber sensation of the church lingered on his bones and he entered the bar feeling a little less cheerful than he would have several months ago. But maybe he was still feeling depressed about his conversation with Liz. He'd liked Liz, and felt as if he'd spoiled something.

He walked into the smoke filled room and was suddenly moved by the serenading vocals of a woman at a microphone. Jazz. He loved jazz. This woman stood so close to the microphone that her full lips were practically pressed against it and the classic style of her voice jumped right out of French jazz history and floated out into the room along with the smoke of the people watching with their cigarettes.

"What's with the cane?" Said a handsome man behind the bar as Philippe sat down. His hair was slicked in such a way that, along with the dress of the woman singing, told Philippe that they were having something of a themed night tonight. The nineteen twenties and thirties were home again.

"I broke my ankle a few months ago. It's almost healed though."

"I broke my ankle once when I was a kid." Said the bartender. Twisted it in a dance class, believe it or not. Never quite got my dance back. He smiled and winked. It was known to those who frequented the place that Jean was a terrible dancer. "What can I get ya? I haven't seen you in a while. A long while actually."

"I've been overseas, I have to admit, I didn't expect you to still be here when I got back." After a moment of perusing the cocktail list, Philippe decided to go with a glass of rose instead.

"Don't rub it in." Said the bartender with a smirk as he poured the pink colored wine into Philippe's glass. "Hey, I know you always like to look good, but why are you so dressed up tonight, and in the wrong way." He gestured towards the theme of the room."

"I apologize, I didn't look at your schedule. No one told me about the theme. I don't come in often enough anymore."

"And therein lies the problem."

"Indeed. And actually, believe it or not I just came here from evening mass at Notre Dame."

"Oh we always get the after crowd from that place." The sarcasm was palpable. "I didn't know you were the religious sort. Something change?" In truth, Philippe had dressed nice for the modeling gig, not the church. But since the look fit in both places, he decided that he didn't feel like talking about modeling this time.

"No. Nothing's changed. I was meeting a friend there, but they stood me up." Of course, Sacha hadn't had any idea that he'd been expected, but the explanation was close enough for short conversation.

"And then you crawled to your favorite bar since looking for love at Notre Dame is ridiculous. I'm happy to hear you're still our biggest disciple. You know, you should learn an instrument, I bet you'd be good up there with a saxophone."

"Actually…" Philippe said, resting his chin in the palm of his hand and putting his elbow on the countertop. "That would be really fun. I should do that. Who do you know that teaches?"

"Depends on which instrument you want to learn."

"What do you think I'd be best at?" The bartender reached out and took Philippe's hand out from under his chin and turned it over to get a good look at his fingers.

"You'd probably be nimble on the piano. Do you sing?"

"I can, but not like her." He looked over at the woman with her eyes clamped shut clutching the microphone for dear life and exhaling with a waver to her vocals that Philippe had absolutely no idea how to do.

"No one has a voice like Monique. But, if you were to learn the piano, you could learn to put vocals along with it. And then you two could sing a duet. But if you played the saxophone, and I think you would look really sexy playing the saxophone by the way, but you wouldn't be able to sing. So that's why I asked if you could sing. I won't ask you to sing for me right now though obviously, but maybe later."

"Why, you think you could teach me?"

"I'm not half bad. But no, if you wanted to sing, I'd send you to Monique. She teaches. But if you wanted to play the saxophone, then I would happily teach you myself."

"And the piano?"

"Well, there's Bernard, but I'm not sure if he teaches. You'd have to ask him." Someone else walked into the door and Jean finally let go of Philippe's hand to take their order. They were a cute couple who'd come in arm in arm from the cold. The woman was wearing a faux fur coat. She'd obviously gotten the theme memo.

Philippe turned to see that Monique had stopped singing and was being applauded by her adoring fans. Philippe clapped too, her voice was beautiful. But as she stepped down from the mic, Philippe was taken off guard when he saw the couple who stepped into her place. It was a man and a woman, the woman wrapped her fingers around her accordion and the man sat on a wooden chair next to her, and held his cello against his chest. They were the same couple who had directed him up the Eiffel tower for the second of Sacha's poem clues.

The man started to pluck at his cello with his fingers and became both the percussion and the base of the music which was much more upbeat than Monique's slow melodic singing. At the Eiffel tower, they had performed songs that tourists would know, this song was obviously one they had made up themselves and it begged the watchers to dance to it.

"So what are your spiritual affiliations? Do you have any?"

"What?" Philippe was broken from his reverie by Jean's return to their conversation.

"Well, if you weren't at Notre Dame for mass because you've signed up for their explanation of truth, then what explanation do you adhere to? If any." Jean shrugged. "I'm just curious."

"I… Well… nothing in particular I guess. I'm pretty agnostic." Philippe shrugged. "It is certainly philosophically possible, but having never met God myself, how would I know?"

"That's a fair point. So you're not for the Hinduism or Buddhism thing either?"

"Well, it's the same thing. It could be true, but who knows? But then there's say, Taoism, which is mostly a set of ideas on how to be the best person you can be. I don't have anything against anything that helps people be better people, I just don't understand why anyone would need a higher being to tell them to be good. Philosophy, sociology, heck psychology, it all says that we do better as a society and as individuals if we're just good to each other, so that seems good enough to me."

"Fair enough, fair enough. But you don't ever feel like you need something more spiritual than that?"

Philippe shrugged. "I think that spirituality is something to be shared with the people you're being good to. I guess, spirituality can be like, sharing your spirit with another. I like the idea that we're all really just one with each other and don't know it. I like to spend the time remembering how to be one with someone. It's like, remembering who we are as one."

"Ah okay. Now his spirituality comes out. It's all about sex."

"Well, sex is a very spiritual experience. But it's just one way. There would have to be others. Otherwise, how would you find that place of connection with say, your grandmother, or your child? It's like the idea of, I love my wife, I love my son, I love my dog, I love my food. They sound similar but are obviously expressing very different things. But I think that they are really just many expressions of what is essentially all the same thing. Does that make sense?"

"You really have thought about this a lot haven't you?" Philippe smiled.

"I really enjoy philosophy. What about you, what do you believe?"

"Um… I actually try not to think about it too much. I tend to go off on a serious head spit if I do and then I start wondering what will happen to me, if anything, when I die. Trying to get comfortable with the idea of just being worm food is no fun, but I just can't quite accept the higher power idea. I have always kind of enjoyed the thought though that we all go wherever would be the perfect place for us when we die and that's what heaven is. I guess I'll stick with that."

"And where will you go?"

"I will go to a place with lots of music, lots of painting and lots of sex and you are totally welcome to visit if you want." Philippe laughed.

"Alright I'll be there, but you might have trouble getting rid of me."

"Ah, whatever, the more the merrier." Philippe smiled and sipped his wine while looking over at the musicians. The faux fur couple had gotten up to dance and the cellist had started singing along with his partner in his sultry baritone voice.

"They're good aren't they?" Said Jean.

"Yeah they are. I've seen them before, playing for tips."

"Yeah. Money is one thing musicians give up for their passion. You know, music is kind of a spiritual experience."

"It definitely is. Especially when shared. Which is why I'd be interested in taking you up on your offer to teach me the saxophone if you were serious about that."

"Yeah, sure, definitely."

"Do you get to play up there at all tonight?"

"Yeah, I actually get to play at the end of my shift. You should stick around and listen to my spiritual experience. Then we can go to my place and I'll teach you some things if you're up for it."

"Sounds fun. A night full of spiritual experiences." The innuendo was received and Jean smiled.

"Looking' forward to it." He said, and then walked away to fix a drink for someone. Philippe sipped his rose and watched as the rest of the music went by, but something bugged him about that duet. Their songs were about love and about hard nights that could be softened by each other, but sometimes a line or two was in there that Philippe couldn't help but feel was about something else.

When Jean came on with his saxophone, Monique piped up with some vocal and the air returned back to normal, but still something was tickling the back of his mind, and he just couldn't figure out what it was.

"So what did you think?" asked Jean later that evening as he carried his sax case over his shoulder on their way back towards his apartment.

"You're a master with the sax, I don't know how I'm going to live up to it."

"Practice makes perfect Philippe, I've been doing this for like fifteen years. And Monique stole my spotlight but that was alright."

"I think she likes you."

"Yeah, I dunno how to let her down easy."

"So what are you going to teach me first?"

"Well, first we have to start with the obvious basics. How's your lung capacity?"

"Not great."

"It'll have to get better then. But you'll have to learn all the finger positioning and such and then how to blow without sounding like a duck." Philippe chuckled. They walked slowly and Philippe's ankle was started to feel sore.

"I guess it's going to be an awkward evening then. I'm not sure I'll be able to get past the duck noises in one night."

"Naw, you'll do fine. It's not that hard really. Just takes some lip dexterity."

"I'm well set then." They laughed and then finally reached Jean's door. Jean started walking up the steps to enter the building but turned around when he noticed that Philippe was still standing on the sidewalk at the bottom.

"Is your foot okay? Do you need help up the steps or something?"

"No, my foot's fine. I'm sorry to get all the way here before realizing this, but I think I need to get home."

"But, what? Why?"

"It's just late. I should have thought about it before. Maybe another time. You can teach me how to play the saxophone. It's just my roommate worries that I'm dead when I stay out too late."

"Some roommate." Said Jean looking disappointed and obviously aware that he was being turned down and Philippe was just making up excuses. "Yeah, get yourself a sax and I'll teach you."

"I'll do that. I really am sorry Jean."

"Don't sweat it. No harm, no foul. I'll talk to you later." And Philippe was left alone on the sidewalk and now he knew that there was definitely something wrong with him. This starting his life over thing really wasn't looking the way he thought it would. Jean would have been a good lay, but for some reason Philippe didn't want a good lay. He'd rather have actually learned to play the saxophone. And he couldn't get that jazz couple out of his mind, and he found himself wondering if they had any music that he could download onto his phone.

So by the time he got home, he had an earbud plugged into his ear and he was listening to various YouTube videos that they had made and was trying to pick out a common theme for their music besides just jazz. He found that they had been playing together for quite a few years and he liked their newer stuff more than their older stuff. Their older stuff was full of angst and soul, which was good, but their newer stuff was full of something else.

He closed the apartment door behind him and plugged their music into a Bluetooth speaker so that he could take the earbud out of his ear and go to the fridge to find something to eat. After the music started on the speaker he looked around and saw that Aimee wasn't home yet but that didn't worry him. He didn't really pay attention to her work shifts.

He opened the fridge and pulled out the leftover duck a l'orange and put some onto a plate. He took a deep breath and started reheating it and wondered what he could do with the last bits of it. Maybe he could make it into soup. He was getting tired of eating it as it was. So he picked up his phone and starting looking up how to make bone broth. While he was noticing that bone broth was actually quite easy to make and thinking that a nice soup would be really good for the winter weather, the door opened, and Aimee was home.

"Hey Philippe." She said as she closed the door and set down her purse and started working on unwinding her scarf from around her neck.

"Hey, welcome home. How you doing?"

"Oh, well…" She hung her scarf up on the hook. "You are absolutely certain that you want to be my baby's legal dad right?"

"Yeah. I haven't changed my mind." He smiled at her and set down his phone. "Do you want some dinner?"

"Oh yes please." She hung up her coat. "But I really hope you don't ever decide to change your mind. I know it's not on paper yet but it will be."

"Yup. I'll sign it." He smiled more, thinking that she simply needed a bigger dose of encouragement on this already decided point."

"That's really good, because I may have just told my dad that you're the baby's father."

"Oh." He blinked several times.

"But I mean, that's okay right? Because that was pretty much the plan."

"That was… yes… that was definitely the plan. Yes. I'm sorry, you just startled me is all." He set a plate of duck on the bar counter for her.

"You're not suddenly having second thoughts right?" She sat down. "Thank you." She said, offhandedly for the food before continuing. "Because, you must have known what that was going to mean right?"

"Yes," he set his own plate down and moved around the counter to sit next to her. "I'm going to sign the paternity affidavit. As far as anyone is concerned, I'm that baby's dad. That includes your father. But it's going to have to start including me because I'm still trying to get my head around it." He suddenly leaned over and kissed her belly and then straightened up and kissed her on the forehead and then smiled earnestly as he looked her in the eye. "I just thought I had a couple more months but it makes sense that it would start now. Especially since your pregnancy is so obvious. Do your co-workers think it's mine?"

She nodded. "Yup."

"Good. Good. That… that's really good, it's um…" The only word he could think to say next was 'good' but that was just too many in a row so instead he stuffed a hunk of duck into his mouth and chewed so that he couldn't say anything. Aimee chuckled.

"You know you're cute when you're nervous." He swallowed and took a deep breath.

"Like a shivering Chihuahua. They're cute." Aimee Laughed. He'd succeeded in making her feel more secure, so he smiled. "So you're talking to your dad again?"

"Yeah, he took me out to dinner. Be quiet, I'm eating for two." As if he were judging her eating habits, which he wasn't. "And we talked. A lot."

"How was that?"

"I mean, about as awkward as you can expect. But when he saw that I was pregnant, I think it sort of gave him a different perspective on things. He definitely didn't approve of my being pregnant, not that I can blame him. I don't approve either, but nothing I can do about that now." She smirked and chewed a bit of duck thoughtfully. "But he does seem to be taking the grandpa thing pretty seriously." She shrugged, "But at least I'm not disowned anymore."

"Well that's really wonderful. I'm glad to hear it." She smiled mischievously at him as she waited to finish her mouthful. She swallowed.

"He does want to talk to you though."

"I… figured that was coming. I can't say as I think your dad has ever exactly liked me, but I don't think he hates me."

"Oh he does. But he never approves of anyone I spend time with. Think's their beneath me. But now he's having to take a closer look at you since you're his grandbaby's father."

"Oh wonderful. Because that doesn't make me nervous. What should I say to him?" Aimee shrugged.

"Just don't tell him that you're not his grandbaby's father."

"Thanks." He rolled his eyes sarcastically. "Anything else helpful?" She shrugged again.

"Aside from that, just be honest with him."

"What if he decides to do the math? I wasn't here when you conceived."

"Say you came home for a visit. He's not going to be interrogating you to find out whether or not you really are the father, he's going to be interrogating you to find out whether or not you'll be a good one."

"Are we sure I'll be a good one?" Aimee chuckled and shook her head.

"I don't care what my dad thinks of you Philippe, I think you'll do a great job with this little guy."

"Well, your confidence comforts me." He smiled and they just chewed on their dinner for a little while. "Hey Aimee," Philippe said after a minute or so, "Would you want to go to the Christmas midnight mass at Notre Dame with me this year?"

"Um..." she said raising an eyebrow and looking a little bit surprised by the question. "Sure. Yeah sure. If that's something that you want to do. That sounds kind of nice."

"Really?" He looked at her, somewhat surprised by her response.

"Yeah. The midnight mass is pretty. I think it sounds nice."

"Well, alright." He smiled. Let's do that then. If he had still been listening, he might have noticed that the jazz duet on his Bluetooth speaker had started playing hymns.

Chapter 48. Burning Bridges.

"So what do you think of the pommel?" Philippe was holding a black cane in his hand with the roaring brass face of a lion on the top instead of a crook. Marcello had invited Philippe to his home for dinner after a shoot and Philippe hadn't been able to come up with a good excuse not to go. There he was again, with Marcello having still learned nothing about the car.

"It's nice." He said, but in all honesty it looked a little too gaudy for his taste. Marcello always liked things to look regal. His house was decked out in gold art frames, black marble pillars, and crimson curtains.

"Nice." Marcello echoed, "How's that for gratitude. It'll look better in the pictures anyway, I don't care what the photographers think. Or the buyers for that matter."

"Now there's business sense." Philippe smiled jokingly. "Really, I appreciate it. The other cane made me look like an old farmer. This one's for Armani."

"There you go. That's a good idea. Maybe I'll get you some pictures for Armani. That would be a good place for that cane wouldn't it. Of course, Armani pictures tend to work better with men who didn't spring for laser hair removal on their face." He winked at Philippe's lack of any kind of facial hair. "You know, this was my father's before he died."

"It's special then."

"Naw. He had a bunch of them. Only ever took this one to important meetings. Made him look more intimidating." Marcello chuckled. "He'd hate me using it for stock photos. But I never was his favorite son." He tapped his chin. "Canes. It could be a new look. Return to an old look. I love when they make old looks new again."

He liked Marcello, but he still hadn't gotten that follow up call from Sacha about the car. Marcello was much more likely to mention the car when he was talking about other fancy physical objects. The cane in this case. Philippe did at that moment have a thought that the car did not legally belong to Marcello. The title was in Philippe's name. So what did he have to be worried about?

Marcello's wrath. That's what he needed to be worried about. Philippe had not bought that car, it had been given to him. At the time he'd felt a little like the Karate Kid when Marcello had handed him the keys. Except that he had learned modeling skills and work ethic instead of Karate. And unlike Mr. Miyagi, Marcello would be angry about a gift lost. At least, Philippe imagined that Mr. Miyagi would be more forgiving. Marcello put a pinch of something into whatever amazing Italian dish he was cooking. The smells of which were causing Philippe's eyes to water, and his mouth too.

"What would you think about stewing bay leaves in that sauce?"

"Bay leaves?" Marcello raised an eyebrow and stopped for a minute to look consideringly at the sauce. His kitchen was enormous. "I hadn't thought of that before. But I would have needed to put them in a lot sooner."

"Next time then." Philippe smiled. He'd have to be careful or his newfound cooking hobby was going to leak into his modeling career. And that wouldn't be safe for anyone's belt lines.

"Yeah well, this was my great grandmother's recipe. But I might be willing to tweak it for the next family reunion eh?" He smiled and winked. "Well anyways, I think that Armani would do good to add a bit of a softer touch. You know a little femininity in men's wear and business wear too. That's what I always think when I look at Japanese suit models. They just look so sleek. I think we could pull that off with you in a European way."

"It's always good to add a little bit of new flavor." He managed to respond to both the family recipe comment and the Armani comment with one word. He enjoyed that.

"Ha! Flavor. Clever. Hey, do you like a good scenic view."

"Always." Smirked Philippe. He knew where this evening would end up. It wasn't as if they got together for cooking dates just for the love of cooking. "Is there any way I can help you in there?"

"Yeah, you can keep your paws off my great grandmother's recipe. Naw I'm kidding, it's time to put the pasta on. Go for it. But it has got to be al dente to watch yourself and don't forget the salt and olive oil." Philippe got up from his chair and started putting on a pot of hot water. "What I was going to say Philippe, is that there's a great view about an hour's drive from here. Even when the sun's down. Especially when there's a full moon and a clear sky which tonight, might I point out, there is. So since all those prerequisites are in alignment, I want to take you up there after our dinner."

"Sure." Said Philippe as he sprinkled salt into the water and turned on the heat. "Sounds nice." They had come to this house for their impromptu dinner date in Marcello's car. So Marcello's next suggestion was not only one that he didn't want to hear, but also one that he hadn't exactly expected.

"Let's take a detour back to Paris and take your car. That thing would drive nice on those roads. Wish I'd thought about it earlier before we'd left. Woulda saved us the trip."

"Oh… Um…" Philippe tried to think of how to carefully choose his words, but just simply his subtle change in tone of voice caused Marcello to stop stirring the sauce, and turn to look at Philippe.

"What?" Marcello pursed his lips and looked as if he was now forcing himself to be patient and give Philippe the benefit of the doubt.

"Well, I… I don't have it anymore."

"You don't have it anymore." Marcello nodded. It was a feigned calm. The sort of calm that was really only holding back the flood gates. He took a deep breath through his nose. "You sold it didn't you. I know you were hurtin' for cash after Veronica died."

"No. I didn't sell it."

"You wrecked it?" Philippe bit his lip and shook his head and poured some olive oil into the now boiling water and reached over for the pasta that was waiting. His hand didn't reach it because Marcello's hand was now gripped around his wrist. Philippe felt suddenly unsafe. Marcello smiled a tense smile.

"What happened to the car Philippe?"

"It was stolen." Philippe swallowed. "I parked it and when I came back it was gone. I reported the theft but they never found it." Marcello stared at him long and hard and then suddenly twisted his arm, driving Philippe down onto his knees. He held him there for a moment of held breath and gritted teeth before finally letting go and taking a deep breath. Philippe stayed on the floor holding his arm, and wondering if it would bruise.

"And yet, the worst thing, is that you decided not to tell me." Marcello reached over to the pasta and put it carefully into the boiling pot, as if the pasta were too precious to break. "Things like that happen Philippe. Cars get stolen. We can't get too attached to material things." He stepped back and looked down at Philippe while he reached over to grab a wooden spoon to stir the noodles. "Sooner or later, all things pass. Cars break down. Houses crumble. And the only way we keep them around any longer is by replacing the dead parts with new parts. So we don't actually keep them around at all. Just their look alikes."

He put the spoon down on the stove top and picked up the one he'd been using for the sauce. "Scoot over Philippe, I need to get into the oven." Philippe scooted just enough to get out of the way. "But look alikes are good, because they remind us of what they once were, and thus, what we once were. They're the combination of past and present, in one material item. Its things like duplicates, and retrofits, and art restoration, that makes us immortal. If we just let those things disappear, then they would be no better than we are, and we would be nothing."

"I was careless. I left it in a bad place." Philippe was staring at the floor level cabinet across from him. He wondered why they were white. They looked tacky in Marcello's grandiose home. Mahogany would have been better. It was true that Philippe had left the car in a bad place, but in his defense, he hadn't expected to be away from it for more than an hour, and certainly not an entire day.

"Get off the floor Philippe, you're not a dog." Philippe pushed himself up against the counter. His ankle was hurting. He wasn't sure why, it hadn't knocked into anything or been stressed in any way. "You're forgiven and it's forgotten. That car has been wiped from your possession, and wiped from my mind." He waved his hand in the air. "When the history books are burned, it is as if history never happened. And for all the good it does anyone, it may as well have not happened." He handed the sauce spoon to Philippe who held it with his bruised arm and then he patted him on the back.

"You get another chance Philippe. I'll even give you another car."

"I don't want another car." His spoon had just touched the sauce when he let go of it, and it clunked gently against the pan as it sank slowly into it. Marcello turned and looked at him hard in the eyes.

"First you rob me, and then you insult me?"

"I didn't rob you, Marcello, the title was in my name."

"I gave you that car."

"I never asked for it."

"If I remember correctly Philippe, the first time I met you was when you were a sixteen year old thief trying to steal that car." Philippe looked away. He'd lost that one. What Marcello said was true. That was how they had met. And that was also how Philippe had gotten into modeling. Instead of calling the police, Marcello had taken Philippe under his wing and made him a model. It was thanks to Marcello that he had met Veronica. In fact, everything that Philippe had managed to accomplish with his life was thanks Marcello and that day when Philippe had tried to steal his car.

"I quit." He barely heard himself say the words.

"You quit? Quit what? Quit stealing cars? Quit smoking?" Philippe turned his eyes back onto Marcello, he could feel his lips and his fingertips shaking.

"I quit modeling. I'm quitting. Right now. I quit." He was shivering all over but he stood his ground under Marcello's hard gaze.

"There are hundreds to take your place." Philippe swallowed. He couldn't say that those words didn't sting. "Go. Get out of my house." Philippe stood stock still for a moment while it sank in. "I said get out!" Philippe nearly jumped out of his skin and then limped around the counter and picked up his cane and started towards the door. "And Philippe, don't ever try to be a model again. In about an hour, your name will be blacklisted. No agency will touch you." Philippe stopped and looked over his shoulder at Marcello. "You can't say things like that unless you mean it Philippe. You have to have a backbone. Now go. I don't ever want to see your face again." Philippe swallowed and turned and grabbed his coat and opened the front door out into the cold.

He closed the door behind him and began to shake violently. He leaned against the stone stair rail and lurched over it, unsure if he was about to be sick in Marcello's roses. He felt like he wanted to be sick but nothing came up and he was just shaking. So he pulled his coat quickly onto his shoulders and wrapped it around himself and then hurriedly limped down the stairs and the driveway. He walked faster than his ankle wanted him to, but he felt as if he couldn't get away fast enough. But halfway towards the road to the nearest bus he stopped and looked up into the air, and just started bawling.

That was it. He was now no one that he had been before. That was the last shred of his identity. Gone in a flash. Gone was the person who had been born in a brothel to poverty and drugs who had turned to theft and lying in order to feel he was worth anything. And now gone was the model, the beauty and high living that he had fashioned for himself. Gone were the connections to a life that was better, and the people who lived there. It was all gone. Now all he had, was him.

The rain started dripping down from the clouds and mixed in with his tears. And then it started pouring and the sounds of the drops thundering against the ground covered up all the sound of his crying until he stopped. And it was still raining, and he was still standing there, quietly. He was soaked from head to toe, but he didn't care. He started walking slowly. Not fast anymore. He felt the squeaking squishing of his designer shoes being saturated with water.

When he finally got home, he was shaking from cold instead of emotions, and Aimee demanded that he take a hot shower immediately. Then with hot tea with honey in their hands, they snuggled up on the love seat with piles of blankets over the top of them and Philippe admitted to her that he was now officially a freeloader. But she somehow, didn't seem to care at all about that. The old life was officially gone.

Chapter 49. Fearful Fatherhood

"So you went and knocked up my daughter huh?" Philippe had barely hung his jacket over the back of his chair when Claud said this, but he was trying hard not to be intimidated by the man. "You know what she said to me?" Philippe slowly lowered himself into the chair across from him. "She said to me, 'daddy, you have other daughters who can be lawyers.' As if my children were like marbles to me. Oh I lost one, but it's alright, I have others."

Philippe tucked his hands into his lap and looked at Aimee's father. His hair was white but thick. Age had worn his patience but his face was strong and his health, better than he could have asked for. Philippe said nothing. Obviously he was not yet being asked to speak. The waitress came by with a menu, sadly oblivious to the tension.

"Thank you." Philippe said quietly to her when it was handed to him. She got no such response from Aimee's father. In fact, she got no response at all. It occurred to him, that Aimee was perhaps rather lucky to have a friend who was willing to weather the 'how dare you knock up my daughter' talk, when he hadn't even done it. But truly he'd brought it all on himself. After all, it was his idea.

"Do you think that I want less for Aimee than for my other girls? That I would want to just cast her aside into something beneath her worth?"

"No." Replied Philippe, sensing that this was one of those, respond, moments. "I don't think that at all."

"I want all of my girls to live up to their full potential." He looked thoughtful. "She didn't have to be a lawyer. She could have been a doctor. Hell, will her intelligence, she could have been a politician." Philippe couldn't help but notice his use of the past tense.

"You think that the baby has put an end to those possibilities?" The man stared at Philippe for an uncomfortably long moment.

"I think, that if she wanted to, she could do anything that she set her mind to. She could be great, the best, at anything. And instead, she chooses this." the term 'this' had so many reference possibilities. Philippe looked down at his menu and wondered why they had come to a cafe as if they might eat anything. He supposed something would get ordered, but it didn't exactly seem like the best time to say, 'I think the sandwiches look good, what are you getting?' So instead he just stared at the menu.

"Yes indeed." Claud continued, "Instead, she chooses to live in that apartment, work at a cafe that takes up time that could be better spent, majors in a career worth pennies, and gets knocked up by you." Philippe took a moment to realize that Aimee's father had barely ever taken notice of him before, and had hardly ever said more than two words to him. So really, in this moment, Philippe was worth more to the man than he had ever been before. Worth the time and energy that Claud was spending insulting him. "So what do you have to say for yourself?"

"Are you looking for a diplomatic solution?"

"Ha." Aimee's father snorted. "Diplomatic." Then he picked up his menu. "Let's order shall we?" Philippe opened his menu since now was apparently the time to think of cafe food. He didn't, at that moment care what he ate. He couldn't say that he was feeling particularly hungry. A salad would be alright, but soup was warmer. Was there a way to communicate through what you ate? What he chose to order, could have an effect on the impression that he made.

Her father set his menu down on the table having apparently decided what he would order. "Why didn't you just use protection? I thought kids were better about that these days." Philippe looked up at him. He was almost offended at the mere consideration that he wouldn't use protection. He was downright uptight about that one. No glove no love. But he actually couldn't be sure whether or not Aimee had used protection. He'd never asked her. Was it a broken condom? Or was it recklessness?

The man sighed and a whole new look came over his face. It was sad and almost a little hopeful. "She told me it'll be a boy." Philippe nodded.

"That's what they said at the ultrasound."

"Don't get me wrong here, I love all my girls and I never wished that they weren't girls. But we had four of them, and we never had a boy. Not one boy."

"It's not like we're going to keep your grandson from you. You can see him whenever you want."

"Damn right I can."

The waitress walked up and looked at them like they had better order quickly or she was leaving. "What can I get for you?"

"Ham and cheese." Barked Claud. "And lemonade."

"The quiche please." Said Philippe, "And coffee."

"Mmm hmm." Said the waitress, and took their menus and walked off.

Philippe folded his hands together and placed his arms on top of the table and leaned forward. "Look sir. What can I do to alleviate your concerns?" Aimee's father put his own arms onto the table and also leaned forward.

"You can convince my daughter to go back to law school."

"No." Said Philippe abruptly. "She doesn't want to go to law school." Claud leaned back in his chair.

"Then I guess I'll have to stay concerned. Concerned that she is going into something so much less than she could be.

"Do you know why she didn't want to go to law school?" Claud lifted his hand into the air as if handing the conversation to Philippe.

"Enlighten me."

"She felt that lawyers sell out to the highest bidder instead of seeking the truth. She wanted to become a journalist so that she could get into the middle of all the world's troubles and find the answers. She could be great at that. She could be the best at that. If she put her mind to it, then she could fulfill all of her potential. And I think that would give her... our son something to look up to."

Food was placed onto the table in front of them. "Thank you." Philippe said quietly to the waitress as she walked away. Claud looked at his sandwich thoughtfully, and Philippe took a sip of his coffee.

"She thinks I sell out to the highest bidder?"

"No. I don't think she thinks that about you."

"And what is it that you think you can you offer her?"

"I don't know." Philippe shrugged. "But goals area a lot easier to reach with two people rather than one. At least with kids they are." Philippe's eyes shifted to the pinkish tannish strange color of the tile and thought of his mother. "I just don't want her to get stuck. I want to help."

Claud sighed and picked up his sandwich. "Well I guess that makes two of us. But it still bugs me that you don't have a job."

After they left the cafe, thoughts swirled around Philippe's mind and the weight of his decision was starting to truly set in. He had just told a man that he was going to be a father. A fact that was true only in action, not biological reality. He was going to have to do everything that a father would do. And he realized, that he had no idea how to do that. He'd wanted to help Aimee, but it hadn't quite hit him that he was going to be helping another little person too.

He stopped just inside the heavy doors of Notre Dame. He looked up at the huge high ceilings. Sanctuary. That was what the room was called. He heard the mumblings of a few tourists who were marveling at the architecture. But that was only the half of it. It was the half that the church capitalized on. But Philippe was feeling something else.

There was no mass and the only sounds were whispered voices and cell phone camera clicks, but Philippe was quiet, and he slowly lowered himself down into one of the chairs and stared unseeingly towards the towering arches and the cross standing at the end of the room with Mary at the foot of it, holding the corpse of her crucified son on her lap.

"What are you thinking about Philippe?" The words were like a whisper in his ear asking him about the contents of his heart. What was he thinking about? He lowered his head into his hands with his elbows digging into his knees. He heard the clack as his cane fell to the floor at his feet.

"What if I made a mistake?" He whispered so quietly that no one could have heard him unless they had their ear pressed against his lips. "I'm not built for this. I don't know how to raise a baby. It was rash and stupid for me to offer that kind of help to her." He wiped some moisture from his eye and folded his hands together and bit down on one of his fingers. His eyes gazed at the back of a chair. It was a sturdy chair. His eyes followed the wave of the wood grains broken by whoever cut the wood and then sewn together again by whatever carpenter had made them.

"It isn't as if she couldn't have done it herself." He continued his whisper, as if the wood grains were listening. "I've seen some very capable single mothers. I've met them. Just because my mother failed, doesn't mean that Aimee would." He wrapped his arms around himself and leaned over in his chair so that he was folded and his gaze was directed towards the simple brown cane lying atop the polished tile floor.

"I can't let her down but…" A tear dropped onto the tile and he could see from its water, which direction the light was coming from. "I don't have the strength." He tucked his hands under his armpits and sat up but his gaze still down, at nothing in particular. "I can't do it." His gaze lifted and was caught again by the cross. He bit his lip and held his gaze for a long long moment.

Then he took a very deep breath and exhaled slowly, and calmly. He felt as though, just admitting that, even to no one at all, had just given him what he needed, to do just what he thought that he couldn't do. He nodded, as if something had been affirmed and decided. Then, feeling suddenly self-conscious in that huge room, he got up, and left the sanctuary. He realized as he walked away, that no one had asked him the question that he'd answered, and he wondered just who he'd been talking to.

Chapter 50. Midnight Mass.

It was packed with people at eleven o'clock at night in Notre Dame. Philippe and Aimee found themselves in standing room only, near the back where the view was terrible. But they had at least managed to make it into the door at all. The rest of the crowd was stuck with an outdoor view. A man stood up front in a robe, introducing the evening and Philippe recognized him immediately as Sam.

Everyone applauded when he stopped speaking and began to make his way down from the stage. Philippe and Aimee applauded along, and then Aimee clutched onto Philippe's arm so that that they took up just a little less space. Organ music started and they could hear the sound of voices singing and echoing like cherubs across the walls though there was yet no one standing up in the front. Aimee reached up onto her tippy toes and Philippe could guess that she wasn't actually able to see the fact that there was no one yet standing up there.

Far past the people out of the corner of the room back behind the cross came the singing procession. The conductor led them, with his arms raised in the air and they followed him in song as they followed him on foot. The cherubic voices of a dozen or two children walked up onto the stage in front of the cross and they all took their places. They were finely dressed, either in long brightly colored robes or little black suits with ties and collars and Philippe found himself envying their childhoods. But he supposed he might not have appreciated the discipline and no childhood was without its steins.

From the corner of his eye he saw Sam making his way towards them, unable to avoid greeting every person he passed. When he made it to them, Sam smiled and touched both of their shoulders gently. His eyes looked at Aimee's face and then wandered down to her pregnant belly and he raised an eyebrow at Philippe and smiled. But he was en route, so he patted Philippe on the shoulder and whispered, "Good to see you." and kept on walking.

"What was that?" Asked Aimee reaching up to whisper into Philippe's ear.

"There's a story there." He whispered back. "I'll tell you later when there's less people."

"Alright." She nodded, and went back to trying to get a better view of the singing. And he would tell her later too. He would tell her all he knew about Father Samuel. And she would be very quiet for a while. Because she was the daughter of a man who believed in justice rather than grace and in punishment rather than mercy. And she would have to choose what she believed. But for now, she thought that he had simply had a sweet little interaction with them, and he was content to let it be so.

They were all songs that Philippe only knew vaguely. Christmas had never been a huge thing with him and his mother. Sometimes she would get him something small, and he was always given a little chocolate Santa which he'd always enjoyed. Right now, he was craving one. But Christmas was something else entirely here. The closest thing to it he had ever attended was the Nutcracker, and this was certainly no ballet.

The music went on and eventually he noticed how Aimee was shifting from one foot to the other. "You have to sit down." He whispered into her ear.

"There's no place to sit." She said to him obviously. He looked around for someone, preferably a man, who seemed to be sitting alone.

"Come on." He whispered. She spotted what he was looking at.

"Oh, no Philippe."

"Come on." He repeated and held her hand against his arm and started walking over to the man. The organ music ceased, and Philippe looked up to see that while it had been playing, the child choir had made its way back to the stage and they were now singing "Silent Night." Another song that he only knew a few words of.

"Excuse me." He said quietly, tapping gently on the man's shoulder. "I'm very sorry. Would it be possible for my wife to sit?" He gestured to Aimee, particularly at her belly.

"Philippe…" Aimee said, feeling on the spot and not wanting to bother the man and not feeling as if her pregnancy should cause people to owe her any favors. But the man practically leapt out of his chair.

"Of course, please."

"Thank you very much." Said Philippe. The man walked away through the crowd into a better standing vantage point and Philippe raised his eyebrow at Aimee and gestured to the chair with a smile.

"I'm not your wife." She whispered as she sat down.

"He doesn't need to know that." Responded Philippe, and just stood next to her.

"It's a better view from here." She conceded.

"Indeed."

"Shh" Said a woman in front of them.

"Sorry." Whispered Philippe and smiled at Aimee.

Then the bells started ringing and Philippe couldn't help but look up as the walls seemed to rattle and vibrate and the singing stopped and everyone was silent as they listened to the tolling of the bells. It was midnight and each toll thundered down upon them. It bugged Philippe, that in that moment, he couldn't remember how many bells there were. That was a fact that he would know, should know, was sure that he did know, and just couldn't think of it. The chanting and the singing started up again, in time with the bells.

It was lucky that he had sat Aimee in the very back row, because just then, he needed to jump aside so that he was standing behind her in order to get himself out of the way. He put his hands on her shoulders and watched as the robed procession of priests and cardinals and whichever other important religious people started walking down the aisle. Right down the middle of all of them. They wore long white robes and towering hats and a few held censors filled with the smoke of incense that plumbed over the sides as it was waved like a pendulum back and forth in the man's hands. Sam was part of the procession, but his eyes were focused on the front of the room as he passed.

They made their way up towards the front of the room and from there, Philippe was lost in the traditional liturgy of it all. Songs and chants were broken up with talking and the censor was waved around the center of the room in ways that Philippe was sure was symbolic, but he didn't know how. There were times when the whole room knew just what to say and they all spoke together. He looked down to see that Aimee was looking in the program for the words. Some of them were there. Some weren't. But she knew the Lord's Prayer, and she said it along with everyone else. Philippe wondered if he was the only one in the room that didn't know it.

"That was nice Philippe. Thanks for suggesting it." The echo of the songs and bells still seemed echo through Philippe's mind as he walked with Aimee. They headed down the stairs to the metro to wait for a train back to home.

"You knew the words. I didn't think your dad was Catholic." She smiled at him.

"Loosely. We went to a couple of services every year. Christmas and Easter mostly."

"This is the first Christmas service I've ever been to."

"Well, thanks for bringing me along Philippe. It's been a few years since the last time I went. I guess I kind of missed it. It was nice." They reached the bottom of the metro stairs and found a place to sit and wait for their train.

"What if we went more often?" He looked at her, feeling her out for her reaction.

"You thinking of getting baptized?"

"Baptized?" He raised his eyebrows. She shrugged.

"I was baptized when I was a baby. You know, so that I'm bound for heaven no matter what I do I guess."

"I guess you can do anything you want then huh?"

"Yeah." She smirked. "That's what I'll tell little Jerome here." She had half-jokingly started calling her unborn baby that. She pulled out her phone and started perusing Facebook. "It's okay with me Philippe." She said suddenly, looking up from her phone. "If you want to start going to church, it's okay with me. If you were looking to me for permission or acceptance or something. I don't think there's anything wrong with you going to church."

"Okay." He smiled and chuckled a little. He realized, that really was what he'd been asking her for. "Maybe you'll go with me sometimes?" She smirked at him.

"Maybe." He smiled and looked down at his shoes. They were starting to get worn, but that, for once, didn't bother him.

Chapter 51. Catholics and Protestants

The vocals of the choir singing Ave Maria were amazing. The acoustics in the room were haunting and awe inspiring. Philippe had learned that Christmas, for Catholics, was twelve days long. That explained that song titled "Twelve days of Christmas" and the various days of Christmas on which their true love gave them something. So the midnight mass had been to celebrate the first day of the twelve day holiday.

Philippe was enjoying the service, sitting in his chair towards the back. He could barely see the choir but that was alright. Not being able to see them gave the voices an ethereal feel to them. Like the song was just seeping in through the walls, or sailing down from the heavens. When they stopped singing, someone would go up and speak. Read a few versus. And then the choir would sing again. Sing and speak, chant and speak, and often the congregants would chime in all at once. Philippe knew he'd learn the words sooner or later.

He was suddenly startled by the unexpected and thoroughly distracting sensation of his phone vibrating. He discretely pulled it out of his pocket and saw that it was a text from Sacha. He was finally getting back to him. It had taken him long enough.

"How do you like it?" The text read. He lifted his head and vaguely scanned around the room. He didn't immediately see him, but when he turned back around, Sacha was just then lowering himself into the seat next to Philippe. Philippe looked at him oddly and decided not to respond to him with a text.

"It's pretty." He whispered at a polite volume. "It's very extravagant." He tipped his head from one side to the other and then back. "Maybe a little stuffy." Sacha looked at him and smiled slightly and then turned his face down to his phone and started typing something. Instead of hitting send, he just showed Philippe what he had typed.

"As always." The writing said. Philippe wondered if he was having more trouble than usual with his stutter or perhaps he just didn't want to stutter in a crowd. Philippe decided to follow suit and respond with a text.

"I didn't expect anything else." He hit send rather than showing the text to Sacha. Without missing a beat, Sacha responded in kind.

"Would you like to visit another place?"

"Why?" Philippe looked up from his screen and looked at Sacha. Sacha looked at him seriously but kindly.

"The Church is bigger than one." Philippe noted the intentional placement of the capital letter in 'Church'.

"I don't know." He responded simply.

"Are you looking for something here? Or someone?" Sacha typed.

"If you mean God, I don't know. I've been trying to figure some things out about myself. This place certainly has ambiance."

"Do you need tourist destinations to find yourself?" Sacha looked at him for a moment and then added another text. "Sam wouldn't hold it against you." Philippe leaned back in his seat and read the text over a few times. This guy was too good. He rested his phone between his knees and ran his thumb across the ridges of the phone case while he considered this point.

Sacha bumped his elbow into Philippe's upper arm to get his attention and then nodded for Philippe to follow him. He stood up and apologized his way past the people watching. Philippe decided to follow suit and they quietly left the iconic cathedral.

"I wanted to ask you," began Philippe when they had made it out to the side walk and he was following Sacha to God alone knew where. He was happy to notice that he was mostly just carrying his cane now rather than using it. "Have you gotten any news about the car? I don't mean to nag. In fact, I don't even really want it anymore." He looked at the ground where he walked as he remembered his altercation with Marcello and how Marcello had offered him another car. What was it worth then? It had just been handed to him in the first place. No matter how much he'd duped himself into thinking that he'd somehow earned it.

Sacha just looked at him curiously with a raised eyebrow. "I... I..." He cleared his throat and put his fist on his chest. "Yes." He nodded. "L... later. After." Whether or not Philippe wanted the car, he was still curious about what had happened to it.

"Where are you taking me anyway?" Sacha cleared his throat again.

"Church."

"You go to more than one?" Sacha just smirked at him. He started up the steps of a church building that was old and rustic and about a hundred times smaller than Notre Dame. Philippe looked up at the words written above the door.

"But… This is a reform church. It's not Catholic. Aren't you Catholic?" Sacha smirked again and gripped onto the door handle.

"You wanted less-ss-ss-stuffy right?" Philippe looked at him and shrugged.

"Alright." Philippe walked up the steps and Sacha held the door open for him. It was a very pretty church. Quaint as compared to Notre Dame, but it had its own sweet feel. They sat in old wooden pews and several people were already sitting. Philippe could tell that they were coming in, during the middle of the service so very quietly, he and Sacha took a place in the back.

"And that is why forgiveness is such a difficult thing." The preacher was standing up front looking very much less bedazzled than the Notre Dame priests, and he wasn't speaking in verse. It wasn't liturgy, it was a presentation. A sermon. A speech. "But forgiving someone doesn't mean that you're saying that what they did was okay. When Jesus was walking to the cross on his way to his death he said, 'Forgive them Father, for they know not what they do.' It's almost unfathomable to think that those people who were crucifying our Lord, were in the same breath, forgiven for it.

Forgiveness isn't about fixing anyone. We've tried and failed. Only Jesus can do that. And it isn't about justice. Jesus is the only just judge. It's about grace. As Jesus said to the adulteress in the Gospel of John. 'Neither do I condemn you. Go and sin no more.' It's about giving up your right to judge. Aren't you glad we have a just judge who wants to forgive us? But be warned. It says in Matthew seven, 'Judge not, lest you be judged. For with the judgement you pronounce you will be judged, and with the measure you use it will be measured to you.' Ouch." The preacher put his hand over his heart. "That smarts. So let's look at our other scripture again for a moment. Matthew six, fourteen and fifteen.

"For if you forgive others their trespasses, your heavenly Father will also forgive you, but if you do not forgive others their trespasses, neither will your Father forgive your trespasses." It's imperative that we learn how to do that. Forgiveness is something that heals our own hearts, so that we can be closer to Jesus. So let's remember that the next time we say the Lord's Prayer. Let's do that right now."

Philippe heard Sacha next to him say exactly what everyone else in the room was saying, without stuttering once. Philippe didn't know the words yet, but he was more amazed by Sacha's ability to say it so clearly. "Our Father, who art in Heaven, hallowed be thy name. Thy kingdom come, thy will be done, on earth as it is in heaven. Give us this day our daily bread," and here's that sticky part folks, "forgive us our trespasses, just as we forgive those who trespass against us." Right. As we forgive. So we are forgiven. Sorry I keep interrupting. Let's finish "And lead us not into temptation, but deliver us from evil. For thine is the kingdom, and the power, and the glory forever. Amen. Let's sing our closing song now."

Some people suddenly stood up from the front row of pews and walked up to the front of the room. It was then that Philippe noticed the instruments. A piano was one, but also there was a drum set, a guitar, a bass, and a microphone. Once they had taken their places, everyone stood up and opened up paper programs containing the words to the song. Philippe stood next to Sacha silently. Sacha looked at the person in front of him and quietly tapped on his shoulder. He was a broad shouldered man with a bald head and glasses and a ruddy leather coat. He turned in his seat and instantly smiled.

"Sacha." He whispered. "You came."

"And brought a f-friend." Sacha whispered. Philippe nodded to the stranger. "D-do you have a spare bull-letin?" The old woman standing next to the man waved and smiled at them.

"Take mine, we'll share." She said and handed the paper over to him and scooted over to look at the broad man's copy.

"Thanks." Sacha said, and handed the paper to Philippe. Philippe opened it and read the words, but he didn't know the song so he just read along. But the band at the front was practically rocking out as if it was their own private concert. The contemporary music was an intense contrast from the classical choral singing and chanting of Notre Dame, but he liked it. He liked them both. He supposed it would depend on his mood.

"Okay everyone," The preacher got back onto the stage once the music had stopped. "We've got some sacraments on the list for today. Well, actually only one. Speaking of forgiveness, our own Lionel Le Chien, as he was once called, has asked for it and received it. He is now Lionel, child of God, and today he's going to claim that name, and get baptized." Everyone applauded and Sacha reached forward and clapped the broad man hard on the shoulder. "Lionel, why don't you come up here?" With a beaming grin as broad as his shoulders, Lionel inched his way past the old woman, who Philippe suspected was his mother, and made his way up towards the preacher. When he got to the front, the preacher also clapped him on the shoulder like a brother and then said, "Welcome home Lionel. We're going to welcome you the way we know best. Is there anything you want to say before we do this?"

"Well uh…" The man obviously was not used to speaking in front of people. "You know, I think that the verse, the bible verse, that really brought me home was uh…" He leaned over to the preacher and said something quietly into his ear.

"Oh yes," said the preacher so that everyone could hear, "That's Mark, chapter seven, verse fifteen." He flipped some pages of the bible that was sitting on the podium and pointed to a spot on the page.

"Yeah." Said Lionel and squinted to read the verse. ""There is nothing outside a person that by going into him can defile him, but the things that come out of a person are what defile him." So it's not what we eat or drink, or drugs or anything, because those pass through us and eventually come out. You know, in the toilet or detox or something. But it's what comes out of you. Like what you say and do. Well, basically it's not the shit, it's the bull shit." Sacha choked on a laugh and there was a general chuckle throughout the room. "Well anyway, that helped me understand that, even though the drugs were killing me, it's what God can put into my heart that will save me. So I said to myself, I want that. That's what'll clean me up."

"Thanks Lionel." Said the preacher, "That's actually a really beautiful description of your journey here and we're very lucky to have you. And very lucky to have someone with such a down to earth understanding of scripture. I do believe that's a gift that God has given you, and I believe that he'll grow you more and more into that gift so that you can share it with others in a way that everyone understands. God bless you. Alright, let's head to the water. I don't know how many of you came in here noticing that the tub back here got filled up."

He went up another step on the back of the dais, slipped his shoes off and stepped into a large stone slab, which Philippe now realized was actually a marble tank full of water. "Come on in Lionel, water's warm. Lionel started taking off his shoes. "Well," added the preacher, "warmish." Lionel climbed into the water with the preacher. The old woman in front of Philippe was smiling and wringing her fingers together as if this was the moment that she'd been waiting for all her life.

The preacher suddenly remembered to take off his clip on mic, and handed it to the guitarist and said something quietly to him. The guitarist nodded and set the mic aside and started playing something quiet and sweet and solo with no singing. The preacher projected his voice well.

"Lionel." He wrapped one arm around the big man's shoulders and put his other hand onto his forehead. "I baptize you, in the name of the Father, the Son, and the Holy Ghost. I baptize you with water, may you be baptized in the Holy Spirit also. You ready?"

"Amen." Was all Lionel said and then he was leaned all the way back into the water, and bought back up on the next breath, which he gratefully inhaled. Everyone applauded.

"Congratulations." The preacher said with a smile and soaking wet sleeves. "You have died to this world, and have been born as a citizen of Heaven." the applause continued. Philippe watched, but he didn't clap. Not because he meant to be rude, but because he forgot. He was too busy trying to wrap his head around what the purpose was of this tradition. He supposed it was a symbol. It was a stamp, a physical act to put an exclamation point on Lionel's decision to follow the faith. It was symbolic, and Philippe wasn't able, in that moment, to even begin to consider the idea that there was any literal truth to it at all.

Chapter 52. Escapism

"I don't really understand forgiveness." Philippe said this to Sacha as they were walking away from the little reform church. Philippe was just following him to wherever he was being led next. "It seems like so many people have been telling me about it, or asking me to do it, including you." Sacha looked at him as if he were trying to remember the exact moment that he could be referring to. "And I really just don't understand what it is that you or they are asking me to do." He looked at Sacha who looked thoughtful but silent and said nothing. So Philippe continued, "I mean, in order to forgive someone, you would have to first be angry at them wouldn't you? That preacher was talking about it as if you needed to set aside your judgements. But what if you're not judging in the first place? I'm not angry at anyone. I'm not holding anything against anyone." Sacha tilted his head to the side as they walked and furrowed his brow slightly.

Philippe stopped suddenly and raised his eyebrows. He saw where they were going. Specifically, he saw the car. Vintage red Mercedes convertible with soft top undamaged and safely pulled up. Tires un-slashed, though they looked like they could use some air. Windows fully intact. He walked quickly over to it and started inspecting it for bumps or scratches.

"There's nothing wrong with it." He said disbelievingly. "Well," he took it back for a moment. "There's a scuff on the right by the headlight but... That very minimal consider what she's been through." He straightened up. "What has it been though?" He looked at Sacha who was just standing there watching him.

"L-Landrs hid it. He m-meant to sell it. Between the hospital and e-everything else, he didn't get around to it." He nodded towards the front right headlight. "Th-that was actually my mistake. I scraped it in an alley getting it h-here. Sorry about that." Philippe shook his head and closed the distance between him and Sacha and threw his arms around him.

"Are you kidding?" He said and squeezed and then let go and walked around the car again to double, triple check over it. Like a new mother checking for all her newborn's fingers and toes. "I really just don't know how to thank you for this." Sacha smiled.

"I-it was yours to begin with. L-Landers should never have had it." Philippe looked up from the car at Sacha with a smile, and realized that there was a very strong chance that Sacha had done this for Landers more than for him. "Th-the keys are at my pad. Do you want to c-come in for tea?" Philippe turned around. He'd been so absorbed by the car that he hadn't noticed where they were.

"Is that your pad?" He asked, gesturing to the apartment building that they stood in front of. Sacha nodded and started leading the way towards the door. Philippe put his hand on top of the car and walked away from it reluctantly, running his fingertips over it as he walked past, for as long as his fingers would reach. He'd almost forgotten how much he loved that car.

Sacha's apartment was very minimalistic, and not in a Feng Shui kind of way, he just didn't seem to own much. It was a small studio apartment, with dusty blinds on the windows and a single size mattress on the floor in the corner with a wide short book shelf next to it that was covered in a disorganized array of books. Several of which were laying open on the floor.

Sacha first slipped off his shoes as he entered the door, as if the carpet needed protecting, but he did it anyway. Then he walked over and reached for the top of the book shelf and picked up Philippe's keys and tossed them back to him. Philippe did managed to catch them, though in the process he dropped his cane.

Sacha disappeared around the hall corner and Philippe looked down at the dirty sneakers inside the doorway and decided to follow Sacha's example and slipped off his own shoes, and took a moment to inspect his keys. Along with the old rustic car key was the key he'd had that went to his mother's apartment. Number thirty-six. Since he hadn't been able to return the key to the apartment owner, he'd had to pay for them to replace the lock. Now the key was useless.

He tucked them into his pocket and left his cane laying on the floor. When he came around the corner, Sacha was just closing the door to the microwave into which he had just put two mugs full of water. After he'd started the microwave running, he turned around and took his coat off and tossed it over the back of a folding chair in his makeshift dining room. His table was a black fold up card table that was bowed in the middle, but Philippe got the sensation that pretty things weren't often much on Sacha's mind.

Sacha leaned against the wobbly card table and flipped open a leather bound journal that was laying there and picked up a pencil and poised it over the top of the page. He looked as if he were waiting for the words to write themselves, but eventually the pencil tip touched the paper and Philippe could see a moment of his creativity at work. Philippe assumed that whatever it was that he was writing was something that just needed to get out onto the paper right now. Either that or Sacha had a habit of writing poetry while he had company. Philippe glanced over at the mattress on the floor. The blankets were just sort of tossed over it. Philippe figured that he didn't often have company anyway.

The microwave beeped. Sacha bit his lip and squinted his eyes and poised the pencil again as if he had just lost his train of thought and thus the next words he'd been about to write were lost. He frowned and tossed his defeated pencil down onto the page and turned around for the mugs of steaming water.

Philippe felt as if he'd just witnessed a strange but intimate internal moment. There was something poetic about the whole thing. Something passionate. That the man would enter the room, and compulsively need to write something. Then once he's started writing, the poetry slips from his mind and he's left to mull over the right words all over again. He wondered if it was that mulling over the words that caused Sacha to stutter. And that was another thing. How poetic to have a poet, with so much to say, that just can't get the words out. So instead he writes. Philippe admitted to himself that the whole internal dynamic of this was a bit of a turn on to him.

"I just have j-jasmine."

"That's fine." Philippe smiled. "The same stuff you had in the alley?" Sacha nodded and started opening tea bags and putting them into the water. He handed the hot mug to Philippe and then gestured to the chair. It was the only chair. Philippe wondered where Sacha had gotten the chairs and table that they had used in the alley. Perhaps he had borrowed them.

"S-sit." Sacha smiled and reached over to the journal and closed the pencil inside. Then he sat down cross legged on the floor near the table.

"Oh I don't mean to put you on the floor." Sacha looked up at him.

"I s-sit here most of the time." Philippe sat down on the folding chair feeling a little bit awkward, but at the same time, a little overly excited to be here.

"Sacha," he started, feeling the need for some small talk. "I like your tattoos, where did you get them?" He reached out and put his finger against Sacha's shoulder where he could see the roaring face of a lion with flames coming out of its eyes. Sacha looked at Philippe's finger and at the tattoo that it was touching.

"We would t-tattoo each other."

"You're a tattoo artist too?" Philippe took his finger off of Sacha's arm and gripped onto his warm mug and took a drink.

"I was. H-he was better." Philippe tilted his head to look a little more closely at Sacha's other arm.

"He did all of them? And you did all of his?" Sacha shook his head and looked at the dragon on his other shoulder. Part of it was scarred.

"No. We a-all did each other." He rubbed his palms over his shoulders and stood up, leaving his mug on the carpet, and walked over to a closet where all of his clothes seemed to be hanging. He pulled out a button up sweater and pulled it on over his arms. Philippe straightened up.

"Oh I'm sorry. I just realized that I'm asking you about something uncomfortable. You don't like them?" Sacha shook his head and turned back around.

"I d-don't like why I have them."

"Oh I see. I'm sorry, I shouldn't have asked." He set his mug down onto the bowed card table and stood up. Sacha shook his head.

"Earlier, while we w-were walking. You s-said you didn't want the car anymore. Why?"

"Well…" Philippe started, but he stared at Sacha instead. It seemed that Sacha wanted to talk about Philippe, but he didn't want to talk about himself. Notable that someone who spends all his time helping people through their mistakes, has trouble talking about his own. Not an uncommon human phenomenon. But Sacha knew a lot more about Philippe than Philippe knew about him. Philippe stepped carefully over the hot mug of tea sitting on the carpet and walked over to him.

"Why do you want to know?" Philippe asked, stopping just in front of him.

"It s-seemed important to you."

"It is." Philippe said and watched as Sacha tilted his head slightly looking just a little puzzled. "I can share with you," Philippe continued. "I'm happy to, but can't you share with me too?"

"I write." Said Sacha flatly. "I can t-tell you my story if you want. But I wonder if it's too different from yours to h-help you."

There it was. Sacha was a helper. He was willing to tell his story in situations where he thought it would help someone, but he was the sort who had no interest in being helped himself. Philippe tended to think that these sorts of people only felt that way out a sense of power and control. There's something gratifying about helping other people and focusing on other people's problems. But sometimes, they needed to be able to let someone else help them. The thing is though, that they will never likely be the person to notice this. What Philippe really needed to do, was just to take down some of Sacha's walls. Philippe smiled and reached out his hands to either side of Sacha's face and then leaned in and kissed his lips.

Philippe found himself lying flat on the mattress but Sacha was about as far away from him as he could be. There was a thud and a splash as Sacha just about tripped over the cup of tea that was sitting on the carpet waiting to be spilled. Philippe blinked as the stars cleared out of his vision and looked over to see Sacha looking thoroughly startled with his hand over his mouth looking between Philippe and the spilled mug of tea as if the two had anything to do with each other.

"I'm sorry!" Said Sacha thumping his knuckles against his forehead. "I-I-I-I-I-I'm an i-idiot."

"Ow." Muttered Philippe in response and rolled over onto his side to sit himself up. He looked at Sacha to see him standing stock still with his fist shoved up against his forehead and his eyes clamped shut, forcing himself to take long deep breaths. "I'm sorry Sacha, I..." but Sacha put up his other hand as if to silence Philippe for a moment and he crossed his arms over himself and leaned against the counter and lowered his head. He took one more big deep breath and then opened his eyes and looked at Philippe.

"I'm s-sorry I pushed you." Philippe shook his head.

"I'm sorry I misread you." Sacha put up his finger and seemed to be physically struggling with getting words out of his mouth.

"That n-n-never crossed my mind." He stared at Philippe for a moment and then made a sudden lunge over to his journal and started madly flipping through pages looking for something. He stopped on one page and read the length of it before, much to Philippe's surprise, he tore it right out of the cover and then with an outstretched arm, handed it over to Philippe. Philippe took it and looked down at it.

Escapism

The spirit and the flesh.
Like two ever burning forces,
The angst of humanity.

In the effort of trying to become
Close to that truth which we yearn for,
We drive ourselves away from it.

I remember a time, when I saw beauty,
I threw myself head long into it.
So close was I to all the answers
That my body heaved and groaned under the pressure.
After it was all over and the night was as spent as I was,
I had lost that beauty which had filled me to the breaking point.
But in truth I had never captured it to begin with.
No, I hadn't even come close.

Escapism.
Creation's existential irony.
In an effort to be close to angels we turn to
Sex and drugs or
Anything to try to force ourselves to see
A little more. To open a little wider.
To fill a little fuller.
To be a little greater.
A little farther away from reality.

It is devastating, excruciating, that what things make us feel full,
Also leave us feeling empty, vacant, alone.

We insist upon our sin because just as we yearn so truly for closeness,

We also yearn in equal measure to be apart from Him.

Apart from God.

We want to feel his love but we use anything and everything else that might feel similar.

That way, we won't have to get too close.

Love burns with cleansing fire,

But escapism is warm, and safe and fleeting.

Our lust for this world will pass,

But we will never escape Love.

Philippe looked up from the page. Sacha was staring at him intently.

"Um..." Philippe reached up and wiped a confused tear from his own face. He felt strange. He felt almost angry or ashamed or perhaps embarrassed. Sacha had just handed him something that clearly stated to Philippe, that the thing he'd always used to help him feel close to people, had actually always been doing the opposite. But if that were true then that would mean that he didn't know what it actually felt like to be close to someone. As far as he was concerned sex had always worked. But if he was so sure of that, then why was he crying?

He decided to assume, given the fact that it had been torn right out of the book, that it was his to keep. So he folded it neatly, making sure that each edge was perfectly lined up, as his lip quivered and his eyes stung, and he tucked it into his back pocket and then looked back at Sacha who was still staring at him intently.

"Um…" He said again, and wiped his eye with his sleeve. "Thank you for returning my car. That means a lot to me." Then he turned awkwardly and walked over to pick up his cane, and slip on his shoes.

"Ph-Philippe." Said Sacha coming to the corner to watch him. Philippe looked up from his shoe. "I d-don't want to have this be between us brother."

"Oh no. No it's fine. It's fine. I just… have to go."

"I'm going to write you a poem about f-forgiveness." Philippe finished slipping on his shoes and looked at Sacha.

"I'll look forward to that." He forced a smile onto his face, and he turned and opened the door.

"God bless you." Said Sacha and the door closed.

Chapter 53. Prodigal Mercedes

Philippe parked his car in the parking space that went along with Aimee's apartment and then turned off the ignition and wiped his eyes. It was strange to be sitting in his car again. His seat felt just as it always had but the sensation was not as comforting as it used to be. It felt like a moment stolen from the past. His car was supposed to be stolen and gone forever, and yet, here he was sitting in it and trying to feel as if it had never been gone.

Philippe got out of the car and closed the door and looked down at it. He walked slowly around it and ran his hand over the scuff on the front right headlight, and then walked around it again, trying to get a hold on exactly what he was feeling. He took his phone out of his pocket and called Aimee.

"Hey." He said, "Will you come down to the parking lot? You'll never believe this." He slipped his phone back into his pocket and waited. The car was so red. He loved that about it. Red wasn't even his favorite color. He imagined it would look pretty cute in baby blue, but there was definitely something evocative about the vintage red Mercedes. The elevator dinged and Aimee stepped into the garage.

"Whoa. It's…" She started.

"Yup. It is." Philippe finished. She walked up next to him and looped her arm into his.

"It looks perfect." Her expression said that this was almost as surreal to her as it was to him.

"Aside from a scuff on the side of the headlight, it is."

"Wow." She raised her eyebrows and nodded. "Congratulations."

"Yeah." She looked up at him.

"You don't sound so sure."

"If I had gotten this car two weeks ago, I'd still be a model. It shows up now instead."

"Good." Aimee shrugged. "That just means your old boss can't use it as emotional leverage anymore."

"Yeah but… it should be his anyway. Part of me wants to take it to him and hand him the title so that it's not here reminding me of that."

"So… you would just give this amazing car back, even though it's legally yours, just because you feel sentimental about it."

"Well, yeah."

"That's like, when high school girl and boy break up and she gives him all his cd's back even though he gave them to her for her birthday and they are totally her favorite albums just because, 'Oh! Every time I listen to them I think of him.'" He looked down at her. She was holding the back of one hand over her forehead in a very dramatic fashion.

"You make it sound so cheesy."

"That's because it is cheesy Philippe. This is an amazing car and it's yours fair and square. You have nothing to be ashamed about."

"Maybe you're right." She crossed her arms as he unlocked his own from her so that he could step forward and reach out and touch the car. "It's just a car."

"Mmhmm. Yup." He looked into the window at the stick shift and the seats and the wheel. He turned around and leaned his rear up against it and looked thoughtful.

"You know, Father Samuel said something interesting to me."

"What's that?" She shifted her weight onto the other leg. He was aware that her proverbial jury was still out on Sam.

"I asked him if he knew why it was that my mum had never gone home. He said, that maybe she was too ashamed to face her parents."

"Why should she have felt ashamed?" Her tone was accusatory, that jury seemed to be just about to come to a conclusion.

"She shouldn't have, that's the point. The tragedy is that she wasn't able to face her parents even though they would probably have just been happy to see their daughter alive. Just like she was never able to talk to me about it, she couldn't go to her parents either." Aimee looked at the car.

"Road trip?" She raised an eyebrow."

"Even if they aren't there anymore. I think I'd like to take my mother's ashes home." Aimee quietly nodded for a moment.

"Alright. I'll go with you."

"You don't have to." He shook his head and his eyes obviously fell down to her belly.

"Oh come on." She rolled her eyes and then smiled. "Just let me find the time off work."

Chapter 54. The Nordins

Philippe reached his hand over to the passenger seat of his car and rested his hand atop Aimee's belly. He swore he'd seen the baby move out of the corner of his eye. It had taken a full month for her to find that time off work and she had basically decided to start her maternity leave at a full month before the due date. So eight months pregnant she lay tilted back in her seat, fast asleep. He'd tried to convince her not to come, but in truth he was happy to have her with him.

Twenty-four hours was what the internet had told them as to the length of time it would take to reach their destination. But of course they weren't driving straight. They'd decided to split their drive into two twelve hour stretches with a hotel stay in Germany, which they did. Of course, it would have been faster to just fly there, but there was something about the drive that Philippe liked. Aside from just enjoying driving, every kilometer closer to his destination helped him feel like his heart was getting more and more ready.

"Aimee." He whispered.

"Huh?" She moaned but Philippe could tell that she wasn't actually awake and hadn't actually heard him. He looked into the back seat where his mother's urn was resting quietly. It had been a long trip and Philippe couldn't blame Aimee for sleeping. The sun was down and they were illuminated only by the lamplight of the residential street that he was parked on. He'd contemplated getting another hotel room and coming back in the morning, but it wasn't too late into the night and now that they were here, he didn't want to put it off any longer.

He sighed and rubbed Aimee's belly for a long thoughtful moment. She may be sleeping, but someone else was definitely awake. He smiled and reached into the back seat and grabbed Aimee's coat which she had stuffed back there. He laid it gently over her and tucked it under her shoulder to keep her warm. When she woke, she could just call him. He leaned over and gently kissed her cheek. She moaned peacefully. He reached back and picked up his mother's urn, and got out of the car.

He hadn't parked in the driveway of the house. He wasn't sure whether or not the family still lived there. He hadn't chosen to try to call ahead or anything because, though he hoped they would be there, he didn't want to go tracking them down if they weren't. If they weren't there, he would just release his mother's ashes, and go home.

He pulled his scarf a little tighter around his neck and felt the crunch of the snow under his feet as he took a step towards the little house. Winter had perhaps not been the best time to make this little trek, but had they waited, there would have been a baby in the equation too, and the whole thing would have been just a little too complicated. It was either right now, or a few years from now. They chose now.

When he stepped up onto the frosty curb, he looked up to see that the lights of the house were still on. He stopped, and just stood staring for a moment. They hadn't seen him yet. Someone inside stood up and walked away from the window towards the back of the house. There was a family in there. Not just two people, but more. He wondered how many, and he wondered if they had anything to do with him at all. He hoped they did, but he braced himself. It had, after all been over twenty years since his mother had been taken from them. Over twenty years during which time anything could have happened.

He took a deep breath for courage and took a step up the short paved driveway. He slipped slightly on the ice and caught himself on the iron stair railing that led up the few steps to their front door. One, two, three, four steps he climbed with slow deliberation. They could have seen a shadow of his approach through the window now, so there was no turning back. They were probably already in there saying to one another, 'hey, who's that at the door?' It occurred to him, just as his hand poised to knock on the door, that he didn't speak a word of Swedish. He doubted that they spoke any French. Perhaps English was a language they could have in common.

He shook the doubt out of his mind, and allowed his knuckles to land on the front door next to a sign that hung on it saying, "Valcommen". He didn't know what that meant but he assumed it was something friendly. Before his second knock landed the door opened, his hand still in the air. The woman who opened the door looked to be not much older than him. She was tall and athletic looking, with short disheveled sandy brown hair and an expression of semi explosive confidence that was probably always on her face. She wore a tank top and a pair of baggy sweat pants and was obviously feeling comfortable for the evening.

"Ja?" She said with a tone of mild impatience.

"Is this the Nordin residence?" Philippe asked in English, figuring that would be the best language to try. He felt like his heart might jump out of his chest.

"Yeah. What do you want?" She answered frankly and looked down at the urn that he was holding under his arm. She raised her eyebrows and looked at him like 'well?' But he was too busy seeing mild tunnel vision. This really was them? He wondered, what was this girl's relation to him? Cousin perhaps? "Okay, so are you like a delivery guy or something cuz I didn't order anything but maybe someone else did. That vase doesn't look like it's full of flowers. So help me out here man, or I'm just gonna close the door on you." Philippe shook his head.

"Sorry I just… I must be your family."

"Vad?" Came a voice from within the room. A boy who looked about fifteen or so stood up from a chair to get a better look at Philippe. He had hair that was obviously dyed black and had been purposely combed directly into the front of his face.

"Get mamma." Said the young woman over her shoulder. He nodded and bolted out of the room. Another young man, likely about the age of the woman also stood up to look at Philippe.

"Well, let him in Syb." He said. His hair was dark brown and combed neatly. He had a gentle face and dark brown eyes and an attractive jaw, or so Philippe noticed.

"Alright then, come in." She said, doubtfully and stood aside from the door.

"Thank you." Said Philippe quietly, entering the room. She closed the door behind him and then crossed her arms over her chest. She looked like she could take him down in a fight, and she also looked like she'd be willing to do so.

"You're not part of the D'Jean family are you?"

"Um, no, I don't think so."

"Oh." Her shoulders relaxed and she looked a little less like she might take him down at a moment's notice. "Well, alright then." She walked away from him, past the man and sat down on a living room couch.

"Sybil don't be rude." Said the man and stepped forward and put out his hand. "I'm Thomas, and that's Sybil, my sister." He shot Sybil a glance as Philippe took his hand to shake.

"Philippe."

"You sound French." Said Sybil to Philippe while giving Thomas a glance in return. There was obviously some sort of silent conversation there that only the two of them were privy to.

"I am French. Well, I grew up in France anyway."

"I didn't know we had family in France." She stated.

"Well…" But at that moment, a portly older woman entered the room.

"What is all this that Hugo is trying to tell me?" She asked as she entered the room, and then stopped and took a good minute to look Philippe up and down. He could see the family resemblance immediately. Her hair was mostly grayed but he could see some bits of blonde still clinging to color. Her eyes were a whitish sky blue and Philippe was startled to see that he very much had her nose.

"Are you Ingrid?" He asked as her eyes continued to put pieces together.

"I am." She said, and looked up at him curiously, waiting for the quiet answer to her questions. A tall thin old man with little hair and much beard came out of the hall behind her and Philippe could see the family resemblance in him too.

"Well then you're… well, I'm your grandson." Sybil stood up abruptly, Thomas took a step back to get a better look and Philippe heard Hugo from behind the old man say, "Vad?" as he tried to squeeze a peak around him. But none of those things was quite as startling to Philippe as the fact that Ingrid gave him a long look and all the color seemed to drain away from her rosy face until suddenly her eyes rolled up into her head, and she fainted.

Philippe reached his hand out towards her but he couldn't really help her while holding his mother's ashes. The old man just barely managed to catch her, along with Thomas who was the next closest. They lowered her down to the floor carefully and the old man started waving his hand over her face and saying her name. Philippe felt stunned and guilty. Not that he assumed this would be easy, but he hadn't expected to see any fainting. He had a moment of wondering if it would have been better for him not to have come, but it was interrupted by Sybil who suddenly walked up to him and put both hands onto his cheeks and turned his face from left to right and back again.

"This just keeps gettin' weirder." She mumbled, more to herself than to him. Ingrid groaned suddenly after a few gentle taps on the cheek by her husband who then helped her to sit up. Thomas said something to her in Swedish and she nodded and allowed him and her husband to help her over to the sofa against the wall where she sat down between the two of them and held her hand to her forehead.

Sybil let go of Philippe's face and ran into the kitchen around the corner. Philippe heard water running as she filled up a glass and brought it back out. Hugo just stood there in the hall with his hair covering half his face, staring at Philippe with his mouth hanging open like Philippe was some strange alien.

"I'm so sorry." Philippe shook his head. "I didn't mean to shake everyone up so much. I don't need to stay."

"No don't go." Said the old man, "We just need a minute. Please," He gestured to the chair across from the sofa and the coffee table. "Please sit down."

"Okay." Said Philippe sheepishly and slowly walked over to the chair. Sybil came back from the kitchen with the glass of water and handed it to Thomas. Thomas tried to give it to Ingrid but she just shook her head which she continued to hold.

"So wait… that would make you my…" Sybil looked thoughtful. "Whoa, that would make you my nephew. How old are you?"

"Sybil!" Thomas rolled his eyes at his sister.

"It seems like a valid question to me." Philippe lowered himself into the cushy chair that felt too soft. He wanted to sit on the edge of it to keep his posture rigid, but the chair demanded that the sitter lean back into it and Philippe was left with very little choice on this point. So he held the urn in his lap, so as not to mush it into the side.

"Wait…" Said Hugo. "How is that possible?"

"Um…" Started Philippe, but luckily for him, he ended up not needing to answer the question.

"Because we had a daughter." Said Ingrid, finally taking her hand off her head and leaning back into the sofa. "Before any of you." She gestured to her three children. "We had a daughter." Hugo got a strange expression on his face as if someone had just kicked his puppy. "But she um…" Here her voice choked and she put her hand over her mouth. Thomas set the glass of water onto the coffee table and reached over to an end table and grabbed a box of tissue and handed it to her. She took the tissue and nodded for a thank you. The old man rubbed her shoulder.

"She disappeared when she was twelve." Said the old man and then looked over at Philippe, obviously considering his existence.

"And… we never knew this why?" asked Sybil, gesturing to herself and her siblings. "I mean, I've never seen photos or anything."

"It was a painful thing Sybil. It wasn't that we meant to hide it from you. I'm not proud of it," He looked back to Philippe, "But we put away the photos on the day we decided to stop looking for her."

"We still have them." Ingrid choked, looking at her husband. Then she smiled through her tears at Philippe. "What's your name dear?"

"Philippe." Sybil answered for him, jutting her head in his direction. "He's French."

"Philippe." Ingrid repeated, putting her hand back over her mouth. Hugo finally came out of the hallway and joined them in the living room.

"So, then I'm not the miracle child?"

"Oh!" Exclaimed Ingrid with a loud chuckle. "You are, Hugo. You see," She turned to Philippe, since he was the one with the least amount of knowledge on the subject. "A few years after Emelia was born, we tried to have another. But we had a miscarriage because I have diabetes. And the doctors told us not to have more children. But after she disappeared, our home had no children in it, so we adopted Sybil and Thomas." She gestured to her two elder children. "But of course, a few years later... You were an accident Hugo. I had to be in the hospital a lot, with the diabetes and with my age. I was forty which is too old you know and tends to cause complications. But we did everything within our power to keep you, and it worked." She smiled at her youngest.

"Ja Hugo, don't worry." Said Sybil, "You're still the miracle baby." Hugo glared at his sister.

"But you..." Ingrid looked at Philippe and furrowed her brow. "How old are you?"

"That's what I asked." Piped in Sybil, but she got an elbow from Thomas.

"Twenty." Said Philippe. He elected not to go into detail about the fact that he didn't know when his birthday was exactly. His legal age was close enough. They were silent for a while. Ingrid and her husband looked thoughtful.

"That's only a couple years younger than us." Said Sybil looking slightly disturbed and patting Thomas on the shoulder.

"Fifteen." Said the old man. And Ingrid bowed her head and put her hand over her eyes. "She would have been fifteen when she had you right?" Philippe nodded.

"Uhg." Grunted Hugo, who was himself fifteen.

"It's not a happy story." Said Philippe looking down at the urn.

"Oh no!" Exclaimed Ingrid, "Is that…?" Philippe nodded, but just then, he felt his phone vibrate.

"Oh, sorry." He said as he reached into his pocket.

"I'm awake now…" read the text from Aimee. "Where are you?"

"Be right there." He texted back and slipped his phone back into his pocket. "I'm sorry." He said again standing up. Ingrid had her hands over her mouth again and was squinting against the tears building in her eyes. "Um… I left my friend sleeping in the car. But she's awake now… I know I've already been intruding on you all, but is it okay if she comes in?"

"You left her in the car?" Sybil said with a frown and walked over to the door and opened it and walked outside. Philippe could hear her calling out, assumedly to Aimee who was probably wandering around the sidewalk waiting.

"When did she die?" Asked Ingrid through tears. Philippe sighed.

"About six months ago."

"Oh." She put her hand over her mouth and looked at her husband. The old man frowned sadly.

"Why didn't she come home?" He asked. Philippe shook his head sadly.

"I don't know. I didn't even know we had family until after her death."

"How did it happen?" Asked Ingrid cautiously.

"Drug overdose." Philippe said plainly.

"Oh." She tapped her heart with her hand and then reached out for the glass of water, obviously wishing that it were something a little stiffer.

Sybil then re-entered the room with Aimee in tow. Ingrid looked mildly faint again when she saw Aimee's huge belly and came to some obviously conclusions. As far as she was concerned, a great grandchild had just walked into the room. She had just acquired two new generations in one night. Philippe certainly wasn't about to set her straight on the matter considering his promise, but it was hard to watch her struggle.

Aimee looked about awkwardly, standing in the doorway with Sybil not knowing what to do with herself. The vacant gawk on Ingrid's overwhelmed face didn't seem to be helping her. Philippe smiled at Aimee with a smile much more joyful than the occasion warranted.

"Aimee. Well, if it's not too uncomfortable for everyone for me to say, let me introduce you to… to well, my family." He nodded to Sybil and then gestured his hand around to each. "My Aunt Sybil, Uncle

Hugo, Uncle Thomas, Grandmother Ingrid and grandfather…" He looked at the old man, having not yet gotten his name.

"Ole." Said the old man.

"Grandfather Ole." He looked around at everyone. "If I have that all correct."

"You do." Nodded Ingrid with tears still in her eyes. With a little help, she stood up and walked over to Philippe. She reached out and he handed her the urn. She looked down at its lilac, flower covered surface and held it like something most precious. But then she turned and set it gently atop the coffee table, and turned back to Philippe and wrapped him up in a long warm hug. "Welcome home." She said into his ear. And then it was his turn to cry.

Chapter 55. Hope Chest

They had insisted that the family didn't need to put them up, but the family had insisted that they stay. So rather than sleeping in a big bed in a hotel next to each other, Philippe and Aimee ended up in single sized beds in separate rooms. Sybil and Thomas didn't actually live in the house anymore but they came home for dinner often so Philippe was allowed to sleep in Thomas's old bedroom which was still mostly as Thomas had left it aside from the books and clothes which he'd taken with him to his apartment.

Philippe rolled over. It wasn't being away from home that made it hard to sleep, his mind just wouldn't stop turning and he was having some trouble coping with the emotions of the evening. His own room growing up had never been so well furnished. Thomas had one of those old wooden desks with the roll top pulled down. His bed had a headboard and a footboard. He had a bookshelf covered with what books and nick knacks he hadn't felt the need to take out of his old room. Comfort items for whenever he returned.

Growing up, Philippe had had a bed where the mattress sank in the middle, his floor had been covered in stuffed animals that he'd acquired, that he couldn't seem to get enough of. His closet had been full of ill-gotten clothing. But this was the room of a child who had wanted for nothing. Thomas had been adopted as a baby but he had been adopted by parents who would bend over backwards for him. Philippe wondered what Thomas's life would have been like if his mother had decided to keep him. He wondered if it would have been something like Philippe's.

He rolled onto his back and looked up at the ceiling. There were stick on stars and planets that had been there for who knows how many years. He wondered which room had been his mother's. It could have been this one. Ingrid said that she still had the pictures somewhere. He decided that, in the morning, he would ask her if he could see them.

But that decision still didn't help him sleep, so he sat up and looked towards the small window. It was curtained given the fact that it looked straight out to a street lamp which was blinding to one trying to sleep. He picked up a well-loved teddy bear that was sitting on the bedside table and had probably been sitting there for years. It reminded him of the teddy he'd had in the brothel. Its fur was mottled and worn, but it had both of its eyes. He set it back down and stood up and went over to his duffel bag and opened up one of the pockets and pulled out the poem that Sacha had given him that day in Sacha's apartment.

He sat down on the bed and read over it again. It wasn't about sex specifically but sex was certainly among the implied. He had never thought of it as an addiction. Well, he thought of it as an addiction the way Father Sam had talked about it in himself. Philippe supposed it was an addiction if you were willing to subjugate someone to get it. But if it hurt no one, then what was the problem? But the poem didn't seem to be considering whether or not it was done at someone else's expense. It was more or less stating that it was done at one's own expense. As if, every time Philippe slept with someone, he was somehow hurting himself.

"It's devastating, excruciating, that what things make us feel full,
Also leave us feeling empty." it said.

Philippe wasn't sure that he could say that sex had ever made him feel empty. But he could admit to himself that he had always sought sex in order to feel full. It wasn't the sex though, it was the people. When else were people willing to be so vulnerable with each other? He'd never much been one for pornography because there was no intimacy there. You couldn't talk to them. You couldn't ask them how they felt about life. No, it wasn't the sex, it was the people. The sex was just a tool for closeness.

"I remember a time, when I saw beauty,
I threw myself head long into it.
So close was I to all the answers
That my body heaved and groaned under the pressure.
After it was all over and the night was as spent as I was,
I had lost that beauty which had filled me to the breaking point.
But in truth I had never captured it to begin with.
No, I hadn't even come close."

He read the verses over again. These ones in particular made him shudder. These ones struck a little too close to home. It took those sweet sentiments he had towards sex and intimacy, and threw it into his face saying that he hadn't even come close to the beauty he was seeking. But what did Sacha know? He had to admit that Sacha had already had far too much insight for his comfort. Even without sex. Maybe in the same way, this poem was a portion of Sacha much more intimate than a night spent in bed. Philippe shuddered to think it. What if he'd gone through life thinking he knew what intimacy was, only to find out that he had never captured it to begin with. No, he hadn't even come close.

Philippe folded up the page and set it back on top of his duffel bag. He'd just remembered that it was currently Saturday night. That meant that tomorrow was Sunday morning. So he pulled out his phone. He needed to find a church to attend. He found one nearby. It was a Lutheran church. But after that, sleep still evaded him and the room still felt strange. So he got up and walked out into the hallway. He wasn't the only one who couldn't sleep. He found Ingrid, standing in the hall looking up at a rope that was hanging from the ceiling.

Are you tall enough to reach that Philippe?" Ingrid stepped back and Philippe reached up relatively easily to grab the rope loop that was hanging from the ceiling. He pulled down to release the folded up stairs to the attic and guided the steps to the floor. He watched Ingrid fiddle with the switch of a flashlight for a moment before finally managing to flip it on. She shined the light up into the dusty darkness. "There's a light up there. But it might have gone out. It's been awhile since we've gone up, Ole and I. But, that's because we're getting old for these stairs. We moved the Christmas decorations into the garage. Will you help me Philippe?"

"Of course I will." He answered and reached out to take her hand. Slowly they made their way, step by creaking step into the darkness. Philippe took the flashlight so that Ingrid could just sit at the top of the steps for a moment. He shined the light around. Piles of dusty boxed were stacked here and there. An old rocking horse was sitting in the corner, covered in cobwebs, the colors of its fur and saddle were faded. Philippe could imagine a tiny version of his mother playing on that, but he quickly moved the light, and finally found a small chain hanging from a light bulb. He reached out and pulled it and a dim yellow light filled the small room.

"Oh it does work. That is nice."

"It is." Agreed Philippe and flipped off the flashlight and looked around.

"Now, I was just looking for pictures. For you, and for Ole and me to look at. And I owe it to Sybil and Tom and Hugo too."

"How come you never told them?" Philippe asked as he reached down to help Ingrid up. She shook her head as she allowed him to help her stand.

"By the time they were old enough to have conversations about such things, everything was already packed up here. I admit, now that you're here, I regret it. Oh. I regret putting them away in the first place. But try to understand, we thought she was..." She didn't finish because of course, she was truly dead now. She steadied herself and walked past the boxes to an old wooden chest with peeling green paint. "I think most of the pictures are in here."

"That's a lovely old chest." Philippe noted. Ingrid sighed a little.

"Yes. It was her… um" She looked like she was searching for the term for a moment. "Hope chest. It was her hope chest." Philippe frowned, saddened by the idea that her hope chest had been repurposed as the burial place for her photographs and memories. Ingrid leaned against the chest and lowered herself down to her knees and undid the latch and slowly opened the lid. "Don't tell Sybil though. I never got her a hope chest. Never got around to it. But I think that the hope chest has somewhat died with my generation. I doubt she would have appreciated it anyway. Head strong as she is." She reached in a pulled out a large photo album and wiped some of the dust from the cover. "Oh, you'll have to help me carry these down later. It's time to bring them back out."

Philippe got down onto his knees and scooted a little closer to her to look. "I'll definitely help you with that." He smiled. "I realized not too long ago that I'm not sure I really knew her. I was too focused on her flaws to notice. So I'm looking forward to seeing the Emilia that you knew."

"Well, I thought I knew her. Every mother thinks they know their child. But she was so young." Her face looked sorrowful but then she perked up her shoulders and opened up the photo album. "Oh!" She chuckled looking down at a photo of a little hairless baby lying stark naked on her belly staring at the camera like she didn't know what hit her. "Oh that's sweet. You'll understand once your own baby is born perhaps."

"Do you think he'll have the same baby butt dimples?" He asked and she turned and laughed at him. Philippe leaned over against the chest and started mulling quietly through its contents. He pulled out a small blanket that was a pale yellow and had satin around the edges. He held it and felt the soft fabric between his fingers and smiled.

"That was the baby blanket we wrapped her in when she was born. You should take it Philippe."

"Alright." He pulled it out and laid it on his lap, still feeling its softness thoughtfully. "Ingrid."

"Mormor." She answered quickly.

"What?"

"Mormor. Call me Mormor if it's alright."

"What is Mormor?"

"Oh! It means Grandmother."

"Mormor." He whispered softly to himself. "Mormor. I never had a grandmother."

"What about your father's mother?" Philippe smiled and shook his head.

"I never knew him."

"Oh I see." She was quiet a moment, adding that piece of information to the story she was beginning to build about what exactly had happened to her daughter. "Then I'm your first Mormor." She said with a smile.

"Yeah. You are." They sat smiling at each other for a long moment.

"You were going to ask me something?"

"Oh yes." Philippe remembered the color of the urn and his mother's lilac dress. "What was my mother's favorite color?" He felt embarrassed to ask her such a basic question. A question with an answer that he had no excuse for not knowing. There were so many questions that he could have asked her that it would have been impossible for him to know beforehand, but as he held onto the little yellow blanket, he couldn't help but ask.

Ingrid stared at him for a moment and her expression felt like it was echoing his thoughts. Why didn't he already know the answer to that question? "Well," She said finally with a slightly furrowed brow. "It changed a few times."

"Oh." Philippe blinked.

"Kids tend to change their minds a lot about such things." She looked thoughtful.

"Well… What was her most recent favorite color? The one she had before she disappeared."

"Hmm. Blue I think. Or at least, everything she wanted seemed to be blue. School clothes and things. Gift ribbons."

"Oh." Philippe smiled. "That's my favorite color. It's always been my favorite color. Baby blue."

"Oh is it. I'll have to keep that in mind. You'll have to give me your address before you leave by the way. So we can mail you gifts and things for the holidays."

"Oh you don't have to do that."

"Nonsense. I'm a Mormor now, and you have a baby on the way. It's my privilege. My right." She smiled and turned the page of her photo album. "Here she is playing on that rocking horse. You know that rocking horse has been through a lot. It didn't come up here to the attic until Hugo grew out of it. Now I suppose I'll have to pull it back out again for your little one to play on when you visit. Oh," She looked up at Philippe as she'd only just met him yesterday. "You will come back to visit us won't you?"

"I'd love to." He leaned in to look at the photo. She was perhaps six or seven. He hardly recognized her. She was sitting on the rocking horse with a bright gleam in her eye and a gleeful grin on her face. She was missing a couple teeth and she was all elbows and knees and her arm was raised up in the air as she played and stared straight at the camera. Behind her was the old wooden desk that Philippe had seen in Thomas's room and on the desk sat a couple of stuffed animals. Perhaps that was her room. But Philippe squinted a little closer and looked at the animals. They were a rabbit and a bear, both with buttons for eyes. They were cute. But the bear, Philippe recognized.

"I know that bear." He said, pointing at the picture.

"Do you?" She looked surprised. "They were a matching set she got from my mother. When we found out she was lost and we were going through her things, that bear was one of the things we couldn't find. She'd taken her backpack, and some of her clothes and she must have grabbed that bear before she left too." Philippe looked up at her.

"She ran away?" Ingrid nodded.

"We'd had an argument. A dumb one. Other parents told us stories about the times when their children had run away, only to come running back home the same night. We prayed she'd come home soon. But she didn't. This is such a small town. We were sure she'd turn up at a neighbor's house, or someone would bring her back to us. Her friends lived just down the street… but no one had seen her. We had already decided to adopt another child, but everything was put on hold for a year while we searched. That was the argument you know. She didn't want another child in the house. I love Tom and Sybil, but had I known…" She looked sadly down at the photo. "Of course, it wasn't Sybil and Tom at the time. It was another child. He never came to live with us. We let that adoption fall through to search for Emilia. Had we known…"

"You couldn't have known." He put his hand on the shoulder of the old woman with tears in her eyes. "You wanted to open your house to an orphan. You couldn't have known. It gladdens me to know that it didn't stop you from adopting again. Sybil and Tom have homes and a family because of your big heart. I wish my mother hadn't run away, but it's not your fault." Ingrid smiled passed her tears and reached up to touch the side of Philippe's cheek.

"She must have been lucky to have you." Philippe looked down. He certainly wished that she had been. "You know," Ingrid continued, "I think that the rabbit is still in here." She reached into the chest and rummaged a little, and pulled out the old rabbit. A little dusty, but still with both its eye buttons. She smiled at it, and handed it to Philippe. He held the little rabbit and ran his thumb over one of the eyes and shuddered a little as he remembered the sensation of popping the buttons off of the rabbit's brother.

"I forgive you." He said quietly.

"What?" Ingrid cocked her head. He looked up at her.

"Oh behalf of my mother. I forgive you for the argument. Thank you for welcoming me into your home." Ingrid choked a little and put her fingers up to her lips. She squinted her eyes shut against the shaking in her chest.

"I didn't know, that I needed to hear that." Her voice quavered and she reached out to Philippe and pulled him into a hug. "Thank you. And thank you for bringing her ashes home. And may this be a home to you too. You're like one of my own. You are one of my own."

Philippe inhaled a wavering breath. He was beginning to understand what power it was that Sam had said was in forgiveness. With a very few words, Philippe had just allowed this woman's soul to find a little more freedom. And though he had never been angry with her, he felt a strange sort of freedom in his own. She pet his hair while she cried, the same way his mother used to do and he felt truly comforted. He wasn't sad that he had never known her. This moment was far too precious.

"Now," She said, leaning back and beaming at him. "Will you help me get these things down those stairs? We'll be able to look at them with everyone tomorrow."

"Of course I will. How often do Tom and Sybil come around?"

"Oh, very often. We have a family dinner on Sundays always, sometimes more often. Sometimes they just drop in for dinner unannounced. It's like they never left. They just don't sleep here much."

"That's sweet."

"It is. I don't mind it. And Hugo gets lonely when they're away, though he'd never admit it." Philippe helped Ingrid get his mother's things down from the attic, though really that mostly meant that he did it himself, and then helped her get down from the attic. And when he finally got back to bed, he slept like a baby just rocked to sleep.

Chapter 56. Neither do I Condemn You

From the pictures he'd looked at on his phone the night before, this church had looked like the perfect picturesque tall white steeple in the middle of the tiny town surrounded by all the little houses. The reality was not disappointing. The church was also surrounded by a small park and trees in a row all around the building. With the snow falling from the sky and crunching underfoot, the whole thing was downright fairytale in its beauty though Philippe imagined that the trees would look amazing once they had blooms cast against the steeples white walls.

"Cute." Said Aimee from beside him.

"It is isn't it?" Said Ingrid from his other side. "Oh I do love when we come. They have a lovely Christmas service." It was just the three of them and Ingrid was dressed in her Sunday best with a little hat that Philippe thought was incredibly cute just perched there on top of her head. She started walking up to the building and Philippe and Aimee followed.

The pews were red with green trim hanging about the place. It looked a little like Christmas all year. But the ceilings were high and ornate and the pipes of an organ could be seen atop the back wall.

There were several people sitting in the pews but still Ingrid leaned up towards his ear and said quietly,

"Though it is much less crowded than on Christmas." Her tone suggested to Philippe that she hadn't fully been aware of that. He had the impression that she was not herself a weekly attender, but had come because his presence there made it a special occasion.

"More room to stretch out." He said quietly to her with a smile.

"That's right." She chuckled and he followed her to a pew about halfway through the room and they sat down.

He of course didn't understand a word of the service, though Ingrid would lean over to whisper a short translation here and there for whatever parts she thought were most important. But the part that was most helpful to him was when she let him know what they were reading, because he then decided to pull out his phone and look it up to read along. They were reading from the book of John chapter eight about a woman who had been caught in adultery. The story goes something like this:

Jesus, a man who Philippe had to admit was someone he knew very little about, went to the temple to teach. The scribes and Pharisees, people who Philippe knew nothing of, brought a woman into his midst, hoping to test him and catch him in some religious mistake. They said, "This woman has been caught committing adultery. The law of Moses," a law that Philippe was oblivious of, "commands us to stone her. What do you say?" For some reason Jesus just sat there doodling in the dust on the floor for a while before he answered and said. "Let him who is without sin among you be the first to throw a stone at her." Then he went back to doodling.

Well everyone just stood around feeling awkward about that and no one threw a stone at her and one by one, they each left the room until only Jesus and the woman were standing together. Finally Jesus asked her, "Woman, where are they? Has no one condemned you?" "No one Lord." She answered. Then Jesus said to her, "Neither do I condemn you; go now, and sin no more."

Philippe looked up at the preacher still talking in Swedish. Ingrid said something in his ear, but he didn't hear it. He was staring at an image that was standing behind the preacher. It was a large picture of a cross with Jesus hanging from it and some women and a man standing beneath him. Now Philippe considered himself to be someone who enjoyed learning, but as much research as he'd ever done about the church, especially in France, he found that he knew next to nothing about Jesus, the major character of their faith. This disturbed him and challenged him.

One thing that the models in New York had never known about him was that he loved to learn things. He was the trivia night master and had spent more time in Wikipedia than anyone ever should. As a student he had discovered that school work was a reprieve from his mother and had sought its escape throughout his school career and had thus been a high mark student. All on his own efforts of course, because the teachers tended not to give him the light of day. The library had been his hideout. But he had also quickly learned that people didn't always care to hear all of the fun random facts about the world so he had been something of a secret researcher.

But now here was something that he knew nothing about. And despite his tiny pool of knowledge, he found he'd been harboring his own judgements on the topic. How could he say that they were wrong when he had studied nothing? How could he say that Sacha was wrong about him unless he learned the perspective from which he was coming? He looked down at the words he'd just read. "Go now, and sin no more." and "Neither do I condemn you."

They almost felt like they were speaking to him personally. He sighed and considered those words and compared the story the poem that Sacha had given him. The two concepts were only vaguely, but Philippe saw a connection. If sex could not lead her nor the poem's recipient to truth, then it made sense to "go and sin no more."

Philippe looked up again at the image of Jesus on the cross. What did he have to offer, that sex couldn't? Philippe couldn't hear anything that anyone was saying for the rest of the service. He devoted himself entirely to research and he spent the entire time glued to his phone. He felt Aimee's hand lower his arm once because he had been holding the phone too close to his face. He found yet another story in the book of John that seemed to have personal relevance. It was John chapter four with the story of the woman at the well.

Jesus sat by a well in Samaria, his disciples had gone into town for food. A woman came by to draw water from the well. He asked her if she would give him a drink. The woman said, "You are a Jew and

I'm a Samaritan, why would you ask me for a drink?" Philippe had to diverge into a little research on this question to find out what the relevance was. As it was, Samaritans were regarded as Jewish half breeds who had married with outsiders. A Jew ordinarily would not have touched her with a ten foot pole. But Jesus was talking to her anyway.

Jesus answered her, "If you knew the gift of God and who it is that asks you for a drink, you would have asked him and he would have given you living water." Philippe felt as oblivious as her about this. Jesus answered, "Everyone who drinks this water will be thirsty again, but whoever drinks the water I give them will never thirst. Indeed, the water I give them will become in them a spring of water welling up to eternal life." The woman said to him, "Sir, give me this water so that I won't get thirsty and have to keep coming here to draw water." Philippe figured he'd probably have a similar response to Jesus's offer. He could tell that he was using an analogy for something, but it didn't seem unreasonable for her to take him literally.

He told her, "Go, call your husband and come back." "I have no husband," she replied. Jesus said to her, "You are right when you say you have no husband. The fact is, you have had five husbands, and the man you now have is not your husband. What you have just said is quite true." At this point Philippe decided to put himself into the place of the Samaritan woman. It was here that he could reasonably start relating the words to Sacha's poem. Sex can't bring someone truth. What can? Jesus's living water.

Jesus went on to tell her "But the hour is coming, and is now here, when the true worshipers will worship the Father in spirit and truth, for the Father is seeking such people to worship him. God is spirit, and those who worship him must worship in spirit and truth." She ran back to her village, leaving her jar by the well, because she was too excited to tell everyone that she had met the Messiah, and what he had said to her. Philippe only had two more questions. What is this living water, and how does it bring truth?

But his thoughts were pushed aside when everyone suddenly stood up and started singing. So he tucked his phone into his pocket and stood up and hummed along. Aimee smiled at him and held his hand and hummed along with him, since neither of them could speak the language.

Chapter 57. Twin-cest

Ole said something to Ingrid in Swedish at the dinner table. Several glances were exchanged. Sybil and Tom, looked at each other and then at their parents. Ingrid looked at Ole and then at Philippe. Philippe looked at Aimee who, also not knowing the language, shrugged. Hugo just kept looking at his food.

"I didn't think of it." Answered Ingrid in English and sort of gestured with her eyes at Philippe and Aimee.

"Oh!" Exclaimed Ole looking apologetic. "Oh I am sorry. Uh… Well, perhaps this isn't actually good table talk."

"Well, you've started it now dad. You can't just back out." Piped in Sybil. "Especially since three fourths of us actually know what you said and I'm sure the other fourth is getting pretty curious." Ole put his hand up.

"Alright. Alright. I concede. Though I do apologize, I shouldn't have brought it up at the dinner table." Philippe shrugged.

"I don't care what's said at the dinner table."

"Well," Ole cocked his head. "You might. But just to get right to the point. We wonder if you would mind if Emilia's ashes were buried."

"Oh." Philippe blinked. He was reconsidering the table talk topic. "Um… I suppose. Why buried?"

"Well, for one thing, we have space in a cemetery. For another thing, it's a more common practice here as well as a legal one. We'd have to gain special permission to spread the ashes without burying them. And for a third thing, she already has a headstone."

"Mmmm!" Exclaimed Sybil with her mouth full of meatball and an expression of disturbed shock on her face. "Oh Mah Gah!"

"She does?" Asked Thomas. "Have we seen it?"

"You have." Nodded Ingrid. "It's over by your grandmother's. But we never specifically pointed it out to you."

"Probably just thought it was some obscure relative." Mumbled Hugo. Philippe could tell that he still thought she was just some obscure relative. Ingrid seemed to miss that though.

"Probably yes." She agreed. "In any case. She has technically already had a funeral. But I still think that, since she is here, and you are here, it would be appropriate." She nodded towards Ole, "As well as legal." Philippe frowned, more to himself than anyone else. It wasn't that he had a problem with it, it just wasn't how he'd envisioned it.

"But…" Aimee spoke up, "It's not like anyone would know if we spread her ashes. Maybe in one of her favorite places to be?" Aimee shrugged. "I know I'm not family or anything so I don't have a say but I did spend quite a bit of time with her. I think that burying her might feel a little caging and she had enough of that in life. Whereas releasing her ashes might be a bit more like setting her free." Ingrid looked suddenly grieved by this concept and Philippe could tell that she'd had no thought at all of cages nor did she know anything about the captivity that her daughter had lived in.

"Then again," Said Philippe reaching over and resting his hand on Aimee's knee, and looking at Ingrid's distressed face. "One of the reasons I brought her to you instead of just releasing the ashes in Sweden was so that she could be reunited with her family. Although, um..." Philippe looked over at the lilac urn. A color he wished he hadn't put her in. "I would request that if we bury her, we turn the urn over and put the ashes themselves into the grave."

"Alright that's it!" Exclaimed Sybil suddenly standing up from the table. "I can't listen to all this burial talk anymore, I'm going for a run." And she made a quick beeline towards her bedroom, which Aimee had been sleeping in during their visit.

There was a sudden general exclamation from Ingrid, Ole and Thomas all at once and Philippe didn't quite hear what anyone said but he was startled by all of the suddenly somewhat terrified faces.

"Sybil!" Ingrid called but Sybil had already turned the corner. She turned back around, "Tom?" But Thomas was already getting up from his chair.

"I got it Mamma." He said and quickly followed Sybil into the other room.

"What just happened?" Blinked Philippe.

"Oh." Said Ingrid shaking her head. "She shouldn't be running."

"She seems very fit." Added Aimee with a raised eyebrow since running was obviously something that Sybil was accustomed to.

"May I be excused?" Interrupted Hugo and looking at his parents.

"Um… yes." Said Ingrid and Hugo got up to take care of his plate. He stopped by Sybil's chair and picked up her plate too. "Thank you dear."

"Sybil has been struggling with a certain kidney disease." Said Ole in answer to Philippe and Aimee's confused faces.

"Yes…" Agreed Ingrid putting her hand on her husband's shoulder. "But she is very tender about the subject."

"What happens if she runs?" asked Philippe.

"Her body has a hard time processing the toxins or something like that. The doctor explained it. But when she exerts herself too much, it does make it worse. She's lost one kidney already. But she was in track all through high school and would even have made it into the Olympics except that when she tried out for it she, well… she collapsed."

"Is there a cure?" Philippe asked.

"Eventually she'll need a transplant. But those are very hard to find… Her best bet would be a blood relative. But she's adopted."

"And the running just causes her to run out of time until that transplant is absolutely necessary." Added Ole.

"What about Thomas?" Asked Aimee.

"Oh they aren't blood related. They were adopted separately."

"But…" Philippe frowned. "She said he was her twin."

"Oh, she likes to say that. They have the same birthday. But they are completely unrelated blood wise. But they grew up together, and they've always been so close. It's almost as if they do have a twin speak sort of bond between them."

"But she doesn't seem to be storming out of the house." Said Ole.

"Tom must have talked her out of it. I wonder what riled her up so much."

Philippe shrugged. "It isn't exactly a heartwarming topic."

"No, but still." Ingrid looked thoughtful. "Philippe, why is it important that your mother's ashes be released rather than kept in the urn when buried?" Her mind was obviously returning to the cage comment.

"Um…" Philippe shifted a little uncomfortably and looked over at the urn sitting in the living room.

"Why don't you go get it?" Suggested Aimee.

"Yeah." Philippe agreed and stood up to go collect the urn.

"There's a bit of history there." Aimee explained to the grandparents while Philippe stepped away. There was a step that went from the linoleum dining room and kitchen area, down into the carpeted living room. Philippe stepped down and started walking over to where the urn had been resting since the night before when they had arrived at the home. He glanced, on his way, at an old grandfather clock that rested against the wall. It looked ancient, but he wondered if the bell inside was broken because he couldn't remember hearing it ring.

It was only a moment, as he walked across the carpet to the coffee table, but it was a moment that he instantly wished hadn't happened. Down that hallway were the bedrooms and the bathroom and the door to Sybil's room was open a tiny crack. But the line of sight through that crack led to a mirror that hung innocently on the wall. But the reflection in that mirror came from the other side of that bedroom where, for a split second, Philippe saw quite clearly, Sybil and Thomas, arms wrapped around each other, kissing passionately. What was worse, was that in that second, he had seen Sybil's eye looking into that same reflection. She had seen him, see them.

Philippe stopped when he reached the coffee table and put his hands over his face. He could hear the chatter at the table. He was pretty sure that they had started talking about the baby but he couldn't quite focus on their words. He was too busy trying, and failing, to wipe his memory of the tiny infectious piece of information that he'd just unwillingly downloaded into his brain. It was like a little virus of the mind and no matter how he tried, he couldn't reset his mental computer to an earlier time before the event.

He put his hands over his mouth and looked down at the urn. He had come to Sweden for his mother. But he was also here for family. And he had just been reminded that families come with their own weird dramas. He reached down and picked up the urn and took a deep breath and turned around to head back to the table.

When he turned he saw Sybil standing in the doorway to her room staring at him with a look of either terror, or murderous rage. Philippe couldn't quite tell which. She put out her hand, and waved for him to come over. Aside from not wanting to, he was rather in the middle of something. So he shook his head just a little and gave her a look that he very dearly hoped said, 'I know what I saw, but I won't tattle.' He lifted the urn to try to make his point. She seemed insistent, but he forced himself to look away from her, and returned to the table.

Chapter 58. Why We Love

Telling Ingrid and Ole what kind of life their daughter had led, was very likely one of the most difficult things that Philippe could ever remember doing. He described the brothel, and there were tears. He described the drugs and there were tears. He told them why he hated the urn that he'd put her in and why he wanted her not to be buried in it. And he tried to explain why he thought she hadn't come home after they had been liberated. That was the most difficult part. She had harbored all that pain in her heart and shared it with no one. For shame she hadn't gone home or told Philippe about his grandparents. Even though that was the thing that would have healed her.

It had been a long night of tears and details. Sybil and Tom had let themselves out without saying goodbye to anyone. But they had exchanged a look with Philippe as they left. Sybil's expression had held a threat, and Thomas's eyes had been filled with only fear and uncertainty. But Philippe said nothing to them, or about them. He had his own business to worry about, and wasn't going to exchange it for petty gossip. That was between them, and he certainly harbored no judgement.

But the next time he saw them was also a bad time for them to bring it up with him. Given the amount of snow that had to be dug through just to reach his mother's predetermined grave site, it was perhaps lucky that they needed only a very shallow grave that would be filled with the dust of her remains.

It was a very small service. Just them and the priest. Any who wanted to were allowed to pour a little of the ashes into the shallow hole as the service progressed. Only Philippe, Aimee, Ingrid and Ole did. It was perhaps fitting, since only the four of them had actually known her. Ole and Ingrid sang a sad lament together. It was in Swedish, so Philippe couldn't understand it, but it was lovely and Philippe was thoroughly moved by it.

It was odd to him to have had a formal service for his mother. He had originally imagined it being just him and maybe Aimee, finding some body of water or a mountain or something. A windy spot to just let her float away, or a stream to let her flow down. But instead it had been a family affair, which seemed appropriate. It would have been selfish of him to have done it alone. But the presence of the priest was especially odd to him. His mother had never been religious, so it seemed strange to give her a religious funeral.

The priest was a woman, wrapped it the vestments of her standing. She had been friendly and gracious. Solemn and sad. And though his mother had not been religious it seemed somehow fitting, that this priest should remind them that from dust they came, and to dust they shall all return. Ashes, to ashes. Dust to dust. His mother's fate was the fate of all of them. It was only how she'd gotten there that was tragic.

And so Philippe stood for a long time in front of the headstone that had marked her death some twenty three years before she had died. The writing on the stone was in Swedish but he had been told that it said "A child, much loved." It was at that headstone that Philippe first contemplated his own mortality. It wasn't so much that he wondered what would happen to him after he died. But it was perhaps the most pessimistic thought he ever had, that he wondered what the point was of living, if we all were to end up dead. But even then, it was more of a philosophical question for him. It was a question that he truly wanted the answer to. And he also found himself believing, that there was very likely, an actual answer to be had.

"Excuse me." He said, turning quietly to the priest who was collecting her things to leave and get out of the cold.

"Yes?" She said with a comforting smile, ready to receive the mournful heart. He glanced at the others who were talking quietly among themselves, also preparing to leave. He had at least a minute.

"What does your religion say about why we live?"

"Why we live?" She looked like she wasn't sure of the exact nature of his question. "Well, we live for God's glory."

"His glory? How would we give him glory?"

"Well," She paused and shifted her weight thoughtfully. "In all truth… we can't. All have sinned and fallen short of the glory of God. We can no more give him glory than we could step from here to the edge of the universe." She tilted her head to the side. "Are you thinking of becoming a follower of Jesus?"

Philippe stared at her. He was baffled. "I don't understand. Why would I?"

"We follow Jesus out of gratitude. Because he loves us, we follow him. He loves you Philippe."

"Why would he love something that doesn't do what he made it to do?" She smiled as if that were the question she'd been waiting for.

"Grace. Grace is forgiveness undeserved and love unwarranted. You see? We love because he first loved us. What else could we do? God is love. If we don't live for love, then what do we live for?"

"I don't know." Philippe was thoughtful. Love had always been Philippe's highest priority. Sacha had suggested that he'd been looking at love all wrong, and now this priest was telling him that God is love. If love was what Philippe lived for, then could he afford not to believe that God is love? If he believed that, then living for love would automatically mean living for God. If he lived for God, that meant that he needed to give God glory, but that was the one thing he couldn't do. We love because he first loved us. Philippe staggered at the paradox. He would only be able to live for God by loving God, and the only reason that he could love God, was because God loved him first. God loved him.

"You seem to be asking yourself some pretty big questions. Why don't you try asking Him instead? You might find some surprising answers." He frowned.

"How would I ask him?"

"Three ways." She held up three fingers. "One is by praying to him." She put down one finger. "One is by reading his word." She put down another finger. "And the last way, is by asking the council of other followers of Jesus. Like me, or perhaps someone else you know. Do you have any Christian friends?" Philippe could only think of Sacha and Sam.

"I suppose I have a couple." He mused about what they had told him about how to love, and how God loves.

"Then talk to them. Or come and talk to me. Or I can even find someone else for you to talk to. Someone that you can bounce your thoughts off of. But also, try praying, and spending some time in the word. And read some biblical commentaries. They aren't perfect but they can sometimes help."

"Alright." He nodded.

She smiled. "I think your family is leaving." He turned to see everyone making their way across the cemetery except Aimee who was looking at him and waiting for him to come along. "God bless you." She added as he turned to walk away.

"Thank you." He said, "You too." and went to join Aimee.

"Do you want to go get some lunch?" He asked as he sidled up beside her and she looped her arm warmly with his.

"I thought maybe your grandparents were planning something."

"Probably, but I just sort of wanted to get away for a little while." She nodded.

"Yeah alright. Sure."

Chapter 59. Epiphany

"You know, you and I have slept around a lot Aimee."

"Yeah." She said calmly, stirring some sugar into her tea. "But now I'm all knocked up."

"Has that stopped you?" Philippe had never been one for keeping close tabs on Aimee's sex life.

"Yeah. I haven't really been looking for anyone to sleep with. I've been too busy focusing on school and work and baby things. It sorta feels irresponsible to try to go get laid right now." She shrugged. "Not that it's stopped women before. I dunno. I just wanna try being a mom for a little while. And I've always been into the wrong guys. I'm not sure I should have guys like that hanging around my kid. I guess I get where my dad was coming from when he was glaring at every boy I ever dated. Guess he didn't want those kinds of guys hanging around his kid either. I gotta start looking for the good kind of guy instead."

"Do you regret it?" She was quiet for a while as she continued to stir her tea and watched the brown liquid flow around and around. Then she slowly nodded.

"I think I do a little. I don't know what I would have done differently, but I guess I kinda do yeah. Why do you ask?"

"I don't think I want to sleep around anymore." She stopped stirring and looked up at her best friend like she couldn't believe her ears. He smiled at her expression. "Just for the sake of argument," He started his philosophical point. "Let's say that Christians are right that people shouldn't sleep around. If we're assuming that's true, then even if it's consensual, do you think that two people could be hurting each other by sleeping together?" Aimee set down her spoon and furrowed her brow and cocked her head to the side.

"What?" She asked simply with a raised eyebrow.

"It's something that someone said to me," He didn't mention Sam's name because he knew how she felt about Sam. "That even if someone chooses to do something, it possible for say, me, to take advantage of their bad decision. If we're believing the Christian idea that it is a bad decision, then me sleeping with someone else, is taking advantage of their bad decision, and they are, in turn, taking advantage of mine. So, inadvertently, we'd be hurting each other." She stared at him blankly, trying to follow his odd logic. He continued.

"And then, being taken advantage of and hurt makes us want to guard our hearts and taking advantage of someone else desensitizes us and makes us callous. I never thought of myself as callous but honestly, I can kinda see it. After looking at my mum. After being molested myself. After looking at Sam and Landers. Even after... You know my friend Liz cheated on her boyfriend with me and I didn't know it but she thought that I did. That didn't matter to her at all but when he cheated on her it was the end of the world." Aimee's expression softened some and she looked thoughtful.

"I'm not sure that your logic really tracks Philippe, but I can kinda see what you're saying. Like sometimes I think I'm trying to feel validated through sex. Looking for certain types of guys and spending energy thinking about guys based on what type you think they are. It's exhausting. It's sort of odd to think of it like people are taking advantage of each other though. But I kind of get the soul sucking aspect of it, even if I love doing it." She shrugged. "I dunno Philippe. I figured that was just part of the human dilemma. You think Christians have a way out of the cycle?"

"Maybe. I dunno." He looked down at his half eaten sweet roll and considered the ways in which baking was different than cooking. Yeast was an odd factor. "I'm thinking of taking the chastity idea for a test drive though."

"Well, maybe you should get yourself baptized and find out. Let me know how it goes." She smirked and pulled her phone out of her pocket and set it onto the table next to her tea, which she sipped. Philippe was thoughtful about this. He didn't believe he could reasonably get baptized unless he fully understood the Jesus factor. Just like he couldn't improvise baking unless he understood the yeast factor. But then again, there were recipe books, and there were science books that could tell him how yeast worked and how much to put into something that he was baking. And there was the Bible and theology books of course, to tell him about Jesus. And Wikipedia for both.

But until then, he could still experiment with some of the principals. He didn't need to sleep around anymore. Strangely enough, for the most part, he didn't even want to. He considered what had happened in Sacha's apartment. Philippe's intention there had been to seduce him. It wasn't as if it were the only time he'd been turned down, that wasn't it. Sacha had not turned him down out of disgust, disorientation or even disinterest. He had turned him down because that sort of relationship was not something he wanted or needed, in order to understand someone. It had been obvious that he thought the relationship could be worth something without it.

But what other kind of relationship was there? In all truth, his mother had been the only person that he'd been at all close to without sex. And he had even on occasion wondered if they would have been closer if sex had been a social option for them. Yet Sacha's poem and thoughts demanded that true intimacy was indeed possible without it. What would that look like?

He acknowledged the growing relationship between him and Sam. But that example was somewhat skewed by Sam's history. There was the incredibly intimate moment that he'd had with Ingrid in the attic with the photo album. But while that could be something worth noting, it was a little too early to tell. He supposed he would just have to try it out with people and wait and see. And probably be extremely awkward while he tried to maneuver through social cues that he wasn't quite as knowledgeable about. He had no examples to work off of in his own life. Only the examples as seen by other people's lives. No, the only relationship that he'd had any intimacy and depth in prior to sex making it that way, was with Aimee. They had been best friends for years before sleeping together.

An epiphany suddenly struck Philippe's mind and he couldn't quite stop his mind from thinking it. He looked up to see his best friend in a whole new light. She was sitting with her head bent over her phone, scrolling through whatever article, news, or Facebook that she was reading. Her nose was peppered with freckles as it had always been. A strand of her auburn hair had fallen into her face but she seemed not to notice. He knew that she would eventually, without noticing it, tuck it back behind her ear to stop it from partially obscuring her vision. He simply knew this about her.

She was not suddenly more beautiful than she used to be. He was not looking at her as if he had never seen her beauty before. Not one thing about her had changed. She was still the average girl he'd always known. And perhaps that was it. She was still his best friend. His most intimate companion.

It wasn't a soul mate thing. If Philippe could be said to have ever had a soul mate, if soul mates even existed, then he knew that he had already met her, and she was already gone. Veronica had been the most beautiful woman that Philippe had ever known and no woman could ever be expected to rival that. So he wondered if this unstoppable contemplation was that of settling with second best. In lieu of Veronica's love, there was Aimee. But Aimee was not second best because Philippe didn't consider her to be of any less worth or value than the beautiful Veronica.

Veronica was the only thing that had parted them. Aimee had been there first. But it seemed more as if there had been two states to the universe. There was the universe in which Veronica was alive, and the one in which she was dead. When Veronica had been alive, Philippe had followed her across the world and would have followed her even farther. He would have married her and the world would have been much different. But she had died, and he was now in this world where he found himself sitting in a pub in a tiny town in Sweden.

He looked at Aimee and wondered, if he would not have eventually found himself here anyway. If Veronica had never entered his life, would he have eventually found himself having these contemplations? He felt that he would have. Eventually he would have developed, and grown, and changed enough as a man to think about this. If he was to consider changing the way he related to people, the only person that he did not want to change his relationship to, was Aimee, and that put him in an awkward position.

Aimee was his best friend. That friendship had first included benefits when they were younger and everyone around them seemed to have lost their virginity in some way or another. Aimee had had boyfriends but the person who she'd given her virginity to, was Philippe. Becoming not a virgin was something that she'd felt the pressure to do, but she'd chosen to do it with the one she trusted most. The one who hadn't pressured her at all. Which was not the boyfriends who wanted it. Philippe would have gladly given his virginity to her in return if he'd had the choice.

Right on cue, Aimee tucked her hair absentmindedly behind her ear and Philippe smiled at that. She had trusted him with her most intimate moments, and he had trusted her with his. No one else had been right next to him through the journey of growing up with his mother. Perhaps he could build another intimacy so strong with another, but why?

Only Veronica had separated that intimacy for a time when Philippe had flown away to New York. Thus far, he and Aimee had seemed to agree that their current little life partnership should only continue unless some similar event should occur. She could reasonably assume that it eventually would. But they were about to embark on a very great partnership with the baby coming and perhaps a stronger solidarity was called for. Perhaps rather than distancing his sexual intimacy with Aimee for the sake of chastity the way he intended to do with everyone else, he should instead seek even more intimacy with her to the exclusion of all others.

Aimee had never asked him to commit to her any more than he was willing. His support of her and her coming child was mutually understood to be inevitably temporary. Veronica would eventually come again, in one form or another.

But what if that didn't happen? What if he could choose that it wouldn't? What if, instead of being swept off his feet by some beauty, he instead gave everything he had to Aimee? What if he took the coming partnership much more seriously, and actually raised that child as if it were his own? What if, when he said that it was his son, he meant it?

If it were his own child, then he would need solidarity between him and his partner. There would need to be a greater measure of trust between him and his best friend. What if he could promise that to her? What if he could make a vow, that Veronica would never be able to call him away again? What if he could make an oath, a covenant, that his commitment to her and her child would be permanent?

Their partnership would never be broken, their friendship could never falter. Aimee could always know that she was giving her love to the one she trusted most, and no social pressures would force her to give it to anyone else. She would never have to feel the need to look for anyone to be validated by. She could be secure in knowing that he would always be there, that he would never leave, no matter how many moments of invalidity she felt. And then, he would always have his best friend, with whom he could always share his own lowest moments.

He looked at the bulge in her belly and felt that the epiphany had finally concluded itself. His heart was now forever altered towards her and he felt as if it was shaking in his chest. He would now have to face the consequences of that fact, whichever way things went.

"Aimee." He said with a feeling of calm that was unexpected. She glanced up at him with a smile to let him know that she was still listening. Her eyes nearly made it back to her screen before she did a double take. He had never looked at her the way he was looking at her now. In all the years that she had known his every minor twitch, this was not an expression that she had ever seen the muscles on his face express.

"Whoa." She said, jumping to her feet as if she had just touched something hot. "Why are you looking at me like that?"

"Well…" Philippe began but was instantly interrupted.

"No." She put one finger up in front of her. "Whatever it is you're about to say, just hold it in."

Philippe chuckled a little. "Why?"

"Because you're about to say something that's going to change the nature of our entire relationship when you say it, no matter how I respond to it." Philippe closed his mouth and just watched her and waited for her to process whatever it was that she was needing to process. She ran her fingers through her hair and scratched the back of her head as she stood there making eye contact with her friend and his expression of fate changing consequence. "Tomorrow, okay? Whatever it is, just sleep on it, and let it sit 'til tomorrow. If you still feel like you need to say it, you can say it then."

Philippe smiled and nodded and took a deep breath. "Okay," he said, "deal." She nodded back at him.

"Thanks." But something had already changed, and they both knew it.

Chapter 60. Forgiveness

Forgiveness,

Bear witness,

Some people never change.

Forgiveness,

Can't win this,

Try and may your brain be deranged.

That time when they left you flat on the floor,

They did it again, just like before,

Forgiveness,

Repeat this,

Just give it away to the Lord.

Forgiveness,

Unclenched fists,

You're a doormat flat on the floor.

Forgiveness,

Your fight's lit,

With red eyes and teeth like a boar.

Do or don't, do or die,

Either way a black eye,

Forgiveness,

Why do this?

Just give it away to the Lord.

Forgiveness,

Now hear this,

It's never okay, what they've done.

Forgiveness,

It's no wish,

That's spoken in vain just for fun.

You can't just say "it alright man, no problem.

It might happen again but it's already forgotten."

Forgiveness,

It's not this,

It's giving it up to the Lord.

Forgiveness,

What point is?

There in speaking this one simple word?

Forgiveness,

My life is

Not changed by the utterance I've heard.

May it free up your heart when you speak it in prayer,

To the killers who hear it may they hear God's voice there,

Forgiveness,

Not judgments,

Just give it up to the Lord.

He sat on a park bench in the chill cold overlooking the lake and read the poem over again. Sacha had sent him a text, the contents of which were only the poem. He thought about his question on the subject which Sacha had endeavored to answer. It had taken him a month to come up with the poem. Philippe realized that the question of forgiveness wasn't a simple one if it had taken that long to try to explain. That said, Sacha's poem seemed to require some contemplation and wasn't really a straight answer.

He looked out over the lake and thought about so many things. He was glad that he'd taken this time to go for a walk. He wasn't quite ready to go back to the house where the family was mourning for a daughter that they had lost more than two decades ago. He wished that Aimee had walked with him, but she had gone back to the house to rest. She had probably left because she needed some time to consider the silent change that had transpired between them. Whatever is was.

Philippe knew what it was. But he felt just as shaken as she. Even more so because it was borne out of his own change of heart. A change that he had never considered before. But Aimee was changing too. He could tell. That baby was altering more than just her body. She hadn't said anything about it. But that was because she was a pragmatist and didn't often discuss things unless she deemed those things relevant. But Philippe was her best friend, because he could see it without her needing to say anything. He could tell that the only reason she hadn't talked about it was because she, like him, hadn't fully wrapped her head around it yet.

He assumed that her changes were far different from his own though. Philippe was noticing a strange and subtle transition in his own heart. Some of it was in ways that he couldn't quite put his finger on. He tried to track back to the moment when it had first begun. He supposed, though he supposed incorrectly, that the change had started with Sacha, when he had gone on that little scavenger hunt. In truth, it had started long before that, but he had no way of knowing it.

But what had changed? Why stop modeling? Because it had felt shallow and strangely he had started feeling like an outsider to those people. He'd left Marcello because his personal freedom had become something that was worth more to him than what Marcello had to offer. Interesting, since it was the first time that he'd noticed that personal freedom was something he'd been lacking.

Why stop sleeping around? Disinterest. At first he'd been worried that something was wrong with him and that he was inexplicably losing his libido. But truth be told, his libido felt strong as ever, he just didn't feel the need to spend it. What he thought he had for those people turned out to be nothing and his libido was a bag full of energy better spent elsewhere.

Like cooking. In the place of the things he'd lost he could see the existence of other things that hadn't been there before. He wanted to cook, sing, play an instrument and raise a baby. He contemplated the idea of starting a video cooking blog when they got back home. That sounded fun. Maybe he really would get himself a saxophone and get

Jean to teach him, in a completely platonic sort of way. He didn't really have any platonic relationships. He sort of wanted one. Just to see what all the fuss was about. Maybe Jean wasn't the best option for that but Philippe's mind was just blowing steam.

But the real question was what had caused all these things to change? What was creating that subtle transition in his heart? Looking back over the events of the last eight months since Veronica's death, he had no idea. Sure lots had happened, sure things had changed, but that explanation just didn't seem good enough.

"'Sup li'l nephew." Philippe jumped out of his thoughts when Sybil plopped onto the bench next to him, crossed her arms over her chest and leaned back like that bench belonged to her. Philippe noticed that she wasn't nearly as bundled as he was, and wondered if her temperature tended to run warmer, or if she was just more used to the Swedish climate. Irrelevant things to ponder at that moment. "Enjoying the view?" Sybil asked, not turning to look at him but just staring resolutely out over the icy water.

"Look," Philippe put his gloved hands out in front of him as if to show her that he wasn't holding any weapons. "Whatever is between you and your brother is none of my business. I didn't mean to see you, and I have no intention of saying anything about things that aren't my business to anyone." She turned to look at him with an eyebrow raised.

"Damn straight." She leaned back against the bench and looked thoughtful a moment. Then nodded her head to the snow. "Cool." She said plainly as if that just about wrapped up everything she wanted to go over. She looked like she was about to stand up and leave, now that they had that covered, but looked at her nephew and seemed to relax a little bit, and leaned again into the bench. "You know we're not real twins right?"

"Yeah." Philippe nodded. "I know that. I'm really really not here to judge anybody." Sybil nodded at him. "You know," Philippe continued, "I do really like Ingrid and Ole."

"Yeah." Sybil smiled. "My parents are awesome. Better than any others I've met." That last sentence had a small tone of animosity that Philippe could tell was not for him.

"Are you and Tom going to come out to them?" Sybil was quiet for a moment and she stared hard with a furrowed brow at the place where her arms crossed each other.

"I want to." She said at length, "Tom's skeptical. You know that was the first time that Tom and I have kissed in ten years or something. It only happened one other time. We've kept that a secret for so long, it'll be hard to unleash it." She clicked her tongue and made a flipping motion with her thumb like unleashing a dog.

"Do you think they'll accept that?" She shook her head slowly.

"No. I think they'll freak. But life's too short." She scuffed her shoe against the snow and ice at her feet. "And if I can't spend the rest of it running, I can at least spend the rest of it with my soul mate, not hiding." She shrugged. "He's a worry wart. But I think it's better to do it than not. I think that, if we do it now, then maybe our parents'll forgive us before I..." She trailed off and stared out over the water.

"You don't… really look like you're dying to me." Philippe said cautiously. She shrugged.

"Without a transplant I will, sooner or later. It's just a matter of time. Can you even imagine how much that blows?"

"I can't." Philippe said honestly. "It sounds hard to walk around knowing that your life has been shortened."

"That," Agreed Sybil, "And the fact that I have to live carefully, drawing it out as long as possible, on the slim hope that I'll survive long enough for a miracle donor to make it all better. In the meantime, life sucks. At least if I had no hope at all, I'd be able to just go out with a bang. Do all my favorite things until it kills me and die happy."

"What would it take to get you a transplant?" She looked down and scuffed her foot against the ice and snow some more.

"There's one guy. My biological father, who could have the right set up to make it work. Andrew D'Jean. But he's made it really clear that he never signed up for that." She snorted.

"I'm sorry to hear that." He hadn't expected this conversation to happen. But it was nice to be talking to another member of the family. She shrugged.

"It sucks balls. But everybody's got something. I'm sorry about your mom. It mighta been nice to have a sister."

"Yeah well. I probably wouldn't exist if things had gone better for her. I'm just sorry that she never recovered. And I'm sorry that I held a grudge for so long. I wish I could tell her that I forgive her."

"You're religious aren't you? I thought you went to church with Mamma the other day." He looked over at her and found himself having a lot of trouble figuring out where she was reading the connection between those concepts. She read his confusion. "I mean, can't you just pray and tell God that you forgive her? Maybe he'll give her the memo." Philippe blinked. It was like she'd read everything. His questions, his pain, the poem, the convolutedness of the concept. She had just summed it all up and handed him a solution in one nice neat little sentence like it was the most obvious thing in the world.

"I… I never tried." He answered, having been struck a little dumb.

"Alright well, while you're at it maybe you'll pray for me too. I haven't been to a church in forever. Maybe God'll check in with me."

"O...kay." Said Philippe, not quite knowing what to think of this girl. She looked at him and smiled as if his agreement to do this for her meant a lot to her and caused her to like him just a bit more.

"You're alright li'l nephew." She reached out and unexpectedly tousled his hair, pushing his hat off of his head. He smiled and leaned down to pick it up. "Burr. It's really fucking cold out here. I'll see you at home li'l nephew." She smiled and stood up and walked away as suddenly as she had sat down. Philippe wasn't sure how he felt about the pet name, but he supposed she'd likely call him whatever she wanted to call him.

It really was cold out though, so after just a few minutes of thinking about what he had just managed to agree to, he decided to get up and go back to the house also. He couldn't very well tell someone that he'd pray for them and then not do it… but he did wonder how he would do it. He spent the rest of his walk back considering this.

Chapter 61. Prayer

He walked slowly into Thomas's room that evening. While Sybil had been the direct sort and had decided to just come hash it out with Philippe, Tom had spent the evening more or less utterly avoiding eye contact with him. Philippe wished that this silly family drama would do him a favor and not get in the way of them enjoying each other. He'd just met Thomas and Thomas was already trying not to talk to him. Philippe knew that he didn't mean anything personal by it though. It was just that looking Philippe in the eye reminded him that his age old secret wasn't so secret anymore. Given that it wasn't Philippe's business, he wished that Tom and Sybil would forget that he knew it. But he supposed that family drama was all part of the package, so in that way, he somewhat enjoyed it. It meant that they were family. He looked at a toy car sitting next to an outdated globe on the book shelf and considered how much history the family had that he had not been a part of.

He turned towards the bed that he would sleep in that night and wondered if kneeling was really a prayerful requirement. He had no reason to think that it was and every reason to think that one could pray in any position that they felt most comfortable. But Philippe got down on his knees and rested his elbows atop the bed and folded his hands and bit down on the edge of his fingers. He looked sideways at the door he'd closed behind him. Some stickers were pasted on the back of it that had probably been there since Thomas was seven or eight.

He knew that he didn't have to kneel, but for his first prayer with intention, he wanted to be better safe than sorry. Besides, it seemed a little more revering. Or rather, he had to admit that part of him thought that God might not listen to him otherwise. But it really didn't matter how he decided to be there, the important part, was that he had come.

"Dear God," He whispered and his lips moved quietly against his fingers but his eyes stayed fixed on the little stickers, shaped like dogs, stuck forever onto the back of that door. "Dear God," He said again, not really knowing where to go from there. "I don't know how to pray." He admitted in a whisper. "But I promised I would. I don't like breaking promises. I don't really like making promises either." He squeezed his eyes shut and pressed his sockets against his knuckles.

"If you're listening, I promised to pray for Sybil. I don't know what for exactly. I guess, because she's unwell, that I should pray that you would make her well." He paused. He thought that this prayer just didn't quite feel right. He pressed his forehead against the covers of the bed and smothered his face into the mattress. "I don't know her very well." He continued, and if anyone had been listening, they would have heard only muffled mumbling. "I'd like to get to know her better. And Thomas. I'd like to get to know him better too. I don't want Sybil to die and I don't want Thomas to feel awkward around me." He scoffed a snort at himself and turned his face to the side so that his cheek was against the blanket.

"Those two things aren't at all on the same scale of importance." He said, "Heal Sybil, it doesn't matter if Thomas feels awkward around me." He took a deep breath. His knees were starting to get uncomfortable and he wondered how anyone could be able to kneel that way for long hours. At least his knees were resting on carpet. He realized that he was staring at the stickers again and he clamped his eyes shut and put his face back into the bed.

"Why is this so hard?" He asked quietly. He wasn't sure if he was asking himself or God. He would have been okay if either offered an answer. "My mum." He took a deep breath. "If… if she's somehow up there, would you please tell her… tell her that I forgive her. And tell her that I'm sorry for holding a grudge for so long." He wiped his eye with his sleeve. "I never thought I was holding a grudge you know. I thought that, I don't hold grudges. I thought I never held grudges but I did. I do. I have." He felt his chest gently shaking against the bed. "I don't want to hold grudges. That's the worst thing." Then a strange feeling came over him. He cried, but he felt like he wasn't crying alone. It felt a little like someone had their arm around his shoulder and was crying, right along with him. He felt, even though he was all alone, that he wasn't at all lonely. Instead he was warm, and comforted, and free to cry his tears.

He crawled up onto the bed as he wept and curled up on top of the covers and heled onto the pillow. He would later find it odd but at the time he barely noticed that he had strangely put his thumb part way into his mouth and was not so much sucking it as just finding it a little comforting to have it there. "Please forgive me for holding grudges." His words were only half formed due to the obstruction of his thumb, but that didn't matter. "Please take away my grudges."

Comforted he cried until he cried himself to sleep. But he found himself awake again and wasn't sure how long it had been. It was dark still, and as quiet as could be. He couldn't remember dreaming but he felt as if he had. He rolled over onto his back and took his pants off to be more comfortable and curled sleepily under the covers he'd been laying on. He sighed as he felt sleep trying to return but he felt he had just a little more to say. He closed his eyes. He wasn't sure if he'd ever stopped praying, but if so, he prayed again.

"Dear God." He took a deep sleepy breath. "Help Sybil. Bring her biological father to his senses to help her. He wouldn't want to be the cause of her death. Help Sybil and Tom. I don't know what they should do, but they say you know everything. Help Ingrid and Ole and Hugo when they find out. Help them to have mercy, and understanding and grace." He yawned a big open mouthed yawn and before slipping off into a deeper sleep, he said, "Amen."

Chapter 62. Birth

"Philippe." He was jarred out of his sleep by the rough shaking of his shoulder. He blinked sleepily up at Aimee.

"What? It's not time to go yet." He said sleepily and squirmed to feel the warmth of his covers. As one's mind when half asleep, comes to woefully wrong conclusions, he had somehow thought that she would be waking up him because it was time to go back to Paris. But had he been more awake, he would have remembered their agreement to stay for breakfast first.

But then something smelled strange and he heard and odd dribbling noise and felt a shudder from Aimee's squeezing hand as she scrunched her eyes closed to shake back the tears. He opened his eyes suddenly to see her face scrunched up in distress and her other hand holding on to her belly. Something wasn't right.

She stood half doubled over him in a t-shirt and her underwear and he looked down to see that the dribbling noise was coming from some fluid dripping down from between her legs and soaking into the carpet. He sat bolt upright and turned towards her and held her arms.

"Aimee you're…"

"No!" She protested through tears. "It's too early Philippe, it's too early."

"Calm down. Let's think about this."

"No Philippe. I don't have anything. The blankets, the onesies, the diapers, the freaking car seat. They're all at home. I'm not supposed to be having it here."

"It's okay Aimee." He put his hand against her cheek. "We'll make it work."

"You don't understand!" She stamped her foot. Something that he hadn't seen her do since the second grade. "It's a month too early Philippe! What if it dies!?" She yelled. Tears ran down her face and drool dripped from her mouth. He could tell that she was in complete hysterics and was not likely to be calming down anytime soon. But also, she was right. The baby was coming too early. The place that they needed to go to, was the hospital.

"Okay, okay okay." He said and kissed her forehead. She half fell into his chest and stood in a very awkward position to hug him and sob. He could tell that she was extremely uncomfortable and she was holding herself stiff against the drippings from her womb. He kissed her again on her cheek and his lips came away wet with tears. "You gotta let me up though okay." She nodded against his neck and moved over and leaned with her hands against the side of the bed. She was bent forward and she rocked herself from side to side.

This feral animalistic view of his friend was strange to him. She had always been the one with the collected thoughts and logical worldview but now her body had taken over her mind and she was a beast, groaning in the night. He got up and walked out of the room and walked quietly but quickly down the hallway. Who knew why he thought he needed to be quiet considering his intention to wake someone up.

He came up to his grandparent's door and knocked lightly. As if that would wake anyone. So rather than knocking harder, he opened the door a crack and peeked in. It was dark and he could see the forms of Ole and Ingrid as silhouetted snoring lumps against the dim light of the window.

"Mormor." He whispered and tiptoed into the room and gently rested his hand on Ingrid's shoulder. "Mormor."

"Huh!" She jumped slightly and looked at him like she didn't quite know what she was looking at for a moment.

"Mormor. Aimee's in labor." She stared at him for a long moment, and then sat up and turned on her bedside lamp and nodded as she rubbed her eyes and processed what it was that he had just said to her. "Mormor, she's a month early. And she's..." He gestured towards the floor between his own legs. "Uh... She's dripping. I think her water broke." Her head continued nodding.

"Yup." She finally said and swung her legs out of bed. "Her water broke."

"She should go to the hospital." Philippe said, thinking perhaps she wasn't quite with him yet.

"Let me get dressed and then we'll drive her. She'll be fine for the moment. Labor is a long ordeal."

"Get dressed." Philippe nodded. "Okay." And he left the room thinking it would be good for him to do similar since he was only in boxers and a shirt. And perhaps it would be good to get Aimee in at least a little something more.

"What's going on?" Asked Hugo who was standing in the hallway looking towards the door to the room in which he could hear Aimee's agonizing voice.

"The baby's coming." Said Philippe passing him by quickly and without a glance to how he was doing. But he heard Hugo's voice make a mildly disgusted or confused sound and then heard the click of his door shutting tight. Philippe went into his room and flipped on the bedroom light.

"Turn that thing off!" Aimee exclaimed, and Philippe instantly obeyed. But he stood there for a moment wondering how he was to go about finding a clean pair of pants in the dark. Any pants would have been fine, of course, but his mental processes needed forgiving in the midst of it all. So he went to his duffle bag and pulled out the first piece of fabric that seemed to be pant shaped. They turned out to be a pair of sweats. Fine. Good enough.

Then he turned to Aimee, still moaning and rocking against the bed. She had moved down on her knees and had her head buried against her hands on the covers in the same position that he had knelt in earlier that night. He didn't like the idea of trying to put a pair of pants on her over the wet stickiness of her legs and feet. He wrinkled his nose at the thought and went back out into the hall to go to her own bag to see what he could find.

"Oh!" He said when he saw Ingrid coming down the hall. "Do you have um… a bathrobe or something that she could wear?"

"Yes. One moment." She said and turned back around. Philippe went into Aimee's room and grabbed her shoes and a pair of socks. He then went back into his own room with Aimee. He put on his own shoes and coat.

"Why is this happening?" Asked Aimee tearfully. "It wasn't supposed to happen like this."

"Come on," He said quietly to her. "Let's get your socks and shoes on."

"I was hoping that it was just gas that was hurting."

"Well," He knelt down next to her and started putting a sock on one of her feet. "It looks like it's not." He wrinkled his nose a little and had to shake himself into determination to get himself to ignore the wetness that he felt on his own fingers as he helped her with her socks. He wasn't sure he had the time to go into the bathroom and wash his hands… but he also didn't want to go wiping the stuff on his pants. There was nothing sanitary about this night.

"We're going to get you to the hospital, so I'm going to need you to stand up."

"What about health insurance? I don't know how the health system works here. What about the paternity affidavit? What about the birth certificate? What about national citizenship?" He finished getting her shoes onto her feet and reached up and put his hand into her hair. He put his cheek onto the bed so that his face was facing hers.

"We'll figure it out as we go." She stared at him, her face full of fear and concern, but finally taking some small comfort in his reassurance. He leaned in and kissed her forehead. "Now it's time to stand up okay?" She nodded.

"Okay." She put her arm over his shoulder and let him help her to her feet. Philippe saw that Ingrid was standing at the door holding a long soft bathrobe with a sweet expression on her face, as she had just been standing there watching this little exchange. He smiled and took the robe from her and wrapped it around his shaky friend. A few days later, Aimee would tell him that she would never forgive him for letting her leave the house with no pants on, but it was all taken in good humor.

"We'll take my car." Said Ingrid as they headed out the door. "I know the way all too well."

At the last minute, Philippe had remembered to run back to their bags and grab their passports. The hospital was a flurry of unknown communication and language barriers and it all moved too fast and was far too full of confusion for Philippe to really understand all that happened to put Aimee in the birthing room. But she did end up in the birthing room, without her robe or her shirt wearing nothing but a hospital apron and a pair of socks designed to keep her from slipping on the tile.

They had her sign a document or two that she didn't have the wherewithal to read, not to mention not knowing the language. Ingrid tried to explain the documents but strangely enough Aimee seemed to lose all her capacity for speaking anything other than French. This made Philippe into a translator, albeit not the best one, but passable enough.

But eventually Philippe found himself just sitting in a chair next to Aimee who was lying on her side on a hospital bed clinging to his hand. With every contraction he lost just a little more of the sensation from his fingertips. But at least she had finally managed to accept the fact that this room was the room she was going to give birth in, so now all they needed to do, was wait.

She opened her eyes after a contraction and looked at Philippe who was sitting next to her, staring at her and madly biting the nails of his free hand. He hated seeing her like this. There was supposed to be something regal and powerful in the experience of birthing another human being into this world, but all that Philippe could seem to see was agony. It was all his nerves could do to keep from having a meltdown each time she cried out in pain. He was here to support her, not the other way around.

"Philippe."

"Yeah." He answered, taking is finger tips out of his mouth and leaning towards her to hear what she would say.

"The sun's up." He looked over his shoulder at the window behind him. Ingrid was sitting in a chair by the window having fallen fast asleep, despite her best efforts. She was holding the soft yellow blanket on her lap. Philippe could remember her leaving the hospital to run back home to get it. Aimee was indeed right. The sun was gently lighting up the beige curtains behind Ingrid. They had been here all night.

"Yep." He said simply, turning back to his laboring friend who was clenching her face in another contraction, squeezing another ounce of life out of Philippe's hand.

"I said," She groaned as the contraction started to lift, "That you would have to wait till today."

"For what?" Philippe raised his eyebrow. "I certainly don't think that we're going to be going home today darling."

"No." She smiled at him. "You were going to ask me something yesterday. But I said you needed to wait till today. Well, it's today."

"Oh." Philippe blinked. "Oh it can wait." Philippe leaned closer and looked into her freckled eye. She didn't have her contacts in and he knew that she could see him better if he got closer.

"Just ask." She smiled weakly. "I'm ready for whatever you got." Philippe doubted that very much. He hesitated and put his other hand on her cheek and held her gaze as she went through another contraction. "What is it?" She said as her jaw unclenched and their eyes were locked.

"You don't have to answer me." He said in almost a whisper. "Not yet. Not now. Besides." He smiled, "I wouldn't mind it if you let me have a chance to sweeten the deal before you answered anyway." Her brow furrowed slightly.

"You're looking at me like that again." In response he leaned into her next contraction and kissed her chapped lips. He'd kissed her plenty of times but this time was a little different. She was in labor and something about it entered him just a little into her experience. But more than that, his intentions were different. It wasn't a sweet kiss of friendship or a passionate kiss to open a night of eroticism. Because in that kiss he was deciding that if given the chance, he would never kiss other lips. That kiss belonged to her only and forever, and that made it different. That made it pass all invisible barriers.

The contraction subsided and their lips parted and her eyes told him that she knew that that kiss had been different than all the ones before it. He would have held his breath for longer but she had asked him, and he was looking at her like that again. So he decided to breathe the words in the birthing room, which would change their relationship in one way or another, no matter her answer.

"Will you marry me?" He whispered and the number of expressions that played through her eyes were uncountable. She had somehow known that he would ask this, but given their history, the occurrence of this question was impossible. So she had doubted her hidden knowledge. And here it was. The impossible question asked, and old emotions uncovered. Her eyes wetted with moisture not born of pain, but then her eyes squeezed shut and she let go of Philippe's fingers and rolled onto her hands and knees.

"Hot!" She exclaimed. "Oh Ow!" She yelled. Philippe stood up, not knowing what to do with himself, and there was a sudden rush of people. Someone with gloved hands appeared behind Aimee and reached into her and then said something that Philippe couldn't understand. Aimee suddenly bore down and leaned back towards her feet with gritted teeth and a high pitched sort of growl in her voice.

Philippe put his hand on her back and couldn't help but lean over to look at what was going on. Nothing visible yet. A nurse came up towards Aimee's head and put her hands on her shoulders and pushed her gently like she was trying to guide her into laying down and rolling over onto her side. Philippe was surprised to see that with sudden ferocity, Aimee lashed out with her arm at the poor nurse and yelled and then began again to bare down.

Philippe put his hand over his mouth when he saw the tiny dark matted hairs of a small scalp becoming visible. He left his viewing point and got as close to being in front of Aimee as he could. He reached out and put both of his hands against her forearms and she reached her hands around his elbows and held them tight, shoving her forehead hard into his shoulder as she cried out and bore down again, using him as an anchor.

Part of him was curious to see as the baby broke through into this world. But he didn't look or remove himself from where he was because most of him was still here in this room, much more for Aimee's sake than for the sake of her offspring. But that perspective changed in an instant. Philippe's heart got caught in his throat when they pulled that tiny baby from Aimee's body, still attached to her by the cord. Philippe couldn't help but to look up to see the doctor was holding his tiny form in her arm, clearing away mucous from his little mouth. He saw Ingrid suddenly next to the doctor's elbow holding the little yellow blanket, ready to wrap him up in it.

"Why isn't he crying?" Said Aimee, not wanting to see. Her face still buried into his neck and her nails digging into his arms. Philippe lifted himself up just a little and held his breath. He watched as all the sound seemed to leave the room. The doctor put some sort of tube onto the baby's face for a moment and then took it off again. It was quiet, but like a clear little bell, the sound of his tinkling little cry, broke through the silence and Aimee suddenly turned around to look and broke into fearfully relieved tears.

The baby, tinier than he would have been if he'd stayed 'til term, was settled gently against her chest with the doctors glowing smile. Ingrid settled the soft yellow blanket over the top of him. Aimee leaned back against Philippe who was still at the head of the bed, and he got a clear view his little face.

He had little tufts of dark hair plastered against his flaky skin. His color seemed a little wrong. His skin was mottled and he was covered in a light gooey film. His crying was quiet. Too quiet for a baby but he was at least crying, and that was good. He was miniature in his proportions and his face was wrinkled and scrunched up against the world. Philippe was mesmerized by this strange creature, and could not look away.

Aimee looked up at him and smiled, every care of those hours of agony washed from her face and replaced with unaccountable bliss.

"He's okay." She said to Philippe. But she seemed to be informing herself of this fact as much as him. He smiled and tore his eyes away from the little thing and looked at Aimee.

"Yeah he is." He said reassuringly. "He's perfect."

"They're saying that they want him to stay for a few nights for observation because of his delay in breathing." Ingrid said to Philippe. She hadn't been able to communicate anything with Aimee in hours and wasn't sure if that time had passed.

"Alright." Philippe nodded. Aimee kissed her baby's sticky head and then wrapped him loosely in the yellow blanket and looked at Philippe and turned a little, obviously meaning to pass the little creature to him. He felt unsure about this. Philippe had about the gentlest hands in the world, but still the he felt sure that the baby was too small and delicate for him to hold. But he ended up in his arms nonetheless.

He held that bundle. He had stopped crying and was wide awake and squinting against the light of the blurry world. Any doubt at all that Philippe had had about playing the father, left him that very instant.

Chapter 63. Names

"Au clair de la lune..." Philippe sang softly as he was walking slowly from one side of the small dimly lit hospital room to the other holding the yet unnamed baby in his arms. Philippe didn't want to let him go, or put him down. And the sentiment seemed to be plenty mutual. The baby was just falling asleep as he sang the quiet notes of the old French folk song.

It wasn't that he'd thought that he wouldn't love the baby, but he hadn't thought that he'd love him quite as much as he did. He almost hadn't wanted to let Aimee hold him when it was time for him to be fed, and he'd been more than happy to take him to allow Aimee to get some much needed rest. Though the rest was interrupted every couple of hours by a nurse needing to check in on them, and needing to wake both Aimee and the baby up to have them feed again. After that night of exhaustion, it would be a long time before she got a real night of rest.

He kissed the little baby's forehead between verses, and then continued singing. His hair had dried out and his skin color had regulated itself in the few days they'd been there... Ingrid had insisted that the baby's hair would probably fall out, but it seemed pretty thick to him. It was dark, almost black, with some of his mother's auburn tinges that Philippe hoped would come out more when he was older.

"Yes." Said Aimee from her bed behind him that she'd been sleeping on. He turned towards her and wondered how long it was that she'd been awake watching him pace back and forth singing lullabies. He'd been far too engrossed in this activity to notice. He smiled at her and walked over.

"I think I'm going to like this." He said to her and looked down at the sleeping bundle, who seemed to him to be breathing just fine. "I wasn't sure how I'd actually feel about him when it came to it. But now it's come to it and-"

"Philippe," She cut him off. "I said yes." He looked up at her and it took a moment of them staring at each other for it to click in his mind, just what she was referring to having said 'yes' to.

"You said yes." He echoed back, and then the weight of it hit him. He actually took half a step back as if something had softly collided with him. A strained giddy sort of giggle escaped from his throat and the smile that lifted his cheeks was completely involuntary. But just as involuntary was when that smile suddenly made way for tears.

"Oh good." Said Aimee, putting her wrist with its medical band over her mouth. "I'm not the only one who wants to cry about that. It's not just me." He walked over to her and she scooted to make some room next to her on the narrow medical bed. Slowly and carefully with the baby still sleeping in his arms, he snuggled in next to her.

"What's making you say yes?" He asked, but at the same time he didn't want to jinx it.

"I've been keeping a secret from myself for a long time."

"Oh?"

"When I was little, I would have a little fantasy about you and me getting married. Don't look at me like that, you weren't the only one. But you were the only one who stuck around." She swallowed and wiped a tear out of her eye and brushed her thumb against the tufts of hair on her child's head. "But you and I were never officially together, and I sort of, decided that maybe that was why you always stuck around. So somewhere along the line, I intentionally friend zoned you, and put it out of my mind. Because that way you would never leave."

"But then I did." He said, finishing her unspoken thought.

"Yeah." She said quietly. "But then you came back." She looked up at him, as well as they'd known each other, her gaze held a certain sincerity that was new, like he was getting a closer look at her than he'd had before. Like they were sharing a degree of intimacy that they'd never shared. He leaned over and kissed her. A kiss not unlike the first one. And they realized that this kiss was one that they would be able to share for their entire lives. A flavor that only their lips could taste.

"I love you." Philippe said in a tone different than he'd ever said it.

"I always have." She replied, though that truth had been buried treasure to her.

The baby raised its tiny arms into the air and made a small grunt that only babies can make. They both smiled and looked down at him and he settled his sleeping fists back down onto the blanket. Aimee worked his arms back into the warmth and tucked the swaddle tighter. The blanket and diapers provided by the hospital were his only clothes for the time being, Ingrid had gone to fix that. After a good night's sleep that is.

"I guess we'll have a little family." Said Philippe with a grin.

"Yeah, what should we name him anyway?"

"Pablo." Said Philippe, "We'll train him up to be the next Picasso."

"Oh stop." Chuckled Aimee shaking her head. "Don't make me laugh, it hurts. How about we go with Jerome." Philippe raised his eyebrows.

"You're serious?"

"Yeah. You like it. But I want his middle name to be Claudius, after my dad."

"Jerome Claudius." Philippe said to the tiny bundle who had yet to care."

"De 'Leon." Aimee added.

"Oh. Heh... no." Philippe shook his head.

"Well, we are getting married right?"

"I actually was thinking of changing my name. De 'Leon was never supposed to be my name in the first place. Maybe I'll change it to Nordin. Or I could take your last name."

"That would be very progressive." She cocked her head and seemed to like the idea. But sighed.

"You should take Nordin. I've had my family my whole life, and you now finally have one. Besides, I like your family more than my family likes you." She smirked. "And then we can go through the pain of changing our names together and it can be a unifying experience."

"Well, alright. But can I be a progressive stay at home dad."

"Freeloader."

"I'm cheaper than childcare."

"Stop. It hurts." She rubbed at the stretched muscles in her belly as she chuckled.

"Jerome Claudius Nordin. I guess he has a name." He looked at Aimee and smiled. The door opened and a nurse walked into the room. Following behind her was Ingrid, carrying a car seat that had some onesies and tiny pajamas in it. Philippe could tell that they were the smallest that pajamas came, and Jerome would still be swimming in them.

"Let's check your urine." Said the nurse and walked over to help Aimee out of the bed.

"Oh, lovely." Sighed Aimee and sat up to be helped slowly into the restroom. Philippe was happy to not be playing translator anymore. Though he knew English well, and French natively, switching between the two was never easy and trying to do it while talking to someone who also had English as only a second language and was thus switching back and forth same as him, had been really quite confusing.

"Well," Said Ingrid, setting the car seat down and tipping her head to get a good look at the sleeping bundle. "They told me that maybe he isn't as premature as we thought. He's quite healthy. He should be able to come home today. Are you ready?"

"No." winked Philippe, "But I am excited to leave this hospital."

"I want you three to stay with us for a few days until Aimee is ready to make the trip. No matter when you leave, it'll be too early for the both of them, but at least a little wait would be good."

"Well, we can't stay too long. Aimee is still preparing to start school in the spring which is just around the corner." Ingrid shook her head disbelievingly.

"I don't have any idea how she can do that."

"Well, she has me." Philippe smiled. "I'll take care of this fella. We're naming him Jerome by the way. We've just decided."

"That's a lovely name." She smiled.

"Jerome Claudius Nordin." Ingrid's jaw dropped just a little.

"Oh Philippe."

"May I?" he asked.

"Oh of course." She looked so awe struck and wanted to share her affection with little Jerome, so Philippe allowed her to lift the little baby from his arms which he just realized were aching and burning from holding him. A sensation that he didn't know wouldn't leave his arms for the next three years. He smiled and swung his legs off the bed to take a look at the pajama options. The one on top was red with little white snow patterns on it, made of a warm soft fabric with a hood and a tassel. It was very possibly the cutest clothing item he'd ever seen. It came with a matching pair of the tiniest socks in the world.

"Oh!" He exclaimed in a cute whimper.

"A church neighbor gave that to us. Isn't that sweet?"

"It's darling."

"Put a onesie under it so that the zipper isn't cold on his skin." The bathroom door opened and Aimee walked out with the nurse.

"You're all good to go." Said the nurse. "Let me check the baby." She walked over and took the baby from Ingrid. She held him with secure arms that were obviously well trained in the juggling of tiny infants. She took him over to a small padded table and laid him down. She checked his color, his breathing, and unwrapped him and checked his diaper. All of this woke the poor baby up of course and he started crying in his little tinkling cry, stretching his arms wide out to the universe. But the nurse seemed unconcerned and even paused for a moment to listen to the quality of his crying.

"His lungs seem to be working just fine." The nurse smiled. "And his color is good, and I think he's ready for some food, and then you are welcome to take him home." She wrapped the wailing naked infant in a new diaper and then loosely wrapped him back in his blanket and carried him over to his mother.

"Finally." Smirked Aimee as he was rested into her arms and she lifted him to her breast. The nurse fussed with making the pillows into a helpful platform for nursing. "We get some you and me time." She winced at first and then watched him nurse. "Daddy has been hogging you hasn't he." She smiled at Philippe and then turned back for her one on one time with baby. Philippe smiled. Never in all his life had he imagined that 'daddy' was a title he would ever hold. But it was his now, and he wanted to keep it.

"Let's go get something to eat." He said to Ingrid. "We can come back when they're done."

Chapter 64. Providence

Exhaustion set in to both of them in the weeks that followed. And when it was time to go back to Paris, the bags under Philippe's eyes almost felt like they were burning as he tried to keep the road under his car at the right angle. Aimee had fallen asleep in the seat next to him and he had agreed to leave the music off so as not to wake up the little sleeping Jerome in the back. Worst agreement he'd ever made. He knew that a little music would perk him up, but he also knew how much worth was in any amount of time that the baby slept. They already were needing to pull over at least once every two hours to feed him, and more often than that to change his diaper. The true inconvenience of Aimee giving birth in Sweden had not been giving birth. It had been figuring out how and when to get home. A couple weeks really wasn't long enough for Aimee and baby to stay in one place after childbirth but if she wanted to get home in time to start the school semester, which she did, then they didn't really have any time to spare. But when it came to a two to three day drive back to Paris, there was no time that was really convenient. It was only three o'clock in the afternoon but they had been on and off the road since four o'clock that morning since they had been awake anyway.

Philippe shook himself. He knew that in the middle of the baby's sleep was the worst time to take a break, but he wasn't sure that he could keep this up. The scenery was beginning to blend together and he was sure that the last street sign had looked like nothing but gibberish. The fact of that thought was sign enough. Of course it had looked like gibberish. It was in Swedish. He had no reason to expect that he could read it.

Unfortunately, the thing that the area most dearly lacked… was anything. There was nothing for miles. No town that he could just pull over to. He would have to stick it out for at least another hour. He had by this point completely decided that they would get a hotel this side of the ferry boat to Germany. There was no way they would go any farther than that on this day. That seemed like a more than reasonable goal. They might even stop earlier. The trip that had taken them two days coming up would take them at least three going down. Philippe was willing to take it even slower if that meant being rested enough to stay on the road.

The road though, was beginning to take on shapes that it shouldn't. It looked like it had waves and was undulating and melting like a Salvador Dali painting. Had Philippe been more rested, he would have been less likely to assume that this phenomenon was a hallucination out of his over tired mind. He would have seen the signs more clearly, and realized that it was no hallucination at all. But it wasn't until his car started jerking violently, waking up Aimee, that he realized that the wavy road was as seen through the mists rising up from the hood of his beloved Mercedes.

"Philippe." Said Aimee, sitting up and looking startled. But Philippe was focused on putting in the clutch and trying to carefully steer the jerking car onto the side of the road before it stopped doing anything all together. He made it barely, though the rear end was still a little uncomfortably angled into the road. But not too much for other cars to just go around a little. The car stopped running and mist kept rising from the hood. Philippe stared disbelievingly at the vapor and then turned the key into the off position just for good measure.

"Shit." Said Aimee flatly as they both just watched the, whatever it was, rising for a moment, silently wracking their overtired brains for obvious options. The baby started crying. Philippe sagged and put his forehead onto the steering wheel.

"It was too old for these long distance road trips." He mumbled. Aimee took off her seat belt and climbed into the back with Jerome and started unbuckling him. Philippe popped the hood of his car and zipped up his coat to go out and take a look. Standing against the cold mid-February in Sweden, he lifted up the car hood and then put his hands over his mouth to warm his fingers while he waited for the mist to clear so that he could get a good look.

Philippe wasn't the worst with cars, but he knew full well that he wasn't a genius with them either. Marcello had given him a bit of a rundown on how the thing worked. He'd polished and named many of the parts, but he could tell that without Marcello there to coach him, his knowledge was a little bit rusty. As far as he could see, the engine had overheated. It probably needed oil or water or both, and there was a chance that it had blown a gasket. He had no water or oil in the trunk though, and if it had blown a gasket, he wasn't in any position to repair it.

He checked the oil. It was low, but not totally gone. He sealed the oil back up and put his cold fingers back up to his mouth again and walked back to the driver side door. He opened it and reached in to unplug his phone from the cigarette lighter.

"What happened?" Asked Aimee quietly from the back seat as she nursed the now contented baby.

"We're going to need to be towed." He answered and rubbed the face of his phone to clear away the finger prints. He felt Aimee slump with an exasperated sigh from behind him. He got back out of the car and closed the door to keep in what was left of the heat. He went back around to look at the engine again. Nothing had changed, though it was steaming less.

He looked down at his phone. No signal. He put his chilly fingers against the bridge of his nose. Of course. He rubbed his eyes and experienced for the first time in his life, a moment of wondering why it was that God was doing this to him. He lifted his hand off his face and looked up and the clear crisp blue sky as if it would give him answers. The sky said nothing. He sighed and slipped his useless phone into his pocket and turned around to survey his surroundings. They really were in the middle of nowhere. In the space between two somewheres. The snow covered the distant hills and glistened in the light as if it were considering melting for spring, but hadn't quite started yet.

As he turned his way around full circle, he finally saw something, just down the road in the distance. From there, it looked like a small house. A very small house. Indeed, it seemed impossible that anyone would live in it for it was too small for much of anything. He squinted his eyes and thought it looked less like a house, and more like an extremely small church. Smaller than any church he'd ever seen. He glanced up at the sky again and swore that its cheeks were rosier from chuckling. He sighed and walked back over to the driver side door and got in.

"Aimee." He said, pulling the door closed to keep in the quickly depleting heat. "I think we're going to have to do a little bit of walking."

"Oh?" She looked about as skeptical as possible.

"There's no phone service. But there's a small building just down the road. It might be warmer there. Maybe there's a phone." He turned in his seat to look at her. "I'd rather you two didn't stay. It's not that far. Wrap him up tight. He'll be okay." She sighed.

"If we must." He pursed his lips and nodded.

"Yeah. I think so." He reached into the haphazard pile of items in the back next to Aimee and found his gloves. "Bundle up though." He added, and they did so. It took just a little longer than he would have liked because Jerome decided to make himself a dirty diaper too. So they had to undress him in the cold, then redress him while he cried from being so cold. But after he was all bundled up, he seemed happier with a full tummy and a clean diaper, and they were able to climb out of the car. Philippe closed the hood before they started walking.

"That building?" Aimee frowned, squinting into the distance.

"It's the only one I can see anywhere." Snapped Philippe.

"A simple 'yes' would have sufficed."

"Sorry Aimee." He looked down at the ground and they started walking. She bumped his arm with her shoulder lightly. She would have held his hand, but her arms were full.

"It's okay." She said and then looked at their destination as it slowly drew nearer. "Is that a church?"

"I think it is." He answered with a small smile.

"It's tiny." He nodded in agreement.

"Aimee… What do you think the odds are that breaking down here wasn't a misfortune?" She raised her eyebrow at him.

"Slim." She said bluntly but then sighed. "What do you mean?"

"I mean, what if it's providence."

"Providence?" Her expression seemed ever skeptical in this time of exhaustion.

"Look." He pointed ahead of them. "There's cars parked out front." He looked at her doubtful face. But she couldn't deny physical facts. There were indeed, two cars parked in front of the tiny church.

"Well," She half conceded, "At least we're blessed to have someone who we can ask for help." He smiled at her. Jerome started squirming and whining. The cold on his face had just become too much and it had overwhelmed the happy full tummy feelings.

"Here, I'll carry him for a bit." They stopped and the squirming bundle changed hands. Philippe raised him up against his shoulder where he could tuck his face a little into his scarf. They started walking again and Philippe sang a lullaby quietly into Jerome's tiny ear. By the time they climbed the two tiny steps up to the door of the miniature chapel, the baby was fast asleep. Aimee grabbed the door handle, and opened the door.

Chapter 65. From Therapy to Eternity.

"Your identity is built on what's happened to you, it's time to put those things in the past. So that they aren't your identity anymore."

"I think I've done that, for the most part."

"Mmm, hmm." The therapist looked at Philippe a little skeptical.

"So how do you like this new therapist?" Aimee, his wife, had asked him earlier that day. He had to admit that the man had nothing on his therapist back in New York. He seemed to some extent to see Philippe as a puzzle worth solving. Philippe didn't see that as a bad quality. But though the man was very logical, he lacked something in the department of empathy, something his therapist in New York had had in abundance.

"If it seems alright to you Philippe, let's talk a little more about your childhood molestation. That's a thing that can have quite an effect on one's life."

"I agree." Philippe nodded. "Honestly though, I'm not sure that it's an area that needs more work. You have no idea how much has changed since the last time I talked about that with a therapist. You know I actually ran into Armel the other day. Very unexpected. But I've found that, I do believe I've forgiven him. And I told him so. He looked a little traumatized by it actually and left as quickly as he could."

"Are you sure that was wise?" The therapist asked.

"Wise? How do you mean?" Philippe looked at the man with his glasses perched on his sturdy nose and his white gray hair combed back and one leg crossed over the other. The man certainly did look dignified.

"I mean that the effect of these things has a way of sneaking up on you. Perhaps even more so if you convince yourself that forgiveness is the way to meet the problem. Did you say that you have children?"

"Yes." Philippe nodded. He had a sneaky suspicion that he knew where this thought was going and he didn't like it at all. "Yes sir, I have two sons."

"And how old are they?"

"Five and two. They mean everything to me."

"And, have you considered at all, what contingencies you might have if you ever find yourself feeling something sexual towards them?" Philippe stared at him blankly. That was exactly where he thought this was going. The therapist continued, seeing Philippe's non response as recognition of the supposed problem. "I'm sure that you would never feel a wish to cause your children any harm. But statistically speaking, the fact that you were the victim of pedophilia yourself puts you at a greater risk of developing those kinds of feelings. I simply want you to be prepared for that possibility. And in the interest of your children's safety, it might be wise to come up with an action plan, should those feelings ever arise."

"Sir," Said Philippe, as calmly as he could. "Perhaps my time and money is not well spent to pay for someone to tell me that I am statistically doomed to molest my children." He stood up and made a beeline for the door.

"Not doomed Philippe," Said the therapist before he made it out. "I never said that. I said that there are workarounds to make sure that it doesn't happen."

"And you're assuming," Philippe rebutted, "That there is an inherent problem in me that needs to be worked around." And turned the door handle.

"And you're assuming that there isn't." The therapist returned.

"Yes." Said Philippe, pulling the door open. "I am." He closed the door behind him and found himself in the hallway. He walked out of the building and towards his car. His face felt hot with an anger that wanted to dissolve into tears. He knew the statistics. He held the door handle to his car and looked in at the two car seats that had become permanent fixtures of his old classy Mercedes. It was ironic that the therapist had said that his past was something to leave behind, only to conclude that his past would dictate the struggles of his future.

He wrenched the door open and got into the driver's seat. He pulled the door closed and gripped the steering wheel. Those statistics assumed that it was impossible to escape the things that had been done to him. But over the years, he had learned better. It wasn't impossible at all. With the right kind of help, it was more than possible, it was miracle. He turned the ignition. At least now he'd have something to talk about at his next meeting.

He drove through the streets of Paris. In his rearview mirror, the setting sun silhouetted the Parisian city scape against its painted colors of pinks and oranges. The Eiffel Tower stood out like a beacon of history. An iconic skyline forever. But ahead of him was an old church building that had been newly reinvigorated with a youthful congregation and on the curb in front of that old and new church, Philippe parked his car.

He walked up the steps to the front door and let himself in. The pews were empty, the lights were off, but Philippe walked right through them without needing to feel for where he was going. He knew the place. He went through a door on the far side of the pulpit and could see a gentle glow down the hall and the murmur of people talking. He smiled with a sigh and felt as if his worries were gently beginning to lift, like he was waking up from a bad dream into reality and he remembered that he had nothing to worry about.

He walked down the hall towards the light and the voices and pushed the door open to a small room with a table and several chairs encircling it. The people in the room looked up to see Philippe enter and smiles and greetings were offered to him. Aimee was sitting on the far side of the table next to an empty chair left for him.

"Oh Philippe," Said one of the women in the room as he smiled and made his way around the table to sit with his wife. "Aimee brought these amazing macaroons and insists that you made them."

"I did." Said Philippe with a grin as he sat down. "Though I can't take all the credit. Jerome helped quite a bit. That's one of his there." They all chuckled. Next to a pot of steaming hot tea, on a tray full of different colored macaroons there were a couple that were more than a little out of shape, though they tasted the same. Philippe pulled the pot of tea towards himself and filled the cup that was already sitting in front of his chair. He set the pot down and looked at Aimee who's face he had also seen delivering the news on the television earlier that day. She smiled and exchanged some silent message of love that explained everything that had not yet been explained. He leaned over and kissed her gently on the cheek and rubbed the belly that he dearly hoped held the life of a daughter this time.

"Well Philippe, now that we're all here," Said a man who was sitting two people to the left of him. "Would you like to start us off?"

"Happy to." He folded his fingers atop the table in front of him and he prayed, for a blessing on the time, the food, and the fellowship, and when he'd said "Amen." He looked up, and the people started talking. And as each person talked, Philippe thought about how he hadn't known any of them five years ago, but now it was as if each of them were family, as dear to him as his own. Their presence though, was only a shadow of something far greater that he knew he was a part of. He smiled a smile free of Botox. He felt the slowly growing wrinkles at the corners of his eyes, on his forehead and at the creases of his cheeks next to his lips. This smile that God had given him to keep. So that he could reflect God's love on his face.

Each person told their story of their troubles or their griefs or their praises. Grandparents in the hospital, new jobs and homes received, struggles with what they felt God was calling them to. Aimee talked about how it had been put on her heart to speak only the truth in her work, but that the media had other ideas. That was her battlefield.

And finally it came to Philippe. He took a deep breath and began with just a few simple words. "Please pray for me."

But who was Luis? Let's take a sneak peek.

Passing Through Fire: Luis's Ghost.

Chapter 1. Abandoned Pizza.

"I've called you here because I have some concerns about your son."

"Well, yes, I assumed as much."

Parents. They always had to go and get so defensive. "Yes. He's been missing a lot of school."

"Well, alright, I'll talk to him about it." She abruptly stood up and turned towards the door. "I hardly see why I needed an appointment for that. You could have just called me."

"Ma'am," the principal said, trying to keep a tone of annoyance out of his voice. "I asked you to come in because there is more to it than that. Him missing school is only one thing." She stared blankly at the principal for a long moment before finally lowering herself back into the chair. She had a feeling that she knew where this was going to go.

"Several of his teachers have expressed some concern about his... mental health."

"What are you suggesting exactly?"

"He's extremely distracted in his classes, has a lot of trouble staying focused. Perhaps a little ADD."

"I tend to be of the boat of parents that thinks that your kid is probably crazy if they're not just a little ADD. I'm pretty sure being distracted in class is pretty normal sir. And I'm not a fan of what I consider to be unnecessary labeling."

"And I clearly hear your opinions on that, but that's not all. Several of the teachers have also spotted him talking, mumbling and whispering to himself."

"You never talk to yourself? I talk to myself all the time. Anyone who says that they don't is lying."

The principal gave a somewhat exasperated sigh at the stubborn defensiveness of this particular parent. "His writing in English has a rather constant theme of death."

"Sir, I'm sorry, but will you please get to your point."

He paused and stared at this mother for a long hard moment. "We think that he may be having hallucinations. Talking to them. Writing about them. Being so distracted by them that he can't focus on his classes. We're concerned with his mental stability, and his grades are truly suffering because of it."

"So, let me get this straight. You think my son is schizophrenic." She sighed and shook her head. This was exactly where she thought this would go. "With all due respect, you and your likeminded people can take your concept of the normal, standardized child, and respectfully shove it up your ass." She stood up and turned towards the door. "It's not weird for a kid to have some imaginary friends. I wish you people would get over that."

"Please ma'am, imaginary friends are normal to a point and I would completely agree with you if he were in the first grade. But ma'am, Luis is seventeen. Imaginary friends aren't normal at seventeen." She gave the principal a long cold glare, and then left the room. She had been avoiding this for years, but maybe it was finally time to talk to Luis about his... abnormalities.

Luis walked into the little shabby house that he shared with his mother. He dropped his skateboard down next to the door and the pile of shoes and wrestled to remove his converse. He added them to the pile and then made a Beeline past the clutter towards the refrigerator because he'd had a long day and also a serious case of the munchies. He was fully aware of his mother sitting on the couch with a notebook on her lap and a pen scribbling madly across the paper.

"Hey mom." He said, and opened the refrigerator. Let's see. Leftovers… leftovers… more leftovers… Did he want pizza, Chinese or shepherd's pie from the day his mom had decided to cook? Pizza.

Definitely pizza. He pulled out a slice and began to unceremoniously shove it into his face.

"Hang on just a second." His mother said in a sort of droll distracted tone to note that as soon as she was done with this paragraph… or page… she would have something to say. He looked over at her. He also wished he had a cola. He didn't have a cola. So he leaned against the counter feeling thirsty and shoving more pizza into his mouth. He had three guesses about what his mother wanted to say. It was either about missing school, failing classes, or being stoned… Any of these options were plausible, not to mention completely acceptable things for her as a mother to want to talk about.

She finally set down her paper with a sudden thud against the coffee table as if to put an exclamation point on the finality of her writing. She took off her reading glasses, slung them on her pinky finger and then with the same hand began to massage the bridge of her nose. She let out a deep sigh while she did this. Her eyes were squinted shut. Either he was really going to get it this time, or that had been a really tricky essay to write.

"You alright mom?" Luis asked as if he couldn't possibly have any idea what this was about and he was absolutely just here for emotional support.

"Just a second." She said quietly. She was gathering her thoughts and transitioning from the writing world to the present one. She was also maybe just a little bit taking an extra moment to get Luis squirming. "I had to talk to your principal again today." She moved her hand under her chin and opened her eyes to look up at him. Her glasses were still just dangling from her pinky finger.

"Oh." He glanced down at his dirty socks and then opened the fridge for another slice of pizza. It was a wonder he was so skinny. He knew he'd probably pay for it in old age if he made it that far.

"He called me into his office Luis. Not just a phone call, he made me go into his office and sit with him." Luis looked at his pizza as if it had suddenly turned into a slime covered eel.

"I'm sorry mom. I know my grades are shit. I just…" He set the slice down on the counter next to him and promptly forgot about its existence. He'd pay for that later too when the ants came calling. "I just can't seem to focus on it. You know? I just… It doesn't seem like… important you know? Like, what is all that math really gonna do me in life you know? What's the meaning of it all?"

She'd gotten over the hope of having a not stoned conversation with him somewhere around fourteen or fifteen. She did her best not to feel like a failure as a parent. She did know what he meant. She also knew that later in life he'd see the purpose of math class. But that was beside the point this time. This time had nothing to do with his terrible grades.

"No, Luis, it's not that. Well, I mean that is a problem. That is definitely an issue, but it's not what he had me come in to talk about today." Oh shit the glasses. She set them carefully down on the coffee table on top of the notepad. Suddenly thirst became way more important to Luis than it had a second ago and he opened the cabinet over the sink to get a water glass. "Luis um… Luis you know you can talk to me about anything right?"

He lifted his full water glass about halfway to his lips and then stopped and just looked at his mother. You know, he hadn't actually had that thought. Not that he necessarily thought that he couldn't tell her anything, he had just never specifically asked himself the question of whether or not he could.

"Uh yeah…" He then chugged the water.

"You know brother, I think she's telling the truth." The spectral image of Louise was sitting on the over cluttered desk across from their mother. The clutter meant nothing to the amount of space that she could take up or not take up. He glanced over at her. She desperately wanted to be known. But he just wasn't comfortable with that. Not yet anyhow.

"Luis I just… I don't really know how to talk to you about this. You've always had imaginary friends. Always. Ever since you were crawling you've had someone to talk to. I have pictures still. Little color crayon doodles that you made of them."

"You kept those?" He set down the empty water glass and opened the fridge. The pizza was gone (except for the poor forgotten slice on the counter) so now it was on to the Chinese.

"Yeah I kept those. Along with your first haircut in your baby book. It's those little things that I like to remember my baby boy with." This conversation was getting a little weird for him.

"You cut my hair?" Luis's hair came down to about the middle of his back. With this new news he knew that his hair had been cut exactly three times in his life. Once when he woke up from sleepwalking to find his hair full of some unexplained stickiness that couldn't be gotten out without scissors, Once when his father said that he had to go 'find his soul' and never came back, and apparently once when he was a baby just so that his mother could have a little tuft in a scrapbook that said the words 'baby's first haircut' under it. As long as he never lost a lock of the stuff to witchcraft he figured he was probably okay.

"Well, when you were a baby I didn't know you were going to want to grow it out." She put her hands up in the air as if to say, 'guilty as charged.'

"Oh, okay." He grabbed some chopsticks out of the drawer and made to head off down the hall towards his bedroom. Cool. The information had been absorbed. She cut his hair when he was a baby and if he ever wanted to talk to her about imaginary friends he could.

"Luis, wait." He stopped before rounding the corner to the hall and turned to look at her. What more could they possibly need to talk about here. "Luis, why don't you just come over and sit down here with me and talk for a bit."

"Um… Okay." He watched as his Louise shifted over to sitting on the coffee table closer to their mother. Luis came and sat down on the couch next to her. He pulled his feet up under him and sat cross legged on the crummy old sofa that they'd had for years. He opened the Chinese and thought about taking a bite but so far his appetite just kept taking abnormal turns.

He looked at his mother who had that 'collecting her thoughts' expression on again, and decided to set the Chinese down next to his sister who looked at the food longingly for a moment, and then turned her attention back to their mother.

Another deep sigh escaped his mother's lips. "Luis. Your principal is worried that you're seeing things. He says your writing has an over obsession with death and that you talk to yourself or you talk to someone who isn't there as if they were. I think he's ridiculous honestly. I mean you're seventeen. Seventeen year old's do some weird things sometimes. I think it's silly to get all worked up over it, but your principal and your teachers are getting all worked up over it." She crossed her arms and rested her elbows on her lap and stared at her knees for a moment. "Luis. Who… who are these… 'friends' that you talk to?"

Nope. That was definitely the question he never wanted to hear. It was time to transform into his slightly more focused and serious self. He cleared his throat. He glanced at the Chinese food wishing that things could just be simple instead, but when he looked over he saw the face of Louise staring hard at him. No. Nothing could ever be simple for him.

"Um… well… you know, that one movie, with the little kid? The once with the guy and they talk and then at the very end of the movie the guy finds out that he's been dead all along. You know? With the kid and he's like, he all whispers like, 'I see dead people.' you know that one?"

"'The Sixth Sense?'"

"Yeah yeah! That one. So um... I guess. I see dead people..."
She blinked at him.

"You see dead people." She just stared. Her head bobbed in a
nod that Luis knew she wasn't aware she was doing. "Right." She
added flatly.

"Yeah. Well, I knew this was stupid and you wouldn't believe
me. No biggie. So, can I go now?" He shrugged as if he hoped to just
shrug the whole conversation off and pretend that it never happened.
"Seriously mom. Don't worry about it. I just... smoke too much pot and
stuff, you know. I'll get my grades up. Don't worry about it."

She was staring right at Louise. But not at Louise. She was
just zoning out in her direction. She was staring at the wall behind her.
Staring through her. But Luis could feel his sister staring back.
Pretending that her mom was looking her in the eye. Wishing that her
mom was looking her in the eye. She reached her ethereal fingers
towards her mother's face but stopped when Luis ever so subtly
shook his head.

"Mom?" He reached out and touched his mother's shoulder.
"Mom?" She shook her head and turned and smiled at him. She
rubbed her cheek where Louise had almost touched her.

"It's okay hon. it's just that... I just want you to be happy."

He smiled comfortingly. "I know mom. Don't worry about it. It's
no biggie. I'll get my grades up and everything will be cool." He
reached forward and hugged her. "I love you mom. You're the best
mom a son could ever have." He kissed her on the cheek and then he
stood up and picked up his box of Chinese. Louise was mad. He

could feel it. She stood on top of the coffee table and glared at him. That would probably come back to haunt him later too. Probably within the next few minutes. Hopefully he'd be locked up tight in his bedroom when that happened.

"Hey mom. Do you need anything before I turn in for the night?"

"No, I'm alright darlin'. I just got to get this article done and then I'll be turning in too. I want to talk more about this later alright? I just need to sleep on it." Just what he didn't want her to say. Maybe she'd sleep it off.

"Alright. G'night mom." He answered nonchalantly.

"Good night sweetheart." he proceeded down the hall and the door to his bedroom clicked shut. She stared down the hallway at it for a good ten minutes or so. It wasn't possible was it? That he was talking to ghosts? It wasn't impossible. She was sure of that. But maybe it was about time to call up his father again.

Special thanks are definitely due to a few people. Special thanks to Cheri Wilke and Justin Wood for being willing to do some friendly editing. Thanks to Sharon Lingbloom, and my co-workers, for putting up with me while I wrote this book. Thanks to Brittany Hunt, for being willing to listen to me read aloud my roughest of drafts. Thanks to the Writers of Restoration for supporting me and rooting for me as I wrote this book. Thanks to you all. I love you all.

L. A. Willard

Made in the USA
San Bernardino, CA
28 November 2018